BEDMATES

Also by Nichole Chase

BEDMATES

AN AMERICAN ROYALTY NOVEL

NICHOLE CHASE

WILLIAM MORROW
An Imprint of HarperCollins*Publishers*

BEDMATES. Copyright © 2016 by Nichole Chase. All rights reserved. Printed in the United States of America. No part of this book may be used or reproduced in any manner whatsoever without written permission except in the case of brief quotations embodied in critical articles and reviews. For information address HarperCollins Publishers, 195 Broadway, New York, NY 10007.

HarperCollins books may be purchased for educational, business, or sales promotional use. For information please e-mail the Special Markets Department at SPsales@harpercollins.com.

FIRST EDITION

Designed by Diahann Sturge

Library of Congress Cataloging-in-Publication Data has been applied for.

ISBN 978-0-06-240519-7

16 17 18 19 20   ov/rrd   10 9 8 7 6 5 4 3 2 1

For my father who served his country well. For my family and friends past and present that heeded the call to help. Thank you for all of your sacrifices.

BEDMATES

Chapter 1

Maddie

Half a bottle of wine, poor planning, and a misplaced desire to save the world. That was all it took for me to end up sitting in an uncomfortable plastic chair in a room lit by harsh fluorescent lights and dreading my inevitable demise. My father's publicist was bound to walk through the grimy front doors of the police department any moment, her face fixed in a scowl, with blood from her last victim dripping down her chin.

I wasn't disappointed. She arrived in a flurry of monochromatic flare. Cruella's brown eyes raked over me in disdain and I knew I was in deep shit. Her name wasn't really Cruella, but it might as well have been. With her scary eyes and penchant for black-and-white clothes, she would give the cartoon character a run for her money. Her real name was Reese Pang and she never paid me any attention except when my father was angry. With the way her eyes snapped with fire, he must've given her a lot of ammunition. I tried to convince myself that it could be worse, but I was pretty sure that if Reese had her way I'd end up buried in a government bunker. As my father's right hand she would be the only person he would trust to come get me.

It's not like the President of the United States could swing down to the local police station and post bail for his twenty-one-year-old daughter without some interesting headlines in the morning's newspapers.

"Want to trade places?" I looked at the cop next to me and raised an eyebrow.

"Not even if you were Bill Gates." The older man shook his head and looked back down at the paperwork on his desk. "That woman looks like she's going to chew you up and spit you out."

"Well, shit." I grimaced. He was right. The only thing left for me to do was to prepare for my inevitable roasting.

The worst part was that I probably deserved it. I mean, what I was doing had been a good thing, but maybe I had gone about it in the wrong way. Dad was always pushing me to look for long-term solutions, but I liked fast results. Passing a bill about animal testing seemed like a waste of time when I could just break into the center and release those poor babies. If only I had normal parents like my friend and college roommate Phoebe.

Phoebe wiggled her fingers at me from where she sat next to her parents. They were filling out paperwork at the desk of another officer. Her mother, Maureen, wore her silver-threaded hair in a long braid and was smiling, while her father, Diego, didn't look fazed as he brushed his dreadlocks out of his face.

Maybe normal wasn't the best way to describe Phoebe and her family. My stepmother, Abigail, called them hippies in a tone that made it clear she didn't approve, but I loved it. I loved every non-normal, plant-loving, vegan way that they were different from my family. They were so completely opposite from everything I had experienced growing up. When Phoebe had been eleven they had taken her out of school and toured all of the states. They volunteered with the homeless, fostered animals, and protested something every other weekend. The only thing that differentiated them from the other people with flowers in their hair was a large trust fund and Diego's uncanny investment skills.

Trying to free animals from torture was basically a family outing for them. If they were mad about anything it was because we hadn't included them.

I on the other hand had gone to private school, wore uniforms, and even attended a class that taught table manners. When I was twelve I'd gotten in trouble for having a fake tattoo. A temporary sticker-style tattoo with my favorite band's name had cost me concert tickets and a night out with my friends. Of course, that had just made me determined to get a real one.

A tiny bird to represent my mother graced my left shoulder. It made me feel like she was watching over me, always with me, even though she'd been gone for such a long time. It was also a nice middle finger to my father who thought tattoos only belonged on gang members.

"Are you the officer in charge?" Reese peered down at the man sitting next to me.

He stood up and adjusted his tool belt. "That'd be me, ma'am."

"Right." Reese set her bag down on the chair next to me. "How can we make this go away?"

"Reese," I hissed. "You can't bribe people."

"I'm not bribing anyone." She ignored me, keeping the officer in the line of fire. "But we can't have this going out to the news stations."

"It can't just go away. There is paperwork and the company is pressing charges." His gaze dipped down to mine, almost as if in apology. It was a look that I received often when I was stuck under the watchful eye of my father's pet dragon.

"No, they aren't." Reese reached into her bag and pulled a card out. "This is the number of their lawyer. He's agreed to drop the charges."

"He was here twenty minutes ago." The officer's eyebrows drew together as he looked down at the card.

"And I spoke to him fifteen minutes ago." Reese snapped her bag shut. "He was more than willing to drop the charges if Madeline and her friend agreed to pay for the damages."

"He did?" I leveled my gaze at Reese. "That lawyer described what we had done as corporate terrorism and now he's willing to just drop the charges?"

Reese curled her lip. "Yes, Madeline, after speaking with me he agreed to drop the charges."

"That shouldn't surprise me." I rolled my eyes. "You probably snarled fire at him."

"I do not snarl at people, young woman." I swear flames danced in her eyes as she looked at me. "I also don't commit B and E in a pathetic cry for attention. And I am thankful when someone steps in to save my ass from a really poor decision."

I jumped to my feet. "Listen here—"

"Can I intervene for just a moment?" Phoebe's father flashed a charming smile but it was lost on Reese.

"I think you have done enough, Mr. Roberts." She turned to look at him. "You've proven to be a terrible influence."

"You're not the first person to say that to me." His smile turned down on one side. "I believe I heard you say the company has agreed to drop charges on the girls if we pay for the damages?"

"Yes, Mr. Roberts. That's correct." Reese looked back at me. "Of course, your father has a few more ideas about how you can repay the community as well."

"Whatever she has to do, I'll do it too." Phoebe moved to stand next to me.

"I think it might be best that you two spend a little time apart." Reese shifted her bag onto her shoulder.

"You don't get to decide who I spend time with. I'm an adult, Reese." Fury tightened the muscles along my jaw.

"When you can act like an adult, I'll treat you like one." Reese pushed her glasses up on her nose.

"What the hell—" I stepped closer to the thin woman.

"Hold on." The officer raised a hand. "The charges might be dropped but I still have to file the paperwork. It's going to be in the system no matter what. Then the ball is in the District Attorney's court."

"I understand the importance of paperwork, sir. Do what you must, but let's try to keep this out of the news, shall we? No reason to let loose lips fly or to give any hints to nosey reporters." Reese kept her gaze on mine. "I'll handle the DA if it comes to that."

"We don't spread rumors here." The officer planted his hands on his hips and glared at Reese's back. "And I don't take very kindly to it being suggested that we do."

"You can take it however you want, just don't let a word of this go public." Reese turned slowly. "I'd hate to have an inquiry done on your past cases."

"Are you threatening me?" His cheeks reddened.

I hung my head and closed my eyes. Things just kept getting

better and better. First I'm a corporate terrorist, then I'm up against the DA, and now my "savior" was pissing off the man that had closed the handcuffs on my wrists. At this rate I was going to be sentenced to life in prison.

"Of course I'm not. I'm just pointing out that sometimes paperwork really is more of a hassle than it is worth." Reese smiled and the hairs on my arms stood up straight.

"No one is threatening you, Officer McCullough. Ms. Reese has an uncanny way of expressing things that can leave people feeling miffed. I blame it on her being related to fire-breathing dragons. Or was it Hitler? I'm not sure. Anyway." Another officer chuckled and I lifted my hands. "I'm glad that the charges have been dropped and I will be happy to pay for the damages we've done. And, and, maybe we can do some kind of community service to help show our repentance."

The older man rubbed his chin and looked at me. "You'd probably get the same sentence if it went to court anyway. With no priors, minimal damage, and no theft, you'd likely just get a slap on the wrist."

"I can assure you that Madeline will be doing volunteer work and working toward repaying her father for the damages." Reese smiled and I fought the urge to vomit. I was in deep shit if she looked so pleased.

"Great. I know a local animal shelter in need of more volunteers." Mrs. Roberts placed a hand on my and Phoebe's shoulders. "Community service is a wonderful thing. All children their age should have to do it."

"Mom, I'm not a child." Phoebe groaned.

"Shh." I elbowed my friend and jerked my head toward the officer. He was watching us closely. No need to give him a reason to change his mind.

"All right—" he started.

"I'm afraid that won't work. Your father has different plans for how you're going to spend your time doing volunteer work, Maddie. Of course, Phoebe is welcome to make her hours as her parents see fit."

"What sort of plans?" I looked at her, feeling like I'd been kicked in the gut.

"You'll be working with the Returning Combat Veteran Affairs program."

"What?" Shock didn't cover what I was feeling. I had no experience with that sort of work. "Dad wants me to work with RCVA? Where did that come from?"

"Jake will be home tomorrow and he's heading a fund-raiser for the program."

"Wait. Just wait." I held up my hand. That was a low blow. Jake hated me and I wasn't exactly his biggest fan. No wonder Reese was thrilled about the punishment for me. And I would be a total failure at planning any kind of fund-raiser, which would be no help to Jake. Baffled, I grasped on to the one thing that I somewhat understood. "Jake is already in D.C.? And setting up fund-raisers? Didn't he just get back from Afghanistan?"

"He's been back for a while and he's quite serious about helping his fellow warriors. A very remarkable young man. I'm sure your father is hoping some of that will rub off on you." Reese looked back at the cop while I stifled a groan. "Is there anything else you need, Officer? It's late and I'm sure both of these girls still have a lot of explaining to do with their parents."

"Uh, no. I guess that's it," Officer McCullough said with a mix of pity and frustration. "If I have any more questions, I know where to find you."

"That you do." Everyone knew my address. It was hard to miss. Giant, white, and patrolled by the military.

Someone brought my backpack over and that was our signal to get the hell out of Dodge. Outside, Phoebe mimed calling me but I shook my head. I'd call her when I got a chance, but first I had to face the music.

Reese's heels tapped loudly on the concrete as we walked to where she had parked. Instead of driving her tiny Lexus sports car, she had borrowed one of the unmarked vehicles from the White House collection. A man in a black suit sat behind the steering wheel and I winced.

Tony was the Secret Service agent that had been assigned to me for the last two years. He followed me around campus and when I did my laundry. He knew everything that I bought at the grocery store. Hell, he probably knew what type of tampon I preferred. He was always watching out for me.

But I'd given him the slip tonight. And he looked pissed.

"Get in the back and put on the hat."

I threw my bag in first before sliding along the leather seats and picking up the Red-Sox ball cap. I twisted my hair around my head and pulled the hat down firmly.

"Sorry, Tony," I muttered.

"Do you have any idea how stupid all of this was?" He turned in his seat to look at me. "You could have been hurt! I could be fired. You've got to stop acting like a rash child."

"They are going to kill all of those dogs tomorrow." I sat up straighter. "Just euthanize them because they were over three years old. They tortured them and now they are going to kill them, then pillage their organs for science."

"Maddie, you know I get it, but you can't go about it this

way." His dark eyes clouded. "I know how much this means to you. You know I do. But there has to be a better way."

I leaned back in my seat and looked at my feet. "I'm sorry I skipped out on you."

"I know." He put the car in reverse and pulled out of the parking spot. "Can't drag your bodyguard to a breaking-and-entering."

I snorted.

"Agent Vasquez might make light of the situation, but I assure you that this is very serious." Reese turned in her seat to look at me. "Did you even think of your father? How this would affect his career and the stress it would add to his already full plate?"

"Jesus, Reese." I sank lower in my seat.

"Seriously, Madeline. You can't do this kind of stuff. You're not Phoebe. You're the President of the United States's daughter. You have an image to maintain."

"I could care less about my 'image.'" I shook my head and couldn't help but sit up straighter. "What I care about is how inhumane and cruel our culture is today. Most people turn a blind eye because they don't want to know where their favorite lipstick came from. Excuse me for caring that it was tested on rabbits and dogs before landing behind the counter of a department store."

"You should care about all of the hard work your father has put into this country. He's lowered the unemployment rates by ten percent and gotten better medical coverage for the armed forces. Not to mention pulling us out of a hell of a recession. He strived to make this country a better place and you are undermining everything he's done!" Reese turned back to face the front as we pulled out on the street. "If you screw up, it gives his political enemies a tool to use against him. And with how tight things are in the polls, he can't afford to have any weak spots. If his new Warrior Bill fails, it will be your fault."

I closed my eyes and let my head hit the back of the seat. When she put it like that, it did make me feel bad. But I hadn't asked to be the President's daughter. No one had asked me if I thought he should run for office. Had he done some amazing things? Hell yeah. More than most people can accomplish in one lifetime. But I'd also lost my dad in so many ways. He was completely gray now and he looked perpetually tired. Our time together was usually spent briefly in limos on the way to an event, quick phone calls, or while surrounded by dignitaries and staff.

And there was Abigail and my stepbrother Bran fighting for time with him as well. Not that I begrudged them the time. I just really missed our fishing trips and hikes.

I missed being normal.

"Is Dad waiting on me?" I tried to keep my voice calm, but I did want the chance to talk to him. Explain myself face-to-face.

"He left at five to attend a meeting and event on the West Coast." Reese's face was highlighted by the screen of her Black-Berry. "He plans on calling you in the morning."

"And my stepmother?" I sighed. The thought of enduring her disappointed looks and tsk-ing was depressing.

"She is in Uganda."

"Right. The food bank."

"Yes. And going smoothly."

Of course it was. My stepmother didn't know how to fail.

"And Jake is back?" I kept my tone neutral. No need to let

her know how much the thought of working with him bothered me.

"He's moving well with his prosthetic and his mom says he
is raring to go."

I looked out the window and fought my frown. "That's not
surprising."

Of course the great and wonderful Jake Simmon was up and
running around, ready to do his mother's bidding like a good
little boy. If mommy asked him to jump, he'd jump.

"What?" Reese hummed as she scrolled through some to-do
list. She'd already dismissed me from her mind now that she'd
said her piece.

"Nothing." But even the perfect Jake Simmon needed a
break from time to time. He'd been back in the States for a year
tops. The guy wasn't a robot, but nothing seemed to stop him.

His mother shouldn't be pushing him so hard even if he was
acting like everything was okay. She should be insisting that he
find a hobby or taking a vacation. But she had a stiff presidential race in her near future. Being immersed in politics for most
of my life meant I could see how waving her injured son like a
rallying flag would be beneficial.

I wasn't sure what made me sicker; the fact that his mother
would use him in such a way or the fact that I understood her
reasoning. Living in D.C. required the ability to see the strings
attached to everything behind the scenes, the lies, and the ma-
nipulations.

Closing my eyes I leaned my head against the cool window.

Yeah. I really missed being normal.

Chapter 2

Jake

Y ou okay?"

I looked up at the douche sitting across from me. "Shut up, Martin."

I kept my eyes locked on the empty seat across from me as the helicopter began its descent to the landing pad. The steady thumping of the blades made my teeth rattle and my heart beat faster. The dickhead sitting next to me said something, but I had no idea what. I nodded my head in hope that he would just shut the fuck up and leave me alone. I'd known Martin for years and never really liked him and at that moment I'd happily have smashed his face into a pulp. I wanted to be alone.

And anywhere but in that helicopter.

No one was going to shoot at us. There were no IEDs at the D.C. airport. I had no reason to feel so worried. But that didn't keep my ass from puckering as we touched down. I focused on my breathing as the helicopter made landfall with a slight jarring that almost spilled my companion's coffee.

"Damn it." The young aide wiped up the few drops that had escaped his cup before looking at the pilot. "C'mon Charles. A warning next time."

"Sorry, Martin. I know how much you love your joe." The pilot flipped some switches and the blades slowed. "Wind picked up in the last hour."

Someone ran toward the helicopter and opened the door. Martin crab-walked out and stood just outside waiting for me.

My fingers gripped the handle of my cane and I slid across the seats, intensely aware of the way my prosthetic leg caught on the floor.

"You okay, Captain?" Charles looked over his shoulder at me, his voice quiet.

"Fine." I caught a glimpse of his face and was relieved that there was no pity in his eyes. Charles was an Air Force pilot and he understood more than most people would. There was an unspoken need for me to not show weakness; for me to feel as normal as possible.

When my mother had sent for me, I hadn't thought she would send a helicopter. Not after what I had been through on the last one. But apparently the most expedient means outweighed her consideration of how I felt.

Not that I'd told her I had a problem being in a helicopter. That wasn't a fucking option. The Simmon family didn't show weakness. We were a tough family full of war veterans. No one needed to know that I hated flying now. That I never wanted my feet—well, my foot—off the ground again.

But no, I wasn't about to admit that to anyone. Especially not to my mother. I'd survived a crash landing, pulling my friends out of the wreckage, and the loss of my leg. I could deal with a helicopter ride. Even if it made me flash back to bloody scenes that made my lungs constrict and my stomach clench.

"Do you need some help?" Martin stuck his head back inside the helicopter and I fought the urge to punch him.

"No." The word snapped out of my mouth before I could think better of it.

Martin frowned but stepped out of my way.

Getting out did wonders for the steel bands that had been wrapped around my chest for the last two hours. I took a deep breath and inhaled the soft scent of roses and jasmine that surrounded the giant building.

I nodded at Martin to soften my earlier response. Just because I hated the prick didn't give me a right to bite his head off.

He looked like he was about to say something else, but stopped. Probably because he thought I might freak out.

I hated that; hated the way people weighed and measured each word they said to me. It didn't help when I snapped like I had earlier.

"Sorry, Martin. It's been a long day of interviews and meetings." With the help of my cane I started walking toward the black cars that lined up by the hangars. "I forgot how much I hate all of this."

Martin snorted. "All for a good cause."

"Yeah." I wasn't going down that road. I had serious doubts about how sucking up to cameras was going to help anything. There had been a time when I would have thought I was doing my duty, that I was really helping people by getting their vote for my mother.

Now, not so much.

The car ride was quick. It didn't hurt that we had a motorcade to get us through crowded roads and red lights. I tried to not fidget in my seat as we passed a group of people that turned to look our way, annoyance etched along their faces. Motorcades were a normal part of life in D.C. but that didn't mean it didn't irritate people.

When we pulled up to the West Wing, I took a deep breath before carefully stepping out of the car.

"Jake!" Ari burst through the double doors and ran at me full speed.

I braced my good leg for the inevitable leaping hug, but there was no stopping the smile that spread across my face.

"Arizona!" Mother's voice rang across the pavement and my littlest sister skidded to a halt. "For God's sake, don't knock him over."

The warmth that had started to spread through my chest instantly turned to ice. Ari slowed and looked up at me with big eyes. She pushed the curly strawberry-blond hair out of her eyes and looked at me warily.

"It's okay, Ari. I'm fine." I held my arm out for her and she sidled up to my side.

"I missed you," she whispered. She buried her head against my ribs and squeezed tightly around my waist.

"Missed you too, monster." I squeezed her with my free arm.

"I'm thirteen now. You can't call me monster." She huffed but didn't step out of my embrace.

"Actually, I believe the definition of a thirteen-year-old girl is monster." I ruffled her hair and chuckled when she swatted at my hands.

"Shuddup." She mock glared at me and part of me relaxed a little.

At least she hadn't changed. Much. She was definitely taller than when I first deployed.

"I'm pissed at you, you know." She stepped away from me and crossed her arms.

"Arizona!" Mother tsked as she got closer to us. I watched as my mother, Madam Vice President Virginia Simmon, walked toward us. Her red hair shined in the lights from the house. There was a photographer with her and I ground my teeth as he snapped pictures of us.

"Why are you mad at me?" I felt my eyebrows pull together and focused on anything but the photographer. And when had she started saying *pissed?*

"I've seen you once since you've come back. Once, Jake! Where have you been?"

"Ah, I'm sorry, monster." My shoulders slumped. "I would have rather been with you."

"Leave him alone." Mother put her hands on Ari's shoulders and smiled at me. She didn't try to hug me, instead ran her eyes over me critically. "You look good."

"Thanks." I started toward the doors. I wasn't going to stand there for her inspection. I had enough of that every time I went back to the doctor and at my mandatory psych evaluations.

"Wait, we need a few more pictures." My mother tugged me back to her side. Her smile looked so genuine it made me sick. "That's it. Roger, make sure you get his cane in the picture, please."

"Mom!" Ari turned to our mother with disgust on her face.

"Hush, young lady. These pictures are important." Every word was delivered with a pleasant expression. "Now, Jake, try to lean a little toward me.

"Are you hungry?" Mom fell in step beside me, her arm still around Ari's shoulders.

"We ate before we left." I didn't look her way as I walked

under the covered path. There was a Marine standing at attention and my stomach clenched. For half a minute he looked like my friend Grange, but I quickly snuffed that thought out.

Stuart Grange was gone. He had died before my Blackhawk had crashed. I could still remember his grunt when the bullet slammed into his gut. My eyesight wavered and I had to fight to keep from being pulled into the memory. It was too much after the long day followed by the fucking helicopter ride.

Ari seemed to sense my thoughts because she wrenched away from our mom and slipped her hand into mine.

"What could possibly be more important than hanging out with me?" She flashed a small smile. "I've barely seen you since you came back."

"You know he's working on the Warrior Bill." Mom shuffled past us once we were inside and motioned toward her assistant. "How did the last interview go? Rolfe can be a real drain."

"Went well enough." I shrugged. The truth was Rolfe hadn't been bad. Instead of the fake sympathy and sad looks from the others, I'd enjoyed his straight-to-the-point questions.

"That's good. You think he'll go with a positive spin?" Mom's eyes took on a shrewd look. "You can never tell with him."

"He shook his hand at the end of the interview, ma'am," Martin offered.

"That's a promising sign." Mom turned on her heel and headed for the office she used when at the White House. She had a permanent setup, but she was rarely at the White House. In fact, she was rarely anywhere the President was for long. That could be attributed to their mutual distaste for one another or to the need to keep the country's two leaders apart in case of some kind of tragedy.

"Why did you have me come here tonight?" I looked down

the hallway, hoping for a sign that my father was present. Another genuine happy face would have been a welcome sight. Or possibly a bed with sun blocking curtains.

"Mm." Mother stopped in her tracks and turned to look at me. She was still wearing that sharp expression and she pursed her lips. "I have a proposition for you."

"That's never good." Ari raised an eyebrow. "I'd be worried if I were you."

"Have you finished your homework?" Mom turned her attention to her younger child. "I had to talk with your Algebra teacher last week. I don't want to have to do that again."

"It's finished." Ari stuck her chin out, like a miniature version of Mom.

"Good. Then have your crew take you home."

"But Jake just got here!" Ari crossed her arms over her chest. "He's my brother too, you know. I'd like to see him for more than five minutes before you send him off on some errand again."

If they both dug in, it would be like trying to move the Rockies. Not wanting to deal with the mounting tension in the claustrophobic hallway, I moved closer to Mom and smiled at Ari.

"When I get done we can catch up on *Doctor Who* before you go to sleep." I raised my eyebrows.

"Ugh. We are so behind. And the new Doctor starts soon. I'll go see if we can watch in Bran's room." She pointed her finger at me. "Hurry up! And don't let her talk you into something ridiculous."

"Arizona, seriously. You're just asking to lose privileges." Mom put her hand on her hips, but she didn't look upset. Truth be told, she liked that Ari was spunky. Said it would make her a good politician one day, while Dad argued it would make her a good commander.

"Right." She rolled her eyes before miming that she was watching me.

"Yeah, yeah. Get outta here." I watched as she flounced off. "And see if you can find me a root beer."

"Got it!" Her steps picked up and turned a corner, heading off into the bowels of the city capitol.

"Ready?" Mom looked at me with a thoughtful expression.

"Let's get it over with."

She opened the door to the large blue room that was the official office of the Vice President of the United States. I took a seat on a low couch and shoved some of the fringe-adorned pillows out of my way.

"I want to amp up our work with the RCVA." Mom leaned against her desk and crossed her arms. "This is our fighting point; the thing that lets the people know we respect their sacrifice and are serious about their care."

"I think they know that." I rubbed the bridge of my nose.

"I don't want them to know it. I want them to believe it." Her voice took on a stern note. "Because we mean it."

"And how do you propose that we amp things up?" I shifted on the uncomfortable couch. "I've done twelve interviews in the last week. Had dinner with five senators. I've slept in my suit for the last two nights and over seventy-two hours on a plane. Not to mention the helicopter ride here. What more do you want me to do?"

"I want you to do a tour." She gripped the edge of the desk on either side of her.

"No." My eyes narrowed. "I've done my tours."

"I'm not talking about Afghanistan." She sighed. "I want you to visit the wounded soldiers around the country, show the media how much we're doing for our veterans."

"You want me to put these men and women on the TV so they can be your martyrs." My tongue felt as if it was wrapped in cotton.

"Martyrs." She pushed off of her desk and sat down in a chair across from me. "I'm not asking you to make them martyrs. They already are."

I undid my tie and threw it on the seat next to me. "That's great, Mom. So now you want me to throw them to the media."

"The media will be fixed on you. You get to decide what stories are focused on, what people take away from this." She leaned forward. "We'll do more as we work through it, but I think this would be a nice way to show our thanks for their bravery."

"I suppose the President knows about this plan?" I ran a hand through my hair. "That he endorses your running platform?"

"He more than endorses it, Jake." Mom sat back in her chair and smiled. "He suggested it."

"Great." I stood up and tossed my cane between my hands for a moment without speaking. "What does he get out of it? He's leaving office soon."

"His take in this is more of a personal note." Mom's face went blank.

"And that is?" I cocked my head to the side.

"He wants Maddie to go with you."

"Why?" Go on a press tour with Maddie? Why flash his daughter on television when there were no electoral votes to obtain?

Did the man hate me? His daughter couldn't stand me. Sending her along was like stabbing me in my good leg.

"She's been in some trouble lately and he thinks she needs some direction." She kicked her shoes off under her desk before shaking her head in amusement. "It's amazing that her father has managed to run the country when he can't control his daughter."

"Still trying to save the world?" Irritation ran through my body. The last thing I wanted to do was babysit Maddie while being my mother's pawn. Maddie was infuriating, sexy, and so far off limits she might as well live on Pluto. The last thing I wanted was to drag her around while limping to photo ops. The last time we'd seen each other she'd accused me of being jealous and a mama's boy. And with the way things had worked out, she most likely still hated my guts.

"Puppies." Mom laughed. "She got arrested tonight."

"Jesus. What was she thinking?" I shook my head. "And you want me to take her on tour with me?"

"It'll be good for both of you." She leaned back in her seat.

I started for the door not wanting to touch that with a stick. Or a cane. I was sick of people deciding what would be good for me.

"Where are you going?" She leaned forward. "We need to outline our plan."

"I'm going to go watch the Doctor and Donna fight with each other while they save the world from Daleks." I opened the door.

"The who and the what?"

"Good night, Mom."

"Thanks for stepping up to help, Jake."

Chapter 3

Maddie

Vibrations ran down the spine of the book my phone was perched on, making a loud rattling noise. I pursed my lips and tried to mentally make the book stop moving. Sniffing, I wiped at my eyes and sat the newspaper down on the table. There was nothing in the columns about my escapades but there was a note about a protest over the death of three dozen test animals.

"He's not going to stop calling." Bran shifted his feet on the leather sofa and juggled his glass of milk between his hands.

I turned my gaze from the book to my little brother and narrowed my eyes. It wasn't like I needed him to state the obvious. I just wasn't sure what to do once I finally answered.

"You can look at me like that all you want, but you know that if you don't answer your phone, Cruella is going to come in here with her phone, and good luck escaping that call." He took a big gulp from his cup.

An imperious voice drew my attention toward the parlor and I winced. "Run, Pongo, and hide the Dalmatians."

My younger brother stood up and drained the rest of his milk. His gangly thirteen-year-old frame had shot up in the last year, making him taller than me. It wouldn't be long before he was as tall as our father.

"For what it's worth, I think he should be proud. No one can say you aren't a go-getter." He threw me a goofy smile over his shoulder as he walked out of the room and I threw a tissue box after him.

"Escape while you can, little boy, or I'll tell her about the online interview you did for your little fan group."

"Hey, it's not like I sent anyone naked pictures." His voice dropped into a laugh as he walked out and I shook my head. "It's not my fault if people send them to me."

I didn't have much time to worry about what he said because a winter chill slid through the room.

"Madeline."

Reese's stilettos clicked on the hardwood floor as she marched in my direction and thrust her phone under my nose.

The tiny phone felt like a lead brick pressing against my palm. I lifted it to my ear and tried to not wince at the sound of my father's exasperated sigh.

"Hi, Daddy."

The door closed behind Reese as she left me alone.

"Maddie." The amount of disappointment packed into one word was a clear example of how my father could affect people. I immediately cringed and fought the urge to chew on my fingernail.

"I'm sorry, Daddy." I whispered the words softly.

"Sorry you got caught?" I could picture him leaning back in his chair and frowning.

"That too." My smile was short-lived. "Mostly I'm sorry for upsetting you."

"That's something, but not enough." My father didn't pull punches.

"I'm going with Jake." This time I didn't stop myself from chewing on my thumbnail. If they wanted me to feel inferior and pathetic, working with Jake was the perfect way.

"It's a start." His eyes would be narrowed, his left pointer finger tapping on the arm of the chair.

"Daddy, you're sending me out with Jake. What more could you possibly want from me? You know how much I hate doing press. This is basically torture. Are you going to throw me in Guantánamo next?"

"You're so dramatic." My father's chuckle surprised me. "I'm sending you with Jake because he needs someone on his side."

I let that sink in for a minute. "Not to punish me for breaking into an animal clinic?"

Part of me wanted to ask if he had put me to work with Jake because he would tell on me if I did something wrong. The only other time my father had been angry with me—truly angry—with me had been the time Jake told him I was spending time with Nate Renson. I'd been told to avoid Nate Renson at all costs and instead had run straight to him with the intent of pissing everyone off.

And I'd succeeded, though not how I'd planned because of Jake and his big mouth.

"That was a fringe benefit." His words were casual, but that was misleading when it came to my father.

"What are you not telling me?"

"Roughly a billion things." His laugh was genuine.

"Dad." I gritted my teeth and tried to stay calm. "What's going on?"

"You're an adult, Maddie. An adult. I can't ground you. Technically I could because I'm President of the United States, but I won't do that. It would only backfire." He stopped for a minute and I took a deep breath. "I love that you're brilliant and passionate. I don't want to take that away from you."

"I get it from you." I closed my eyes.

"You get it from your mother." His voice took on a wistful note.

"She would have been holding the flashlight." I smiled, even though tears gathered in my eyes.

"That is quite likely true." He chuckled. "Then again, she would have been frustrated by your short-sighted plan."

"I had an organization willing to try and rehabilitate them." I frowned and thought about the people I'd need to contact.

"They've been locked in cages for years. They don't know how to interact, to be normal dogs. The chances that they would ever be able to live a normal life are beyond slim." He sighed. "You mean well, but you can't just throw them out in a yard and expect them to play fetch."

"I'm supposed to just count them as a lost cause then?" My eyes drifted back to the newspaper on the table. "I guess it doesn't matter. They're dead now."

"Maddie." He took a deep breath. "I'm sorry."

"The only thing they did wrong was be born, Daddy." I hoped he hadn't heard the catch in my voice.

"Then you have to stop the process. Change it so that there are no more animals born in cages."

"What do you mean?" I lowered my voice.

"Find a sponsor and take it to the House."

"Propose a bill? They get stopped in the Senate every time someone tries." I shook my head. "Too many people try to add unimportant things and it drowns."

"Then make sure it doesn't drown."

I could hear someone talking in the background and knew that my time was almost up. When your father is the President there aren't a lot of long heart-to-heart talks. So I waited while he sorted out whatever someone needed.

"I have to go." His voice had lost some of its warmth and I knew he was slipping back into the role of Commander-in-Chief.

"If I can get a bill through the Senate you'll sign it?" I gripped the phone tightly.

"I'll sign it. I have no one I need pander to." I could imagine his smile. He believed in his job, his role in the world, but was more than ready to be free of the strings that came with his office.

Wheels spun in my head. I hated politics, but knew they were sometimes a necessary evil. Did I really want to get involved with that hellish nightmare? You started out selling tiny bits of your soul to accomplish some good and before you knew it, you were so entrenched there was no hope of escape.

As if reading my thoughts my father lowered his voice once again and said, "It's the only way to make it permanent, Maddie."

"I don't want to fall down the rabbit hole."

"Then don't." Someone started talking in the background and I knew my call was over.

"I'll talk to you soon, Dad."

"Wait. You're the daughter of the President, Maddie. Use it.

Own it." His words were edged with intent, reminding me that he was the leader of the free world. "You've given up a lot over the years and might as well get something you want out of it."

"I'll think about it."

"Don't think about it, Maddie. Jump in and make it happen. That's what you do best. I love you."

The phone clicked and I sighed before setting it back down on the table. I glanced back at the article about the slaughtered beagles and fought my tears. I'd failed them.

A quick knock was followed by the door opening and someone stepping into the room. Quickly wiping at my eyes I stood up and turned around, tripping slightly on one of the high heels I'd grudgingly worn. I was expecting one of the aides; instead I fell into Jake's arms. The last person in the world I would have ever wanted to see me in such a weak moment.

Tall, striking Jake Simmon. He dropped his cane, letting it clatter to the ground, and steadied me with both hands. I stared into his brown eyes and found that my throat had gone dry. How many times had I fantasized as a teenager of being this close to him? Far too many.

His face looked sharper and the white scar under his right eye gave him a roguish air. Standing so close to him made it hard to ignore the way his suit jacket fit tightly across his chest and how tight the muscles of his arms were under my fingers.

As he studied my face, my heart hammered. I shouldn't like being around Jake. That was a dead-end road that I had roped off years ago, but being around him was always a shock to my senses. He'd been gone so long I'd lost my immunity to his charm, which was something I'd relied on during the campaigns and endless dinners. He wasn't the poster child of the perfect political son for no reason. He was gorgeous before, but now there was something dangerous under his eyes that made my knees weak. Jake wasn't that perfect, pristine boy anymore. He had grown and matured.

And from the way my pulse was racing, I obviously liked what I saw.

"Have you been crying?" Warm fingers touched my cheek and I jerked in surprise at the sparks that danced through my blood. I couldn't remember if he had ever touched me except for obligatory dances at celebrations and fund-raisers. "What happened? Are you okay?"

"No, I'm fine." I stepped out of his reach and rubbed under my eyes. Tearing my gaze from his I leaned over and picked up his cane. "It's allergies."

"We've known each other too long for you to lie to me." He let his hand fall back to his side. I handed him the cane and stepped back. "Someone told you that I was on my way, huh? We all know how much you hate me. I'm surprised you didn't jump out of the window."

"It was an option." I rolled my eyes. I guess I wasn't the only one that remembered our last meeting hadn't been pleasant. "I also considered hiding in the closet, but was too slow."

There! Take that, perfect Jake Simmon. I was quick on my feet today.

"So, you know why I'm here." The way his eyes ran over me as if taking stock was obnoxious.

"I'm your bodyguard. When the crazy women start running after you, I'm to dive in the way." And damn if they wouldn't come running when they saw how he looked all grown up and rough around the edges.

"I'm glad they have a plan." He scratched his chin. "Getting bombarded with underwear and bras is a health issue."

"If they got to know you, it wouldn't be a problem."

"What does that mean?" His head cocked to the side.

"I thought you lost your leg, not your brain." My eyes widened, but it was too late to take it back. Why was it that I said the most horrible things around him? Even when we'd been younger I'd had diarrhea of the mouth. Especially around Jake.

He threw his head back and laughed. "I don't think they're after my brain, Maddie. Thankfully the part they're most interested in is still fully functional."

His lazy smile and sparkling eyes had me swallowing hard.

Heat crept up my neck and I fought to not look away. "Well, good for you."

There went my witty responses. Really, what was I supposed to say to something like that?

I'd always suspected he'd hated the attention he garnered, but maybe I'd been naive. There was no denying his appeal to women. When he'd cut his hair for the Marines there'd been girls crying on the news asking him to be allowed to grow it back. As if his wavy hair was a national treasure.

Steeling my nerves I let my eyes run over him. He was different from the teenager that had stolen a million girls' hearts—different from the boy that I had secretly wanted. In the past, he'd barely acknowledged the attention he'd received from the girls—and the women. But something had changed; and not just his extremities. There was a darkness behind his eyes that made my heart ache, despite his pompous attitude. I'd seen it on the news when he had first returned to the States and was sad to see it still lurking deep down.

The difference also affected how he held himself, the relaxed confidence in his movements. Despite his injuries he knew that he was capable of handling himself no matter what was thrown his way. He moved toward the water pitcher and poured himself a glass of water and handed me one as well. I realized I'd been staring and took a gulp of water as I looked away.

Where was everyone? Weren't we supposed to be having a meeting? I was never alone for this long without some aide asking if I wanted anything. A third person would help make my awkward banter a little more bearable. Being alone with Jake Simmon typically led to arguing and hollering.

Before he'd left for officer training, he'd told my father about Nate Renson and I'd called him all sorts of names. Including jealous. Heat curled up my neck and I tried to calm my nerves.

"If it was a guy, you're more than welcome to borrow my cane to deliver a few lumps." He took a sip of his water. Why would he think it was a guy? I looked over at him and was surprised to see the appreciative look on his face. I tried to ignore the way his eyes ran over my body and the goose bumps they left behind.

That was new and not exactly welcome. Had he been gone so long he was willing to ogle anything with boobs? He'd always treated me like I was his ugly third cousin.

"I don't cry over men." I shot a covert look in the large mirror over the mantel. The navy dress and nude heels were a far cry from my normal outfit of jeans and t-shirts but that was the only difference. I still had bland hair and a boring figure. My face was symmetrical, but nothing of interest. I was average in every physical way. My only redeeming point were my eyes. Despite my lackluster hair, I'd been gifted with thick, dark eyelashes that surrounded my hazel eyes.

"Is that so?" One side of his mouth turned up in a sardonic smile. I itched to punch him in it.

"Crying over men is a complete waste of time." There, that

sounded mature and worldly, right? I sat back down and tried to ignore the fluttering in my chest as he walked toward me. If he hadn't been holding his cane, I wouldn't have noticed his slight limp.

But it was definitely there.

"Ah, I should have known better. I seem to remember you used them to piss off your father."

My eyebrows shot up and I snorted. "Yeah, that's me. I'm only after one thing."

"Several of the senators' sons will never recover from the heartbreak." His eyes twinkled at me as I tried to not gape at him. "You only showed interest in the ones that would piss off your family."

What on Earth was he talking about? What senators' sons? The only time any of them invited me to do anything was out of obligation, or some gross need to score with the President's daughter. No, at every gala and fund-raiser, I'd been left with no dance partners.

Except for when Jake would escape the masses of giggling women and perform his obligatory dance with me. And those had been humiliating. *Look at the President's gangly daughter, poor thing. She can't find anyone to dance with her. Oh, look! Dreamy Jake is so gallant and is offering to dance with her. Blah, blah, blah.* I'd seen it on every face that looked our way.

"It wasn't a man." He frowned at the paper on the table next to me. "What about puppies?"

"Puppies are an entirely different matter." I glanced at the newspaper. Men could fight for themselves, puppies didn't have that luxury.

"And those were the ones you meant to save?" He sat down across from me and propped his cane against the side table.

"Yes." I looked down at the cup in my hands. A silent alarm and one key-code is all that stood between me and their freedom. But I had failed and now they were all dead.

"You tried, Maddie. Sometimes, that means more than anything else." He watched me with haunted eyes. "Sometimes knowing you tried is all you have."

I met his gaze and wondered what had inspired the pain in his eyes. I only knew what the news had said about his accident. I couldn't imagine the horrors he must have faced. Had people been depending on him?

"What did the police say when they realized they had arrested the first daughter?" He smiled and I knew he was trying to lighten the mood.

"Asked for pictures." I took another sip of my water.

His laugh was a surprise again. It wasn't the polite chuckle I remembered from years ago. It was a hearty, honest laugh that made his eyes twinkle. It also came much more readily than it would have in years past.

"How many phones did Cruella confiscate?"

"I didn't bother to mention that little tidbit. I'm sure I'll be hearing from her when the picture of me in handcuffs being held in the air by three smiling officers starts circulating." I hid my grin behind my water glass.

"You're trying to kill her, aren't you?" His laugh filled the room again. "I hope someone is following her with smelling salts when that happens."

"Oh, give me some credit. I didn't really pose for any pictures." I smiled remembering the way the cop had fumbled with my wallet when he saw my name. "They were all very proper."

"That's a shame. Maybe we can get one during the construction." He settled back in his chair.

"Construction?"

"I'm tired of television shows and pointless interviews. I don't want to just talk about veterans and the troubles they face when coming home. I want to do something about it."

"You want to get your hands dirty?" I leaned forward excitedly. This was something I could get behind.

"I can't go back to sitting behind a desk and smiling for cameras." The raw truth to that was etched in his face. "My mother wants me to promote this new program, but I want to do it my way. With your help."

"Look at you, you rebel. If it means I won't have to wear these ridiculous shoes, then you can count me in." I kicked the shoes off and smiled at him. "What are we building?"

"Houses. So many veterans come back with nowhere to go." Passion lit his eyes. "They should have somewhere to call home."

"We could also add ramps, make modifications to established homes." I looked around for a pen and paper. "That would give the media plenty of picture ops that wouldn't require high heels or long interviews. They can just watch us actually *doing* something."

I grabbed a legal pad from a desk and sat back down. "The program already has something along those lines in place, right? All we need to do is pick families that can handle the media attention and then dig in."

"Mom has arranged for a publicist to work with us. They can work on contacting the media and arranging the camera stuff." He leaned forward with a wicked smile. "Then we can work on getting dirty."

My eyebrows shot up and I looked back at the paper hoping to conceal my blush. He didn't mean that to sound so . . . naughty, I told myself.

"Your cheeks are red, MadLibs."

When I looked back up at him his smile had grown. I hated that nickname and he knew it.

"You just try to keep up, golden boy. And don't think I'm going to cut you any slack because of that." I pointed at his prosthetic leg with my pen. "I'm not going to take it easy on you."

"I wouldn't have it any other way." His eyes sparkled and I had the horrible sensation that I had just fallen into a different sort of rabbit hole.

Chapter 4

Jake

Maddie stood next to me, a giant fake smile plastered to her face. Oddly, it was her fake smile that made mine genuine. Over the last week, I'd grown used to her carefree smile as we made plans to work with the charity, but it was nice to know I wasn't the only one hating being up on the stage. Flashes from cameras partially blinded me as we waited behind my mother for her to talk about her great plans to fix the country; starting with our commitment to the RCVA.

"My son, Jake, is living proof that our soldiers are willing to give everything for their country. It's time we give back!" My mother stepped back from the microphone and waved me forward.

The crowd cheered and clapped when I hugged my mother and she whispered in my ear. "Make me proud."

I watched as she stepped back next to Maddie and wrapped an arm around the younger woman's shoulders. Maddie's smile tightened but she didn't step away. Considering the amount of venom my mother tended to level at the young woman, I had to admire her fortitude.

"I've had the great pleasure to serve our country over the last six years." The clapping grew and I clenched the podium a little tighter. "But I think there is still more work to be done. Here. At home. Our veterans are coming back after giving everything they have, to find they have no home to call their own. Some of them are still waiting for prosthetics, medical help, or don't have enough to eat. We need to change that. Here in D.C., in our own backyard, there are five hundred or more homeless veterans. Some of them are mentally ill or physically incapable of working. Are we the type of people that expect sacrifices from others but aren't willing to help in return?"

Some of the people shouted *no* in agreement while others clapped. I shifted my weight off of my prosthetic just a bit and nodded at the people before me.

"I didn't think so. It's time to shoulder some of their burden as they have done for us." My stomach clenched and I fought to not lose my focus. Some of the men and women living on the streets carried a much heavier burden than I did. "My family has a long history of serving and that isn't about to change. We're working to serve our veterans. Housing, ramps, food. We're going to help."

The applause was deafening and I could feel sweat trickling down my neck. I swallowed and tried to focus on the teleprompter. Get through this and I'd be done. No more speeches. No more teleprompters.

No more D.C. bullshit. Just good old-fashioned hard labor. A chance to do some real good.

"And you get to help, too. That's why you came, right? Don't worry, I'm not going to ask you to roll up your sleeves and grab a shovel—though I won't turn you away." Chuckles filled the room and I wanted to slump against the podium. "There is no delicate way to put this, folks. We need your money. We need funding. As much as you can give so that we can give back to those in need of some compassion. And just so you don't think I'm asking something of you that I wouldn't do myself, here's my check."

Reaching into my tuxedo jacket I pulled out the envelope that contained my donation. An aide ran forward with a box and I dropped it in the slot.

"Now, let's get back to dancing, eating, and enjoying this fantastic music!" I smiled as they all clapped, bowing my head toward the orchestra as they started playing once again.

"Thank the fuck that is over," I whispered under my breath. If I never gave another speech it would be too soon.

"Well, if I don't win the presidency, it's comforting to know that another Simmon will occupy the White House eventually." My mother wrapped her arms around me and kissed my cheek.

"You better win, because that was my last public speech." I gritted my teeth and looked for a way to escape my mother.

"Oh, hush. You're exactly what this country needs." She let her arms drop and stepped back to look up at me. "What do you think I've been grooming you for?"

"I don't think you should be grooming anyone." I smiled down at her. "Not even a poodle."

"Are we really going to do this right now? Remember who you are, Jake." My mother's eyes glittered angrily at me.

"Hey, Jake, would you mind walking me to the bar? Senator Franklin is over there and he's a bit handsy." Maddie smiled at me before turning her bright attention toward my mother. "Madam Vice President, you won't mind if I steal your son away for a few minutes, will you?"

"Of course not." My mother smiled at Maddie before turning to look back at me. "The rules are still the same, Jake."

"Geez. I forgot what a witch she could be." Maddie's voice dropped as she slipped her hand through my arm and turned us toward the bar. "The rules are still the same, Jake." She parroted my mother's words perfectly. "What does that even mean? Do you really need to be reminded to brush your teeth still?"

"We drink to be social not to be drunk." I leaned down so I could say the words quietly. That was the truth, but not all of it. My mother was more than okay with me working with Maddie if it gave her the President's support, but I wasn't to be involved with her in any other way. Maddie was not a suitable companion in my mother's opinion.

"Ah. We have several of those rules as well," she sighed.

"I remember . . ."

"I bet." Her little nose wrinkled as she frowned.

"Maddie, save me a dance?" Jason Franks placed a hand on her shoulder and I noticed the way her eyes tightened.

"I'll try to find you," she replied. As soon as he moved away she rolled her eyes and I had a feeling that she wouldn't be looking for him too hard.

"That was one of your rules, wasn't it? A dance at every function?"

"Yes." Her voice took on a pained tone. "I hate those damn rules."

"I'm happy to help out," I offered.

"Always the shining knight." She laughed softly. I looked at

Maddie from the corner of my eye as we moved through the crowd, smiling at people. In the sea of black tuxedos and form-fitting dresses she looked like a bohemian fairy princess. The champagne-colored fabric hung from one shoulder and the loose material barely hinted at her lithe form. Her light brown curls were pinned to one side of her head and she was wearing the barest amount of makeup.

I was reminded of the time I'd had to go to her high school's performance of *A Midsummer Night's Dream.* She'd played the Fairy Queen Titania and it'd been the first time I'd really noticed she was beautiful. Now I could imagine her flitting between trees in a dreamlike glen, petting bunnies or something. Maddie didn't fit in here. She was a breath of fresh air amongst all of the tight-fisted, self-important people filling the ballroom. Surrounded by political sharks was the last place she belonged.

"Do I have something in my teeth?" She glanced in my direction as we skirted some of the dancers.

"What?" I signaled to the bartender when we escaped the crowd.

"You're looking at me funny." She touched her mouth. "It's broccoli, right? I knew that vegetable tray was a bad idea."

"The dress is beautiful," I admitted before I could think better of it.

"Oh. Phoebe picked it out." She looked down at her dress and brushed the skirt. Color filled her cheeks. "My stepmother hates it, which is a big plus."

"It's not just the dress." I cocked my head to the side. "You've grown up while I was away. You don't look like a stork anymore."

"A stork? Geez, thanks." She scrunched her nose and snorted before leaning forward peering at my face. "You're only a couple of years older than I am, you know."

"Can't I give you a compliment?" I frowned but motioned to an open table and pulled a chair out for her.

"No, Jake Simmon doesn't give me compliments. That would upset the balance of the universe." She leaned back in her chair and took the glass of wine the bartender presented. "The Jake Simmon I know would have pointed out that my hair looked like a bird's nest and how it matched my *stork* legs."

"I'm not the same Jake Simmon." I tried to not cringe. Did she really remember me as such an asshole? I'd kept her at arm's length when we were teenagers, but I didn't remember being a bully.

She looked up at me with a frank expression, her eyes traveling over my face. One side of her mouth pulled down in a delicate frown. "I suppose you aren't."

Her eyes seemed to look right through me, touching upon my darkest secrets. Did she know about my friends dying? That I'd been conscious the entire time I was trapped under the helicopter, listening to my friends scream in pain? Did she realize I'd been too weak to save them? Not a skilled enough pilot to save us all?

They'd all died and I was sitting at a gala drinking alcohol like the world was perfect. They were dead while I shook hands and posed for pictures. That deep hole in my chest opened up and I tried to push it away but that didn't work. I could feel my heartbeat picking up and I decided to try and fill the hole rather than ignore it.

I gulped down the last of the chardonnay before signaling for a beer. "Do you want something else?"

Awkwardness filled the air for a moment before she answered.

"Nah. I'm a lightweight." Her cheeks turned pink. She lifted her full glass and shook her head. "The last time I drank wine I broke into a pharmaceutical testing company and ended up in handcuffs. Not my brightest moment."

"We've all had a few of those moments." I settled into a comfortable position, glad that she hadn't shut me out or started probing my sore spots.

"Really? I can't imagine you doing anything that stupid." She chuckled before taking another sip of her drink.

"At boot camp there was a drill sergeant that was a total pain in the ass. Not the normal drill sergeant crazy. The kind that made us contemplate killing him and hiding his body in a swamp. I think he was even worse because of my family." I nodded at the waiter when he set my beer down next to me. "He was a weird guy. You know how some people can't go without their phone or ChapStick? He was obsessed with his deodorant. After getting drunk one night I had a brilliant idea."

"You did?" She smirked.

"Don't sound so surprised." I laughed. "One of my care packages contained a roll-on stick of muscle relaxer. Peeling the stickers off was so easy." I pulled the label off my beer and shredded it. "Switching them was even easier. He couldn't put his arms down for days."

She winced and crossed her arms as if she could imagine it happening to her. "Did you get caught?"

"I was too drunk to remember that my name was written on the bottom of the bottle in black marker." I laughed. "I spent the next day hungover and scrubbing all of the company's vehicles with my toothbrush."

Her smile highlighted her eyes in a nice way. "Still, not exactly a felony."

"True." I tipped back the beer bottle. "Maybe that'll change hanging out with you."

"I can't promise a felony, but maybe a lawsuit. All of those nail guns just lying around waiting for me to trip on them." She looked away from our table, focusing on the people dancing.

I set my beer down and looked over to where the couples twirled. "Is your boyfriend over there? The one that made you cry?"

"You plan on ratting me out if he is?" She looked back at me and frowned. Ah, so she was still angry that I'd told about that rat bastard Nate and his plan to get in her pants. "And no. A politician is the last person I would want to date."

"And what kind of person are you looking for?" I nodded at a congressman that waved in our direction. "A hippie? Astronaut? Someone in Greenpeace?"

"I don't have time for that sort of stuff." Her eyebrows pulled together and nose wrinkled. I had the oddest urge to reach over and smooth the tiny lines out.

"Too busy saving the world?" I raised an eyebrow.

"You're one to be talking." She snorted and set her mostly full glass on the table. Her hand shook just a little and I wondered what had made her jumpy. "So, you think I'm into Greenpeace guys. What's your cup of tea, Jake? Athletic? Movie stars? Fake boobs?"

"You forgot theater girls, goth chicks, and girls with Daddy problems." I tipped my drink in her direction. I still couldn't get the image of her as a Fairy Queen out of my head.

"I should have known." She chuckled and lowered her eyelashes. "You love to play the hero."

"At least I didn't date any political children. Did you date anyone that wasn't a D.C. brat?"

"I've sampled the buffet." Her cheeks pinked, but her eyes didn't leave mine. "But I tend to steer clear of people in the limelight. I've got enough of that as it is."

"You're saying you like regular boys."

"The Yin to my Yang." Her smile grew. "Something to balance out the crazy."

"And do you have a lot of time for dating, Maddie?" I looked around the room before letting my eyes drift back to the woman in front of me.

She snorted. "No. Not at all."

"All work and no play, huh? What are you majoring in again? I don't think they have a degree in saving the world."

"Sure they do. Environmental Science." She took a sip of her drink. "With a focus on sustainability."

"Sustainability? Like farming?"

"Sure. Water, energy, food sources."

"Sounds like you need a cape or something to go with that degree."

"I'll get to pick one out at graduation."

"That's soon, isn't it?"

She nodded her head. "One more year and I get my official adult card."

"And you're stuck spending your last summer vacation with me." For some reason I didn't understand that thought brought a smile to my face.

"Lucky me, huh?" She chuckled.

"This is nice." I chuckled and gestured to our table. She'd provided a nice distraction from the tension gripping my shoulders.

"The fund-raiser?" She looked around the room in confusion.

"I meant talking. I don't remember the last time we've sat down and talked." I leaned back in my chair. That wasn't true exactly. The last time had been yelling and hollering, not talking.

She stared at me with wide eyes. Silence fell between us and I felt the need to fill it.

"I mean, you're one of the few people that gets how lame this scene can be." I gestured at the air. "You can relate to all this crazy."

"We haven't, not really." I almost didn't hear her over the people around us.

"What?"

"You said you couldn't remember the last time we sat down and talked." She cleared her throat and met my gaze. "We've never really sat down and talked. We've yelled at each other but never really talked."

"Sure we have." I shrugged uncomfortably.

"No, we haven't." Her lips curved slightly. "We've only ever talked when we had to for campaigns or press functions. Otherwise we stood next to each other for pictures or you made fun of what I was wearing."

"That's not right." I scratched at my collar. "We've talked."

"No, we haven't, but you were right about one thing." She cocked her head to the side and her smile grew.

"What was that?" I leaned forward, enjoying the way her smile lit up her eyes.

"It would be nice to have a friend to relate to." She looked around the room and her smile faltered. "Not a lot of people understand what it means to be us and the things we have to put up with."

"No, not really." I looked over my shoulder to see what had distracted Maddie.

The human version of Barbie was headed in our direction and most of the male heads in the room turned to follow. Her red dress was painted on, making her fake blond hair glow. The way her hips swayed in the mile-high heels had drawn more than its fair share of attention. "Ronnie." Maddie looked at the woman, her features perfectly schooled into boredom.

"Maddie, it's good to see you." The woman leaned forward and mimed kissing Maddie's cheek. "You look absolutely darling. That dress is very sweet."

I might be a guy, but there was no missing that back-handed compliment, even if I disagreed. Where this Ronnie woman flaunted her curves, the way Maddie's dress merely teased at them was just as sexy.

"Thank you, Ronnie. So many people show up to these things dressed like prostitutes." Maddie ran her eyes over the other woman and tsked. "But the theme does suit you."

"Are you going to introduce me to your friend?" Ronnie turned toward me, obviously done pretending to be nice.

"Oh, how rude of me." The scorn in Maddie's voice was unmistakable. "Jake, this is Ronnie something-or-another from the Vox station. She attempts to report stories she thinks are real and a lot that aren't real. Ronnie, this is Jake Simmon, the Vice President's oldest son, which you obviously had no idea about."

"Veronica Whitmire. It's an honor to meet you, Jake." She held her hand out and I shook it gently. "You're a true hero."

"The pleasure is mine." I tried to ignore the way she squeezed my hand.

"You've had an excellent turn-out tonight." She sat down in the chair next to Maddie and leaned forward. "It was an excellent speech."

"Thank you." I smiled and looked over at Maddie. She was watching Ronnie with thinly veiled distaste. I looked back at the blonde and wondered what I was missing.

"Are you looking for something in particular, Ronnie?" Maddie narrowed her eyes. "A quote maybe?"

"Sure. A quote would be great but a dance would be even better." She smiled at me from under her lashes.

"Uh, I owe Maddie a dance, but then I'm free." I took another sip of my drink and looked over the reporter. I was rusty, but she was definitely hitting on me.

"Sorry, but my dance card is full." Maddie picked up her glass and smiled at Veronica. "Jason Franks and I have some things to talk about. And I promised Leo that I'd dance with him as well. Which means Richard Tanner will expect a dance."

Frowning, I focused on Maddie. "Jason? Senator Franks's son? The man whore?"

"Sadly, it's a common trait amongst politicians' sons." She tucked her purse under her arm. Ouch. I was pretty sure that barb had been meant for me. "You know how it is. Politics makes for interesting bedmates. I'll see you at the construction site."

She turned and left our table without looking back. Franks's face lit up like he had won the lottery and I frowned. Had she meant that they were screwing? Or just that she was putting up with him for some political gain? But the Maddie I remembered never played political games. Was it that she hated me so much that she'd rather be groped by that bastard? I'd always given her an out when it came to the dancing. She'd always seemed horrified by the rule and it'd been a simple thing to take her for a spin on the dance floor.

Hadn't we talked while dancing? A joke about the idiots taking our pictures or the fat ambassador that had brought her, the vegetarian, an animal skull as a gift. Surely we'd talked some. Not just about business.

"Well, how about that dance then?" Veronica leaned forward a little more, putting her ample cleavage on display for me.

"You know, I'm not really in a dancing mood." I focused on the woman in front of me. In fact I wanted the fuck out of this place. "How about that quote?"

"I'd love the chance to do something on you." Ronnie cocked her head to the side. "A story or interview about how you're adjusting. I imagine it must be hard."

"You know, hard is an interesting word." I snagged a glass of wine from one of the revolving waiters and handed it to her. Maybe I could blow off a little steam tonight. "I'd be happy to show you how I'm adjusting. When do you have time?"

"Tonight would be wonderful." She glanced over at Maddie who was dancing with Franks. The asshole's hands drifted too low on her back and I watched as she moved them back up to her waist. The woman in front of me cleared her throat gently. "If you don't have any obligations that is.

"My flat is only a couple of blocks from here." She leaned forward and lowered her voice. Her hand reached out and traced the cuff of my sleeve. I flicked my eyes to where Maddie was dancing with Franks before turning my attention back to the bombshell next to me. I let my eyes focus on the ample cleavage thrust in my direction. It had been too long since I'd had sex to pass up the offer.

Draining my beer, I threw some tip money on the table and grabbed her hand. "Sounds like the perfect place to get to know one another better."

As we left the building I deliberately made sure I didn't look back at Maddie. Even if I had no idea why that mattered.

Chapter 5

Maddie

So your father didn't send you to Guantanamo?" Phoebe's voice asked from my phone speaker.

"This is much worse." I wrapped a rubber band around the bottom of my braid and looked in the mirror.

This was me. No fancy dresses or small talk. No hours spent in front of a mirror while someone curled my hair. Faded spots on the knees of my favorite jeans, a long-sleeve t-shirt with SAVE A TREE, CLIMB A LUMBERJACK on the front, and my hair pulled back into a braid added up to the perfect outfit.

"It can't be that bad. Maybe he's changed." Her voice was optimistic, but then again it was always optimistic. It was one of the things I loved about her even though it drove me batty at times.

"He's still Jake Simmon. He might look a little different, but he's just an obnoxious guy." A stupid guy. A really hot and stupid guy.

"You'll be doing something that'll help people and maybe

you won't have to do much with him. You can pose for pictures and then go beat things with a hammer." She laughed. "It's like therapy."

"You're not helping, Phoebe."

"Sorry. But look at the bright side. You don't have to wear a fancy dress or make lots of boring small talk. You can wear your favorite work boots and keep your head down." Her voice took on a chipper note. "And I mentioned beating things with a hammer, right?"

I picked up the phone and turned it back to handset mode so no one walking by would hear our conversation.

"I wish I was going on the trip to South Africa with you." I frowned at my reflection.

"I'll just be wearing work boots on a different continent. Our family vacations are never very relaxing." Her voice took on a tired tone. "All work and no play."

"Don't pretend like you're bummed on my account." I snorted. "You love it and I know it."

"I tried," she sighed. "Just promise me that while I'm gone you'll try to find the bright side. It's not all bad."

She was right about that much. I wouldn't have to dance with anyone, which was a plus. What had I been thinking telling Jake that I was going to dance with Jason Franks? Jason was a lecherous asshole. I hated his guts. And yet, every time I opened my mouth around Jake out popped something idiotic. Not today though. Today I'd keep my head down and focus on helping. Besides, it'd been obvious he was going to screw Ronnie the Bimbo when they left together. If I got tongue-tied around him again, I'd just remember he was like every other guy: a raging horn dog interested in fake breasts and sexy dresses.

If fake boobs and wearing tight dresses made Ronnie happy,

that was all good and well. I just couldn't stand that she used it to get ahead. Or maybe it was the fact that she had slept with two of my exes in an attempt to get information about me. No one had shared anything worth reporting, but they also hadn't turned her down. Which she'd been happy to tell me all about.

"That's what you're wearing?" My stepmother stood in my doorway and watched me with a frown.

I took a deep breath and pulled my thoughts back to the present.

"I have to go, Phoebes. Let me know you're okay over there."

"Take care of yourself, Maddie." The phone clicked off and I dropped it on my dresser.

"I'm going to a construction site to work. What else would I wear?" I picked up my work boots from next to my bed.

"I thought you were interviewing families, telling their stories for the news." She walked over to my dressing table and picked up the Carhartt jacket I'd picked out to wear.

"We're helping actually build the homes these families need. It's a great opportunity to do something hands-on." I sat down in a chair and pulled one of my boots on.

"That sounds like a good plan."

I looked up at Abigail in surprise. "You think so?"

"Yes, I do." She picked up one of my college sweatshirts with a grimace before folding it and setting it on my dresser. "It'll still give the press something to look at while driving attention toward the troops that actually need it. Not a bad plan at all. Much better than what Jake's mom was planning."

"Heh." I picked up my other boot and slipped it on.

"I'm sorry about the dogs. That entire process is a shame." Genuine pity laced her words. "Your dad said that you were going to propose a bill."

"I'm considering it." I looked at her warily as I finished tying my boot.

"You should do it."

Abigail had come into my life when I was young enough to need a mother, but old enough to resent a new one. My teenage years had been ugly. Especially when my father had told me Abigail was pregnant only a few months after the wedding.

She had taught me about tampons and been team mother when I played volleyball. But she wasn't my mom. And despite the things she had done for me, she'd never tried to fill that void left behind by my real mother. She *couldn't* fill that void. Where my mother had been calm, patient, and a complete hippie, Abigail had been the exact opposite.

I'd spent hours going over how to make the perfect seating chart and what not to say in public. She'd always given exactly what was expected of her when it came to me and nothing more. It had taken years for me to understand that she wasn't what I had needed as a child, but she'd been exactly what my father had needed. She was completely different from my mother—from me. Abigail was driven and had given my father a purpose and a direction in which to move.

"You could wear a little makeup even if you're working outside. There will be cameras."

She was also incredibly vain.

"I'm not wearing makeup just so it can drip down my face and get in my eyes while people snap pictures." I checked the rubber band at the end of my braid before straightening my shoulders. "I'm going to work, not impress."

"It's always your job to impress, Maddie." She reached over and brushed some of the loose hair out of my face. "You're the President's daughter."

"Not today." I picked up a baseball cap. "Today, I'm just a felon doing community service."

"For the love of God, Maddie, don't say that where anyone can hear you." She followed me out of the room. "This isn't a joke. You could have caused your father a lot of problems. You know that, right?"

"What do you want?" I went to the kitchen in the family suite and pulled out a bottle of water.

"I want you to start acting like an adult." She crossed her arms over her favorite gray power suit.

"I'm taking responsibility for my actions." I frowned at her.

"How about thinking of the consequences before you do something so stupid." Her mouth pressed into a line and her eyes snapped at me. "I had to cancel my world hunger tour so I could be home to keep you in line."

"You shouldn't have canceled anything. I'm sorry you felt like I needed babysitting, but I swear I'm not doing anything else that stupid again. Besides, no one knows about any of it. They all just assume I'm helping out, not doing community service." Guilt crushed my shoulders. Even if Abigail and I didn't always get along, I knew that she had worked really hard to promote awareness of world hunger.

"Oh, they know." She pushed the newspaper that was lying on the kitchen island toward me. "Someone spilled."

I looked at the newspaper and clenched the water bottle in my hand.

"America's Daughter Arrested." I read the headline out loud and looked over the article before checking to see who was the author. "Son of a bitch!"

Veronica Whitmire's name was listed right there for the world to see. I was going to kill Jake Simmon with my bare hands. Or maybe I'd use one of those nail guns I'd joked about last night. I'd give them all a real reason to print a story about me in the paper.

"Abigail," I started.

"Don't. It was only a matter of time." She shook her head. "That's why I'm here."

"Who is going to take care of the food bank?" I tried to swallow my anger. My anger could wait. My dumbass stunt had just affected a really important program.

"The Vice President will be taking care of my next stop. We'll see after that. I don't want to get halfway across the Atlantic Ocean and find out you decided to rob a bank." She checked her watch. "I'll leave you to your job. I'm meeting with the Lilarian ambassador to prepare for the Prince and Duchess's arrival."

"When are they coming?" That was a topic shift I could get on board with.

"Six weeks? Eight? I'll have to check my calendar. I have a ton to take care of beforehand. I know you dislike official dinners, but I'd appreciate it if you could make this one. The Duchess is only a few years older than you."

"Sure." I agreed automatically, feeling guilty that I'd messed up her tour. "Kind of neat to have America's Duchess coming to the White House."

"Makes it sound like she should be the one hosting us, doesn't it?" Abigail lifted one of her perfect eyebrows.

"Yeah." My weak smile wasn't convincing either of us.

"Well, I'll see you later."

"Wait."

She stopped and looked back at me.

"I'm really sorry. You're right. I wasn't thinking about consequences and I'm really sorry that you had to come back here. I know how important your work is to everyone."

"Thank you." She cocked her head to the side, her eyes appraising. "You're a lot like Helena. She was much more likely to ask forgiveness than permission."

I stood there as she walked out, emotions tumbling through my stomach. Had that been a compliment? An insult? Probably an insult.

But even more importantly, why had she acted as if she'd known my mother? She hadn't met my father until after my mother had passed away.

I could barely focus on the drive to the building site. Tony had bundled me into a car and I hadn't heard a word he'd been saying. My mind vacillated between what my stepmother had said and rage that Jake had sold me out to sleep with a reporter.

I shouldn't be surprised Jake had thrown me to the wolves. He liked to tell on me when I did something wrong. But this seemed off even for him. I thought we'd had a good conversation the night before and wouldn't have assumed it was him if it hadn't been printed by his hookup. I guess being in the Marines had really changed him and not in a good way like I'd hoped.

As if things weren't bad enough, Cruella called and I had to go over what I would say to the press. If I tried to ignore them all day, the stories would just get worse. When it came to the media, the one thing you could count on was a headline to snowball out of control.

By the time I got off the phone, we were out of the city. The SUV was in a suburb where the cherry-blossom trees flowered and people jogged down the sidewalks. I cracked the window to breathe in the fresh air and was rewarded with the sounds of yelling voices.

"Is that coming from the building site?" I looked over at Tony.

"Yes." He leaned over to look out the front seat. "They've been in place since four this morning."

"Who? The volunteers?" I craned my neck and looked out the window. "Shit. This is because of the paper."

Media vans lined the street and I wanted to melt into my seat. I pulled my baseball cap down a little further and took a deep breath. Well, I guess I was just getting what I deserved. Despite the wine that night, part of me had known breaking into a building was a bad idea. A really bad idea.

"I'm so stupid," I muttered.

"What was that?" Tony looked over at me with a smug expression.

"You heard me." I made sure my shoulders were back and confident as we drove past the news vans. "I'm stupid. I shouldn't have tried to break those dogs out. I never should have ditched you."

"Did it ever occur to you that I could have helped?" Tony's smug expression seemed to grow. "If anyone could have gotten you into that building without being caught, it would have been me."

"Uh huh. And you would have helped if I'd asked?"

"I didn't say I would actually help you. I wanted to know if you thought of asking me." His grin was so wide I could see his dimples. "I would have put you on lockdown."

"And that's exactly why I didn't ask." I rolled my eyes.

Fourteen years my senior, Tony treated me like I was his little sister. Which was good in some ways and really bad in others. He wasn't as stiff as some of the suits that worked in the Secret Service, especially when not in public, but it also meant that he went above and beyond when it came to checking out the guys I dated. That joke about having your father cleaning his gun on the front porch when your date shows up had nothing on Secret Service Agent Tony. Weeding out the serious guys is a lot easier when you have an ex-special ops agent that explains he knows how to torture people while glaring at the poor guy that dared to ask me out.

I didn't think Tony had ever actually tortured people, but I also didn't want to look too hard. Phoebe had spent a lot of time wondering about it, but that was because she had a crush on him our freshman year. As far as I knew, she'd never gotten up the courage to ask him. Especially once she met his longtime girlfriend, a hot-shot lawyer.

"Ready?" The humor in his expression was gone. His eyes scanned my face and I knew that if I hesitated he would make the call to pull out of the place.

"Gotta face the music sometime," I answered. "Is Jake here?"

"He arrived before us." He reached out and tapped twice on the car window.

Another agent opened the door and Tony climbed out first. I stepped outside and made sure to have a pleasant expression on my face. I'd learned early into my father's campaign that I suffered from resting-bitch-face. That meant I had to concentrate at public events or I looked like I was pissed off. Of course, having RBF meant there were still photos of me that looked like I was contemplating stabbing people. Knowing that I didn't photograph well also meant that I was a jump ahead when I needed to pretend to not want to stab people.

I gave a small wave to the cameras and was relieved when an older woman wearing a tool belt and carrying a clipboard came over to shake my hand. Her dark hair was pulled back from her face and her jeans had patches on the knees.

This was a woman I could understand.

"Hi, I'm Trina Scott." She held out a hand and I shook it.

"I'm Maddie. Thank you for letting us help, Trina. I'm a big fan of how you get stuff done." I'd received an e-mail the night before from the public relations team giving me a rundown of everyone important. Trina Scott had a master's degree and used to run her own business before starting the non-profit Returning Combat Veterans Affairs.

"Thank you. I'm pretty good at bossing people around." The woman tucked her clipboard against her chest.

"Looks like your volunteers don't mind." I noticed the group of people near the concrete slab, arranging tools and piles of wood. "Do you have a lot of repeat helpers?"

"We have a few, but I think it's safe to say we have such a large group today because of you and Mr. Simmon." Trina turned toward where Jake stood talking to reporters.

"Let's make sure we put them to good use then." I put my hands on my hips. "I'm going to go say hello to the media real quick, but then I'm all yours."

"You might regret that!" One of the older men hollered in my direction.

"Shut it, Kremdenski!" Trina raised her voice. "You might scare her away. You gonna do her work too?"

"I'll just be over here, stayin' out of trouble." The man pointed to a work van. Good-natured chuckles filled the work space.

"Mm hmm. I better not catch you napping again." She

winked at me. "That's the site foreman. He thinks he's a comedian. Good luck with the vultures, I've already paid my tribute."

Jake was working the cameras but I knew that if I didn't
make a statement now, the headlines would only get uglier. I
envied his ease in front of all the people judging him, looking
for weaknesses. He made it look easy while I was busy trying to
remind myself to smile.

"Maddie, why did you do it?"

"Were you making a political statement?"

"Is it true that the police officers handcuffed you?"

I gritted my teeth in what I hoped looked friendly and didn't
look at Jake as I stepped forward. Getting revenge was at the
top of my to-do list. Perfect Jake Simmon was going to pay for
spilling my secrets to his sex-kitten.

"Hi, David." I smiled at a couple of the reporters I knew.
"How's your son, Jan?"

"He's good. Playing soccer. Can you believe it?" The woman
pushed her glasses up a little and smiled.

"He's what, two years old?" I pretended to be shocked. "Isn't
that a little young?"

"Six," she snorted. "He still carries around the stuffed eagle
you gave him though."

"Geez, six? It's been that long?" I shook my head.

"Goes fast."

"All right, give me your question." I let my shoulders slump
in mock weariness. "I know that's what you're waiting on."

"Did you really try to break into a pharmaceutical company
to rescue dogs?" Jan asked with a small smile.

"Yes." I stood up a little straighter so everyone would know
I wasn't playing. "Despite my good intentions, what I did was
wrong. I've paid to fix any damages I've caused to Sabre Phar-

maceuticals and am devoting all of my free time to volunteer work. After a lot of talks with my father and the people in charge at Sabre, I see how my efforts actually hurt my goals. So, in the future I will be pursuing legislation."

"Have you proposed a bill?" One of the newer reporters leaned forward, pushing David to the side. He rolled his eyes and someone muttered about newbies.

"Not yet, but that is one of my goals. Sabre euthanized twenty-six dogs this week, fourteen cats, and dozens of rodents. Unfortunately, even If I'd been able to save those poor animals, most of them would not have been able to adjust to life outside of a cage." I took a deep breath. There was no backing down now. "My goal is to stop animal testing before it even begins."

"Do you have a sponsor yet?" David took his spot back.

"Not yet, but hopefully soon." I held up my hands. "That's all I've got for you guys today about that stuff. Right now I'm excited to roll up my sleeves and help build one of our American Heroes a new home."

"But—" The new reporter tried to push her way back to the front and David moved so she couldn't get by.

"Do you know who this home is going to?" David raised his voice. You didn't get to be a senior reporter for an important paper if you didn't know when to ask certain questions and when not to.

"Not yet, but we're hoping to meet the family in a few weeks." Jake moved so that he was standing next to me and I tried to not bristle. "In the meantime, we're always happy to have more help. Anyone here know how to install sinks?"

There were some laughs and the group started to disperse.

"How about I trade you some plumbing skills for an exclusive?" David cocked his head to the side, eyes trained on Jake.

"I don't know, David, are we going to have to hire someone to come back and redo everything you did?" Jake raised his eyebrows.

"Worked for a contractor when I was in college." David shrugged. "I'm not certified, but I can do a lot of the grunt work."

"E-mail the coordinator and we'll work something out." Jake reached out and shook the reporter's hand.

"Well, I'd love to offer the same, but I'd likely break the whole house." Mary laughed.

"There are a lot of other ways you could volunteer," I offered.

"I'll look into it. I don't mind working for a good cause." She motioned me a little closer. "Off the record, how are you?"

"I'm good. Embarrassed." I trusted Mary, but I also knew I had to be careful what I said out in the open. "But okay."

"If it's any consolation, I think what you did was pretty brave. Stupid, but brave." She patted my arm and I laughed.

"Definitely stupid," I agreed.

"If you need help with the bill, let me know. I might be able to call in a few favors."

"Are we bartering?" I frowned. Being friends with reporters was dangerous, but I'd always liked Mary. She'd been a new mom when we first met and I'd taken to her maternal glow.

"No, though I'd get fired if I turned down an interview." She chuckled and her glasses slid down her nose a little. "In the fifteen years I've been at the *Post*, I've made a lot of connections, and honestly, I just hate the thought of those poor babies being mistreated. No animal should have to endure that."

Her eyes got a little misty and I watched as her hand drifted down to her stomach.

"Mary Peterson, is there something you want to tell me?" I looked pointedly at where her hand rested.

"Oh, gosh. Well, yes, but it's still really early." She smiled.

"Congratulations!" I hugged her, but kept my voice down. "But now I feel like I'm taking advantage of your hormones."

"Oh, take advantage of them." She waved her hand in front of us. "Might as well be good for something!"

"Thanks, Mary." I gave her another quick squeeze. "Please tell your family I said hi."

"Take care of yourself, Maddie."

"Yes ma'am." I watched her head toward a photographer.

"Well, that didn't go too bad." Jake's warm voice slid over my skin and I almost jumped.

"Jesus, Jake. Don't sneak up on people." I took a deep breath. My heart was beating out of my chest and I was pretty sure it didn't have anything to do with being angry at him. But I was pissed, I reminded myself. Really, pissed. I just wasn't blind.

"I didn't sneak up on you." He crossed his arms, his eyes glinting with humor. "I've been standing here the whole time."

"Oh, great. Looking for more secrets to spill?" It took every ounce of self-control to keep from poking him in the chest. I focused on the earplugs that were dangling from a string around his neck.

"What?"

"Don't play innocent, Jake. In fact, just don't talk to me. Acting like we're friends is a waste of time. Especially if you're just going to run over and tell your new girl all my secrets." I leaned toward him, barely able to keep from launching into a tirade where everyone could hear us. " 'No one else can really relate to our lives. It's nice to have someone to talk to.' Blah, blah, I'm a big asshole, blah, blah, blah."

"You think I told the reporters about your run-in with the cops?" Anger simmered just under the surface of his polite mask.

"Let's see. You go home with Bimbo Reporter Number One and the next day she releases all the juicy bits of my stupidity for the world to read. So, yeah. I think you were so gung ho to hop in her pants, you gave her just what she was looking for." I started walking away but he kept pace with me.

"You're right. I gave her exactly what she wanted." Cold fury laced his words and my stomach took a nasty nose dive. "Funnily enough, you never came up in the conversation."

My cheeks flamed and I tried to stomp down on the cold pit forming in my stomach. "Whatever, Jake. Go tell it to your reporter. She's going to be jealous when she finds out you promised David an exclusive."

"You're the only one that sounds jealous."

I froze midstep before turning to face him. He'd just used the words I'd thrown at him all those years ago. "You're so arrogant! I point out the obvious and your only defense is that I'm jealous? Of what? You? Get a grip, Jake. If I want to screw someone, you'd be the last person on my list. No, you wouldn't even make the list."

"You say that, but I remember how you used to look at me." He crossed his arms and my mouth fell open. "You said we never talked, but I remember you would just clam up around me, and stare with those big eyes."

"Wow. Afghanistan really turned you into an asshole." I noticed Tony standing off to the side and waved him away. "No matter what I may or may not have thought of you years ago it has no bearing on the present. You're just another man whore. You threw me under the bus to get a piece of ass."

"It keeps coming back to me sleeping with Ronnie, but the fact is, I didn't tell her about your little drunken felony. In fact, we were too busy to discuss much of anything." He rocked back a little and I almost—almost—put out a hand to steady him, but I caught myself. It would serve him right to fall on his ass. Stupid, arrogant asshole.

"Who else would have told her? Veronica Whitmire, the worst reporter in D.C.?" I crossed my arms. Body language be damned. Let anyone watching us think what they wanted. There was no reason we needed to pretend we liked each other. "You handed her a golden ticket. She's gone from bottom of the totem pole to countless stories."

"I'm sure I'm not the first person to be interested in what she was offering." His jaw tightened and he leaned down toward me.

"Oh, you're right. Absolutely spot on. She's offered it *all* to most of my exes too. That's her thing, Jake. She's nothing but a glorified call girl. Only you leave secrets on the nightstand the next morning instead of cash." I leaned forward too and lowered my voice. "At least none of them gave her any dirt on me. They just had a good time and moved on."

"Shit." He rubbed a hand along his jaw and stared up at the sky for a second. "I didn't know about your exes."

"Whatever, Jake." I started to walk away but his fingers curled around my shoulder. "My exes don't matter. You throwing me to the wolves is what matters."

"I didn't tell Ronnie anything about you and the police."

"Save it." I shook my head.

"Look, I'm being serious. I was just looking to blow off a little steam. That's it." He frowned. "There wasn't much talking. She must have known about everything before we hooked up."

"Sure." The way he talked about screwing Ronnie so casually made my stomach sick.

"I'm serious, Maddie. I wouldn't have done that to you. I meant what I said last night. Most people can't relate to our lives. I wouldn't stab you in the back." He ran a hand through his hair. "In fact, when I heard about it on the news I came early to try and deflect some of the reporters."

I blinked. He had tried to save me? If it hadn't been Jake, who else would have known? And out of all the reporters, why would they have given that story to Ronnie?

"You've ratted me out before, Jake," I reminded him.

"I didn't rat you out, Maddie." He groaned. "That was years ago, you know. And I was trying to protect you from that little prick and his father."

"And score points with your mom? All I heard about for months was how perfect you were and how stupid I was." My fingers clenched. "All I'd wanted was to be a girl for a little while, Jake, not the President's daughter. Like you said, blow off a little steam."

"He was just using you," Jake explained. His eyes darkened and in the back of my mind I wondered just how deep his hero complex went. He was still upset about that?

"I'm not stupid, Jake. I knew he was using me. I *wanted* to be used." I glared at the man in front of me and threw my hands in the air. "I was tired of being invisible. For just a little bit I wanted something that was about me."

"You aren't invisible." His eyebrows drew together. "And you deserved better than that jerk."

"It's over. I wouldn't have even brought it up if you hadn't done it again." I was regretting this whole conversation more than the actual arrest. I never should have told him why I'd agreed to go off with the senator's son.

"I didn't tell anyone about the arrest. This is different. And no matter what you think, I didn't profit from telling your dad about that night and I didn't need to share your secret to get in Veronica's pants."

"Ugh. Arrogant ass." I muttered a bunch of nonsense under my breath, mainly curse words I didn't want the media to lip read on the news.

"I might be arrogant, but you know I'm honest. I never lied about who told all those years ago and I wouldn't lie now." He stood up a little straighter. "Give me some credit, Maddie."

I frowned and watched him with narrowed eyes. He was right in more ways than one. He had never hid the fact that he'd told about my late-night rendezvous and he didn't need my dirt to sleep with the bimbo reporter. Not a woman in the world would turn Jake down. They'd have to be stupid.

Though I was starting to wonder how stupid Jake actually was if he slept with Ronnie.

"I hope you wrapped your cucumber," I blurted out.

"What?" His eyes were so wide I thought they might pop out of his head.

"Before you went dipping in her salad dressing. There's no telling what kind of fungus you might have caught." Heat rushed up to my cheeks.

His laugh was so loud and infectious I was shocked it came from him. "Don't worry. I took my own Saran wrap."

"Good plan." I tried to keep from being disgusted by the fact that he had actually fucked Ronnie and tried to remind myself that he'd been gone for the last six years and hadn't had to deal with her.

"Look, we're going to be working together a lot. It'd be nice if we could get along." He leaned his head down to look in my eyes. His warm brown eyes pleaded with mine. "You make me laugh, Maddie, and that's something I've come to appreciate over the last few years. Friends?"

"No." I shook my head. Could I trust him? Had he really shown up early to try and cover for me? "I don't think so."

"I thought we were on our way to being friends last night." He must've sensed that I was caving because his smile grew. "You saved me from my mom, I came out here to save you from the press. That's what friends do, right?"

"Jake—no." I shook my head. He'd sold me out. I couldn't really think Veronica had just happened to get that story from someone else, could I?

"C'mon, MadLibs." A hint of his boyish charm peeked out at me and I rolled my eyes.

He screwed Ronnie, accused me of being jealous, and now wanted to be friends. Why was I even tempted?

"You're on probation." The words fell out of my mouth before I could rethink them.

"Probation? I can work with that." He nodded his head, a sly smile creeping onto his face.

"And I wasn't jealous." I poked him in the shoulder.

"C'mon, you were a little jealous." He stood up straight and his dimple flashed.

"Not even a little." I said it a little too firmly and his grin grew. "And if I find out you were the one that spilled to Veronica, I'll make your life a living hell."

Chapter 6

Maddie

The phone rang and rang. I had to fight the urge to curse out loud. There were a ton of people still moving around the worksite and I didn't want to cause a scene. I'd gotten a voice mail from one of the private shelters I volunteered at during the semester. They were short on help and someone had vandalized a storage shed.

"Jonah," I said when the phone beeped for my message. "The shelter needs more hands. Give me a call."

Jonah was one of the few friends I'd made at school other than Phoebe. He was quiet and reserved but great with animals. I hoped he'd help.

I tucked my phone into my back pocket and stared off into the distance. We were wrapping up here for the day, so I might be able to go over to the shelter and get a couple of hours of work in before I collapsed. Those animals would need their kennels mucked and medicine dispensed. Flora, the owner, had her hands full or she never would have called me.

I looked down at my hands and grimaced at the blister on my thumb. I'd need to get a Band-Aid on that or it'd get infected.

"Everything okay?" Jake grabbed a paper cup from the top of the water cooler next to me and poured himself a drink. I watched as he threw his head back and swallowed the contents of his cup. His dirty shirt stretched across his sweaty chest and I found my eyes tracing the hard lines.

"Uh, yeah. I just need to go help a friend." I tore my eyes away from him and looked down at the dirt as if mesmerized by the brown stuff I was kicking with the toe of my work boot. "One of the shelters had an unfriendly visitor last night."

"What happened?" Jake sat down on the bench and threw his arm over the water cooler.

"I need to help out a friend."

"Hold on." He lifted his sound-cancelling earphones and pulled out the earplugs he was also wearing. "Sorry, I didn't hear you."

"Jerks ripped off the doors and stole some of the containers. It rained last night and a lot of the supplies were ruined. They need some people who know how to handle the animals to do those chores while the others take care of the damage." He handed me a cup of water and I took it. "I figure I'll run over there and help divvy out the medicine and pick up some of the slack."

"You don't hesitate to put in long hours, do you?" Jake shook his head.

"I can't just tell them no." I looked over at him. "They need help."

A loud bang filled the area and Jake jerked, wincing as he ducked his head. I stayed very still, filing the incident away in my brain. I wasn't sure why, but the look on his face made me wince. It was several seconds before he seemed in control of himself and looked back my way.

"You're starting to sound like me." His laugh was weak, but I ignored it.

"That's a scary thought." I frowned.

"My point is, you could tell them no, but you aren't." He stretched his legs and groaned, rubbing where his prosthetic attached to his leg. "When do we go?"

"I guess I'll go now. Just need to let Trina know." I drank the rest of my water and put the cup in the bin. "I've already got my tools packed up."

"Let me clean up my stuff. We can take my truck." He stood up with a grimace.

"What?" I looked at him as if he was crazy.

"You need help." He shrugged. "I'll help."

"No, it's okay. I'll be fine." I shook my head a little too hard and my ponytail whipped me in the eye. I grimaced and blinked back tears. "Ow!"

"Here." Jake pressed something to my eye. "It's no big deal. This is what friends do, right?"

"You're still on probation," I snapped and batted away his hand. That's when I realized he had lifted his shirt to wipe away my tears, exposing a wide expanse of well-muscled abdomen.

"Then I still need to work it off." He smiled at me and my frown deepened.

I had to stop doing stupid things around Jake Simmon. In fact I just needed to not be around Jake Simmon. Looking at him made my brain leak out my ears. Talking to him left me equally amused and tongue-tied. I couldn't think straight around the man and he was busy chasing tail all over D.C. Yes, the last thing I needed was to spend more time with Jake while he tried to be my friend. It just muddied the waters.

"No, no, no. I'm fine." I waved my hands to emphasize my point as if all the *no*'s hadn't made it clear.

He reached toward my face again with his shirt. "Stop swatting at me or you're going to get more dirt in your eyes. Be still, Madeline."

I froze when he used my whole name. It was rare for anyone to use my full name and when he did, something odd happened in my stomach. He dabbed at my face while I tried to ignore the way my blood pressure rocketed with his proximity.

"Now, ten minutes and I'll be back. Then we'll go feed the puppies and whatever." He moved off toward a toolbox leaving the "whatever" to hang in the air.

There were so many fine things I could think of to fill in that whatever. That was the whole problem. It was more than a problem; it was a red hot mess. I needed Jake's help, but I didn't need Jake's help. With him lurking around I'd likely stab myself with medicine meant for a dog. That was the definition of a problem.

Trina took a second from her paperwork to wave me off before yelling at someone about the cost of lumber. I checked my phone, but still hadn't heard back from Phoebe. My security detail for the day was waiting for me to decide what to do when Jake caught me.

His warm hand grasped my shoulder in a friendly grip and steered me to his truck. He put his tools in the back before opening the passenger door for me. He climbed into the driver seat and turned the key before fiddling with the air-conditioner. Cool air blasted from the vents and I sighed in relief. It had been hot and muggy today.

"Where are we going?" he asked as he put the truck in drive.

I gave him the address and rubbed at my face. I was hot, tired, and in dire need of a good bath.

"I've got some bottled water in the cooler in the back." Jake pulled out from the worksite. Our familiar black sedan escort right behind us.

I looked in the back row and found a bright orange cooler filled with cool bottles of water. I snagged two before turning back around in my seat just in time to see his eyes running over my ass. My cheeks heated and I took a breath. That was exactly the problem with spending time with Jake. If he didn't seem interested in turn it would be much easier to shake off this crush I seemed to have developed.

"Here you go." I handed him a bottle before opening mine.

"Thanks." He smiled, obviously not bothered that I'd caught him looking, and untwisted the top of his drink.

"I guess I should be thanking you." I frowned and took another drink of my water. "I was figuring that I would have to muck stalls by myself."

"Muck stalls. Yeah, not fun by yourself." His nose wrinkled. "Not fun no matter how you look at it really."

"Oh yeah. There are eighteen dog kennels, six dog runs, and several cats." Maybe it wouldn't be so bad to have some help. Especially if it meant Jake had to roll around in dog poop. "Of course, they also take reptiles."

"Reptiles?" He jerked his eyes in my direction.

"Yeah, people abandon them. Flora takes them in and tries to find them homes. It's better than people just letting them go in the wild. Most of them aren't adapted to survive here." I shrugged. "And we don't want them to run wild. They could take over and run out the native species. This is a good alternative for people."

"Or, they could just not buy them." Jake shook his head.

I shrugged. "Kids want different things."

Reptiles didn't really bother me, but not everyone appreciated them—or how much work they required.

Feeling like I needed to fill the silence I reached for the radio. Mumford and Sons coursed through the car and I looked at Jake in surprise.

"This is what you listen to?"

He shrugged. "I like it."

"I would have had you pegged as a country music listener." I leaned back in my seat and watched as the streets flew past.

"I like a little bit of everything." He smiled at me before looking back at the roads. "Just depends on my mood."

"And what sort of mood requires Mumford and Sons?"

"I was feeling a little homesick." He shrugged.

"Virginia?" I asked.

"Yeah. D.C. has some amazing things, but I miss the open space. Sometimes the city feels claustrophobic." He rolled his shoulders as if the city was pressing down on them right this moment.

"I can understand that." I nodded my head. I missed my real home too. "We have these lives here in the capitol that are so in your face, you know? The last time I went back to Colorado I felt like I'd entered an entirely different world."

"Exactly." He lifted his water bottle. "The Mumfords just ease the tension a bit."

I watched him as we drove and wondered when was the last time he'd gotten to go home and relax. It had been over a year since I'd been back to Colorado. The thought made my chest hurt. I couldn't think of home without associating it with my mother.

"I wonder if the weather has changed there, yet." I rubbed at the dirt caked on my fingers.

"I bet it would be cooler than here," he said.

"True." I frowned. "I should go visit soon. Take some flowers for my mom."

"You still do that?"

"Not as often as I should." Guilt lodged in my throat and I had to fight to swallow it down.

"You know, she wouldn't care about that." He reached over and squeezed my hand before moving back to the steering wheel.

"Thanks." His touch had been so sweet and gentle. "I think the act is more for those of us still here. So we don't feel like we're forgetting."

He nodded his head but didn't say anything. I wondered how many graves he had put flowers on. Part of me wanted to dig up information on his time in the Marines and on the accident. The rest of me said that was wrong for a lot of reasons.

We didn't speak the rest of the drive and I let myself relax. I must have dozed off listening to the music because it wasn't until Jake shook my shoulder that I realized we were at the shelter.

"Are you sure you want to do this? You look exhausted." His concerned face hovered close to mine and I blinked furiously.

"What?" I sat up straight and rubbed at my face. "I'm fine."

"You don't know how to stop, do you?" He reached out and brushed some of the hair off my face. "You'll run yourself into the ground at the pace you've set."

"Look who's talking," I grumbled. No one had ever accused

me of being pleasant when waking up. "Why are you so close to my face?"

"Thought I might have to kiss Sleeping Beauty awake." He sat back and smiled so big I could see all of his teeth.

"By your own admission, I'm no Sleeping Beauty. I look exhausted, remember? You can save your kisses." I felt discombobulated when he flirted with me and I resorted to being snippy. "I'm sorry. You're helping me and I'm being grumpy. Ignore me."

"Oh, I do." He chuckled as he climbed out of the truck. "And even tired and grumpy, you're still a beauty."

I didn't know what to say to that. My skin ran hot at his comment and I wondered why just a few words from Jake could get me hot and bothered so fast. His casual comments tended to knock me off my feet. With a sigh I opened my door and hopped out, stretching my arms behind my back.

"Maddie!" Flora ran out the front door, Puz the dog on her heels. "Thank goodness. The new volunteers are hopeless. One of them fed the dogs some cat food and I had to send them back to take the food away."

"I bet that went well." I shook my head. "Flora, this is Jake Simmon. He offered to lend a hand."

"We'll take it." Flora pushed her cat-eye glasses up on her nose and shook Jake's hand. "It's nice to meet you, Jake."

"Happy to help." Jake looked down at where Puz was sniffing at his pants. "I guess I'm not the only one missing a leg."

Puz was a poodle mix that had lost his hind leg in a car accident. He'd been such a mess the technicians had started calling him Puzzle. After the dust had settled and he'd lost his leg, the name had stuck. It had seemed appropriate considering that he was missing a piece.

"Oh, we get a bunch of animals with missing appendages, but Puz hasn't found his forever home." Flora smiled down at the dog. "Sit, Puz."

The shaggy poodle mix sat down next to Jake and cocked his head at Flora. Puz was a medium-sized dog with nothing remarkable about his appearance except for his big eyes and friendly personality. The fact that he had taken to Jake didn't surprise me. Flora trained service dogs and Puz had benefited from his time at her house.

"Are you looking for a dog, Jake?" Flora smiled up at him. She'd been in the game too long to look hopeful, but I could see the wheels turning in her head.

"Nah. I don't have much time for a dog." Jake shook his head. "Wouldn't be fair to them."

"You'd be surprised how they make room in your life," Flora explained. "Well, if you ever do decide to get a dog you should considering adopting."

"Absolutely," he agreed.

"I've got to get back to the shed. We lost a lot of supplies and I'm going to have to make a trip to the bulk store." Flora patted her graying hair and sighed dramatically. "I'm just glad it was mainly food and not medicine that we lost. Those are locked up inside."

Flora fluttered back to the door with us on her heels. "Thirteen, seven, and six need insulin. Twenty needs antibiotics. Oh! And there are two cats with urinary infections. Thanks for helping, Maddie. I just can't trust the new people with this stuff."

"It's no problem," I said.

"I mean, they can't even get the food right!" Flora grabbed a clipboard and shoved it in my direction. "I've got the outside dog runs taken care of, but the cages all need a good clean."

"No worries, Flora. We'll take care of this." I turned the frazzled woman toward the back door. "Go keep an eye on the new kids. I'll take care of the stuff in here."

"C'mon Puz. Let's see what they're doing now." Flora started toward the door, but Puz didn't follow. She looked back at where the dog sat next to Jake and frowned before looking back to Jake. "Okay, fine. Stay here. Just means I won't have to give you a bath tonight."

I looked down to where Puz leaned against Jake's leg and then up to the man next to me. His face was calm, almost serene, so I wasn't sure why Puz was behaving as if Jake was suffering from some sort of attack. Maybe the dog just took an instant liking to Jake. Maybe Jake was just one of those people that animals took to.

"I'll keep an eye on him, Flora." I waved at the woman. "Go, before they order something stupid."

"You're right. There's no telling what they think cats should eat."

Once she was gone I gave Jake some jobs to do and went about administering the medicine listed on the clipboard and giving each of the animals a good once-over to make sure they weren't having any problems the vet needed to be called in for. All the time, I kept a sneaky eye on Jake and Puz. The dog followed him everywhere, never letting the man leave his sight.

As we went about the chores I mulled over what that meant. Puz could be sensing Jake's homesickness, but his response was rather intense. Of course, Puz wasn't a fully trained therapy dog. He'd just picked up some of the training while at Flora's.

Maybe Puz just liked Jake. It wouldn't be the first time a dog had picked their human instead of the other way around. In fact, it usually worked best that way. With that thought in mind I went back to my work.

"That's pretty good." Jake's deep voice drew my attention to the back of the building. When I heard a thump and loud laugh I got up to investigate. Surely he hadn't decided to seduce some volunteer.

That would be a big kick in the shins. Especially since I'd been so impressed by the way he'd dove into those kennels without blinking.

"No, don't do that. C'mon," Jake said. His voice was happy and I hesitated. Did I really want to see him with some girl I'd have to work with another day? "Stop licking me."

I frowned.

"I said to stop." His voice got stern and then softened. "Okay, okay. I need a bath anyway."

"What the hell are you doing?" I rounded the corner to see him sitting on the floor and wrestling with Puz. "Oh."

"What's wrong?" Jake looked up at me and Puz mimicked him. "Are you okay?"

"Uh. Yeah. Sorry. I, uh, didn't know what you were doing." I rubbed my hands on my pants.

"So you said." Jake ruffled the fur on Puz's head. "This guy wanted some attention."

"Puz is pretty awesome and seems to really like you." I leaned against the concrete wall.

"He's okay." Jake shrugged in that way guys had when they agreed with you but didn't want to admit it.

"Do you have dogs back in Virginia?"

"Some of the horse trainers do, but we never had a house dog. We were gone too much for that." Jake held Puz still so he could look in his eyes before flipping up his gums to look at his teeth. Puz wagged his tail through the inspection. "Has a bit of an underbite."

"That happens from time to time." I rolled my eyes. "Lots of people pay big bucks for dogs bred to have underbites."

"I didn't say it was bad. Just an observation." Jake shook his head.

"Why don't you take him home?"

"I can't take care of a dog. My backyard is barely five feet across." He scratched behind Puz's ear. "And I'm gone all the time."

"You could do a trial period. If it doesn't work, then you can bring him back."

"That would make me feel like an ass." He shook his head. "Better to let him stay so a family will find him."

"Well, if you change your mind let me know." I didn't bother to hide my disappointment. Puz was a great dog but I knew people were put off by the potential health issues he would deal with in old age.

"Why don't you take him?" Jake looked up at me and I noticed the way he draped his hand around Puz's neck.

"Abigail is allergic." I shrugged. There had been a time when I'd resented that, but the woman couldn't help having allergies. "I don't have my own place yet, so no pets."

Jake stood up carefully, his face tightening as he put his weight on his prosthetic.

"Does it still bother you?" I nodded at his leg.

"Sometimes." He rubbed at his knee.

"Like after a long day of construction work and cleaning dog kennels?" I squashed the automatic guilt. He had insisted on coming. It wasn't like I'd asked him.

"That's about right." He rolled his head back and forth on his shoulder. "Nothing a hot shower won't help."

"Flora's already gone. Let me lock up." I headed for the front desk. It was dark outside which meant we'd been working for hours.

I made some notes and taped the paper to the computer monitor so it wouldn't be missed. I was worried about one of the cats but it wasn't anything that needed immediate attention. There were a few forms to sign and I gathered up some paperwork on Puz. It wouldn't hurt to send it home with Jake. My gut said that they were a perfect match and it had nothing to do with their missing legs.

"Take these." I slid the papers across the counter to Jake while I totaled the credit card slips from adoptions that had happened earlier in the day.

"Puzzle?"

I glanced at him quickly before going back to my work. "Yeah, Puz. Those are the forms you'll need if you decide you want to take him home."

"I told you I didn't have the time for a dog." I noticed he was looking through the paperwork, no matter what he said. "Why did they name him Puzzle?"

"Because he's missing a piece." I shrugged without looking up. I tucked a paper clip on the credit slips and shoved the bunch in the slot on the safe.

"Poor dog." Jake chuckled. "Tell them you're more than the sum of your parts, Puz."

He reached down and scratched the dog under the chin.

"Oh, he has everyone eating out of his hand." I cocked my head to the side and smiled brightly. "If you aren't going to take him home, will you put him in his pen?"

"I thought he lived with Flora." Jake frowned.

"Only until he was healthy enough for adoption. Puz is a perfect little guy and ready for a home. So he stays here with the others. Flora spends a lot of time training service dogs and just can't handle any more mouths at home." I tossed the key for the cage at Jake. He caught it with his right hand. "He's in number eight."

"C'mon, Puz." Jake started to walk down the aisle of kennels with the dog on his heels.

The little dog followed along, his tail wagging. I peered over the edge of the desk, watching them go. Jake opened the gate and motioned for Puz to go inside. Knowing Puz the way I did, I could imagine him looking up at Jake with those giant brown eyes while curling up on the cement.

I chewed on my bottom lip and hoped that my ploy worked. My gut was screaming that the two belonged together and Jake was just being stubborn. Besides, if it didn't work out, I'd bring the dog back—no harm, no foul. Puz would have gotten a little vacation from the shelter and no one would be upset.

If I could have a dog, Puz would already have a home, but that wasn't a good reason to not see him happy now.

"Damn it." The whisper reached my ears and I ducked behind the desk to hide my smile. "C'mon Puz."

I swiped the papers from the counter and stamped the last page. I set it on top of the desk with a pen and pretended to be busy.

"Does he have a leash?" Jake picked up the pen and scribbled his information on the paper.

"I've got one you can borrow. There's a pet store on the way to town." I picked up a yellow leash and set it next to him.

"You're dangerous, Maddie." Jake looked at me and his dimple flashed.

"I have no idea what you mean."

"You're good. Sometimes I think there is no way you're related to your father and then I leave a shelter with a three-legged dog unsure how it all happened." He shook his head with a smile. "It's obvious you inherited the McGuire magic."

"Hm." McGuire magic? "Puz is up to date on all his shots and I'll get you his medical records later. He doesn't have any allergies and gets along with other animals and children. He's house trained and leash trained. So you won't have to worry about that. If you want to change his food I'd do it slowly so you don't upset his stomach but, otherwise, he's an easy dog to care for."

"Right." His warm brown eyes narrowed on me. "Let's go. This is your fault so you have to help me pick out his stuff at the pet store."

"Sure." I came out from behind the desk and put the leash on Puz. "What are friends for?"

I opened the front door for Jake and Puz but didn't miss his smile when I called him my friend. If Puz liked him, then I really couldn't hold on to my doubts. Especially after he spent two hours cleaning dog crap to prove he was my friend.

Chapter 7

Jake

Soft skin covered in a sheen of sweat pressed against my chest. "Jake." Plump lips tore from mine in a gasp of pleasure and I looked down into hazel eyes rimmed with gold. Electricity flooded my body as our gazes met and I jerked awake with a gasp.

For the second time this week I'd dreamed about being inside of Maddie McGuire; feeling her move beneath me. The one woman that barely tolerated me, the one woman I wasn't supposed to have, had started to haunt my dreams.

"Damn it." I gripped the sheets and fought the urge to rip them to pieces.

I couldn't have Maddie McGuire, not even if my body seemed to think I should. I'd thought it was hormones, pent-up lust from being out of the game for so long, but even sleeping with a sexy-as-hell redhead three weekends ago hadn't been enough to knock my system back into line. Neither had the curly-haired lobbyist the week before. I'd been trying all the different flavors since I'd been back to normal—as normal as I'd ever be without my leg—and nothing eased the burn I had for a hazel-eyed, sharp-witted woman I wasn't supposed to want. A woman I didn't deserve.

Well, every flavor except Ronnie again. I'd told her I wasn't interested in a follow-up but she still called every few days offering to do more and more for me. I just couldn't bring myself to even be interested. Seeing the pain on Maddie's face over Ronnie had made it all but impossible to think of the leggy reporter with any sort of interest. In fact, I hadn't been able to dig up any interest in anyone lately. After spending the time with Maddie picking out stuff for Puz at the pet store, I'd barely noticed any other woman. I was screwed. Or rather I wasn't screwed, which was the problem.

Watching Maddie over the last few weeks had been intriguing. Much more intriguing than I had thought she would be. She had grown out of her shell and was so much more comfortable speaking in public. When I'd left for officer school she'd barely been able to mutter a sentence in front of the cameras without turning red. But now, it felt as if she'd stopped hiding. No longer was she trying to be the perfect daughter, she'd simply found a way to be herself without apology.

And the media and public ate it up. They called her refreshing and honest. She might not care much for the attention, but the world couldn't seem to get enough of her blunt personality. People loved her open manner, the fact that she spoke with everyone as though they were equals. Pictures of her sweaty and hauling materials around the worksite had filled the news shows and papers. She was one of them.

Ironically, she was exactly what my mother had hoped I would be for her campaign.

Maddie didn't shy away from getting sweaty. She might be a D.C. debutante but that didn't stop her from earning blisters with the rest of us. She hadn't hesitated to do whatever had been asked of her. There had been moments when I'd been ready to rest but kept pushing because Maddie never stopped. I wasn't about to rest while she toiled around the worksite. By the middle of the week I was more than a little sore.

Stretching in bed, I grimaced as something caught on the left side. They'd removed all the shrapnel embedded in my side but the scar tissue hurt when pulled at the wrong angle. I could deal with the scar tissue; it was the phantom pains in my leg that drove me insane.

There was a scraping noise and I looked over at the floor to see Puz holding his leash in his mouth. Shit. He needed to go out and it was raining.

With a groan I sat up in bed and threw the covers off. I took a few minutes to massage just below my knee before attaching my prosthetic. I stood up carefully, letting everything adjust before walking to the kitchen. I'd bought the brownstone sight unseen before coming back to D.C. The thought of moving back into the Vice President's home had caused my blood pressure to rocket.

"Come on." I clipped the leash to Puz's collar and took him downstairs. I grabbed the obnoxious little poop bags Maddie had insisted I buy and took the dog for a quick walk around the block.

There was no way that I could have dealt with seeing my mother that often. It was bad enough that I had to have daily chats with her henchmen. Someone from her campaign office came every morning to update me on how things were going, if they needed more quotes for marketing, or photo ops with other wounded soldiers.

I knew that while doing things my mother's way I was also getting to do something good for my fellow military. Of course, some days it was easier to hold on to the positive aspects and other days it was almost impossible to keep from pounding my fists onto the countertops while being told what to wear and when to smile.

Puz grunted when we reached the wet pavement and stopped to take a giant dump next to my neighbor's flower.

"Dude, that is nasty." I scooped up his mess and threw the little baggie in the nearest trash can. I wasn't carrying that around the whole block. "No more pizza for you."

By the time we'd gotten back to the house Puz had peed on every house, tree, and signpost. I was starting to worry he'd be dehydrated at this rate.

I filled his bowl of water and added food to his dish, but the dog ignored it and crawled back onto the giant pillow that was his bed and wriggled under the throw blanket he'd stolen from my couch. I took the time to scramble eggs and drink a glass of orange juice before changing into work clothes. By the time I'd checked e-mail, there was a Secret Service agent at my door waiting to take me to the construction site.

"I'll be back tonight and the housekeeper will check on you this afternoon." I pointed at Puz who peeked out from under his blanket. "Don't growl at her purse again. It's just a handbag, got it?"

The dog snorted at me and then closed his eyes, signaling that he was done listening to me. I sighed. I was going to have to clear out a shelf for the housekeeper to put her things. Apparently the first day she'd come over Puz had spent the entire day growling at her bright yellow ostrich purse, and she was worried he'd tear it up.

Not that I could really blame him.

Mom's flunky was waiting in the Suburban to enlighten me on the days itinerary. I barely listened, just nodded at the right intervals. The family receiving the house was supposed to be coming today and there would be media.

I rubbed my sweaty palms on my jeans. This was why I had agreed to do any of this stuff for my mother. Meeting the family benefiting from everything shouldn't make me nervous. At least it had stopped raining.

The press was waiting when we arrived. Considering that it was barely eight in the morning, I imagined some of them really hated their job.

"Has the family arrived?" I looked at the pencil pusher across from me.

"Um, no." He scrolled through his phone. "Looks like the Holland family is about thirty minutes behind us."

"Holland?" My gut clenched and I really looked at the other man in the backseat. "Cyrus Holland?"

"Yes." He drew the word out, making it obvious that I should have already known that fact. "Your mother had his family moved up on the list. She thought you would appreciate it."

Cyrus Holland was the only surviving member of my team. We hadn't talked since I saw him in the hospital in Germany. He'd just come out of another surgery and I was being bundled off in a private plane for the States. He'd lost both an arm and a leg on my mission as well as suffered a head injury. When I'd been trapped under the wreckage, I'd heard his screams of pain, him crying for his wife, and meeting his eyes in that hospital had been the most difficult moment of my life.

And now I was going to face him again . . . In front of a dozen cameras and reporters.

That made the giant glass of orange juice and panful of scrambled eggs I'd eaten that morning a terrible idea. The bile in the back of my throat seemed to mock my earlier appetite.

Blood thundered in my ears and I took a few deep breaths while I counted to ten. One of the Secret Service agents opened the vehicle door and I was left with no option but to climb out. I waved for the cameras before slowly making my way to the clump of people talking where the front door would eventually stand. Anxiety spiked through my veins and I felt like bolting.

But I wasn't at the point where I wanted to punch things. That meant I could turn it around.

"Lovely couple. They have a little boy and another on the way." Trina was looking at her clipboard, going over her daily rundown for the volunteers. "We're expecting even more media, but that's nothing we aren't used to at this point."

"Thanks to Captain Hottie-pants," one of the volunteers mock whispered.

"Hey, now. Leave my pants out of it." I held my hands up and smiled. At least I think I was smiling.

"Your pants? I was talking about Maddie." The short brunette laughed. "Have you seen those jeans?"

"Oh." I leaned back. Talk about putting my foot in my mouth.

"Would you like some water?" Kremdenski the foreman offered. "To ease the burn?"

Trina threw her head back and laughed loudly. Yes, I could turn around my bad mood. It was hard not to when surrounded by such good people.

"I'll heal on my own, thanks." I shook my head and couldn't

help a rueful smile. "Speaking of our illustrious coworker, when will she be here?"

"Maddie's been here for two hours." Trina nodded to one of the work trucks. "She wanted the house to look homey."

"Hard to do when we just barely got the drywall up," Kremdenski huffed.

"Two hours?" I tucked my hands in my pockets and watched as Maddie walked from the truck to the house carrying a large box. "What is she doing?"

"We laid out samples for the family to look over. It's nothing over the top, but she insisted that they get to choose paint colors, cabinets." The short girl that had teased me earlier spoke up again. "She sent me to the Home Depot to get welcome mats."

"Heh." I watched as she carefully climbed the stairs and noticed the brown mat at the door's edge.

"She's something else, isn't she?" Trina tsked. "Pretty sure she'd let me work her into the ground if I tried. Just watching her makes me want another coffee."

"How do you want to handle the Holland family when they get here?" I changed the subject, because thinking about watching Maddie made me want to do lots of things and none of them included coffee. I wasn't sure that was the direction I needed to focus while balancing on a sharp edge of anxiety.

"Let's get them straight to the house. The press can have their go afterward." Trina smiled. "I heard this was one of your boys."

"I wouldn't call him my boy, but yes, we served together. I didn't find out until this morning that his family was getting the house." I counted between breaths, hoping my agitation didn't shine through. "I haven't seen him since Germany."

"I've talked with his wife several times this week and she's a sweetheart. Couldn't be more excited to get the house." Trina cocked her head to the side. "They lost their home right after Cyrus got back to the States. Medical bills, loss of work, you name it. They just couldn't keep up. A real shame."

"How'd they make it to the top of the list so quickly?" My gaze drifted to the road. It would be okay. Even if Cyrus hated me, it wouldn't be the first time I'd spent a few hours working with someone that hated me.

"Well, being that he's a double amputee, they were already pretty far up, but when we found out they were expecting another child it gave them a little boost." Trina tapped her ever-present clipboard against her thigh. "They were living with her parents in a two-bedroom home in Norfolk. They needed their own space."

"How has his recovery been so far?"

"Slow but steady. Still not able to work, but he's in good spirits. Really looking forward to being a stay-at-home father for a while."

"That's positive." The road seemed to open up as another black sport utility vehicle made its way to the construction house.

Someone dropped something heavy behind the house and I ducked, ready to take cover. It wasn't until someone cleared their throat that I realized I was freaking out. Loud noises triggered my fight-or-flight instinct every time. I'd need to get some earplugs if I wanted to make it through the day without scaring anyone.

"Look happy, people! They're here. Sandy, go let Maddie know it's time." Trina reached out and touched my shoulder. She didn't say anything but I nodded my head so she would know I was okay.

The brunette took off running toward the house and disappeared inside. I watched the SUV as it pulled up to the curb and one of the PR leaders opened the door and another pushed a wheelchair around to the sidewalk.

A pretty blonde woman climbed out of the car slowly, before helping a toddler out. The child clutched one of her hands while her other slipped around to her lower back. Someone said something from inside the car that made her laugh before she shook her head.

The goon that had been following me for the day jerked his head in their direction and I sighed. They'd looked happy. And here I was to throw them in the limelight and ruin their moment.

"Kyla?" I said the wife's name on a croak and cleared my throat. I'd remembered because it had been burned into my brain the day I'd been stuck under the helicopter. Cyrus had called for her until he passed out. It had haunted my dreams for months afterward.

"Oh my Lord, Cyrus! He's really here!" The woman turned to me and threw her arms around my neck. "They said you'd be here, but it just didn't seem real!"

"It's nice to finally meet you," I said. I gave her a gentle hug in return, aware of how her belly pressed against me.

"Jake?" Cyrus stuck his head out of the SUV. Panic hit me at the sound of his voice. "Shit, they didn't need to drag you out here for this, man!"

He climbed carefully out of the car. He was wearing a prosthesis attached to his right shoulder and another just below his right knee. Not once did he glance at the wheelchair. Instead, he moved confidently toward me and threw his good arm around my neck. I was shocked by the warmth in his eyes.

It was hard to connect the pain and horror from the past with this little family on a sunny day.

"It's good to see you, man. I wasn't sure I'd ever see you again after Germany." He touched the scar along his cheek with a rueful smile. "And not just because of this."

"It's good to see you, too." The funny thing was that despite all of my pent-up anxiety it was a relief to see him smiling. "Are you going to introduce me to your family?"

"You met Kyla, she's a hugger." He held his hand out to his wife with a grin. "And this here is Korbin. He'll be three in a month."

"Just in time for his little sister's arrival." Kyla patted her stomach.

"It's nice to meet you, Korbin." I held my hand out to the little boy but he hid behind his mother's leg. Considering the clamoring of the press and all the cameras I didn't blame him. "I heard that you're getting your very own big-brother room. Are you excited?"

"Trucks!" Korbin peered around his mother's leg.

"I promised him a truck room." Kyla blushed.

"That sounds like a good plan." I nodded my head. "Are you ready to see your new house? It's not finished yet, but it will be ready for you soon."

"I feel like I'm on one of those television shows." Kyla fanned her face. "I can't believe we're getting a house. I don't want to cry but I'm not making any promises."

"This is awesome, man." Cyrus shook his head. "We really appreciate it."

"C'mon, I'll show you the house and introduce you to the crew from RCVA." I headed toward the house, sad that there wasn't a pretty lawn in place. Now that I thought about it, it didn't seem very homey. "Watch your step, there are nails everywhere. We'll get them all cleaned up once we're done."

"It's beautiful." Kyla smiled, her eyes already glimmering with tears.

"Look at that porch, Korbin. We're going to have fun watching the planes go by from there." Cyrus ruffled his son's hair.

His limp was still pronounced, but that made sense considering the amount of damage he had suffered. Fitting a prosthetic took time. I'd gotten lucky.

Or more likely, I'd benefited from being the Vice President's son. Physicians had jumped at the chance to use me as a walking billboard. Not all returning veterans had the same attention or the same deep family pockets.

Maddie appeared at the front door, bouncing on the balls of her feet. A giant smile split her face when she saw the family.

As if she'd known them her entire life she bounded down the stairs and grabbed Kyla in a hug before turning to Cyrus to pull him in.

"I'm so excited to meet you." Her voice was muffled.

Cyrus looked at me with big eyes before mouthing, "Who is this?"

"Maddie, maybe you should introduce yourself before you assault every family."

"Oh my gosh, I'm so sorry. I just feel like I already know you. Those files the RCVA have are pretty complete. Spooky amount of detail actually." She stepped back and held out her hand to Cyrus. "I'm Maddie McGuire. It's a pleasure to meet all of you."

"Maddie McGuire?" Kyla looked from me to the energetic woman in front of her. "You're President McGuire's daughter? Cyrus, that's the President's daughter!"

"Guilty." Maddie smiled.

"And that's only one charge," I muttered under my breath. I was rewarded with a sharp elbow to the ribs.

"Hey now, those puppies need help." Cyrus laughed and pushed my shoulder. "Don't give her a hard time. Besides, I remember you feeding the strays in Afghanistan."

"Cyrus, I think we're going to get along very well." Maddie beamed at the man next to me. "And, I'd like to point out there were no actual charges. Okay, I can't wait anymore. You guys go in and check it out. We'll give you a few minutes before we show you all the options you have."

"Options?" Kyla looked confused.

"Paint colors, cabinets, and flooring. I put all the samples in the kitchen. This way you have a little say in what your home looks like." Maddie moved to stand next to me. "Go on. I can't wait to hear what you think."

Cyrus took Kyla's hand as they walked up the stairs and I made a mental note to make sure the railing was in place before they came again. There was a wheelchair ramp in the back of the house, but he'd need something to hold on to if coming in from the front.

I heard them whispering to each other quietly as they went through the front door. I pushed my nerves away and looked down at Maddie.

"The welcome mat was a nice touch."

"Thanks. Last night I couldn't stop thinking about how a construction zone doesn't really look like a home." She shrugged. "It's better this way because they get to make it their own. Give it their own spin. But I can't imagine it actually feels like coming home."

"It was very thoughtful." I bumped her with my elbow. "For a felon."

"Thanks. That's really sweet coming from Captain Hottie-pants."

"I thought that was your nickname." I frowned.

"Gullible much?" She snorted. "Though I do look really good in these pants."

She gave her ass a little shake and my blood heated up. I let my eyes travel down over her dusty flannel shirt to the dark jeans that cupped her ass. She was right. Those jeans were enough to make me salivate.

The vivid image from my dream flashed through my mind and I had to fight back a groan. Maybe it was just the fact that I couldn't have her, but at that moment I wanted nothing more than to pull her to a dark corner, grip that perfect ass with both hands, and kiss her until she couldn't think to tease me anymore.

Something must have shown on my face because she blushed, tucked some of the loose hair behind her ears, and looked back at the house. The fact that she was shocked by my reaction made me want to show her just how much I liked what I saw.

"Yes, you certainly do." I moved a little closer, lowering my head close to her ear. "Very good."

She jerked her gaze up to mine and I watched as her pupils dilated. Little Maddie had grown up and I wasn't blind. But she wasn't the kind of woman you took for a quick roll. She was the kind of woman that could drive you crazy with little looks in a dress that showed nothing but one shoulder. Her personality shined through everything she did. It would never be just sex—though I was pretty sure that would be amazing.

There would be movie marathons, popcorn fights, and pillow talk with her.

Maddie was the kind of woman you kept forever.

And I wasn't looking for that type of relationship. Right now, all I could focus on was today. Forever wasn't in my vocabulary. Especially not with someone my mother had outlawed.

"We've got press shots soon." Maddie licked her lips and tilted them closer to mine. Biting her bottom lip, she reached up toward my face and used her thumb to brush the corner of my mouth. "You've got a little something right here."

My hand went to my face, checking for drool. Her throaty laugh had me look up in time to see her wink before she took the stairs two at a time.

"Minx," I muttered.

"Captain Hottie-pants."

I might not be looking for forever, but damn if Maddie wasn't tempting.

Chapter 8

Maddie

Kyla picked up one of the paint chips and held it up in the fading light.

"I really like this one," she said. "What do you think, Cyrus?"

"I love it."

"Really? What about this one instead? It's very sophisticated." She held up a bright purple card and raised her eyebrow.

"You're right." Cyrus nodded his head while looking over pictures of refrigerators in a magazine. "Sophisticated."

I bit the inside of my mouth to keep from laughing.

"We could do the trim in this green color, too."

"Yeah, that sounds—wait. Green?" He looked up and I couldn't stop my laughter. "For the trim?"

"You better pay attention or you're going to end up with a house painted like a gypsy caravan." Jake leaned back against a wall.

I'd noticed that he'd started favoring his left leg after the press interview and there weren't exactly a ton of chairs in the construction zone. Cyrus had finally given in to using his wheelchair and we'd found a stool for Kyla. There wasn't much left for us.

"The contractor said I needed to pick out the appliances by Monday." Cyrus frowned. "I don't want to end up with a leaky ice maker. If my phone hadn't died I would be looking up reviews online."

"We've got all weekend, Cy." Kyla rolled her eyes.

"I'm sorry today's gone on for so long. You've got to be exhausted." I looked over to where Korbin had fallen asleep in a stroller. He had a crayon gripped tightly in one fist while the coloring book had dropped to the floor next to him.

"Don't apologize! Are you crazy?" Kyla looked at me with big eyes. "Um, I'm sorry. You're so normal I forget that you're the President's daughter. Obviously you aren't crazy."

"Eh. The jury is still out." I gathered up some of the pamphlets and slipped them into a large envelope. "I put my number in here too. If you think of any questions or are worried about anything, don't hesitate to call. Some of these contractors will run you over if you don't put your foot down."

"Oh no, everyone has been so nice. I almost feel bad for taking the time to choose stuff. I know there are lots of people waiting for homes." She giggle-snorted. "But if anyone gives me trouble, I'll be sure to call you."

"I'm serious. They give you a hard time and I'll give them the old one-two." I mimed punching.

"Can you imagine? It would be like having Princess Kate calling the plumber because I don't like the toilet seat! I'm just happy to have a toilet seat to call my own." Kyla held her stomach as she laughed. "Who knew we'd be hanging out with American royalty today?"

"Don't forget the hour-long photo session while people screamed inappropriate questions at your face." I sighed.

"It wasn't bad, but I dread the pictures. Being pregnant really messes with my good side." Kyla stood up and stretched.

"Every side of you is perfect." Cyrus looked at his wife with genuine love. "And I personally really enjoyed the questions about whether or not my junk still worked."

"We've got our proof right here." Kyla rubbed her stomach.

"Damn right." Cyrus laughed.

"You two are adorable." I held up my hands. "But I really don't want to hear about what positions you used to get pregnant."

"I guess that's our cue." Cyrus rolled forward and took the large envelope.

"We really need to get Korbin back to my parents. It's almost five and I need to start dinner." Kyla looked at her watch. "I'm making pork chops."

"Then we definitely need to go." Cyrus smiled at Jake. "You should come over sometime. Kyla's cooking isn't to be missed."

"Housewarming party when we move in," Kyla announced. "It'll be great and you'll get to see everything put together."

"Does Korbin like dogs? Jake could bring Puz over to play." I smiled smugly at Jake.

"I saw that in a paper," Kyla explained "You adopted a three-legged dog!"

"It was Maddie's fault." Jake held his hands out as if innocent of some crime.

"Yes, I forced you to fall in love with the half poodle and

take him home." I rolled my eyes. "I forgot to send you some bows for his ears."

"I'm not putting bows on that dog. He's a guy." Jake jerked his head in a definite denial. "Absolutely not."

"Yes, you have to bring the dog. Korbin will love him." Kyla laughed before whispering to me, "And I bet I can scrounge up some bows for his ears."

"C'mon on. Those pork chops are calling my name." Cyrus headed for the back door with the ramp.

Kyla picked up the coloring book and tucked it next to her son. "Thank you again for everything you've done."

"Thank the RCVA. They're the ones making this possible. We're just here to get people to pay attention." I shrugged.

"That's important too. If people don't realize there is a problem it can't be fixed." Kyla looked toward where Cyrus was rolling down the ramp.

"Is everything okay?" Kyla was so sweet I hated to see the worry on her face.

"Usually." I watched as she pushed her sorrow away. "There are bad moments, but this house has been a big help; gives us something to look forward to. Living with my parents isn't easy, there just isn't much room."

"I can't imagine."

"Most people don't realize that the real damage is inside, where no one can see it. It's not physical." She lowered her voice. "His arm and leg? Those are an adjustment, they slow him down some, but eventually he'll be back to his normal pace, you know? The other stuff is a lot harder to fix."

I nodded, thinking about her words. My eyes drifted toward where Jake stood next to his friend. Did he have those same type of scars under the surface? If so, he hid it well.

"But don't let me be a downer. This has been a great day."
She smiled brightly. "Did you see Korbin's face when he picked
out a room? He was completely over the moon."

"He's an adorable little guy." I looked down at his sleeping
face. "And so smart."

"Thanks, he makes it easy to get up each morning." Kyla
pushed the stroller down the ramp and toward the front of the
house. "When I found out about Cy, Korbin was the only thing
that kept me going."

"Seems like your family has been through an awful lot."

"We've been very lucky. It could have been so much worse."
She smiled and her entire face transformed into something an-
gelic. "He's still here with us. So I think we've been far luckier
than anything else."

"You're a strong woman, Kyla."

"Nah. It's just about how you look at things." She cut her
eyes at me with a sly smile. "Speaking of looking at things, I've
noticed the way Jake's been eyeing you."

When she burst out laughing, I could only imagine my expression.

"Uh, no. Not what you think." I shook my head. "Not at all.
Nope. It's just, normal looks. Probably annoyed looks, actually.
We don't get along so well."

"And now I know I'm right." She chuckled softly. "If you
ever need to talk, I'm happy to listen."

"Er, thanks?" I frowned.

"Anytime."

After having them bundled up in their car, I went back to the
house to make sure everything was off and cleaned up so the
crews wouldn't have an issue the next morning.

I was throwing an empty soda can away when I heard the

soft scrape of a shoe behind me. Despite the logical part of my brain that knew no one would get past the Secret Service guards I immediately went into panic mode. Turning around I threw the garbage bag at the person standing behind me and dove for a broken two-by-four on the ground.

"What the hell are you doing?" Jake swatted the black bag out of the way.

"How the hell do you move so quietly with a fake leg?" I threw the board at him, adrenaline still ringing in my ears. "Shouldn't you make some kind of sound when you move? A dragging sound, shuffling noises, or something?"

He knocked the board out of the way with his cane. "I'm missing a leg, not a zombie. Do you want me to groan and walk with my arms out?"

"Clear your throat or something. Don't just sneak up on people." I waved my arms in the air.

"I will remember to clear my throat next time." He held up his other hand, which had a six-pack of beer. "Peace offering?"

"Thanks, but I don't drink beer." I took a deep breath and knocked off some of the dust from my jeans. "Never got a taste for it."

He sat the case down on one of the worktables and pulled a bottle out. "My friend owns a microbrewery and this is an ale, not a beer. Made from apples."

"Apples?" I looked at the label. "I didn't know you could make beer out of apples."

"Ale, not beer. Want to try it?" He held a bottle out to me. "If you don't like it I won't tell Tame."

"Your friend's name is Tame?" I took the bottle from his hand.

"Nickname." He popped the top off his bottle and leaned

back against what would eventually be the kitchen island. "Got it in boot camp."

"He was in the Marines with you?" I looked at the bottle before reluctantly twisting the lid. "Was he a pilot too?"

"No. Special forces." He took a swig from his bottle.

"So, how does one get a nickname like Tame?" I sniffed at the bottle before taking a small sip. It wasn't as bad as the other things I'd tried.

"You'll have to ask him," he chuckled. "Not my story to tell."

"Some kind of military thing?"

"Something like that." He nodded at my drink. "What do you think?"

"Not bad." I cocked my head to the side. "So, do you happen to just carry a six-pack of your friend's ale around with you all the time?"

"I sent one of Mom's goons back to my place." He reached down and rubbed his knee.

"Expecting a rough day?" I took another sip.

"Honestly? I wasn't sure what to expect today." He ran a hand through his hair. "I haven't seen Cyrus since Germany and . . ."

Silence filled the room and I looked down at my shoes. "I can't imagine what that was like."

"I wasn't sure if he would be upset to see me. I had to leave him in Germany." He looked down at his drink. "He was stuck there in a hospital bed with no family and I was surrounded by the Secret Service and shipped off on a private plane."

"And you thought that he'd, what, hate you for it?"

I watched as his jaw clenched but he didn't say anything.

"Jake, he can't hate you because your mother is the Vice President." I sat the ale down.

"Or it's the perfect reason to hate me." He shrugged and drained the last of his bottle. "Doesn't matter."

"No, I guess not. Seemed like you guys got on just fine." I took another sip of the ale and found it was growing on me.

"Well, he didn't try to kill me with a plastic bag and a stick. So that's something."

"Oh, shut up." I laughed. "You scared me."

"Good thing you have terrible aim." He shifted his weight to his other leg. "You could have given me a splinter."

"You deserve a splinter for sneaking around." I glared at him. "You almost gave me a heart attack."

"A herd of stampeding buffalo could sneak up on you. You get lost in your head."

"I do not. I was just picking up everything before I left." I brushed my hair out of my eyes. "I figured that you left when your friend did."

"You thought I'd leave you with all the mess?" He picked up the plastic bag and dumped his bottle inside. "I'm on probation, remember? Can't let my friend down. Of course I was staying to help clean up."

"Get on with it, then." I motioned toward the spacious living room. "The reporters left their trash everywhere."

"Don't the people on garbage detail get a yellow vest or something?"

"Nope. But I could tape a nail to the end of your cane so you can stab the trash."

He laughed. "Thanks, but that's the last thing I need."

"So, how is Ari doing?" I changed the subject, feeling the need to fill the silence. "We've been watching *Buffy the Vampire Slayer* when we can."

"Is that show still playing?"

"Of course it is. You can stream it on pretty much any device." I moved through the kitchen, trying to make sure that no tools were left plugged in or littering the floor. "It's a classic."

His chuckle floated to my ears from the other room. "I'm really behind on television and movies."

"Your sister, Ari, can catch you up. We talk about it all the time."

"Is Ari old enough to watch that?" He picked up the trash bag and started to stuff empty cups inside.

"She's thirteen now." I laughed. "She can get in to see most movies on her own at this point."

"So, there's a lot of violence in something like that, but what about sex?"

Heat rushed to my cheeks and I silently berated myself. He slept with Ronnie. Might still be sleeping with Ronnie. Just the mention of the word *sex* shouldn't make my entire body hot.

I took a deep breath and picked up a piece of scrap paper.

"Maddie?"

Aw, shit. I hadn't answered his question.

"Hm? What?" I kept my head down, praying for more trash to occupy my attention.

"I asked if there was any sex." His shoes came into view and I looked up slowly.

"Oh, there will be." I met his eyes. "But not yet."

His eyes widened just a smidge, his nostrils flared ever so slightly, and I realized how what I'd said sounded.

"I mean, um, that I wouldn't mind—" Shit, that was worse. "I promise to cover her eyes."

"What wouldn't you mind, Madeline?" His voice dropped an octave, making my heart speed up. Madeline, not Maddie or MadLibs.

"I, um—what?" My voice was breathy as he took a step even closer to me.

"You mentioned something about sex, I believe." He reached out, using his fingers to brush some of the hair out of my eyes.

"I did? I mean, yes, I did. On the show." I fumbled over the words. "Buffy! That's what I was talking about. I wouldn't mind having sex with—damn it—I mean I wouldn't mind seeing—shit. No matter what I say this sounds wrong."

"Nothing wrong with sex." His eyes twinkled and I realized his hand was still on my face when he lifted my chin up.

"I—I—know that."

His thumb ran over my bottom lip. "Then why do you have such a hard time talking about it?"

"I don't!" My spine stiffened. "Sex doesn't scare me."

"Then it's me." He lowered his head close to mine and I swallowed the lump in my throat. "I make you nervous."

I swallowed again, my throat scratchy like sandpaper. "No you don't."

"Yes, I do." His hand swept around to the back of my neck. "I always have."

"I was, what, seventeen when you left for officer training?" I tried to calm my racing heart. "So what if I was a little nervous around you?"

"So you admit it?" His eyes twinkled and his mouth moved a little closer to mine.

"I admit nothing." I jerked my chin up.

"Are you nervous now?" His body pressed closer to mine and I licked my lips. "Am I making you nervous?"

"Yes." I whispered the word, not taking my eyes from his.

"Is it a good nervous?" His eyes grew serious. "Or are you scared of me?"

"I'm not scared of you, Jake." I touched his chest and noticed that my hand was steady despite how fast my heart was beating. "You never scared me."

"You're one of the rules, you know." His lips moved toward mine and I ached to close the distance.

"Rules?"

"That's what my mom was reminding me of at the fundraiser. I'm not supposed to want you." His breath fluttered across my face.

"Do you . . . want me?"

"Yes." That one word was drenched in ragged need. His warm lips pressed against mine and electricity rushed through my body.

The hand on the back of my neck tilted my head so he could kiss me better and I melted against him. I'd waited for this moment most of my life and I sure as hell wasn't disappointed.

The kiss wasn't rushed, wasn't abrupt. It was slow, lingering brushes of lips, as our breaths slid over each other. It was an intense, raw moment as we tested unknown waters and what we found only increased our determination. When his tongue swiped across my bottom lip in a request for entrance I opened on a sigh. His free hand caressed my hip before sliding around to the small of my back, tucking me against him.

The feel of his hard body pressed against me made my head spin. Every delectable inch of him was hard in just the right way. As his mouth danced over mine, fire ran through my veins. Everywhere that he touched me came alive and I wrapped my arms around his neck, hungry to feel more of him pressed to me. This was what I'd been looking for all these years. I felt alive and appreciated with each stroke of his tongue and touch of his hands.

His arm tightened around my waist and my feet left the ground. I gasped as he sat me on the unfinished kitchen island. Dark brown eyes drilled into mine as his hands slid down to cup my ass before gently spreading my legs so that he could fit between them. He pressed against my center and I couldn't help but groan as he pulled me tight. Wrapping my legs around his hips I pushed even closer, trying to relieve the building ache.

He groaned into my mouth and I took the moment to nip his bottom lip. I'd wanted to do that forever; to feel it plump between my teeth. One of his hands squeezed my ass tighter and he grinded his erection into me, causing my head to fall backward on a gasp of pleasure. Each move against me made me gasp louder, and my eyes fell shut. With one hand he pulled my hair free from the rubber band before tangling his fingers in it.

"God, you taste good." His voice was raw, harsh, and it sent shivers down my spine. He ran his nose along the column of my throat before nipping gently below my ear. "Should have done this forever ago."

"More." I shoved his jacket from his shoulders in demand.

He shrugged it off and slid his hands under my baggy shirt, brushing the skin with his fingers, coaxing even more fire into my veins. I fisted my fingers in his hair, my hunger insatiable. I'd always been attracted to him, but now I'd opened Pandora's box and I wasn't sure that I'd ever be able to close it.

As his fingers inched higher along my skin, the less I was grounded to reality. The only thing I could think of was his hands on my flesh, the taste of his kiss, the feel of his hard body pressed against me.

"Maddie?" My Secret Service guard called my name.

I jerked away from Jake as if I'd been burned. I knew that

my eyes had to be huge and I was breathing heavily as I pushed hair away from my face.

"Maddie, your car is waiting. You're supposed to be—" Tony stopped at the door and cleared his throat. "My apologies."

He disappeared back into the dark before I could respond.

"Damn." Jake closed his eyes before stepping away from me. His frustration was apparent in the way his jeans gripped his obvious erection.

I took a few breaths and tried to will away the heat in my face. He reached out a hand to steady me as I slid down the counter and he adjusted his shirt to hide the bulge in his pants.

I stared into his eyes, my breathing still not even, and pulled my own shirt back into place. His hair was all out of place and I thought about smoothing it back into place but that felt awkward. Now that my blood was cooling, I wasn't sure what exactly any of this meant.

"Maddie." He stepped forward.

"Tony is right. I'm supposed to be back at the White House." I dragged a hand through my unruly hair. "If I don't leave now then I'm going to be late for one of my stepmother's dinners."

"Will you be here tomorrow?" He took a step toward me.

"Tomorrow is Saturday." I smiled. "No one will be here to-morrow."

"Right." He stared at me for a minute before his face split into one of his famous boyish grins. He tucked his hands into his pockets and his shoulders relaxed.

"In fact, I think we're both going to be at the State Dinner tomorrow night."

"I forgot about that." He frowned. "I hate those things."

"Maybe it won't be so bad," I offered. "Heh. I don't think I've ever said that before about a State Dinner."

"Maybe it won't." His smile returned. "Are you going to wear that dress again?"

"Dress?" I cocked my head to the side. "The one from the fund-raiser? My stepmother would kill me."

"That's a shame." He took a deep breath as his eyes ran over me.

"You wouldn't prefer something red and skintight?" I chewed on my bottom lip. That made me sound jealous and petty.

"I'd prefer anything that you wear." He took a step closer to me.

"And if Ronnie is there?" I ran my hand down my shirt.

"I knew you were jealous." He reached out and grabbed my hand, pulling me toward him. "I haven't seen her since that night."

"You didn't answer my question." I frowned up at him.

"If Ronnie is there, I wouldn't notice." He leaned down, his lips brushing mine. "I'll be too busy looking at you."

Chapter 9

Maddie

W hoa," Ari whispered. "He's even hotter in person. I didn't think that was possible."

I covered my mouth to keep from laughing loudly. Alex d'Lynsal, Prince of Lilaria, was a few feet from us talking with my father.

"He's married," I whispered back. "And a dad."

"That doesn't make me blind." She sighed, a dreamy look on her face. "He's totally my Man Crush Monday pick."

"Man Crush Monday?" I reached out and pinched her arm. "Get it together, Simmon. You're starting to drool."

"And Samantha! A real-life Duchess." I was a little worried she was going to swoon. "They're so romantic."

"That's it. I'm going to send Bran to get smelling salts." I leaned down so only she could hear me. "I'm worried you're going to faint."

"Don't you dare," she growled. Looking over her shoulder

she gripped my arm. "I'd never live that down. He already makes my life hellish."

"Ari," I warned. If anyone heard her curse at the event she'd be in serious trouble. Though I completely sympathized about my brother. Bran would never let her live it down. That's why I'd threatened to use him.

"You know it's true. Yesterday—"

"Oh, look alive. Here they come." I stood up straight and managed to keep my hands from smoothing my dress. My stepmother hated when people did that in public. She felt that it made them look nervous, which in turn made them look weak.

"Madeline McGuire, my daughter." My father's face was calm, content. In a room full of the world's who's-who, he was completely in his element.

"A pleasure to meet you." The Prince lifted my hand and bowed over it. Oy, if my stomach didn't tumble a bit at the gesture. "I'm Alex d'Lynsal and this is my wife, Samantha of Rousseau."

"It's an honor." I smiled, hoping that no one could see me blush. Ari had been right. The Prince was even hotter in person.

"It's so nice to meet you, Madeline." Samantha shook my hand, pulling me in closer to whisper in my ear. "I'm a big fan of how you break into buildings to save animals."

I couldn't help the loud laugh that escaped. She might be a duchess, a princess, and a mother, but there was something mischievous in her eyes. It didn't hurt that she seemed to have a natural ability to put people at ease. I wondered for a minute if that was something she had learned or if she'd always done that.

"And I'm a big fan of your conservation work," I finally responded.

There was a high-pitched giggle next to me and I turned to

look at Ari with big eyes. From the tips of her ears to the collar of her formal dress was flushed bright pink. Alex held her hand in his and wore a bright smile.

"Don't forget, you promised me a dance." He squeezed her hand and she turned so red I was worried she'd have a stroke.

"He made the Queen of England swoon, poor Ari had no chance," Samantha whispered. "I better go save her, but we should talk later."

"I'd be delighted." I smiled and for once honestly meant it.

I watched as they moved down the line to shake hands with the Vice President. The heavy weight of someone's gaze landed on me and I looked up to see Jake watching me.

My breathing picked up a little and I touched the material of my gown. We hadn't spoken since last night at the construction site. For the first time in a long time, I'd spent hours fretting over what to wear for the dinner. My stepmother had sent a red ball gown that I had immediately rejected. I didn't want him to compare me to Ronnie the Randy Reporter.

After several phone calls and texted pictures to Pheobe I'd decided on an elegant deep green dress that reminded me of Grace Kelly. It had taken a lot of pep-talking from my bestie, because it showed more cleavage than I usually wore. The round skirt draped nicely around my legs without looking like a Cinderella dress. The gown had off-the-shoulder straps which kept it from looking too risqué and despite my misgivings about the amount of skin I was showing, I felt sexy. Almost desirable.

And from the way Jake's eyes raked over my body, he seemed to think so as well.

Yeah, Prince Alex might be a real-life Prince Charming, but he didn't compare to the real-life sexy soldier staring at me. My cheeks warmed and I gave him a small smile. Now that I was face to face with the man that caused me a very long, sleepless night my nerves rattled even stronger in my stomach.

We'd shared a stolen moment last night, but was that all it was? My mind had been cruel, stuck on a never-ending replay of his hands on my body, his lips pressed to mine. When I wasn't thinking about how it felt to be pressed against him, I'd agonized over every word he'd said as if I was a teenager again.

I couldn't exactly ask him what it meant right now. Not with a million people watching our every move. Though with the royals present we might not be the center of attention here. But even if I could ask him right now, how would I go about phrasing it?

I took a deep breath. It didn't matter. One kiss didn't exactly equal a label or definition. One kiss was something that happened, that just was; it wasn't more than that kiss. Not yet anyway.

The Prince held his hand out to Jake and he turned his gaze from mine and said something to the royal. I started to look away and that was when I saw Jake's mother watching me with a blank expression and would have stumbled if my stepmother hadn't spent so many years drilling me on how to act in these situations.

Instead I smiled brightly and followed behind my father as if I didn't have a care in the world. It really hadn't sunk in last night when he said that I was one of his rules—that his mother didn't approve of me. I'd always known that she disliked me. I'd heard Virginia talking with my stepmother about boarding schools. It wasn't until Abigail had said I'd be needed in the campaign that I'd realized they'd been talking about me.

The awkward, troublesome child that needed charm school had been me. While my stepmother hadn't disagreed with Virginia, she had given me a guilty look when she came out of the room to see me sitting on a chair near the door. Neither of us ever said a thing about that day, but it had shaped how we treated each other for years.

"I have to sit next to Bran again." Ari glared at her table. "When do I get to sit at the grown-up tables?"

"I usually don't get to sit at the grown-up table." I frowned, glancing at the name cards around the large head table.

My heart skipped a beat. I was sitting next to Jake. He was talking with the Prince and Duchess, one of his real smiles on his face. He'd shaved for the dinner, where yesterday he'd been a bit scruffy. I sort of missed the rough edge it had given him.

I'd especially enjoyed the way it had felt sliding along my skin.

"Do you want to trade?"

I looked down at Ari, surprised she was still next to me. I was too busy fantasizing about her big brother's hands and mouth. We usually stuck together at these kinds of events. I loved her like she was my little sister, but right now my mind was decidedly fixated on a different Simmon family member.

"What?" I looked down at her and frowned.

"Trade? You can go sit with Bran and I'll take your spot next to Jake." She widened her eyes and smiled sadly. "I've barely seen him since he got back and I missed him so much. You get to see him all week."

"Nice try." I laughed. "The only reason you want to sit next to your mother is because of the guy with the crown."

"Dang it." Without a blink she turned away and went to her table.

I watched as she pulled out her seat and slumped down in the chair next to Bran. She'd get an earful if her mother caught her sitting so unladylike. Unlike me, Ari, Jake, and their middle sister Caro had all gone to charm school. Ari knew better than to get caught slumping at a big event like a State Dinner.

"She'll be fine." Jake's low voice crept over my skin.

I breathed in deeply as I turned around and slapped on my politician's daughter smile. "I feel a bit guilty."

"Because you get to sit next to the Prince?" His eyes ran over my face, down my shoulders and all the cleavage before sweeping down to the floor. "You know, I didn't think I'd like any dress better than the one you wore the other night, but this is my favorite so far."

"Thank you." I said it quietly and couldn't help the blush that crept up my neck. "And she said she wanted to sit next to you because I'd been hogging you for the last few weeks."

"Did she?" He chuckled. "I'll make it up to her later, because I'm hoping to spend a little more time with you tonight."

"Is that so?" I arched an eyebrow.

"Very much so." He lifted my hand and guided me toward my seat next to his. "Is your dance card already full or do you think you could squeeze me in for a dance."

"Hm. I'll have to check."

He pulled my chair out for me. "Please do."

We had to sit through the normal hoopla that occurs at these political dinners. Speeches of welcome, jokes about people attending, and of course the typical pleas for partnership.

Usually I had a hard time keeping my eyes from crossing with boredom during these events, especially the fake pandering, but tonight I was on edge. It had nothing to do with the talks of unity and everything to do with the sexy ex-Marine sitting next to me.

We were sitting close enough together that I could feel the

warmth radiating through his jacket arm. If I looked at the tiny hairs on my arm, I would swear they were standing up and pointed in his direction, as if trying to close the distance between us. When his arm shifted on the table and accidentally brushed mine I almost jumped out of my seat. The reaction was completely out of proportion and I ended up rubbing my arm in an attempt to rid myself of goose bumps.

I looked at him in surprise and hoped that no one noticed my lack of composure. Jake's head was turned toward my father but his eyes were trained on me. Had he felt the shock too? Or, more likely, had he just noticed that I'd jerked away from his accidental touch.

In a room filled with some of the world's most powerful and famous people, Jake looked as if he belonged. He was every bit as handsome as the Prince sitting next to him. Jake easily compared to the movie stars that sat at the tables around the room. Tall with wide shoulders, thick wavy brown hair that was growing out nicely, and eyes that made me want to drool, he was the most gorgeous man I'd ever laid eyes on.

"Samantha, where is your gorgeous daughter?" My stepmother leaned around my father to ask the Duchess.

I looked down at the plate of greens in front of me and tried to remember when it had been put there. It was time to focus on what was happening around me. I didn't even remember the speeches being wrapped up before they served the food.

"She's with my friend at the embassy." Samantha's smile was strained. I couldn't help but notice that she'd picked up the slightest hint of the Lilarian accent. "I'm afraid she's not quite ready for a State Dinner."

"Did you see what happened when we were visiting the

Prime Minister in Canada?" Prince Alex's laugh was contagious.

"I told you her stomach was upset. She's teething." Samantha blushed.

"Oh no." I grimaced.

"All over the place." Alex laughed. As if it was completely normal to throw up on Prime Ministers.

"And then she laughed." Sam covered her eyes for a moment. "So, all the pictures are of the Prime Minister staring at his suit in horror while Martha is laughing her little head off."

"I'm sure he wasn't upset," my father offered. "He has five children himself, doesn't he? It can't be the first time he's been spit up on. That's one of the joys of parenthood!"

"Besides if he'd just laughed it off, it would have been a great photo moment. His numbers could use a little help in the popularity polls." My stepmother began cutting up her salad. "Didn't you have an incident with a baby when you first went to Lilaria, Samantha?"

"I'm sure your reaction was genuine." I frowned apologetically at the Duchess. "I remember reading the articles about the baby that had an accident."

"Maybe this was karma then." She laughed. "I can't believe that story made it all the way over here!"

"You're always in the newspaper or on the news." I shook my head in sympathy. "When you had Martha, they sold souvenir cups, dolls, everything!"

"They did indeed." My stepmother frowned.

"It's pretty weird to see miniature sized dolls of my child." Samantha wrinkled her nose. "Honestly? It's a bit creepy."

My stepmother frowned and patted her mouth with her napkin. She was covering one of her disapproving looks. Discussing your dislike for something in public wasn't something she deemed appropriate. She lived by the golden rules; especially if you have nothing nice to say don't say anything at all.

I wholeheartedly agreed with Samantha though. I'd had a doll named after me in a popular brand and it still gave me the willies. They even had clothes that matched outfits I'd worn during important events. If Chuckie gave little kids nightmares, seeing a doll version of myself certainly came close. Having hundreds of dolls that looked just like your baby must be a mother's nightmare.

"Jesus, what is it that they call those things goblins or whatever trade for babies?" My father turned to look at the Duchess. "No wonder you think it's creepy."

"Exactly! Changelings!" Samantha pointed at my father and nodded her head vigorously. "It's terrifying."

"Oh my." My stepmother looked up, genuine concern in her expression. "I hadn't thought of it that way. That must give you nightmares."

Apparently she was feeling compassionate tonight.

"I had nightmares that people would swap out Martha for one of those dolls." Samantha shook her head. "It's ridiculous, but I just couldn't help it. It's easier now that she's so big."

"And never stops making noises," Alex added. "She's constantly bossing us around."

"A born royal." My father lifted his glass in salute.

"She can speak some, but you never know if it's going to be in English or Lilarian." Samantha shrugged. "And if she doesn't know a word, she makes it up. Usually while pointing at whatever she wants."

"I'd love to meet her sometime." I smiled at the young mother. "She has the most beautiful eyes in the pictures I've seen."

"She gets those from her dad." Samantha turned to look at her husband with a small smile. There was so much softness and warmth in her gaze it was as if the rest of the world had disappeared.

I wondered how it felt to have someone else be your anchor to the world. It was obvious from their small movements, glances, and touches that their union was solid. This hadn't been a political match or convenience. There was so much love shooting between those two that it practically filled the entire White House throughout the meal.

And take it from me, that was a miracle. Most of these people here spent the majority of their lives clawing at one another's throats.

Don't get me wrong. My father and stepmother loved each other, but it wasn't that all-consuming type of love. There was warmth and comradery, but it never seemed as if they needed each other—more like they helped each other.

It wasn't necessarily a bad relationship because they were happy, but it wasn't what I wanted.

As if cued by my thoughts, Jake shifted next to me and I looked up into his dark eyes. His intense gaze was unnerving and I felt as if he was searching for something in me, seeking something in my own eyes. In the distance I was aware that music had began to play and that people were moving about the room.

None of that mattered. I couldn't tear my eyes from Jake's.

It wasn't until my father moved past me with Samantha's hand tucked in the crook of his elbow that it dawned on me everyone was standing. There was a moment of panic as I scrambled to my feet. Jake's eyes brightened and a small smile curved his lips as he took my arm and helped steady me as I stood.

His tall, wide frame next to mine was hard to ignore. I wasn't short at five nine and in heels I was more than on the tall side, but he still towered over me. I tried to focus on my father and the Duchess as the music started.

They glided across the floor and I watched as my father joked with the young woman that had stolen America's hearts. I'd seen countless pictures of her dancing with monarchs and the famous but if I could make an assumption, I would say she seemed a little awestruck by dancing with the President in the White House. If I hadn't spent so many years living here, I might feel the same way.

Samantha might be a royal in another country, but she'd been born American and the White House was the only real castle in the United States.

Halfway into the song, Prince Alex and my stepmother moved on to the dance floor, swaying to the music. The clicks of cameras accompanied the music and there must've been fifty cell phones pointed at the dancers. This was a moment that wouldn't be forgotten by history.

My father dipped Samantha and her giggle was contagious. I let my eyes run around the room and noted all of the smiles. It didn't matter what party the people associated with, or the jobs of investigative journalist and style correspondent; they all were smiling. Every eye was trained on the people in the center of the room.

Except for the security.

And Jake. He wasn't watching the dancers or the people around us. Jake was watching me.

"Did you check your dance card?" His deep voice made me shiver.

"As a matter of fact I have." My voice sounded a little breathless and I fought this insane urge to bolt from the room. We'd danced together a million times.

Yet, this time I knew that it would be different. I wouldn't be the President's daughter dancing with the Vice President's son. This time it would be Maddie and Jake in front of a ballroom full of people. His hands on *my* hips, his eyes on *my* face.

"And?" His eyebrow rose up. "I'm dying here, MadLibs."

"What?" I tilted my head back so I could see his face clearly.

"I just asked the prettiest girl in the room to dance with me." He lowered his voice. "And she hasn't answered."

Pleasure flooded my body and I tried to keep calm, but there was no keeping the faint warmth out of my cheeks.

"That's just mean." I turned toward him and pretended to frown. "What sort of girl would do that?"

"One that's too good for me." His reply was so serious, so sad I reached out and touched his arm. That hadn't been a flirtation, he didn't think I should be with him.

"She'd be stupid to think that." I said the words quietly.

"She's a lot of things, but stupid isn't one of them." He chuckled and I immediately sensed the shift in his mood. "She's brave, thoughtful, and patient."

"You really think a lot of this girl," I murmured.

"Do you know what the best part is?" He stepped closer to me and licked his bottom lip. My blood heated up as I remembered how it had felt to have those lips pressed against mine.

"What?" I was quickly turning into one of those light-headed, silly girls hanging on his every word.

"She's a felon." Humor lit his eyes and even though he constantly pointed out my stupidity I couldn't help but find the amusement in it too.

"You're going to have that put on my gravestone, aren't you?" I took my hand from his arm and rolled my eyes.

"I don't know about your gravestone, but I did have it printed on pamphlets to hand out tonight."

"Oh, shut up." I couldn't help but laugh.

"Miss Madeline? Would you do me the honor of a dance?"

With wide eyes I turned to see Prince Alex smiling at me in all of his princely charm. It was a bit like being blinded by the sun and if I wasn't already obsessed with the man next to me, I might be fighting Ari for her Man Crush Monday pick.

I was all too aware of the flashes from cameras as the Prince faced me.

"I—" I stuttered on my response. Could I tell a visiting Prince no? I looked over at Jake and fought for the right words. "I was just about to dance with Mr. Simmon."

"Actually, my mother is signaling me." Jake reached out and squeezed my hand. "You've been reprieved."

I looked over to where the Vice President was talking to several people. Her eagle eyes were trained on us and despite her pleasant expression I could almost feel laser beams shooting from her eyes.

"Ah, oh. Okay." I tried to not look upset. I mean, my consolation prize was a dance with a real-life prince. That shouldn't be disappointing. "Thank you, Alex."

"I should be thanking you." With a deft touch he swung me on to the dance floor, leaving me a little breathless. "There is a rather persistent reporter trying to get a dance. While normally, I do my duty, this one has a way of annoying me."

"Would you like me to have them removed?" I looked over his shoulder and saw a familiar blond head at the edge of the dance floor.

"That won't be necessary. Unless you see Samantha making a beeline for her. Then you might need to call security to protect her." His laugh was full of pride.

"Only if I got to stay and watch." I lowered my voice. "That particular reporter is a thorn in my side."

"Ah." He tilted his head in understanding. "Some of them have a way of getting under our skin."

"More than one way," I sighed. "But I'll do my best to steer you away from her when I can."

"I'll owe you a favor," he declared. "How shall I pay you back?"

"I have no idea." I laughed. "I don't think I've ever had a prince owe me a favor."

We continued our trip around the ballroom and I realized that Alex was such a great partner I hadn't tripped or stumbled once. I cast a conspiratorial look around the room, wondering if Ronnie would go after Jake since the Prince was occupied. Sure enough she was laughing at something the Vice President had said and jealousy gripped my stomach.

"He hasn't taken his eyes off you since I stole you away," Alex said.

"I'm sorry?" I looked up into sparkling blue eyes and if my mind wasn't obsessed with a pair of dark brown ones I might have felt a bit swoony.

"Jake Simmon. He hasn't stopped watching us." Alex spun me out on the floor before pulling me back to him. I was aware of the people clapping and the flashes from cameras, but none of that mattered. He had mentioned Jake was watching me. "Or rather, he hasn't stopped watching you."

"Oh." I bit my lip and looked down at the Prince's bow tie. "It's nothing."

"I know that look well, and it's never nothing." Alex picked up his pace just enough that we flashed past a group of watching women. "That's the look of a man that's found what he wants and has decided he's going to go after it. It's a look I wore while chasing Samantha. The reporter isn't going to get any of his attention."

"She already has," I responded before I could think. Something about Alex made it easy to share with him. Maybe it was because we had more in common than I would have originally thought.

As a young preteen I'd read the tabloids about him and reading about him and Samantha had been a guilty pleasure when I'd gotten older. One of the maids would slip me the magazines under my pillows. It had been like watching a real life fairy tale unfold.

"Ah." He frowned and looked away. "Are you and he together?"

"No." I shook my head but I wasn't actually sure. "At least we weren't when that happened."

"I see." He spun me around again and everyone clapped. "Well, I haven't known you long, but I'm going to offer some counsel, if you don't mind."

"Shoot." I smiled at him.

"Americans and their shooting." He shook his head. "Men can be incredibly stupid. Especially when it comes to the people that matter."

"Don't take this the wrong way, Your Highness, but I've noticed." I laughed. "Present company excluded of course."

"No, you're right. I've had more than my fair share of stupid moments." His gaze turned serious. "Sometimes we have to make mistakes to know when we've found something good."

"I guess we'll see," I replied. "I think our song is almost over. Senator Fletcher is behind us and I think you'd enjoy chatting with her."

"Are you stacking my dance card?" He chuckled.

"Just helping a friend out." I patted his shoulder.

"I already owe you a favor," he pointed out.

"True." And if he and Senator Fletcher hit it off, this would go a long way toward helping fill that favor.

"You're crafty." He looked at me with appreciation. "Something you inherited from your smart father. She's a horse person, correct?"

"Thank you, and yes, she is." I smiled, but not because of the compliment. "What if I'd suggested Senator Riley?"

"I would have danced with him and talked about the whales that he loves so much." His eyes twinkled.

I'd been careful to not mention if Riley was male or female. "And have you memorized a dossier on everyone in the room?"

"Not everyone. But most of them."

"Modest, aren't you?" I laughed, not caring who was watching or taking pictures. Alex made it easy to feel comfortable in front of everyone.

"No, not usually. You and Samantha can commiserate together over my ego. She would love the chance to talk with you without a million people watching." Step, step, turn. Step, step, spin. He never missed a beat. "Dinner before we leave, perhaps? You could bring your fellow."

"I would like that. Thank you."

"You're welcome." He looked around the room. "How do you feel about a flashy finish?"

"What do you mean?" But my question was too late.

With the certainty of an experienced dancer, he spun me across the room, before pulling me back and spinning me under his arm. Before my brain could catch up with the rest of my body, he had me tucked against him and dipped me back. The song ended exactly on time and I wondered if he had planned it that way from the get-go.

People cheered and I knew I was blushing by the time he lifted me back up, but I didn't care. Dancing with Alex was probably one of those moments I would never forget. I wish I could go back and high-five the teenage girl that I used to be.

He bowed slightly to me before tucking my hand in his arm and I steered him toward Senator Fletcher. She was a large wildlife fan and if I'd played my cards right, I might have just found someone to sponsor my animal cruelty bill.

"Senator Fletcher, may I introduce you to His Royal Highness, Prince Alex?" I smiled at the older woman, well aware that people would be surprised by my move. If I had a reputation amongst the press and the politicians it was that I avoided anything resembling political maneuvering.

But since I'd announced that I was going to propose a bill, I needed to use some of the political training I'd received.

"It's an honor, Your Highness." She held her hand out to him. "I've read a great deal about you and your wife's charity work. You've done a great deal in your country to promote education about animals."

"Thank you." Alex shook her hand. "Please call me Alex."

"And you must call me Laura." She smiled and I wondered if his smile had the same effect on her as it did everyone else. She looked so calm and casual.

"Laura, I think we have a lot in common. Would you care to talk while we dance?"

"Only if you promise to not dip me." She tucked her hand in his arm with a smile. "I'm not as flexible as Maddie."

"I'll take good care of you, ma'am."

I caught a pair of narrowed green eyes glaring at me and I touched Alex's arm before he could get away. "I think Ari would be thrilled to have a dance lesson after Senator Fletcher."

"I'll keep my eyes open." He winked at me.

I watched as he led her out to the floor and other women sighed. He really was pleasant to look at and smarter than he was pretty. Turning to look for Ari I saw her making her way out of the room and I hurried after her.

"Ari, do you have a moment." She looked over her shoulder but didn't stop. "Please, Ari?"

"What?" She turned around so quickly that her hair fanned around her face and I hesitated. I knew Ari was thirteen but this was the first time I'd seen any hint of angst that came with the age.

"I was going to ask a favor." I took a step closer and realized that she'd had a growth spurt. I didn't have to look down very far to meet her eyes.

"Are you serious? First you get Jake. Now you got the Prince. What else do you want? My allowance?" She leaned forward and it was frightening to hear those words come from her suddenly smiling face. It was as if reality didn't line up quite right.

"What are you doing?" I pointed at her face. "You're smiling while yelling at me."

"Mom doesn't like it when I look angry in public." Her smile slipped just a little. "I'd rather not spend the rest of my week being lectured about it."

"Ah. Yeah, I got that lesson too." I moved a little closer and was relieved when she didn't pull away. "I'm sorry about Jake. I didn't know they were going to stick him with me for community service. Maybe you'd like to come out and help one day? Then you could spend some time with him and you'd see we really don't talk that much."

"I can come out and help?" Her eyes widened.

"Sure. We need all the hands we can get and I know that Jake has missed you."

"How do you know that if you don't talk?" Her eyes narrowed.

Damn. "Well, he mentioned during dinner."

"Uh-huh."

"But that's not the favor I was going to ask. Prince Alex asked me if I would get you so that he can dance with you." Hope dawned on her sweet face. "See, there are so many people that he *has* to dance with, he didn't want to miss out dancing with you."

"Really?" Her voice rose a little louder and one of the men near us looked up.

"Yep. You need to be on the edge of the dance floor, ready."

"I can do that." She started off toward the dancing but I grabbed her arm.

"You know how these things go, Ari. Everyone is trying to get their picture with the Prince and Duchess. So, help him pick someone nice to dance with after you, okay?"

"No problem. Belinda is here and I know she is a good dancer."

Belinda was on the Supreme Court and just happened to be Ari's godmother. The woman was a saint, friendly, and would help pass the Prince off to someone else nice.

"That's my girl."

She started to walk off but stopped.

"What is it?" I looked around worried. Had someone managed to snag Alex?

"I'm sorry I yelled at you." She twisted her dress around her finger.

"It's okay, you were right. Alex is dreamy."

"No . . . I meant about Jake. He's different. I'm worried about him and you . . . I see the way he looks at you and how he talks about you. He likes-likes you." Sadness crept into her gaze and I couldn't help pulling her into a hug.

"We're all looking out for Jake. He's been through a whole lot."

"People always talked about how you two would eventually grow up and get married." Her lip trembled. "But I'm not ready to lose him again. Not yet, anyway."

"Whoa." I backed up so she could see my crazy expression. "No one is talking about getting married. I haven't finished college yet. And even if Jake does like me, that doesn't mean we'll get married. I mean, that's a big leap."

"It's fine if you get married. I love you. I'm just not ready yet, okay?"

"No matter what happens between me and Jake, no one will take him from you. That's not possible, because he loves you so much." I squeezed her arm. "Okay?"

"Yeah." The music started to reach its peak and she wiped at her eyes. "Oh my god, I have to go."

Her tone immediately shifted into an excited squeal and she tore away from me. I watched as she situated herself next to the dancing couple and noticed that Jake was dancing with the duchess. They were both laughing, but as I watched his eyes darted in my direction and my stomach did a little dance.

"Nice touch with Fletcher." My father moved next to me and I jumped in surprise.

"Thanks, Dad." I couldn't help but laugh. "He knew exactly what I was doing though."

"I'm not surprised. Alex is bright and quick on his feet. He's going to make a good king one day." He looked down at me and I immediately felt like a ten-year-old girl, awed by the love in his eyes.

"I missed you." I wrapped my arms around his waist and sniffed at the familiar smell of his aftershave.

"Missed you too, Maddie." His arms pulled me tighter against him and I let myself have a moment where he was just my father and I was just his daughter. "Are you still mad at me for sticking you with Jake?"

"It's my own fault." I shrugged and pulled away, surprised by the mischievous glint in his eyes.

"Little Ari doesn't seem to think either of you mind working together. In fact it sounded like she said you were getting married." He draped an arm around my shoulders so I couldn't run away. "Is there something you want to tell me?"

"Dad." I frowned at him.

"Not that I can blame the poor boy. You're gorgeous, of course, brilliant, and completely unaware of it." He leaned down and kissed my head.

"That's not true. You tell me those things all the time." I couldn't help but smile at him.

"Still, I suppose it was only a matter of time. I should have made you guys do something harder so you wouldn't have any energy left." His eyes danced and I knew my cheeks were on fire.

"Dad! Could you please keep your voice down?" I glanced around to see who was listening and wasn't surprised to see everyone near us watching. "Jake and I are friends. That's it."

I bit my lip. I didn't lie to my father. Not ever. But friends was the only thing I could say for sure.

"Really? That's it?" His eyes danced and I fought to not roll my eyes. "If you say that's it, then that's it. Apparently, Little Ari misunderstood the longing looks and little touches at dinner. The floating hearts above your heads were from someone else. I get it."

I stood on my tiptoes and kissed his cheek before whispering. "President or not, I swear I will gut you if you don't stop."

"You could try," he mused. "Or you could pay me off with a dance. What do you say, sweetheart? Dance with your old man?"

"I demand two dances and won't take one less."

"I thought you understood bartering better than that." He threw his head back and laughed as he steered me toward the dance floor. "Very well. Two dances and not one less."

I knew how to barter better than he thought.

I'd just scored two dances with the most important man in the room.

My father.

Chapter 10

Jake

The crowd was starting to thin out but there were still enough people to make for a loud room. A very loud and drunken room, which was wreaking havoc with my anxiety. The President and first lady were entertaining a few congressmen and their wives with small talk, but my attention was focused on the group sitting at a table in the back.

Maddie was leaning close to the Duchess whispering between giggles while the Prince talked with one of the older senators and a Supreme Court justice. She looked so happy and carefree, it was a look I'd come to covet. I was envious that she was sharing it with other people. She haunted my thoughts all the time now. I hadn't been able to concentrate on anything for weeks.

The band was playing the music meant to send the remaining people away and the clock was not far from crying midnight. I looked to where my littlest sister slumped against my shoulder and smiled. She might be growing up, but she was still playing the part of Cinderella. I started to heft her into my arms to take her to one of the cars but she woke up before I could stand.

"What are you doing?" She rubbed a hand across her eyes and smeared some of the makeup she was wearing.

My heart gave a sad thump as I looked down at the mix of little girl growing into a woman. I'd missed so much while being in the Marines. Our middle sister was pre-med and away at college now. I hadn't been old enough to appreciate having a little sister when I'd been home, but now I could see what all I'd missed.

"I was going to take you home."

She pushed away from me and looked around the room. "I normally ride back with Mom."

"She's gone to her office. There's no telling when she'll be done."

"I'll be fine. I can crash with Bran or sleep on one of the couches." She shrugged.

"Aren't you a little old to have a sleepover with a boy?" I frowned and looked around for Bran. At thirteen his hormones would be more than active and I wasn't sure how I felt about him being around my baby sister. Especially alone at night.

"Ew." She scrunched up her nose. "That's gross, Jake. It's *Bran*. It's not like he's a real boy."

I bit my tongue and just shrugged. Bran was a real boy in all the ways I could think of, but I didn't see how arguing was going to change anything.

"I don't want you to have to sleep on a couch. I can take you back home."

"Are you going to stay over?" She cocked her head to the side.

"No. I'll go back to my place in town. I've got to take care of Puz." Having an excuse to get out of things had been an unforeseen benefit of having a dog.

"That's a waste of gas then." She stood up and stretched. "I'll get a ride with Beryl."

"Beryl?" My sister had a whole life I knew nothing about and I was starting to resent that I hadn't been there to see her form it.

"My agent. She's cool." Ari flipped her hair over her shoulder. "I'll text Mom and let her know."

"Are you sure?" I frowned and stood up. I should be taking care of her, someone should be taking care of her. She had a family after all. "Is Caro still away at school?"

"The last I heard she was at the farm. Not sure if Mom knew that though. She'd have insisted she come to the event." Ari shrugged.

The farm. That was our quaint term for a sprawling estate in West Virginia where our family raised horses.

"Well, let's not rat her out." Caro hated everything about D.C. but had a hard time standing up to our mother; an even harder time than Ari and I did.

"I wouldn't do that." Ari sighed and it sounded so much older than it should.

"I know, monster." I pulled her against me in a hug and leaned down to kiss the top of her head. "I know."

"You should talk to her soon, you know. I heard Mom talking to someone on the phone the other day. I think she's going to try and get her to enlist." Ari's green eyes narrowed and my fingers tightened on her shoulders. "I don't even know if Caro knows what Mom is planning for her."

"It's not going to happen so don't worry about it." I hugged her again.

"There's Beryl, I'll go ask her to get me a ride home."

"Text me when you get there." I looked at her sternly.

"Geez, overprotective much?" She rolled her eyes, but there was a small smile pulling at her cheeks.

"Go get some sleep." I pushed her toward a woman in a black suit. The female agent had short hair and was short enough that she wouldn't stand out among a bunch of young females—as long as you ignored the gun under her jacket and the way her eyes scanned every person near Ari.

"She misses you." Maddie's voice was soft.

"I know." I watched as she moved to stand next to me. "Are you done conspiring with your new friends?"

"I told them I had to make good on a promise." A soft smile curved her lips and I fought the urge to pull her against me and bury my face in her hair.

"And what's that?" Unable to help myself I reached out and touched some of the hair lying on her shoulder.

"Well, I think the band is going to call it quits soon, but I think we have time for one dance." She looked up at me with those bright hazel eyes that had been haunting my dreams and my heart jerked in my chest.

"Wouldn't miss it." I held my arm out to her and led her to the dance floor.

I nodded at the orchestra and they switched gears. The song was smooth, not too fast, and not too slow. There was commotion behind us and I realized that the Prince and his lovely wife were making their goodbyes.

Which meant most of the people were not watching us as we moved across the dance floor. I lifted our joined hands and settled my other hand on her waist. I wasn't as smooth a dancer as I'd been before the accident, but I was still confident. The doctors swore that I would eventually be able to do everything I'd done before without any snags.

I stared down into Maddie's bright eyes, watching as the golden flecks caught the light and sparkled, and the rest of the world melted away. As our bodies moved with the music and the sounds reached our souls it felt as though we were the only people left in the room. It should be impossible, but I was dancing with Maddie for the first time. Really dancing with her.

I was all too aware of how small her hand felt in mine and the way she bit her lip and looked away as if she was nervous. I'd never forget how my hand felt holding her waist or the fact that I didn't have to crane down to look in her eyes.

There were no flashy dance moves between us; no twirls or dips. Instead we floated together as the music seemed to bind us, bringing our bodies into sync. I'd used to take great joy in spinning the women around the floor, but I wasn't quite ready to test my leg and at the moment I wanted nothing more than to keep Maddie close to me.

There would be no spinning this woman away. She fit against me too well.

"You're quiet tonight." Her bright eyes peered up at me. "Tired?"

"Not really." I was tired but holding her was quickly giving me renewed energy.

"All talked out?" Her hand on my arm tightened a little and I wondered what she was thinking.

"About politics I am," I sighed. "So much posturing."

"Then talk to me about something else." She smiled and my heart beat a little faster.

"I'd rather just look at you." I reached up and touched her cheek. Despite growing up in D.C. there was so much innocence in her doe-like eyes. I'd thought of her as a fairy queen at the fund-raiser and now I felt entranced by her eyes. Her presence was like a magical balm for my mind and heart.

"You're going to make me blush, Simmon." And she did. Her cheeks pinked and I couldn't help but chuckle.

"What do you want me to talk about then?" I cleared my throat. I'd talk about whatever she wanted if it would keep her near me. I felt raw after a night at the White House being my mother's show horse, and Maddie eased the burn.

"Well, I don't know. What was the last movie you watched?" Her cheeks were still pink and I felt my chest puff out a little knowing that it was because of me.

"I haven't gotten to any movies lately. I've been catching up on some television shows." I looked as I heard the distinctive click of a camera. The royal couple had made their exit which meant the reporters were free to look for other stories. "I added *Buffy the Vampire Slayer* to the list, you know."

"You won't be disappointed," she said, and laughed. "So, other than television what have you been doing now that you're back in the city and not gallivanting around on your mom's behalf?"

"Well, I have physical therapy and doctors' appointments." I frowned, not wanting to explain that I had to go to mandatory psych appointments. "Video games. I go to the gym a lot. I've also taken up swimming."

"Swimming?" Her brows furrowed and I fought the urge to rub the little lines away. We'd already caused enough trouble dancing alone with the reporters now free to watch.

"Swimming." I chuckled and let my thumb rub her lower back. "It's good exercise."

"Do you need a special, er, attachment?" The red in her cheeks darkened. "That's probably a stupid question."

"I've gotten a lot worse questions." I pulled her a little closer. "I don't need a prosthetic to swim, but I do have one if I'm going for something extra strenuous."

"And do you do a lot of marathon swimming?"

"Not yet. I just started."

"I didn't realize you were such a gym groupie."

"Exercise keeps my mind clear," I responded. I hadn't meant to say that. Normally I just told people that I liked to be active, move. Saying that I needed to keep my mind clear opened me up to speculation about my mental state. And that was the last thing I wanted to deal with.

"And you need help keeping it clear?" She cocked her head to the side and I knew I'd screwed up. Worry clouded her beautiful eyes and I hated that it was there for me. She'd been the only person to not handle me with kid gloves.

"Sometimes." I shrugged. "We all need a break from time to time."

The music ended but I was reluctant to let her go. She stared up at me with a soft smile and again I had that urge to crush her against me so I could soak up everything sweet and innocent in her expression.

"Thank you for dancing with me." I had to pry my hands off of her tiny waist.

Her musical laugh filled the room.

"What's so funny?" I walked with her away from the dance floor.

She chewed on her bottom lip before answering. "I guess I never would have thought you'd ever be dancing with me except out of duty."

I stopped walking, surprised by her statement. "You really do think I hated you."

"I don't think you hated me." She looked up at me and I could see the uncertainty swirling in her eyes. "I think I was a frustrating obligation."

I wanted to tell her that wasn't true, that I had wanted to dance with her. But the truth was that I'd been young and blind.

"I was stupid but I never hated you."

Her laugh surprised me. I'd sort of expected her to tell me that it was okay.

"I'm sorry." She rubbed fingers under her eyes. "But you're the second person to tell me that today."

"What?" I couldn't keep the confusion from my face.

"That you're stupid."

Apparently my expression was quite comical because she burst into another bout of laughter and tears squeezed from the corners of her eyes. She lifted a finger and poked my shoulder before laughing so hard she snorted.

With wide eyes she covered her mouth with her hand and chortled some more. Despite my confusion, witnessing her glee was like being bathed in sunlight. She could call me stupid and I was still bewitched by her. Snort and all.

She really was a fairy queen.

I wanted to kiss her so badly I wasn't sure I could control myself. Lacing my fingers with her hand I pulled her through the remaining stragglers toward one of the large staircases to the second floor.

She followed along, still giggling, and picked up her skirts like Cinderella. "Where are we going?"

"I'm not sure." I looked down the hallway toward the residential quarters and turned in the opposite direction.

I pulled her around a corner and waited, listening to hear if anyone was nearby but nothing could be heard but the distant voices of the people downstairs. The room was lit by soft table lamps, casting sharp shadows along the yellow walls of the East Wing sitting room.

"I think we're a little old to play hide-and-seek," Maddie whispered as she touched my chest.

"That depends on who we're hiding from," I replied. There was more than a hint of hunger in my voice. I backed her into the wall and cupped her face in my hands.

"Oh?" Her eyes widened and seemed to almost glow in the shadowy corner I'd found to tuck us away.

"Oh."

I dipped my head down so I could capture her mouth and almost groaned in relief at the taste. Soft hands slid up my chest and under my jacket, tracing the hard lines. Her eager lips tore at my resolve and I let go of her face so I could pull her body against me.

Her soft sigh as she fit alongside me sent a surge of adrenaline through my body. With each touch, each caress, the rational part of my brain shrank.

I ran my hands up her sides until my thumbs were brushing the undersides of her pert breasts. She gasped and it took a lot of willpower to keep from moving my hands higher. I wasn't going to fuck Maddie against a wall in the White House. I mean, I really wanted to fuck her. Just not here, not like this, and not right now. I fought to rein in my hormones and slow our kiss. Now wasn't the time for more. I needed to sort out just what it was I felt for Madeline McGuire.

Her eyes were dark with passion as she leaned back against the -wall and looked up at me. She licked her kiss-swollen lips before giving me a shy smile. Even now after being almost ravaged, color high in her cheeks, she still looked like something that belonged in a fairy tale.

What was I doing with this woman? Heartbreak was the only possible outcome and I figured I already had enough broken parts. And I certainly didn't want to cause Maddie any pain. I didn't deserve to be with someone like Maddie after the rest of my team had died because I hadn't been good enough. I should end this now. I should push her away and keep her from pushing my boundaries. I should leave her alone so she could find someone deserving.

But I didn't want to—which was the whole problem.

"Maddie?" My voice was much deeper than normal and I cleared my throat.

"Yes?"

My mouth froze. I wasn't sure what I was going to say. Run away from me? Beg her to take me? Convince her to let me fuck her until she couldn't see straight?

"Jake?" Worry creased her brow and I didn't keep myself from reaching out to smooth the little wrinkles away this time.

"We should do something tomorrow." I already had my fair share of problems, but apparently I was going to add lady trouble to the list. What was I doing asking her out on a date?

"What did you have in mind?" She cocked her head to the side.

"Uh . . ." Smooth, Jake. You asked her out with no plan.

"You know, in all the years I've lived here, I've never been to the Smithsonian. I'd almost given up on seeing the dinosaur skeletons." Bless her, she threw me a lifeline.

"How do you feel about food trucks?" I ran a finger down

her arm before twining my fingers with hers. "I have a friend that started his own business."

"Another Marine friend?" She left her hand twined with mine but used her free one to straighten my bow tie.

"Navy." I smiled. "If I'm not mistaken he has a spot near the Smithsonian National Museum of Natural History."

Since Afghanistan I'd avoided crowded places as much as possible because they made me antsy, but I'd do it for Maddie. God help me, I'd do anything for the woman.

"Perfect," she said. "Science and food trucks. Sounds like my idea of the perfect day."

"What time can I pick you up?" I sounded like a fucking schoolboy. Eager and pathetic. Maddie messed with my equilibrium. I was completely off balance when it came to her.

"Why don't I meet you at your place?" She looked up at me with guarded eyes.

The thought of having Maddie in my town house, alone, without anyone to interrupt us gave me pause. I didn't think that had been what she was suggesting but my brain was more than happy to explore the possibility.

"Or I could just meet you at the museum." She chewed on her lip, uncertainty floating through her eyes. "I could always get someone else to go with me if that's not your thing."

I was busy fantasizing about getting in her pants and she thought I was trying to get out of the date.

"You already said yes. You can't back out now." I couldn't help but smile. "You're stuck going on a date with me."

"A date with Jake Simmon," she mused. "I'm not sure how I feel about that."

"And I've got a date with the President's daughter. I'm the one that should be nervous." I laughed. "Come to my place a little before lunch and we'll get some Brazilian *pasteis* and *briga-deiro* before we go look at the dinosaur skeletons."

"And the Hope Diamond." Eagerness lit her eyes.

"Isn't that thing cursed?"

"Phfft. Curse, schmurse. That thing has been present for so many of the big events in history. Can you imagine what all it's seen?"

"You're such a nerd," I teased. "Who knew that Ms. Rebel had a dorky side?"

"Just wait. I'm going to bore you out of your mind tomorrow with inane facts." She wiggled her eyebrows.

"I look forward to it."

Chapter 11

Maddie

Clothes were not my forte. Makeup and hair were not my strong suit. I was so far out of my comfort zone I'd almost wished I could ask my stepmother but that would have led to too many questions. I looked down at the slim jeans and heels I'd decided to wear and shook my head at myself.

Me in heels. Voluntarily. Who would have thought it?

At least I had been able to pair them with a comfortable sweater and blazer that I had borrowed from Phoebe months ago and never returned. I'd topped the whole thing with some of the jewelry I'd accumulated over the years—things that had been given to me.

"You look like you're going to hurl," Tony said.

"Thanks, you look nice too." I glared at my guard.

"You always look nice, Maddie. I don't think that's what got you all wound up." Tony shrugged. "You're all jittery and you're sweating."

I wiped my upper lip and grimaced. Reaching up, I turned

one of the air conditioner vents in my direction. Digging in one of my pockets I pulled out a hair-tie and dragged my hair into a ponytail. I didn't want my hair to be stuck to my sweaty face for our date.

I took a deep breath and leaned back in my seat. This was a bad idea. Going on a date with Jake Simmon opened me up, exposed me in ways that scared me. But it was also exciting and made me feel special.

"You've got a stupid grin on your face now."

I stuck my tongue out at Tony. "So?"

"I'm just noting your mood swings." He chuckled. "You aren't normally so high-strung."

"When are you going to get a different job?"

"Who knows? Maybe I'll just stick with you and Jake and then be a bodyguard for your little baby Presidents."

I sucked in air so fast that I started coughing.

"Breathe, Maddie. I'm just joking." Tony reached over and slapped me on the back. "Actually, once your father steps down I've promised Dahlia that I'd go to the West Coast with her."

"The West Coast?"

"She has family out there and she wants to be near them when we have kids." He shrugged. "Her family has a lot of connections out there and I won't have any trouble getting a job."

"Tony!" I practically jumped in my seat. "Dahlia's pregnant!"

"What?" His eyes widened and then he shook his head vehemently. "No, no, not yet."

"Why not? Having trouble downstairs?" I darted a quick look at his crotch intent on making him uncomfortable.

"Jesus, Maddie." For the first time I saw him blush. "No, that's not a problem."

"Then what's the holdup?" I frowned.

"I wanted to wait." He shrugged. "Just in case."

My stomach dropped and I looked out the car window. He meant in case he was killed protecting me. Here I was worried about a date and Tony had put his entire life on hold so he could protect my family.

We pulled up to an old brick row house with green ivy climbing the walls. Tony started to open the door and I put a hand out to stop him.

"Thank you, Tony."

"I always open your door, Maddie."

"You know what I mean." I squeezed his arm.

"You're welcome," he said. "And don't be nervous. You're going to knock his socks off."

He hopped out and held the door for me. I tucked my purse under my arm as I climbed the steps and told myself to breathe. Tony stood at the bottom of the stairs, a polite but safe distance away from me. Taking a deep breath I raised my hand to knock on the door right before it was yanked open.

"Hey." Jake shoved a hand through his wet hair and that's when I realized he wasn't wearing a shirt. Puz stuck his head between Jake's legs and gave a happy yip.

"Hi." My eyes ran down his chest, over the hard lines and sharp planes of his chest and abdomen. A thick maze of scars trailed down his left side, disappearing into the waistband of his gym shorts. He was wearing a prosthetic that curved into a metal C and I noticed that he was holding a toothbrush limply in his hand.

"You look great." His deep voice was huskier than usual.

I looked up to realize he was staring at me with a slightly dazed expression and I was suddenly glad I'd taken the time to dress up a little.

"I think I might be overdressed," I teased.

"You look perfect." He took a step back so I could come in. "I'm sorry. I overslept."

I didn't say anything, unsure how I felt about that. I guess I was the only one that was anxious about today. Instead I reached down and petted the dog. I'd missed seeing him at the shelter the other day, but I was glad to see him settling in so well.

His foyer was bare except for a small table littered with mail and pocket change. There were a couple of leashes strewn across a rack on the wall for Puz.

I'd half expected to find his home perfectly decorated, something his mother would have had done for him while he was gone. It was refreshing to find it empty of the telltale signs of a professional decorator. That meant this was really his home.

Most of the walls were bare except for some pictures in mismatched frames and a large painting of a valley that had a classic red barn surrounded by trees. I'd been to that farm before and suspected his sister Caro had painted it.

"How is Caro doing?" I spun in a slow circle, taking in the details of Jake's home.

The couch was large but not leather like you would suspect. Instead it was a soft gray and looked like the perfect size for napping. There was a throw blanket and some pillows haphazardly strewn on the floor. The giant dog bed was in a corner with a blanket of its own. Game controllers littered the table in front of a giant television and an empty water bottle sat on the wooden floor near a comfortable-looking easy chair. The kitchen was further back in the house, but I could smell the aroma of coffee from where I stood.

"I haven't talked to her much," Jake replied.

"She's pretty busy with her class load." I shrugged. "I haven't talked to her in a while either."

"I suspect she's using school as an excuse to stay as far away from here as possible." He moved around the room, picking up the pillows and throwing them back on the sofa. "Sorry about the mess. Power went out last night and my phone died so I had no alarm."

"Don't worry about it." I gestured to the television. "I'll watch some TV while you get ready."

He walked over to the giant chair and dug around in the cushions until he found a remote. I let myself really look at the scars on his side and back, while I knew he wouldn't notice. I *knew* that he'd been hurt badly—that he was lucky to be alive, but it was different being faced with the actual evidence of his suffering. It was a miracle that he had healed so much in such a short amount of time. It was a wonder that he was even here.

"It's a pretty simple setup." He turned around and I jerked my gaze toward the windows behind him. "This is the guide button."

"I know how to use a remote." I laughed.

"I'll be done in a minute." He looked down at me and smiled softly. "I'm glad you're here."

"Yeah? Why's that?"

"You're just so easy to be around." He shrugged as if that summed up the whole world but I had no idea what it meant.

"And . . . that's a good thing?" I frowned up at him. He

gave me butterflies and I stumbled over everything I said but he thought I was easy to be around.

He stepped closer and I found myself nose to chest. His fingers tilted my chin up and his lips fluttered over mine. I let my palm rest on his skin where I could feel his heart beating rapidly. He didn't touch me except for the fingers on my chin and his lips on mine.

When he stepped back, his brown eyes were dark. "It's a good thing."

Before I could think to ask anything else, he was gone, taking the stairs two at a time. My fingers drifted up to my lips and I stared at where he had just been, the remote in my other hand forgotten.

I'd never been kissed like that before; with so much tenderness and awe. My heart flipped around in my chest for a minute before I turned away from the stairs and looked at the big television. The sofa was as comfortable as I thought it would be and I sank deep into the cushions. So deep that I worried I might need a rope ladder to climb back out.

Instead I kicked my shoes off and crossed my legs under me. This way I'd be able to get up without flailing around like a baby duck. Puz jumped up next to me and curled into a tight little ball against my side. Judging by the dog hair on the cushions I figured it was a regular occurrence so didn't make him get down. The television had a lot more options than the one I used at college, but it didn't take me long to find something to watch.

By the time I heard him coming back downstairs I was completely engrossed in *The Goonies*. I was a giant sucker for the movie. It was my go-to answer for sick days or bad test grades.

"Do you want to eat first or—"

"Hey yooooou guuuyss!"

Puz barked loudly, apparently surprised by the hollering on the television. I fumbled with the remote trying to turn the television back down.

"The Goonies?" He chuckled. "You still watch that movie?"

"Once a Goonie, always a Goonie."

"I remember you watching that on Air Force One. You had food poisoning and your dad sat next to you while reading stuff. He'd pause the movie whenever you got sick."

"Oh, God. I forgot you were there." I covered my face with my hands. "Not exactly something I wanted to come up on a first date."

"A first date," he mused. "I think this is exactly what we should talk about on a first date. Tell me something else embarrassing."

"You probably know all of my embarrassing stories, that's my point."

"Then we can skip that part." He held out his hand to help me off the couch.

"Good, because I think there are a lot more embarrassing stories about me than about you." I slipped my feet back into my shoes and looked up at him. "Pretty much everything I did was embarrassing."

"That's not true." He tucked his phone into his back pocket.

I picked up my purse and frowned. "Pfft. You never had anything go wrong. I on the other hand trip all over my words and had a seagull poop on me in Florida."

"Puz, be good. I'll be back later." Jake reached down and scratched the dog behind his ears. The fondness in his eyes made my heart light. I liked seeing the two happy together.

"'Bye, Puz." The little dog disappeared before we were

out the door and I had a feeling he was reclaiming his spot on the sofa.

"You might have had a hard time then, but you don't any longer." Jake opened the front door for me and I went out ahead of him. Tony was standing at the SUV with the door open and I noticed another black Suburban behind the one I'd been in earlier. Thankfully most people wouldn't blink an eye at a security detail in this city.

"What do you mean?" I slid into the backseat and waited for him to get in too.

"People love you. They think you're refreshing."

"Pfft." I waved my hand in the air as if that got rid of what he said. "You still know all my embarrassing stories."

"Do you remember when we were late for the interview at my family's estate? I told everyone that I lost track of time while I was riding?" He slid in next to me and I tried to not think about how close he was.

"I'd forgotten about that." I shook my head. "I'd gotten a thorough verbal dressing down for being late."

"Sorry for that." He looked at me with a sheepish grin. "I didn't want to tell anyone that I'd lost my horse."

"You lost your horse?" I couldn't help but laugh.

"Remember when we were racing and I told you guys to go ahead?" He ran a hand through his hair.

"Yeah. I just figured you needed to go to the bathroom." I shrugged. Guys were lucky in that sense.

"Bax wouldn't cross the stream so I tried to force him."

"He threw you?" My eyebrows rose in surprise. Jake was a superb horseman. Everyone in his family was brought up on a horse.

"Knocked me on my ass good." He shook his head. "Hurt

like a motherfucker and then he made me chase him down. I couldn't sit for a month."

"Is that why you insisted on standing behind the chairs?" I chuckled. "I just thought you were being arrogant."

"It's so refreshing to hear how much you thought of me." He frowned and rubbed a hand over his jaw.

"You made it easy," I explained.

He chuckled and bumped his shoulder into me.

"Wasn't it raining that night?" I asked.

"I looked like a swamp monster when I finally got back to the barn." A wide grin split his face. "I had to bribe one of the stable hands to trade clothes with me. That's another reason I didn't sit down. His pants were about three sizes too small and I'd busted a seam. If I'd sat down my balls would have been on display for *20/20*."

"Now that would have been amazing." I laughed. "Do you realize how much slack I would have gotten if you'd free-balled it on national television? I'd be an entirely different person."

"Then I'm glad I stood arrogantly behind you," he joked.

"Why's that?" I swayed as the car moved through traffic.

"I happen to like who you are now." He stared down at me with serious eyes and my stomach did a flip that had nothing to do with the car and everything to do with the intense gaze focused on me.

"Good to know."

The rest of the ride was quiet and I tried to not squirm. I still wasn't sure how to act around Jake. There was this sense of history that made me want to relax and just fall into him. But there was also this new facet of sexual tension and intrigue that we'd never shared before and it made me feel like an inexperienced twelve-year-old.

Our SUV stopped in front of a small park encircled by vans and trucks of different sizes and colors.

"Shade owns the *pasteis* truck under the large tree," Jake said.

I looked over at the long line that stretched out from a teal-and-orange truck with a bright green canopy.

Tony opened the door to our vehicle and we climbed out. "You certainly can't miss it."

"You'll understand when you meet Shade." Jake chuckled and put a hand on the small of my back as we walked toward the group of people.

I recognized several people in line, politicians and well-known lobbyists all waiting for their *pasteis*. The smell drifting from the truck made my stomach rumble.

"Hungry?" Jake asked.

"I didn't eat much at breakfast," I answered. One of my heels stuck in the grass and I shifted my weight to my toes.

"I had half a cup of coffee. I can't wait to dig into some *pasteis*."

"Might be a while with that line," I pointed out.

"Nah." He waved at a small woman at the woman who pointed at the tables near the trees. "May won't make us wait."

"May?" She must've been the tiny woman that waved at us.

I sat down at one of the picnic tables and picked up one of the leaves that had floated down to land on the planks.

"His sister. She'll send someone out with food for us." He sat across from me and leaned his arms on the table. "It's one of the benefits of knowing Shade personally."

"Am I going to meet this infamous Shade eventually?" I spun the maple leaf between my fingers.

"Infamous is a good term." Jake shook his head.

"You keep making this guy out to be some kind of over-the-top phenomenon."

"Phenomenon. I'll go with that." A deep gravelly voice had me twisting in my seat and I watched as every single Secret Service guard put a hand on their gun.

As I met the eyes of the mountain-sized man standing next to our table I could understand their anxious frowns. The man that must be Shade was taller than Jake by a few inches and was bald as a cue ball. Scruff lined his jaw and heavy black eyebrows lined his large strikingly green eyes. Tattoos curled down his gigantic arms ending with dragon heads on his wrists. His black shirt looked a smidge too tight under a dirty apron.

"Shade." Jake stood up and slapped the massive man on the back. "I wasn't sure if you were working today."

"I work every day." The large man set down the tray he was carrying and wiped his hands on the apron before extending one to me. "It's nice to meet you."

"And you." I shook his hand, marveling at the sheer size of the man. If you were to throw a bucket of green paint at him, he could pass as the Hulk. An extremely hot Hulk.

"Shade, this is Maddie McGuire. I've been bragging about your *pasteis*. Maddie, this is Gabriel Silva Vitriono."

"Call me Shade and they're all right," he said. With a shrug he pushed the tray closer to me. "I know Jake likes them spicy but May said he had someone with him so I brought an assortment."

"They smell delicious," I said. "I didn't realize how hungry I am."

"You're not going to be disappointed." Jake picked up a *pas-*

teis and took a big bite. Some of the sauce seeped out the side of his mouth and he caught it with his thumb.

"You were always a slob, man. Don't embarrass yourself in front of your date." Shade's deep voice rumbled across the table. "She looks classy."

I inhaled to laugh and accidentally sucked in a piece of lettuce. Shade slapped my back with one of his ham-sized hands until I could breathe again. I couldn't imagine Jake as a slob, but maybe he'd been more relaxed around the guys while on tour.

"You've got a nice laugh when you're not choking on lettuce." Shade smiled at me and his intimidating face transformed into something more than handsome.

"Back off, Shade." Jake mock glared at his friend.

"Can't hurt me for having eyes, my friend." Shade raised his hands in the air but winked at me. Heat rushed to my cheeks and I looked down at my *pasteis*. He stood up and rubbed his hands together. "I'm going to go back to work before May comes out here and drags me back by my ear. I'll send some more napkins for the Neanderthal and some drinks in case you choke on more lettuce."

"Thanks, Shade. It was nice to meet you." I smiled up at him and realized why he was nicknamed Shade. He was so large he literally cast a shadow that you could take shade in.

"My pleasure, *bela*. Come see me anytime." He shifted his bulk so Jake couldn't see his face and wiggled his eyebrows.

"Shade." Jake growled. Only this time I wasn't sure it was so friendly.

"I'm going, friend, I'm going." Turning away from our table he headed back to the truck with a deep laugh. "See you around, *bela*."

"That is an interesting man." I watched him leave and all of the women's heads turned in his direction. He had a dark aura of danger that was more than enticing. "I'm guessing his name is ironic. A joke?"

"Oh, he's a joke all right." Jake stared darkly after his friend. "But he makes some really good *pasteis*."

"That he does." I took another bite of my *pasteis*. "These are delicious."

"His one redeeming quality."

"I thought you were friends." I raised an eyebrow.

"We're friends. That doesn't mean I don't want to wring his neck sometimes." He glared in the direction Shade had walked.

"Now, don't be jealous." I reached out and patted his arm. "I'm sure you make good *pasteis* too."

I couldn't keep the smug smile from my face. It was nice to know that Jake Simmon could be a bit jealous over little ol' me. He looked up at me with sheepish eyes and smiled.

"It's not the *pasteis* I'm worried about," he explained.

"The *pasteis* are the only thing you should be worried about." I took a big bite of my lunch and sighed. "Because they're delicious."

The rest of our meal was spent stuffing our mouths and listening to the breeze whisper through the trees. After a while we picked up our trash and went back to the waiting SUV's.

The museum was hopping as usual. It was a Sunday afternoon and there were a lot of families and tour groups. Our security detail dropped back a little, but there was no missing the fact that they were following us. Considering our late start to the day, we only had a few hours left to peruse the sights.

"Where do you want to start?" Jake handed me a map.

Eagerly I opened it up to scan the pictures. I really was excited about seeing the museum. I loved history; learning how things had grown, shifted, and affected the world over time. If you didn't see how things started and evolved you could look at the end product and think it was magic. It was only with all the little pieces of the puzzle that you can put the whole picture together.

I looked up at the African Elephant in the middle of the museum. It wouldn't be long before those amazing animals had disappeared from the Earth and no one would know why unless they stopped and looked at how humans had hunted them and destroyed their homes. This exhibit would be the only chance future children would have to see an elephant.

Unless someone started speaking up and making a difference.

"You look upset," Jake said. He moved into my line of sight and touched my shoulder.

"What? No. I was just thinking," I explained. "I think we should start on the first floor and work our way up."

"That sounds like a good plan." He looked at the map in my hands. "The mammals exhibit is over here."

I looked at the massive lion up on a pedestal. "Such a magnificent creature. I hate to see it stuffed."

"I met one of the curators once. At a dinner or something," Jake said. "She told me that a lot of the animals were donated after being confiscated from poachers or had died from natural causes."

"You're trying to make me feel better." I shot him a thankful smile. "But I know that a lot of animals are actually trophy kills donated to the museum."

"Maybe," he agreed. "But a lot of the things in here are also fabricated—re-creations to show what the animal would look like in real life. There are also a lot of children that would never have the chance to see one of these animals without having a museum to go to."

I stopped and looked at an orangutan behind glass. I couldn't help but be amazed at how human-like the animal really was. These animals deserved so much respect. I hoped that this exhibit really did expose children to more of the world so they'd be aware of how their actions affected everything.

We spent time looking at all of the animals and I read the little signs. Occasionally we would be jostled by children clamoring to get closer to the exhibits, but it never seemed to bother Jake. I guess being the older brother to two younger sisters had increased his tolerance for children.

It wasn't until a few adults got near us that I noticed his eyes narrowing and how he seemed to pull into himself, staying close to me as if worried people would try to hurt me. A few tourists pressed close against him to get a picture of a tiger frozen in midleap and I saw his jaw tighten. I looked around to see where every one of our guards were and noticed that Tony was focused on Jake as if he was the current threat.

Twining my fingers with his I pulled him away from the group and toward another exhibit that was less crowded. The farther we drifted from the large groups the more tension slipped from his shoulders. I'd seen it happen a few times over the last few weeks, when there'd been too many people around. He'd even left the worksite during the drywall installation but I hadn't realized that it had been for any reason other than to run an errand.

When his thumb ran over the back of my fingers in a gentle caress I realized we'd moved past the most difficult moment. His expression had relaxed and his shoulders weren't tight. Guilt flooded my system as I thought about how he must feel being around a ton of people. I shouldn't have suggested the museum, but it was the first thing to pop into my head last night.

"What's wrong?" He leaned down close to me as we peered at examples of early humanoids.

"I shouldn't have suggested coming somewhere with so many people." I frowned down at the plaque in front of me.

"Why?"

I looked up at him and saw in his eyes that he already knew the answer. I could also tell that he didn't want me to really answer. For one of the few times in my life I didn't blurt out my first thought but took a minute to weigh how my response might affect him.

"After all of those people last night we probably both could have used a break from crowds." I didn't want to lie to Jake. I wasn't going to, but that didn't mean I couldn't temper how I answered questions that obviously mattered to him. "I forgot how pushy tourists could be."

"I'm having fun." He pulled me close and tucked me under his arm. I couldn't help the goofy grin that broke across my face.

"I'm sure that learning about Homo Erectus and the different classifications was something you were just dying to know more about." I poked his side. "Now you know all sorts of details about Eugene Dubois and his expedition to discover our evolutionary ancestors. You're probably thrilled I've filled your brain with all these facts."

"I'm spending time with you, I'm happy." He smiled down at me and my heart fluttered.

"No wonder you're such a ladies' man. Do you say that to all the women?"

"I'm saying it to you." His eyes dropped to my mouth. "No one else matters."

Heat filled my cheeks and I looked back at the description on the case in front of us to try and collect myself. "You've got a silver tongue, Jake Simmon."

"It's easy with you, Maddie. All I have to do is tell the truth." Lifting my chin he pressed his mouth to mine, giving me a chance to see just what he could do with his tongue. I'd been kissed before but there was something different when Jake touched me. It was like being plugged into an electric current. Any time our skin met parts of me came alive that I didn't know hadn't been working.

When he pulled away from me I felt as though every cell in my body had been lit on fire and I hadn't taken a breath in years. I wanted nothing more than to wrap myself around him and dive in for a repeat performance.

Tony cleared his throat and I looked around confused. With Jake's hands on me, I'd forgotten there was anyone else around, much less the fact that we were in the middle of a museum.

I looked around the area we were standing in and saw several people with cameras pointed in our direction. One of the little boys had his mouth wide open as one of the Secret Service guards moved in his family's direction. Tony tapped his watch and Jake nodded his head.

"Er, I think we may have just made tomorrow's news." I looked up at Jake as I unwound my arms from around his neck. The flash from someone's camera phone made me wince. I hated being caught unaware.

"Well, it won't be the first time." He wound his fingers with mine as he pulled me toward a door. "Just the first time we'll be doing it together."

"Where are we going?" I lengthened my stride so I could keep pace.

"You'll see." He smiled back at me, his eyes twinkling.

We took the stairs quickly and it dawned on me that he wasn't using his cane.

"You haven't been using your cane lately," I mused. "Something new at the doctor?"

"Working at the jobsite has been better than all of the physical therapy I've done over the last year. My doctor has been talking about making everyone do physical labor to speed up their progress."

"If anything they'll probably just double their efforts so they don't have to spend days digging trenches or running plumbing."

"Which is probably his actual intent." Jake laughed.

At the top of the stairs I noticed that the crowds were starting to thin. "Are we too late? Is it closing time?"

"I think so." Jake started walking toward the gem and precious stone section.

"Would you rather see the dinosaurs? I feel like I took up all our time downstairs." I pulled him to a stop. The entrance to the Fossil Lab was behind us.

"We'll make time." He smiled and kept walking.

"But—"

"Come on, Maddie. We live here, we can come back and see the dinosaurs another time."

"You're awfully sure we're going to have a second date." I couldn't help but poke a little at his ego. "What makes you think I'm having a good time?"

"Well, I'm having a good time." He looked at me from the corner of his eye. "And I've got an ace up my sleeve."

"An ace up your sleeve?" I frowned.

He smiled down at me. "I might not make good *pasteis* but I have a few other tricks."

We rounded the corner and I was surprised to see an extra detail of security. Several men in business suits and a woman wearing a polo shirt stood in front of a glass case.

"What's going on?" I frowned and looked around the room. Had someone made a threat against us? It wouldn't be the first time I'd been rushed by a bunch of guards to be herded into a corner so they could protect me.

"Remember when I said that I knew someone that worked here?" Jake's eyes shined in the special lighting.

"Yes?"

"This is my ace." He steered me toward the glass case where a large blue diamond stared up at me.

The woman in the polo shirt smiled brightly while she went through unlocking the case.

"Are you serious?" I turned to look at Jake.

"If you dare with the curse looming." He wiggled his eyes brows.

I laughed and threw my arms around his neck. "You're really something."

"Hopefully it's something good." His smile widened.

"I'll let you know."

"Miss McGuire?" The woman standing at the case was wearing gloves and holding a pair out for me. "Would you like to hold it?"

"Yes," I breathed. I handed my purse to Jake and took the offered gloves.

"I'm Sharon." The woman held her hand out to me. I shook it, feeling funny about the gloves. "Are you a jewelry fan or a history buff?"

"History." I looked at the necklace lying on the velvet blue stand in front of me. "Definitely a history buff."

"Then you know all about the curse," she stated.

I looked up to see her smile. She didn't believe in the curse either.

"The curse only affects the owners so I have nothing to worry about." I let my eyes roam over the glistening facets. "Can you imagine what all this diamond has seen?"

"It would certainly have a lot to say." Sharon motioned for me to move closer. "Go ahead. It's heavier than it looks though."

I looked back at Jake before turning my attention back to the gem in front of me. With shaky fingers I lifted the stone from its perch and lifted it to eye level. The diamond definitely had more heft to it than I expected. The stone was a gorgeous deep blue that seemed to go on forever. It had imperfections, but nothing that could hurt the awe it induced.

Unearthed in India, this very stone had once graced the neck of Marie Antoinette, before making its way to Britain, and then the United States. I could only imagine what it had been witness to over the years.

"It's fantastic." I held the necklace up to the light. "I can't believe I'm holding a piece of history."

"Try it on." Jake stepped close to me.

"Oh, I don't know." I looked over at Sharon. "I think I'm lucky to just be holding it. There aren't many people in the world that can claim that now."

"You've got your hair pulled up, so it won't be difficult to put it on and take it off." Sharon held her hands out for the necklace. I passed it over with gentle fingers.

I looked at Jake in question. Was I really going to get to wear the Hope Diamond?

He pulled the gloves from my fingers before slipping them on himself. He stepped behind me and I heard him murmur something to Sharon.

Before I could ask what he was doing I felt the solid weight of the necklace settle around my neck. I let out a long breath and looked down at the stone lying against my collarbone. There was the sound of a clasp clicking and I had to concentrate to keep my hands from drifting up to the glittering jewel and all of the gold that surrounded it.

I turned around to look up at Jake. He was watching me with fathomless brown eyes that seemed even deeper than the blue of the diamond.

"It suits you." His deep voice was barely above a whisper.

"I feel so . . . I don't know. Decadent." I smiled up at him and put my hands on his chest to keep me from touching the diamond. "Thank you."

"So, am I getting a second date?"

Someone chuckled behind us and I smiled.

"I think so." I laughed. "I'm not sure how you're going to top this though." My hand fluttered up toward the necklace and I managed to keep from touching it. "I can't believe I'm wearing the Hope Diamond."

"Where's your phone?"

"My phone?" I reached into my back pocket and pulled out my cell phone.

He took a step back and lifted my phone. "Pictures or it didn't happen."

Chapter 12

Jake

I deserved a fucking medal. It should be big and it should be blue. Just like my balls. I hadn't laid a hand on Maddie since our good-night kiss in front of the White House a few days before. We'd worked side by side on the house for Cyrus and his family, while flirting shamelessly, but I hadn't done anything where other people might see us. I'd been dodging my mother's phone calls since she called after our picture had shown up in the *Washington Post*.

The media shit storm generated by our kiss in the museum was like being swept up in a hurricane. There was no way we could go anywhere and do anything that wouldn't lead to a million more pictures and speculation. Not to mention the constant picture taking. Some website had a picture of me with my eyes half closed and my mouth open as its front page.

"VP's Drunken Son Mauls First Daughter." Had to love the sensationalism.

So here I was, trying to cook dinner for us. I didn't know

how to cook, but how hard could it be? Dinner at home seemed like the perfect plan. We wouldn't have a million people looking at us with speculation and best of all, we'd be alone.

Unfortunately, my plan for our second date had exploded into a mess in my kitchen. Apparently frying foods wasn't as easy as the directions in the book made it sound. It certainly wasn't a tidy venture. The housekeeper was going to kill me and Puz was busy licking everything he could reach with his tongue. Nor was it safe. I had welts up and down my arms. I'd yelped more than I had when they'd picked shrapnel out of my arm. Those little bits of oil stung like a motherfucker.

The doorbell rang and I groaned. Apparently I'd run out of cards up my sleeve.

Darting to the window at the back of the kitchen I threw it open and waved the tiny dish towel in my hand around in the air in an effort to dissipate some of the smoke. The doorbell echoed through the house again and I threw the towel on the counter before making my way to the foyer.

I opened the door and a cloud of smoke poured out into the crisp D.C. air. Maddie waved her hand in front of her face before smiling up at me.

"Ah, honey, you cooked." Her gold-flecked eyes smiled up at me and my heart gave a dangerous thump. She was wearing jeans and a t-shirt. Her hair was pulled back in one of those ponytails she favored. Like usual she was wearing very little makeup and no jewelry.

She was gorgeous.

Puz ran out from between my feet and she picked him up before kissing him on the nose and tucking him against her chest. A man shouldn't be jealous of his dog, but I wish she'd kissed me hello instead.

"Well, I tried." I held my hand out to her and pulled her inside. "It didn't go so well."

"Dare I ask what you were burning?" She went straight to a window that faced a brick wall at the back of the house and threw it open. Puz danced around her feet in excitement.

"Country fried steak and mashed potatoes." I grabbed the other window and threw it open. "Well, steak for me. I tried to fry the portabello mushrooms for you."

"You fried mushrooms?" She choked out a laugh. "You didn't try to fry the mashed potatoes, did you?"

"You're not supposed to fry those?" I widened my eyes.

"Jake . . ." She turned to look over at me before narrowing her eyes. "Har, har."

"Give me some credit. I know you have to beat the potatoes with a spoon before you boil them in a big pot." I reached out and pulled her to me. She chuckled and pressed her hands to my chest.

"Maybe we should order out. " Her fingers spread across my chest before tightening a little. It reminded me of a kitten pawing something interesting.

Puz gave up on getting attention and disappeared. Good man. I wanted some time alone with this woman.

"Unless you only want mashed potatoes that would prob-ably be a good idea." I leaned down and nuzzled her neck. She made a sound of pleasure and my dick jumped in my pants.

"I don't care what we eat," she whispered. Her hands on me tightened and I got the inkling that I wasn't the only one dying to be alone again.

I could think of a few things I wouldn't mind putting in my mouth but I kept that thought to myself. Instead I lifted her chin and claimed her mouth with my own. I'd been dying to do that for days and I groaned with the taste. I pulled her a little closer and let myself take what I wanted. She melted against me, one arm around my neck while her fingers clenched in my shirt.

I pushed her against the wall between the windows and pulled her shirt up so I could touch her soft skin.

She gasped and the sound lit a fire in me. I grazed her sides with my fingertips before stroking her stomach.

Her mouth on mine was just as hungry. She nipped my bottom lip between her teeth before soothing it with her tongue. Maddie poured everything into her kiss and I loved it. There was no holding back, no patience. It was how Maddie treated everything in life.

It was exactly what I needed.

I let myself drink her in, drown in her. She was like a spring day after a painful winter. With Maddie I felt good—I didn't have to keep myself in check. For everything I took, she gave freely. There were no games, no maneuvering to see what the other person was after.

It was just Maddie. Because Maddie was what I wanted and it seemed that I was lucky enough to be what she wanted.

That truth scared the shit out of me, but I wasn't going to let that stop me now. Instead I blundered forward blindly, consuming as much of her as I could. She was my water after being in the desert for so long.

Running my hands up her back I traced her bra clasp before running my hands back around to the front where I brushed my thumbs along the bottom of her breasts.

She sucked in air which gave me the chance to plunder her

mouth even more. The taste of her, the feel of her, and the sounds she made curled around my brain like an enchanted fog. I couldn't think straight.

When she pressed toward me, her back arching, I filled my hands with her tight breasts. She groaned into my mouth and I lost all sense of reality. The only thing that existed was Maddie and how she made me feel.

Needing more I shoved her bra up so I could touch the delicate skin hidden underneath. I kneaded the plump flesh with my fingers as fire tore through my blood. Her head thumped back against the wall and I used the opportunity to yank her shirt over her head and remove the frustrating material of her bra.

Once I had her exposed I looked down at her and felt the blood drain from my head. Her pert breasts were capped in soft pink tips that made my mouth water. She grabbed my shirt and pulled me toward her, slamming her hungry lips against mine. With one hand I reached up and cupped one perfect peak before brushing my thumb across her tender flesh. She shivered and I did it again.

My dick was straining against my jeans, begging to be set free from the rough material. With each caress of her lips every cell in my body screamed to strip her down. Take her. Claim her. Make her mine.

My hand tightened on her soft skin before I gently pinched her nipple between my fingers. She groaned and pressed harder into my hand. I rolled the pebbled peak between my fingers before pinching it a little harder. She groaned so I did it again and she whimpered against my mouth. Her fingers on my chest dug into my skin through the material. I switched breasts, lifting the other one in my hand, enjoying the weight of it as it filled my palm. I let my fingers move over it, massaging it while I devoured her sexy little sounds.

She pulled at my shirt, trying to get it over my head. Grabbing her hands I pinned her wrists against the wall above her head with one hand and used the other to grip the back of my shirt and lift it over my head.

I tossed it behind me and let my eyes roam over her. Her jeans rode low on her hips exposing the planes of her stomach and the sweet little indentation of her belly button. I couldn't wait to run my tongue there and much lower.

I still had her hands pinned above her head and her eyes were dark with desire.

"I swear I've never seen anything sexier than you looking at me right now." I pressed my body to hers, enjoying the way her breasts strained between us. "I don't want it to ever go away."

"Then kiss me again," she whispered. And I obliged. I wanted nothing more than to give her every reason to keep that heated look.

I didn't let go of her hands, enjoying the way it made her breasts point forward, the hardened peaks scraping across my skin. Using my leg I spread hers so I could press closer to her hot center. She groaned loudly into my mouth, her hips straining forward.

Using my free hand I reached between us and flicked open the button on her jeans. Her little gasp of surprise went straight to my dick and I pressed against her, rubbing so she could feel my excitement. Without pause her hips strained forward, grinding against me and I dropped my head to her shoulder.

"I want you, Maddie. I thought I could be patient but I can't." I ran my nose up her neck as she shivered and I used my teeth to tug on her ear. "I want to touch you, taste you. I want to be inside of you. I want to watch you as you come. Can I have that? Can I have you?"

She groaned and her hips bucked against mine again, making my eyes close in pleasure. Heat speared through my body when I opened my eyes again to find her gaze.

"Then take me." Her words were so sure, so strong, I didn't think twice. I pushed her zipper down and slid my hand in the front of her pants. I was greeted with soft lace and delicious warm heat.

I traced the wet spot in her panties with my fingers before using my thumb to rub her hard little clit.

"Oh, fuck," she groaned. She bucked against me, straining forward.

My cock was already harder than ever before, but hearing her curse while I touched her almost killed me.

"You like that?" I bit her ear again, her hands still trapped above her head.

"Yes." She opened her eyes and looked right at me. "Don't stop."

I was nowhere ready to stop. Instead I dropped my head and captured one of those gorgeous tits with my mouth and rolled my tongue over the peak while she bucked against my hand.

"Oh, fuck."

I looked up at her expecting her eyes to be closed, instead they were trained on me as I traced her sweet skin with my tongue. Christ, the woman was perfect.

I pulled my head back a little so she could see my tongue as I licked her and her whole body vibrated with pleasure. Carefully I moved my hand under her panties so I could slip a finger deep inside of her while my thumb rubbed small circles along her sweet spot.

"Fuck, fuck, fuck." Her hips jammed forward, trying to get even more. I rewarded her with a second finger and her groan was like honey to my ears.

"You have a naughty mouth, Madeline." I stood up straight and ran my lips over hers, all the while smoothly moving my fingers in and out.

"You—" She groaned and gasped for a breath. "Just. With you."

"I like it." I bent down and bit her shoulder and she swore under her breath. "Louder, Maddie. Tell me what you want, sweetheart."

"Don't fucking stop, Jake." Her wet pussy clenched around my fingers. "I want more."

I groaned against her skin, dying to be inside of her, but loving every moment of this torture. I'd drag this out as long as I possibly could.

Letting go of her hands I shoved her jeans and panties roughly to the ground before dropping to my knees. I let my eyes travel up along her exposed skin, over her breasts, to lock with her large fairy-like eyes. Slowly, so she knew exactly what I was doing I opened my mouth and trailed my tongue along the wet crease between her legs.

"Jake." My name formed by those lips was pure magic.

Leaning forward I pressed my mouth to her skin, trailing my tongue over the spots she seemed to like the best. Her pants of pleasure and the whispered curses were my road map.

She was sweet, so sweet, and I couldn't get enough. Everything about Maddie drove me crazy, but this, my mouth at her core was perfect. Her hips strained against me and she tangled her fingers in my hair while she demanded more from me.

"More."

I lifted her leg and placed it on my shoulder, exposing more of her sweet flesh for my exploration. Her curses were getting louder and I slipped a finger inside to move in time with her thrusts. She threw her head against the wall and moaned loudly.

"Jake. Fuck, that's so good. So good. Fuck. Fuck." I loved hearing the dirty stream of words coming from that delicate mouth. The contrast was intoxicating. I'd put them there and had more than a little pride in that fact. "Oh God. Fuck. Jake, I'm so close."

With my free hand I reached up and cupped her breast, squeezing it. She gasped and her hips jerked forward. I pressed my tongue against her clit before sucking it into my mouth.

"Holy shit." The curse was ripped from her mouth. "Fucking fuck. That feels good. So good. Don't stop. Fucking good. So good."

Her moans were fast, interrupted by pants of pleasure. Her hips ground against my face, her fingers locked in my hair as she raced toward her peak. There was no sound sweeter in the world than Maddie urging me on, her mouth wrapped around my name as pleasure overrode her sense.

I let loose of her clit, my fingers still keeping rhythm as she strained against me. I rubbed little circles over it with my thumb and turned my face toward her thigh so I could sink my teeth into the delicate skin there.

She gasped, her hips moving faster.

Her moan was loud enough that I wondered if anyone else would hear her.

"Come for me, Maddie." I blew across her clit before sucking it back into my mouth and flicking it with my tongue. My hand was covered in her slick liquid and I added another finger to the one already pumping in and out of her.

"Oh, fuck. Oh, fuck. Yes. Jake. Fuck. That's it." Her fingers tightened in my hair to the point of pain but I didn't stop. My dick was going to be bruised from the zipper of my pants, but there was no way I was going to stop what I was doing.

"Jake!" She came hard, her pussy clenching around my fingers, her hips bucking against the wall and slamming into my face. Her juices leaked down my hand and her whole body twitched in pleasure. I pulled my fingers free and slid my tongue inside of her, desperate to catch every last drop.

She groaned with each stroke of my tongue but her fingers relaxed in my hair. I looked up at her, my mouth still on her warm skin. Her eyes were bright and the muscles in her face were relaxed. Those fairy eyes followed me as I continued to lick her, not wanting to miss anything.

"You keep that up and you're going to have to finish." Her husky voice made my dick strain painfully against my pants. I pulled my mouth away and rubbed her clit with my pointer finger.

"I plan on finishing."

Her eyes darkened and I felt her leg on my shoulder shift so she was spread open even further. Leaning forward I kissed her, using my lips and tongue to drive her past the contentment of her earlier orgasm.

"If you keep doing that—" She groaned loudly when I sucked her clit back into my mouth. "I think my other. Leg. Is. Oh, fuck. Going to give out."

I looked up at her and was surprised to see her squeezing her own breast.

"I've got you," I murmured against her skin. I kissed her inner thigh down to her knee. Carefully I slid her leg off my shoulder and climbed to my feet. "I'm not done with you yet."

Her eyes clouded with uncertainty for a minute and I waited to make sure she hadn't decided this was a mistake.

When she stood on her tiptoes to press her lips to mine I let her kiss me until I could barely breathe. Her tight breasts pressed against my chest, moving and teasing me. Pulling her tight against me, I lifted her feet from the ground and turned toward my dining room table. I shoved the stupid place mats out of the way and sat her down.

She squeaked a little at the cold surface but went right back to kissing me. She reached for my pants and tugged at the button until she could get it free. I let her touch me, keeping my hands to myself as my dick fell free of the denim.

She pulled away from the kiss to look at my cock and her eyebrows rose in surprise. Her fingers reached out and barely touched the sensitive skin as she trailed them from the head down the shaft. When she gripped me at my base with a firm hand I hissed in pleasure.

"I guess you're proportional, huh?" She cocked her head to the side and looked up at me with big eyes. Her hand twisted as she tugged upward on my dick and then again as she slid her hand back to the base. "Big all over."

"You trying to fan my ego, Maddie?" I had to swallow before I could get the sentence out. I watched as her fair-skinned hand ran over me.

"Just stating the obvious." She leaned forward and flicked her tongue across my chest. "You do it justice."

"All I want to do is you." I leaned forward, bracketing her seat on my table with my arms. "I meant what I said, Maddie.

I plan on being inside of you and watching you come. I want to fuck you until you can't stand up."

"Now who has the dirty mouth?" She looked up at me with those big eyes and heat in her cheeks.

"You going to get shy on me now?" I lifted her chin and rubbed my jaw against her cheek, trying to focus on anything other than her hand on my dick.

"No." She whispered the word and turned her face toward me for a kiss.

I pressed my lips to hers, letting her taste the remnant of her pleasure still there. To my surprise she flicked her tongue out over my lip before sucking it into her mouth.

"I like the way I taste on you, Jake." She pulled back and squeezed my shaft a little harder. "I like knowing what you did to me."

"Fuck, you're going to kill me, Maddie." I brought her face back to mine and thrust my tongue into her mouth. She sucked on my tongue before tangling it with her own. I let my hands roam over her body, spreading her legs and pulling her close to me. My dick pressed against her stomach and I groaned at the sensation. She reached lower, cupping my balls in her hand, her pointer finger rubbing that rough spot just behind them. They tightened painfully and I groaned.

Breaking our kiss I pulled her hands from my cock and shook my head. "You can't keep doing that."

"Why's that?" She looked up at me and pulled her hair down from the rubber band holding it out of her face.

"Feels too good." My breathing was heavy as I watched her hair swing free, some of it curling around her tight breasts. "I don't want to come in your hand, Maddie."

"You keep talking about fucking me and I'm starting to feel

impatient, Jake." She leaned back on the table slowly and as I watched one of her hands trailed to that sweet spot between her legs. "You better do something about it."

"Fuck." My brained drained away and I only had the sense to dig in my back pocket for a condom. Apparently it was my turn for obscenities.

"Yes, Jake. Fuck me. Now." She slid two of her fingers into her wet center and I swear my mouth fell open.

Never in my wildest dreams would I have thought sweet, innocent Maddie McGuire would be such a siren. Her fingers circled her clit while her other hand cupped her breast before pinching the nipple.

"Who are you?" The condom in my hand was all but forgotten as I watched her touch herself. "You look like one of those mermaids sent to lure men to their deaths."

Her hand moved over her skin, the wet sounds reminding me of my needy dick. I reached a hand down and stroked my shaft as she moved on my table.

"I'm the same girl, Jake. You just didn't see me." The wild fairy queen watched me. Her eyes were bright with some emotion I couldn't name.

I sure as fuck saw her now. I'd never seen anything so clearly in my life. Maddie. The annoying girl I'd had to take pictures with as a teenager was a sex goddess. I knew there was something sexy under that wide-eyed exterior and bright blushes, but fuck if I had known this was what had been waiting for me.

"Jesus Christ."

"Nope." She laughed. "Just me."

I ripped the condom open and worked it over my thick head

with a little pop before rolling it down and over my shaft. I was so hard I was worried the condom was going to cut off the blood flow.

"This isn't going to be gentle, Maddie, but I'll make it up to you." I lifted her leg and pulled her to the edge of the table. "I want you too bad."

"I don't want gentle," she told me.

I pressed my head at her opening and she lifted her hips so I sank in just a little. Pulling back I rubbed the tip of my dick across her clit, listening to her groan before pressing at her center again. She moaned, her eyes closing briefly before flashing open as I slid home. It wasn't gentle but I honestly hadn't been in control for a second. Her hot pussy clenched around me and I forgot to breathe.

"Fuck," I whispered. "Fuck."

I threw her leg up over my shoulder so I could sink all the way down to my base. Her eyes widened and her mouth opened on a gasp. I didn't move, just looked from her face to where we were joined. God, I'd never felt this way with another woman; as if we'd been made to fit together. It was like she'd been born just for me and I'd been a blind fool for years.

My breathing was heavy as I lost myself in the sensation. She was tight and hot, squeezing me without moving. I let my hands slide down to her hips and over her stomach before cupping her breast.

"Are you ready?" I pinched her chin delicately between my finger and thumb so I could see her eyes clearly.

"Been ready." She gasped as I pulled back and then slid home again. "Just waiting on you."

Fool. I'd been a fucking fool.

"Not anymore." I moved again and her back arched off the table. "Fuck, you're gorgeous."

She gasped and clutched her breasts with both hands. "You make me feel gorgeous."

I pulled back and slid back in as she groaned. I found a rhythm that worked and gripped one of her hips to keep her in place while I rubbed her clit with the other hand.

"Fuck, you feel so good Maddie." I wanted to touch her, all of her. This wasn't going to be enough to satisfy me.

No I wouldn't be satisfied until I'd touched, kissed, licked every part of her.

"Harder, Jake."

I did as she commanded. Anything for my fairy queen.

I slammed into her and the table moved under us. I didn't let that stop me as her groans grew louder. She was writhing on the table, her back arched, her hips only still because I had hold of them.

Her tits jumped in her hands, moving as she fondled herself. I wanted to touch those too, but was out of hands.

"Squeeze your tits, Maddie." She did as I asked and I couldn't stop my moan. "That's it, squeeze them for me. God, I want to suck on those."

She squeezed them, her fingers leaving little marks before she let go. I was about to tell her to not stop, but she didn't leave me hanging. She licked her deft fingers before pinching her hardened peaks and flicking them with her thumbs. I groaned and she repeated it.

"Ah, fuck. Maddie." My dick jerked inside of her and I knew it wouldn't be long before I couldn't hold back anymore.

She reached between us with one hand and rubbed her clit.

The feel of her fingers moving where we were joined had me losing control. I slammed my hips into her, racing toward the finish. Needing to pump into Maddie while she moved under me, making those little sounds.

"Fuck. Yes." She was groaning, her breathing fast and high. "Harder, Jake."

I obliged. Sweat pebbled on my chest as I thrust into her over and over. Her fingers traced the opening where I moved before going back to circle her clit and I wasn't aware of anything else.

Her body stiffened on the table, her hips bucking wildly, and I lost it.

"Fuck, Maddie." I pumped into her before holding her tight against me as I shot load after load into her. I slumped forward, unable to keep myself upright and braced myself on my arms.

She looked up at me and there was so much in her gaze I couldn't understand. It was like getting lost in a whirlpool. I swallowed and reached out to trace a finger over her cheek.

I couldn't think of a single thing to say. Not a word.

"Jake?" She ran her hands over my arms.

"Yeah?" My voice was rough and I tried to clear my throat.

"The table."

Her hair was spread around her like it had come to life while we'd made love. The fading sunlight glinted in her eyes and there was a soft blush covering her cheeks.

"Jake." She squeezed my shoulder. "The table."

"What?" I looked down and was surprised to see that the table was a good five feet from where it had started.

"I think we—"

Before she could finish one of the old legs collapsed and we rolled to the ground in a heap of arms and sweaty skin. Puz came barking before sniffing around us.

"Broke it." She looked down at me from where she'd landed on my chest and started to laugh.

That was when I realized I was in dangerous territory.

My heart thumped painfully in my chest, in a way that had nothing to do with the table, and I pulled her down to kiss me.

"Jake?" She pulled back to look at me with an odd expression. Puz seemed interested in something near her head.

"Yeah?"

"Were the mashed potatoes on the table?" She reached up and touched something clumped in her hair.

It was my turn to laugh as I folded my arms around her.

Chapter 13

Maddie

My phone beeped from the bedside table and I cracked my eyes open. I lifted my arm to turn the phone off but I hit the table with my elbow.

"Shit on a brick that hurt!" I cradled my arm and looked down at the spectacular bruise that decorated my skin.

"You 'kay?" A heavy arm tightened around my midsection and despite my throbbing arm I felt all light and gooey inside.

"Yeah, I'm okay. Hit that stupid bruise." I wiggled a little so I could reach the phone without dislodging his hold on me.

"'Tupid table," he grunted. I had a bruise on my left arm that covered my elbow and ran down to my wrist. Jake had received a giant bruise that trailed from his shoulder down to one butt cheek.

There would be a lot of ibuprofen in our future.

Picking up my phone I swiped the screen open, barely registering that it didn't have its normal password lock in place.

WHAT THE HELL DO YOU THINK YOU ARE DOING?

The text message was right there for me to see before I put two and two together.

Shit.

"Um, Jake. It's your phone." I rolled over to hand it to him. "Sorry, I opened it thinking it was mine."

He grunted and held out a hand for the phone. "S'okay."

I put the phone in his hand and rolled back to my side and pulled the blanket tighter. I felt exposed and it had nothing to do with my lack of clothing. People knew what had happened, that we were together. Somehow Jake's mother had found out I was at his house. I looked around the room for a clock but didn't see one. How late was it? We'd only just fallen asleep.

Jake looked at his phone before tapping on the screen quickly.

"I should go." I started to sit up but he pulled me closer.

"Don't. It's no one's business but our own what we're doing."

I bit my lip and fought the urge to ask him what were we doing. His mother hated me and I knew that I was one of those scandalous political children. I was from a first marriage and broke into buildings. I was a loose cannon.

"No, don't get that look." Jake rolled over on top of me, settling his hips between my legs. He'd taken his prosthetic off when we'd made it to the bed.

There had been no hesitation as he took it off and leaned it against the wall. Honestly, it hadn't bothered me at all. I'd been more mesmerized by the sharp angles and planes of the rest of him. It was the scarring that ran down his side and back that troubled me the most. Not because it made him any less beautiful but because it reminded me that he almost hadn't made it home.

"Stop it." He nuzzled my neck, his breathing tickling me. "No thinking. No worrying. No anything."

I managed to weasel a hand between us so I could trace his thickening cock. "No anything?"

"I take that last part back." His breath tickled my ear and I couldn't help a giggle. "Oh, do that again. I liked that."

Unable to help myself I laughed when his fingers ran along my side, tickling me. I wiggled to try and get free before doing some tickling of my own.

His bark of laughter was short and loud, his fingers digging under my ribs making me flail. My foot hit the bedside table and the lamp crashed to the floor in a loud noise. He froze and something shifted in his eyes. His hands on my sides tightened and I sucked in a pained breath.

"I'm sorry." I looked up at him and had the strangest feeling that he was somewhere else. "Jake?" The way his eyes were focused past me told me that he wasn't trying to hurt me. I wasn't even sure if he was aware that I was still with him.

Puz sat up from his spot on the floor and whined softly before coming closer and putting his paws on the edge of the mattress.

His breathing was slow and shallow as if he'd been hurt. There was panic in his eyes that hadn't been there two seconds ago.

"Jake? Did I hurt you?" I reached up to touch his shoulder and he jerked away from me. The movement was so sudden and he was so fast that I flinched.

Rolling over he sat up, his gaze locked on the end of the bed. Puz jumped up and leaned against his human, making soft noises.

I sat up slowly and pulled the sheet up to cover my chest, my hand pressed where my heart was beating rapidly. Unsure of what to say I sat there quietly until his breathing seemed to even out. Even then I didn't move. Confusion and doubt swirled in the pit of my stomach. No one had said that Jake suffered from PTSD but I was starting to think someone should have. I only knew what I'd heard on the television or during talks my father gave, but this shift in mood was definitely a flag.

After a few minutes he moved to the edge of the bed and scooped up his shorts from the floor. Puz stuck close, never letting him get more than a foot or two away from him. He pulled on his clothes and then strapped on his prosthetic. I tried to not watch, worried that it was me that had sparked something. The crash of the table had definitely upset him.

"Do you want some breakfast?" He stood up without looking at me.

"Sure." I tried to keep my tone light but I was still scared to move. I didn't want to think of Jake as an injured animal, but there was something there, some vibe that he was exuding that made me anxious.

"I'm fine, Maddie." He turned to look at me and his skin was a little too pale, his eyes a little too dark. "I'm sorry if I scared you."

"I thought I hurt you." My voice trembled a little and I realized that I had been scared. By the sudden change when I was at my most vulnerable.

"No, Maddie, you didn't hurt me." He took a deep breath and shoved his fingers through his hair. "C'mon. Let's get some food."

I wrapped the sheet tighter around me. I should get up, but I didn't have any clothes to put on. Mine were still downstairs and I couldn't bring myself to follow him naked. Swinging my

legs over the edge of the bed, I tried to keep the blanket covering all my bits and pieces.

My feet twisted in the silken material and I started to go
down when strong hands caught me.

"Maddie." Jake said my name softly, almost like a prayer.
He tucked me against his chest and pressed his lips to my hair.
"I'm sorry. It doesn't happen often. Sometimes . . . sometimes
it's hard to remember where I am."

"I'm worried about you, Jake." I closed my eyes because they
felt unusually wet. Puz leaned against our legs and I wondered
who he was trying to comfort.

"That's the last thing I want. I like that you don't treat me
differently, Maddie. Don't start now, okay?" There was a plea
in his voice that couldn't be mistaken. He needed me to treat
him like everything was fine. He needed me to be his normal.

That was a really big job.

My heart ached, because I wanted to help Jake, wanted to
find a way to make it all better. But that wasn't what he was
asking of me.

"Please? Just treat me like you always have." He didn't pull
back to look me in the eye and I knew it was because he didn't
want to see anything bad there.

"I'll treat you like I always have, Jake, but only if you promise me that you'll talk to someone else." I lifted my head and
waited for him to meet my eyes. "Well, as normal as I can considering what we did to your kitchen table."

"If you keep doing things like we did on my kitchen counter
I'll talk to anyone you want me to." His smile was weak, but
there.

"It's not who I want you to talk to. It needs to be someone

you're okay with talking to. I'm serious, Jake. I'll keep calling you arrogant and pick on you for having to take your leg off to go through security, but you have to promise me that you will find someone to talk to."

He snorted and some of the clouds in his eyes receded. "I don't have to take my leg off to go through security."

"You should! Who knows what you could be hiding?" I pursed my lips. "They used those little wands on me before they let me see my dad at the Pentagon. But you? No, you can just waltz around anywhere. It's obnoxious."

"That's my girl." He ran his fingers through my hair but they got tangled.

"Ow." I lifted my hand to my head.

"Maybe we should clean the mashed potatoes out of your hair before we go downstairs." He leaned down and lifted me in the air before throwing me over his shoulder.

"Jake!" I reached down and smacked his ass.

"Oh, yeah." He chuckled. "You know what I like, baby."

I laughed until I snorted which made him laugh in turn.

"It's like having a pug for a girlfriend." He set me down in the bathroom and turned on the water in his shower.

My heart sped up and I watched him carefully. "A pug?"

"You know, those little dogs that snort all the time." He turned toward me and started to unwrap my sheet and snorted like a pig in example. Puz had followed us into the bathroom, his eyes on Jake.

"Girlfriend?" I licked my lips and tried to not look overly interested.

His hands stilled and I felt his gaze run over me.

"Yeah. Girlfriend." He tipped my chin back so he could look

me in the eyes. "You're a little mean to me, but that's okay, because you're fucking awesome in bed."

"And don't forget on tables."

"And against walls." He pulled the sheet away from my chest and looked down at my breasts. He growled in appreciation but let loose the sheet so it could fall back in place. "But that's not all I like about you."

"Hm. We covered beds, tables, and walls. What else could be left?" I raked my fingers over the scruff along his jaw. "My wit is a given."

"Are you fishing for compliments, Maddie?" He stroked the column of my neck, his thumb resting against my pulse.

"I think I was being pretty obvious about it, but yeah, I wouldn't mind hearing the good parts since we already know how mean I am." I trailed my fingers over his chest but I was careful to avoid the scars on his side. I didn't want to trigger another episode by drawing attention to a vivid reminder of his accident.

"Madeline McGuire, you're a bright star in a sea of black." He cupped my chin and looked down at me. "You're a balm to those that need soothing. You don't play games or pretend to be anything other than you. It's refreshing. You make me laugh and have such a carefree spirit it puts everyone at ease. Your taste in movies is questionable, but you never complain if someone else picks what you're watching. You're much smarter than you give yourself credit for and have a knack for understanding other people. You give everything in you to the things that matter and to the people you care about."

With each sentence I felt my eyebrows rising further and further. That was how Jake saw me? He was suffering from serious delusions.

"Tangling with me could cause you problems. You're the Golden Boy, the perfect political son, and I get arrested breaking into buildings." I shook my head. I wanted nothing more than to explore a real relationship with Jake, but I couldn't help feeling that I would hold him back.

"You already know I have problems. I'm not the Golden Boy anymore, Maddie, and honestly, I'm not interested in pretending to be. And from where I'm standing you're the last person I need to worry about." He trailed his lips across my jawline.

"What about your mom?" At our ages it would have been a ridiculous question. But when you consider who our parents were, it was a relevant topic.

"I'm not her pawn to maneuver around." His jaw tightened. "She doesn't get to choose who is important to me."

"I don't want to be a bone of contention between you and your family." I shook my head.

"The only person that has an issue is my mother and that has nothing to do with you and everything to do with her campaign."

I fought to keep a frown from my face, because I knew that was absolutely not true. Virginia Simmon hated my guts. My breeding wasn't good enough for her son. My mother hadn't been from an influential family. My father met her while he was touring hospitals and schools for his Senate reelection. She'd been with my grandmother and he'd fallen in love with how she treated the people around her.

My stepmother had the pedigree that Virginia thought so important and she doted on my half brother, no matter what he got caught doing. But me? I was always on the wrong side of things.

"Maddie?" Jake cupped my face and made me look up at him. There was a large stab of uncertainty in his eyes. "We can take things slower."

"No." I shook my head. How long had I wanted to feel the way I did when I was with Jake? Like I was special. "I want to try this—us—out."

"Good." A bright smile bloomed across his face just before his mouth pressed to mine. The eagerness in his touch quickly dissipated any of my doubts. I raised my hands to rest on his broad shoulders and the soft sheet fell to the ground in a whisper. His hands ran down my arms over my hips and down my ass before pulling me closer.

My breasts pressed against the bare skin of his chest and I fought to not moan. Without hesitation he cupped one of them in his hand, kneading it gently with his fingers and groaned. There was something empowering in the knowledge that I inspired that sort of lust. His impressive erection pressed against my stomach through his gym shorts and suddenly I couldn't think of anything more important than getting my hands on him. Running my fingers down his chest, I traced his hard abs, loving how they tightened under my touch.

"Off," I said against his mouth and pushed at his pants.

"Yes ma'am." I pulled back so he could do as I asked. "I'm not sure I've ever enjoyed being bossed around so much."

His eyes twinkled as he reached out for me but I stepped out of his reach.

"Uh-uh." I held a finger up and made a circle. "I didn't get to look at you last night."

His eyebrows rose before his mouth pulled to one side in a smug smile. Lifting his hands, he turned slowly in front of me. I let my eyes run over the muscles of his chest, his back, and his perfect ass. I hadn't seen a lot of male backsides in person, but I was pretty sure that Jake was a prime specimen. Well-defined muscles ran the lengths of his legs. His prosthetic barely registered in my mind. When he made a complete circle I was left staring at an even more impressive erection. When I'd told him he was proportional I hadn't been lying. Jake was a tall, well-muscled man. And his dick was no different. Long and so thick it made me wonder how he had fit inside me.

"Do you like what you see? Not exactly what I used to be." His smile slipped just a little and it wasn't just his body that made me ache and yearn, it was the way he wore his heart out in the open for me. "No more perfect boy."

"Perfect is boring. I like the man you've become, so much more than the boy you used to be." I stepped forward and trailed my fingers down his chest and around to his scars. I traced them with my fingers, ignoring nothing as I examined them. "These are part of you, Jake. That makes them special."

The truth was, that I wasn't sure *like* was the right word. My heart was precariously close to falling over the edge and I wasn't sure there was any way to stop it.

"I don't deserve you," he whispered. His eyes darkened and I knew he was thinking about something that had happened.

"I get to say who deserves me." There was more force in my words than I had meant to use. To ease the bite in my tone I placed my hand over his heart.

"You make it hard to argue with you," he said. Leaning down he kissed me on the head before pulling back to brush at my hair. "Let's get you cleaned up. Then I'm going to make breakfast."

"Maybe we should order breakfast." I smiled up at him.

"Such a comedian." He stepped back and unstrapped his prosthetic before using the support bar to get in the shower. He reached out and pulled me in so the warm water could slide over us both.

I turned my face up to the water and let it run down my body. When I opened my eyes Jake was watching me with a hungry look.

"You know, you're a lot dirtier than I realized. This might take a little while." Picking up the soap he poured some in his hands and lathered it up. Running his palms over my shoulders and down to my breasts he smiled. "Yep, this could take some time."

Backing me up against the wall he chuckled when I hissed at the cold tile. With deft hands he spread the soap over my skin, trailing down my stomach, and then around and up my back.

I snagged the soap from the rack and worked up my own lather. There were a few things he needed cleaned as well.

Later that morning we sat on the floor in his living room, eating things that we had cobbled together in his kitchen. I grabbed the butter knife from the jar of peanut butter and slathered some on my toast.

"You know, this isn't really that bad." Jake had sliced some strawberries to go with our toast and one fried egg. "I'm surprised I had this much food."

"You need to go to the grocery store."

"I eat out a lot." He shrugged and shoved some of the toast in his mouth.

I couldn't keep my eyes from running over his muscled chest. "And you look like that?"

"I go to the gym a lot," he explained.

"Hm." I don't think being healthy was his main objective for going to the gym. If I wasn't far from the mark, I would bet it was because he needed to take his mind off things. "Well, maybe if you eat better, you won't have to go to the gym so often."

"Are you offering to cook for me?" He looked up at me from under his thick eyelashes.

"Um, no. At least not full time. But maybe the next time we have dinner in, I could try to make something." I drained the rest of my orange juice.

"How about tonight?" He brushed the crumbs from his hands before popping a strawberry in his mouth. Puz sniffed around the crumbs looking for something to eat.

"Can't." I frowned. "I have a meeting with Senator Fletcher." Now that I thought about it, I wasn't very hungry.

"For your bill?" He rested his elbows on the table and leaned forward. He'd said he didn't like talking politics so I didn't elaborate too much.

"I'm not sure. She called and asked for me to meet with her." I was seriously hoping that this meant she was interested in sponsoring the bill. At this point I was still just sitting with a notebook of ideas and no real plan of what to do.

"She knows her stuff and has a lot of influence." Jake leaned back on his hands, his shoulders dropping back and giving me a great view of his chest.

"I need someone that knows what to do." I looked down at my plate and frowned. "I honestly have no idea where to start."

"You're the President's daughter, of course you know what to do." Jake popped one of the strawberries in his mouth.

"That's just it. I really don't." I started to pick at my fingernail. "I've avoided everything to do with politics. I had to Google how a bill even works."

I'd spent so much time avoiding anything remotely political my entire life and now I was embarrassed by the fact.

"Maddie, most people would have to Google how a bill works."

"Most people aren't me. I made a dumbass decision and now the only way to make it right has me staring down the rabbit hole. This is how it all starts."

"How what starts?" His eyes narrowed.

"People trying to do something good, make change for the better. Then they start dealing with the devil so that some sort of pretend bill that vaguely resembles the original bill gets passed and nothing actually changes." I leaned back against the couch and chewed on my thumb. "Then people pat you on the back and smile and pretend that you've actually accomplished something except the only thing you've done is sold your soul for an act that didn't actually occur."

"A bit melodramatic today, aren't you?" Jake reached under the coffee table and gave my knee a friendly shake.

"I've seen it happen so many times. Most of these people in D.C. started out with a big dream and lots of hope." I shook my head. "Look at them now."

"You have a big advantage though." Jake squeezed my knee before letting go. "You know what's on the other side of that slippery slope."

"Exactly. It's staring me in the face." I pushed my toast around on my plate. "Anyway, I have to try."

"No, you don't." He leaned forward and grabbed my hand. "That's what makes you special, Maddie. When you realized that you had to do more to protect those animals, you didn't hesitate. You jumped right in."

"I'm not feeling so sure right now."

"Not MadLibs McGuire." Jake reached across the table and grabbed my hand. "Maddie, no one is going to get away with any funny business with you at the helm."

"I'm not sure." I took a deep breath. "But you're right. I decided to jump in so there's no backing out. Someone has to do something for those animals."

"That's my girl." His smile was honest and such a contrast to the pain that had haunted his face earlier.

"I need to get going." I stood up and picked up my plate. I reached for his but he grabbed my hand.

"Leave that." He tugged me down toward him and snagged my plate from my fingers. He pulled me on to his lap and wrapped an arm around me. "I'll take care of the mess."

"Hm. What are you going to do about the dining table?" I let my head fall back against his chest and listened to the steady thumping of his heart.

"I'll get a new one. You can help me pick it out." He rubbed his cheek against mine. "That's one of the benefits of having a girlfriend, right?"

"And what if you don't like what I pick?"

"Honestly?" He chuckled and it made my body bounce. "As long as the chairs are big enough to hold me without breaking I don't care."

"It'll need sturdy legs." I turned to look at him.

"Good point." He moved his mouth close to mine. "Maybe some place mats for cushion."

"You should start a list." I pressed a kiss to his bottom lip.

Cradling my head in both of his hands he kissed me back.

When he finally pulled away it was with a sigh and a look of regret.

"Go, before you miss your appointment." He looked at me seriously but made no move.

"I'd rather take you grocery shopping." I sighed.

"Not a chance." This time he gave me a gentle push and I climbed out of his lap.

He walked me to the door and we waited while the car got close enough that I could duck into it without having to walk half a block.

"There's my ride." I picked up my purse and stuffed my phone in the back of my jeans.

"Call me. I want to hear how it goes." Jake grasped my shoulders.

"Really?" There was no hiding my surprise.

"Yeah. This is important to you." He kissed my temple before pulling back. "And Puz has a definite interest in the outcome."

I paused and debated my next words. "You're going to do what we talked about earlier?"

I wanted to know that he was really going to find someone to talk to. I needed to know it.

"Yes, I'll find someone." His eyes tightened, but he didn't freak out and Puz didn't move a whisker.

"Then I'll let you know." I grabbed the waistband of his shorts and tugged him closer so I could plant a big kiss on him before opening the door and dashing out.

Tony was off, so there was a different agent with me in the car today. She didn't talk, so I let the ride pass in silence while my brain went from giddy to dark thoughts. Remembering Jake's hands on me, the way he had cradled me as if I was the most important thing sent my soul soaring. Then it would plummet when I remembered the blank terror in his eyes at the sound of a lamp breaking.

By the time we got to the White House I wasn't sure which way was up and which way was down. I'd never felt that way in a relationship. I'd been excited to spend time with past boyfriends, butterflies and all, but there hadn't been this sense of importance or dread if things went wrong. Maybe that had been because it hadn't really mattered in the past.

I was so lost in my thoughts I didn't have time to avoid the trap that had been set for me.

"Maddie, the Vice President would like a word with you."

I looked up at her chief of staff with big eyes before looking around the large hallway for an escape.

"I'm sorry, I'm in a hurry. I'll give her a call later." Shit on toast. I should have been ready for this. "Sorry, Zach. I've really got to go."

"No ma'am, that won't do. It's urgent." He put a hand under my elbow and started steering me to the suite of offices the Vice President used when at the White House.

"I have an appointment." I tried to pull out of his grip but his fingers tightened.

"I'm sure it can wait. The Vice President is very busy but has made time to chat with you."

"Let go of my elbow and I'll go." I snatched my arm away and noticed the female agent that had been tailing me moved between us. "When did you get demoted to henchman?"

"She doesn't trust anyone else with this meeting." He reached for my arm again and the agent stepped in his way.

"Sir, please keep your hands to yourself." She was my height, with brown eyes and short brown hair.

"Jesus, Maddie. You're making a scene." He lowered his

hand and glowered at me. "I don't like this any more than you. Let's just get it over with."

I met his stare with my own and tried to think of a plan. I pulled my phone out of my pocket and looked at the time. Desperate for help I sent a quick text to the only person other than my father that wouldn't balk at rescuing me from the Vice President.

"She can have five minutes." I stuffed the phone back in my pocket and sent a covert look at my agent in shiny armor. She nodded her head briefly and stepped back. She would make sure I got out of that office in a reasonable time.

Without looking back at Zach I took off toward the VP's office. She was waiting in the hall, her arms at her sides and wide smile on her face.

"Madeline, thank you for coming." She put a hand on my shoulder and steered me inside before closing the door behind us. "I know you're very busy."

"Not as busy as you are." I frowned and rallied my defenses for her attack. She might be smiling but I knew better. I'd seen the text message she had sent Jake.

"Possibly." Virginia sat down at her large antique desk and folded her hands with a small smile. "I know you're working on a bill to stop animal testing. That's a lot of work. Certainly something new for you."

"It's not something I thought I would do in my life." I sat down in the chair across from her and was careful to not fidget with anything.

"The greatest politicians often end up serving their country because of a calling to make things better. I'm not surprised that your father passed down his desire to change things for the better." Her words were calm, supportive, and I steadied myself, waiting for the stab of her forked tail. "You'll make an excellent politician."

"Thank you, but that's not my goal. I just want to protect the animals, that's it."

"Have you found someone to sponsor your bill?" Her smile almost glowed and I hoped she couldn't tell that I was sweating. "I've been approached by several people that are interested in helping you."

"Odd that they didn't come to me or my father." Breathe in, breathe out. I'd never been in a fight, but there was a battle of wills happening in this office and I didn't want to lose.

She waved her hand in the air as if that wasn't a big deal. "The President is busy. They probably just didn't want to bother him."

"Virginia, you and I both know that's not true. I have no doubt that my father's office has been inundated with calls from people jumping at the chance to help the President's daughter. Who wouldn't want to be owed a favor from the President?"

She leaned further back in her chair and cocked her head to the side without comment. I could keep explaining or I could play her game and try to wait her out. I looked down at my watch and settled back into the chair. I had three more minutes before the agent would interrupt. If she wanted to spend those three minutes playing a staring contest that was fine with me.

"I suppose you're right." Virginia picked up a pen and wrote a few things on a paper before sliding it across the desk. "These are the people that I think would be the most help. They have a great deal of political backing and are interested in helping you."

I looked at where the paper lay on the desk and felt the slippery slope under my feet give a little.

"What do you get out of this?" I crossed my arms and didn't pick up the paper. "You want your name on my bill?"

"No, the credit is all yours. It would be a great stepping stone for you. The rebellious child turned righteous before moving on to make the tough decisions so other children don't feel they need to break the law." She held her pen suspended between two fingers. "You're on the brink of following in your father's footsteps. People will flock to you."

"I'm not interested in politics." I kept my voice even. "I only want to help the animals."

"Of course. We all want to help them. I Googled what they do to them the other day. It's horrifying." She gave a small shudder. "But think about it. Even if you don't pursue politics, this bill could make you the voice that speaks for these animals. I just want to help."

"I'm still trying to figure out what you get out of this." I narrowed my eyes at her. "I might not want to play the game, but I know the rules. What do you want for your help?"

"I'll help you with the bill. It's going to take a lot of negotiating and in the meantime, you let me help you clean up your image."

"What?" The only thing stopping my eyebrows from flying off my face was my hairline.

"If you want to date my son, then we need to make some changes." She smiled brightly and I fought the urge to strangle her.

"I'm not changing who I am for anyone." I looked at my fingernails on one hand and pretended to be bored.

"Then we have a small problem." The Vice President sat up a little straighter.

"And why is that?" Deliberately I lifted my hand and gnawed on a hangnail.

"I'm running for office, Madeline, and you're not an appropriate partner for my son. He needs to be with someone that has unquestionable integrity and class."

Ouch. Score one for the she-devil.

"You lack polish and grace. Your familial ties are good enough, of course, but after that stunt you pulled . . ." She tsked. "I was hoping to make this beneficial for both of us. I help you and in turn you do a few simple things that I ask. Nothing big of course, I don't want you out speaking for me. But, quietly supporting me in the wings wouldn't hurt. The press seems to love you, but you can't stay with Jake the way you are now."

I stared at the woman as if she had grown a few extra heads. "Jake is a grown man. You don't get to say who he invites into his life."

"You're smarter than that." The friendly mask dropped and she practically spat venom at me. "I'm going to be President, Madeline. As a woman, that means my house has to be impeccable. There can be no dirty laundry, nothing out of place, and no whispered comments about my son's wild girlfriend. Everything. Must. Be. Perfect. You're not going to fuck it all up when I'm so close."

There was a knock at the door and I clenched my hands.

"Come in." Virginia's smile was back in place.

I looked over my shoulder at my father's fierce publicist, Reese. She nodded at me but said nothing. Neither did she come all the way in the room or close the door. She did however motion to her watch as if reminding me of something.

"I have a meeting." I stood up, careful to not look at the list of names she had bribed me with. "Excuse me."

"Of course." Virginia stood up and walked around the desk to place a hand on my shoulder. "I don't have to tell you that this is strictly confidential. If you don't want my help it's going to cost you in some way. Just remember, Madeline, I always win. You can play with me or against me."

I ground my teeth so hard I wasn't sure I'd have teeth left by the time I got out of the office.

"I'm not playing anything, Virginia." I smiled and patted her hand on my shoulder. "It was so nice to see you. Have a great week."

Turning on my heel I left the office and headed for the residential wing. I wanted as much space between me and that vile woman as possible.

"Thank you." I darted my eyes in Reese's direction. She might be a bitch to deal with, but she'd come through for me when I needed her. Maybe I'd been too tough on the woman.

"No problem. I never turn down a chance to needle that woman." Reese frowned at the stack of paperwork in her arms. "I have to say, it sounds like you have a bigger problem than getting out of her office."

No shit, I thought.

The Vice President had just declared war. If I didn't get in line with her ideas, I'd have to choose: my animal rights bill or Jake.

Chapter 14

Maddie

Y ou truly think we can get the bill passed?" I looked up at Senator Fletcher as she moved around her office.

"Oh, yes. With what we've outlined we'll have a good chance." Senator Fletcher poured me a glass of water and walked around her desk to sit in one of the seats next to me. "I'd like to tell you that the bill will definitely pass, but I want to make sure you know that it's not guaranteed. This also isn't a fast process. We may be able to cram it through the House quickly, but the Senate is much slower."

"I know." I took a sip of my water and tried to not grimace. From the outside it could look as if bills were passed quickly, but it was an agonizingly slow process from the inside.

"Maddie, if you start this, are you going to see it through?" Senator Fletcher watched me carefully and held up a hand when I started to respond quickly. "I know it's important to you, but this could take years. In essence, you're marrying this bill and the process."

I frowned and chewed on the inside of my cheek. That was a scary way of looking at the whole process. Yes, I wanted to better the world for the animals and for everyone else, but did I want to hitch myself to the cause for eternity? I was young. Who knew what life would throw my way in a couple of years.

"It's okay to take some time to think about it, but if you're serious we need to form an exploratory committee. That can help us set up a plan to move forward, give us a feel for how people will respond to the idea." She sat back in her seat and took a drink from her own water glass. "Big Pharma is going to fight us tooth and nail. No one likes change, especially when it's going to cost them a lot of money."

"Yes, I've thought of that." I frowned down at my glass. "I hadn't really thought about how long it could take to get the bill passed. I knew it would be an uphill fight, but wasn't thinking about it in terms of time."

It could very well take more than two years to get it to the Senate. My father would be long out of office by the time it reached the President's desk. If against all odds it actually did reach the President's desk.

That thought made my frown deepen.

"Of course not. You've still got a year of college left."

"It's not just college." I set my glass on the table between us, careful to use the frilly coaster. "I want to be very up-front with you."

"Oh?" The other woman narrowed her eyes. "Please do."

"Virginia invited me to her office today to chat about the bill." My fingers squeezed into a fist. "She had a list of people that would help get the bill passed."

"I see." Senator Fletcher raised an eyebrow. "And what did she want in return?"

"For me to fall in line." I sighed and sat back in the chair deflated. "Either I shape up or ship out when it comes to Jake. She made it quite clear that I wasn't welcome with her son unless I make some big changes. How did she put it? If I wasn't playing with her I was playing against her."

"That's a lot to ask of someone. Especially if your relationship is as new as I expect it is."

"New is an understatement." I shook my head. "I'm not going to change who I am to make her happy. If I change who I am so she will be happy, I've lost much more than I've gained."

"And you have no definite proof that she won't decide to vote in a different direction if it suits her needs in the end."

"Good point." Leaning forward I propped my arms on my knees and cradled my forehead. "I could do everything she asks, but still end up screwed. Of course, if I don't even make an effort to stay on her good side, the bill is as good as dead no matter what."

"I wouldn't be so sure about that." The senator sat forward and patted my knee. "The VP has some sway in things, but not enough to deny the public what they want. This is where you have more power than she does."

"How can I have more power?" I dropped my hands and looked at Fletcher with surprise.

"She has to cater to those people that helped get her to the top. Virginia owes people favors as well and I assume that list will grow as she fights for the Presidential nomination. On the other hand, you are debt free, politically speaking. You can rally the people to pressure their representatives to vote in favor of your bill. After all, we're supposed to vote the way our constituents want."

"I sure don't feel like I have the upper hand." I grimaced.

"Oh, it's not going to be easy. It's going to be a fight, but I think we can win." She smiled and her eyes lit up. "After all, we have Good on our side. We're fighting for the underdog, literally. And if there is one thing I've learned about America and its voters, it's that they love a good underdog story."

Hope filled my chest and I took a deep breath for the first time since I'd left the Vice President's office.

"Let's do this. Let's form the exploratory committee and save the underdogs." I sat up and smiled. Yes, I was ready to fight for the rights of those animals that couldn't do it themselves.

"Put on your armor, my dear. We're going to war."

It was dark by the time I left Senator Fletcher's office. My back hurt from being bent over a table and going through papers for hours. My eyes were scratchy and stinging from reading countless resumes and searching on the internet. A lot of work went into forming an exploratory committee. I only wanted people I could trust; people that I knew would really care about the animals.

My stomach grumbled as we drove through the dim streets and I asked them to go through a drive-thru. I was too hungry to wait until we got home and I could make something.

As I devoured the reheated burger in the backseat, I pulled out my phone and decided to text Jake.

ME: Fletcher is in. We're forming a committee and I think I got married.

JAKE: Seems a little sudden.

ME: She said I had to commit to the bill long term, that it was a marriage of sorts I'd have to see through. So I'm married to a bill.

JAKE: Congratulations to you and Bill.

ME: What if the Bill wants to have little bills and amendments one day?

JAKE: You probably should have discussed that before eloping.

ME: But it was so beautiful. There was tons of paperwork and a dry erase board to act as our witness. Everything I had dreamed!

JAKE: Lucky woman.

ME: LOL. Seriously, I'm just glad I have someone that knows what they're doing in my corner.

JAKE: I knew she would help. She loves animals.

ME: I've got to hire a secretary. There's so much to do.

JAKE: A secretary? Look at you, Ms. Fancy Pants. Make sure she's hot.

ME: Don't worry, he will be.

I giggled when he sent back an emoticon with big eyes.

ME: Now that I think about it, all the guys working in Fletcher's office were hot. It's probably a requirement.

JAKE: It's good to be at the top. I wonder if they wear loin cloths and feed her grapes.

I giggled thinking of the serious expressions of the men working in her office. They would look angry and determined to feed her only the best grapes while planning exactly how quickly they should move their palms leaves while fanning her.

ME: What are you doing?

JAKE: Watching Puz try to chase his tail. Want to come over and eat? Dinner and a show!

ME: Tempting, but I just ate. I need to get back to my place so I can take care of a few things.

JAKE: Damn. I tried.

ME: Watching a three-legged dog chase his tail is one hell of a temptation.

JAKE: Are you saying my cooking isn't a temptation?

ME: Let's just say it's a good thing you're pretty.

JAKE: LOL. Not pulling any punches, huh?

ME: You like it.

JAKE: I think that makes me a masochist.

ME: Not surprised.

JAKE: You're on a roll.;)

ME: I'm in a good mood.

JAKE: So you're mean to me. I see how this is going to work.

ME: Would you rather me play nice?

JAKE: Does nice involve kissing and less clothing?

ME: Now that is tempting.

I chewed on my lip. There was nothing I'd like more than stripping Jake down and spending a little time between the sheets. Or in the bathroom. Or maybe on that big, comfortable sofa.

Lord, one night and the man had turned me into a sex fiend.

JAKE: You're thinking about me naked, aren't you?

I couldn't stop the burst of laughter that sent a mouthful of soda across the car. The agent looked down at her slacks and picked up a napkin to dab at the moisture.

"I'm so sorry." I grabbed some napkins and tried to pat her knee. "So sorry. I didn't mean to spit on you. I'm awful."

"It's fine, Miss McGuire."

"I'm really sorry." I dug in my fast food sack for some more napkins. "I shouldn't be allowed in public."

"It's really okay." She smiled. "Must've been a funny message."

I laughed and nodded my head, but the truth was I really was picturing Jake naked now. The light on my phone was blinking to indicate I had a new message.

JAKE: I was right.

ME: No, but I spit coke all over my new agent.

JAKE: Score!

ME: Haha. It's late. Get some sleep. We've got a lot of work tomorrow.

JAKE: Yes, ma'am.

ME: Ew, don't call me ma'am.

JAKE: Goodnight, MadLibs.

ME: Goodnight, Golden Boy.

Chapter 15

Jake

It had been over two weeks since I'd freaked out while Maddie had been in my bed. I still wanted to kick my own ass for scaring her. Her eyes wide with fear and her bottom lip quivering haunted me. I'd never hurt Maddie, I'd just needed her to be still.

Hell, I wanted to kick my own ass, period. She hadn't asked again if I'd found someone to talk to, but it weighed in the back of my mind. If I went to the Marine psychologist, anything they labeled me with would end up on a permanent record. Not to mention it would be Sunday reading for my mother.

That was not something that I wanted to happen. My mother was the last person I wanted to know that I wasn't functioning at one hundred percent. I could only see her doing one of two things: locking me away with round the clock monitoring or spreading the information in an attempt to garner more support.

My fingers clenched on the leash in my hand.

Puz looked up at me with a worried whine and I reached down to pet his head. The dog had weaseled his way into my heart with little trouble, but I still occasionally wondered how I'd ended up with some kind of poodle mix. Maddie had tied little red bows in the fur behind his ears the other night. Puz couldn't have cared less as long as she was paying him attention, but I'd almost resorted to cutting them out when I couldn't figure out how to undo the clips.

Little red bows on a half poodle added up to a whole lot of poodle. I'd been in the Marines and a poodle didn't exactly fit the image. No, a German shepherd or maybe a lab would have been my first pick.

Instead I'd fallen in love with a half poodle missing a leg and the woman that had picked him out for me. Yeah, I was in deep shit considering that I'd managed to do the exact thing I'd been attempting to avoid. There was no denying how I felt about Maddie.

Puz stopped to look at a little toad jumping down the stairs in front of our brownstone and I held his leash tightly.

"Don't lick that, Puz. It'll give you a nasty stomachache."

The dog looked up at me and I swear I could see in his eyes that he didn't believe me.

"I'm serious, Puz. They secrete toxins to keep predators away."

The dog sneezed and shook his head.

"Fine, go ahead and lick him. Learn the hard way."

Puz looked at me with solemn eyes before moving up two steps and tilted his hind quarters to pee on the toad. He'd already gone so much that he could barely squeeze a sputtering dribble out.

"I didn't mean you should piss on it! Geez. Go, toad! Don't

just stand there." I moved my toes toward the little green guy and he hopped off into the bushes. "Is it a full moon tonight? What has gotten into you?"

Puz sneezed again and took the last few steps to sit next to the front door.

"You're done, right? Got it all out of your system?" I shook my head and dug my keys out of my pocket. "I don't know why I'm talking to you. You're probably wondering the same thing, huh? It's not like we speak the same language. Otherwise you wouldn't have tried to eat that squirrel last weekend."

Puz had two stitches on his top lip where the squirrel had taken a good bite out of his flesh. He'd gotten blood all over the seats in my truck because he wouldn't be still on the way to the vet's office. Then he'd lay on the table and whined while the nurses fussed over him. The little monster had eaten up the attention. When they were done he'd hopped up and bounded around as if nothing had happened while I paid the bill.

Maddie had brought him a squirrel-shaped chew toy that night. I'd had to cut the squeaker out and then try to sew it back together just so I could get some sleep. Thankfully she hadn't seemed to notice the lack of noise on her last visit or she was bound to buy another one just to annoy me. She liked to do that.

I smiled to myself. And I loved it.

Maddie pushed me, needled me, kept me on my toes. She also seemed to have an infinite amount of patience when I had rough days. It was as if she understood where my lines were and when to not cross them. With her around I didn't have to pretend I was perfect. She accepted me for who I was.

I hadn't had any sort of panic attack or anxiety-induced anger since we'd started spending so much time together.

Maybe I didn't need to talk to anyone about it. It wasn't like I wanted to drag up all those painful memories and relive them while someone else took notes.

Wouldn't that be counterproductive?

I got Puz settled for the day and left the grocery list for the housekeeper on the kitchen island. It was so much easier to pay her a little extra to have her run that errand. Maddie had started keeping a running itinerary on the board next to the fridge. She had listed things like avocados, pasta, and special cheeses. It was fun to go food shopping with Maddie because she knew what she was doing. I just stared blankly at the wall of cans and debated which Chef Boyardee pasta would make the best lunch.

Not exactly a healthy way to live, which is why I had been going out to eat at some of the healthy places around town. That wasn't an option now that Maddie and I were dating. The media swarmed us whenever we went anywhere together. I hoped that would calm down eventually.

There was a knock on my front door as I grabbed my stuff to leave. I opened it expecting to see one of the PR people with an itinerary, but instead my youngest sister looked up at me.

"Hey monster." I pulled her into a hug. "What are you doing here?"

"It's a teacher work day so I'm off from school. I thought I could come help at the house." She squeezed my waist and looked up at me. "That's okay, right? Maddie said I could help."

"Yeah, I just didn't know it would be today." Puz jumped around our legs trying to get my sister's attention. He had fallen in love at first sight of my sister. His little tail wagged so fast I thought it might fly off. "You better tell him hello before we leave or he'll pout all day."

"There's my big guy!" She reached down and scooped the furry beast in her arms while he peppered her face with kisses. "I missed you too. Yes I did. I missed you!"

"Do you want anything before we leave?" I wrinkled my nose when he stuck his tongue in her ear. "Something to drink? Sanitizer for your face?"

She laughed and sat Puz back on the floor before wagging her finger at him. "Be good, Puz. Be good and I'll bring you a treat next time. Yes I will!"

"He's a dog, not stupid." I rolled my eyes while she baby-talked.

"This is how you talk to dogs, Jake!" She punched my stomach. "Isn't that right, Puz? You talk to them like they're sweet little babies, because that's what they are. Isn't that right?"

"If you keep talking like that I'm going to hurl." I gently pushed her out of the doorway. "Go lay down, Puz. Get in your bed."

He looked at me and sneezed again before walking to his giant cushion. His little tail was wagging so hard I was worried he would knock himself off balance.

"Why is he sneezing? Is he sick?" Ari looked up at me with worried eyes.

"The stitches tickle." I put an arm over her shoulders as we walked to my truck. Our constant companions, the Secret Service, followed just a few steps behind.

"Poor Puz. I can't believe you let a squirrel get him!" She glared at me as I opened the passenger door for her.

"Let him? Are you kidding? I couldn't keep the dog away from the little bastard! Puz got exactly what he wanted: a mouth full of squirrel. And the squirrel got a mouth full of Puz. How is that my fault?"

"You shouldn't have let him get so close to it."

I closed the door and rolled my eyes as I went around to my side of the car. "It was in my backyard. It's not like I had him on a leash and took him over to a tree and said, 'sick 'em!'"

"How am I supposed to know that?" She crossed her arms, but there was a small smile on her face.

"Did you decide to do manual labor because you wanted to punish me or because you missed me? Because right now, I'm not sure."

"Why can't it be both?" Her smile turned smug.

"God, puberty is a bitch. I should send out apology notes to everyone I badgered when I was your age." I laughed.

"They wouldn't be able to read them. Your handwriting is atrocious." She reached for the radio controls and fiddled with them until she found a station she liked.

We lapsed into a silence and I thought about how much I had missed being around my sisters. They drove me crazy on a regular basis, but that's what sisters were supposed to do. They were also a comfort because they knew you better than anyone else. You didn't have to explain why you were thinking or doing something because they already knew what your reasoning was behind it all.

Of course, that didn't stop them from pointing out when they thought you were wrong.

Trina fell in love with Ari as soon as we got to the worksite. It wasn't long before she was wearing a hard hat and carrying a clipboard like the older woman. It wasn't like my sister was a stranger to telling people what to do. She'd been doing it since the day she was born. It would take a strong man to handle her when she grew up.

The house was almost complete except for a few odds and

ends. We needed to put on switch plates and touch up some of the paint. One of the French doors that led to the backyard was crooked and would need to be adjusted, but all in all things had really pulled together.

"It's amazing how fast it went." Maddie's warm voice had me turning around to look at her. Those fairy eyes sparkled up at me in the morning sun and I bent down to give her a quick kiss.

I would have loved to have taken longer to savor the moment, but there were already a ton of cameras pointed in our direction.

"Good morning." She smiled up at me.

"Good morning." It would have been a much better morning if I had woken up with her next to me.

"I'm sorry I didn't make it over last night. I was at Senator Fletcher's office until almost eleven." She frowned and I noticed the dark circles under her eyes. "There are so many rules and things to organize. They poll everything! What words to use, when we should submit the bill, who makes a solid supporter. This morning I woke up and thought I needed to poll what jeans I should wear."

I turned her around and looked down at the denim cupping her ass. "These pollsters have good taste."

"Shush." She laughed but it ended on a yawn.

"Why don't you take today off?" I took the paint can that she had set down near our feet. "We're only doing touch-up things today."

"I'm fine." She rubbed at her face. "I just need some coffee."

"Maddie, what time did you go to sleep last night?"

"Um, a little after one." She shrugged and held her hand out for the paint can but I moved it out of her reach.

"So this morning, not last night at all."

"What's your point, Simmon?" She narrowed her eyes. "I had a late night but I'll trudge along."

"A construction site is not a safe place when you can barely keep your eyes open." I put the paint can down on a bench and turned her toward where her agent was standing. "Tony, Miss McGuire needs to go home."

The man already had Maddie's jacket in his hands. "I told you to call out today. You look exhausted."

"Don't gang up on me." Maddie jerked the coat out of his hands and shoved her arms in the sleeves. "And thanks for the compliment."

"It's not his fault you haven't gotten any sleep this week." I brushed some of the hair away from her face.

"You know what I've been working on and there is so much more to do." She rubbed her hands over her face again. "I'm in so far over my head."

"The senator is going to make sure you have someone on your side the entire time." I pulled her into a hug. Damn the cameras and the press. They already knew we were dating. A little PDA wouldn't be shocking now. "I also have a lot more confidence in you than you apparently do. Nothing stops Maddie McGuire when she puts her mind to it."

She snorted and I pressed a kiss to the side of her head. "My little pug."

"Jerk." She laughed against my chest.

"My little felon pug." I chuckled and jerked when she dug her fingers into my ribs.

She stood up on her tiptoes and pulled my face down to hers for a kiss. Her warm mouth made my blood heat up but I kept it short and sweet. She needed to go home and get some rest. There was no reason for her to stay here where she might get hurt.

Maddie sighed and pulled away. "I'll call you later."

"You better."

"C'mon, Maddie." Tony motioned for the car.

"Tell Puz I got him a new squirrel." She winked at me before scampering off to the black SUV.

"Tony, make sure she gets some rest." I stepped toward the man.

"I'll make sure Maddie does what she wants to do." The man squared his shoulders and gave me a good look over.

"Okay." It was going to be like that, I supposed. Tony had been Maddie's guard for a long time and I remember my father mentioning how it was odd to have such a long-term assignment.

I narrowed my eyes and reassessed the man in front of me. He was older than I was but still in good shape. It was easy for me to imagine another man falling in love with Maddie. She made it easy. In fact, I was surprised there weren't a hundred men trailing behind her.

"Whatever you're thinking, stop. Maddie is like my little sister." His deep voice was laced with amusement. "And I watch out for her like she's my little sister."

"So, you're making sure my intentions are honorable?" I ran a hand over the back of my neck.

"Something like that." Tony nodded his head. "Don't screw up, Jake."

I didn't know what to say so just nodded my head.

"Jake! They're going to let me use the nail gun!" Ari's voice floated back to me and I jerked.

"That was one of the most frightening things I've ever heard.

Go take care of your sister." Tony nodded at me again before going to get in Maddie's car.

Worried that my sister might accidentally nail someone I jogged to the house and went to help. The last thing I wanted to do was explain how my little sister killed someone at the worksite.

Chapter 16

Maddie

Where did you get that thing? It's huge." I stared in the door with wide eyes.

"That's what she said." Cyrus laughed from his wheelchair.

Jake laughed from where he was leaning against the back of a giant couch. "You missed all the fun. You should have seen us trying to get it in the house."

"Did you take out a wall?" The couch was almost the size of the living room, with just enough space for a coffee table and television.

"My aunt bought it for us as a housewarming gift." Kyla breezed into the living room and I envied how perfect she looked. It was as if she wasn't about to have a baby any minute. No matter the fact that it was hotter than hell outside.

"I'm sorry I wasn't here in time to help."

"You'll make it up to me somehow." Jake wrapped sweaty arms around me and I squeaked.

"I'm not worried about you," I answered.

"Well, we're not upset either," Kyla shouted from the kitchen. The woman hadn't stopped moving since I'd arrived.

"Has she been like this the whole day?" I looked up at Jake.

"Yes. If we could bottle that energy and sell it, we'd be rich."

"She's nesting," Cyrus explained. Despite his earlier joke I noticed that he had circles under his eyes.

"You doing okay?"

"I'm fine." He waved his hand in the air. "Didn't sleep much last night."

"Excited about the house?"

"Yeah." He smiled, but it only enhanced the paleness of his face.

"Well, what can I do to help?" I shot a look up at Jake and caught his frown. He was looking at his friend with a worried expression.

"You'd be best asking Kyla. I'd probably tell you the wrong thing." His laugh was a little more genuine. "Never get in the way of a nesting mother."

"Right. Then I'll go get my orders from the General." I mock saluted and went in search of his wife.

Three hours later I was sitting on the floor in the closet of the nursery, cleaning the baseboards. My back ached and my knees would have bruises, but there wasn't a speck of dust on any baseboards in this house.

"Thank you so much, Maddie. I just can't get down there and then back up." Kyla handed me a bottle of water and I threw my latest Clorox wipe in the plastic bag with the dryer sheets I'd been told would help repel dust.

"It's no problem." I greedily drank the cold water. "I've learned a lot of tips for when I get my own place."

"Oh my God. I bet you've always had maids." Kyla covered her mouth with her hand. "And I threw you to the wolves! Baseboards are a bitch!"

I laughed. "I've never cleaned baseboards, but I was expected to keep my own room clean. I also had a dorm at college but never really worried about how clean it was."

"I'm so sorry, Maddie. I treated you like another military wife."

My laugh trailed off and I looked at the water in my hands. She was right. While a lot of people were out in the world being adults, I was still living at home with my father, and doing idiotic things like getting arrested.

And even if I couldn't admit it out loud I could admit that I was jealous of what Kyla and Cyrus had together. Marriage had always been something I thought I'd want later in life, but being with Jake made me question things; made me want things.

"I didn't mean that the way it sounded." Kyla chewed on her lip. "That came out all wrong."

"No, it's fine. You're right. I haven't had a lot of real world experience."

Kyla carefully lowered herself down to the ground next to me.

"Don't do that," I protested.

"Hush. I hurt your feelings, I saw it on your face." She put an arm around my shoulders and pulled me close for a hug. "I'm sorry. You have a lot of real world experience that doesn't include cobwebs and baseboards. You know how to talk to dignitaries and what happens during a nuclear explosion."

I laughed so hard that I snorted. "You think I would know what to do if a nuke went off?"

She frowned and her nose had cute little wrinkles. "Well, I

wouldn't know what to do! You're the President's daughter. I figured you'd been briefed on protocol or something."

"Um, no. I'd cover my mouth with my shirt and try to find a Secret Service agent. Maybe they would know what to do." I couldn't stop laughing. "I'd probably crab-walk around like an idiot scared out of my mind. I mean, what would you do if there was a nuclear bomb?"

"Call you!" She laughed. "So find out what the plan is."

I laughed some more before standing up and holding out a hand to help the pregnant woman.

"You know, this is a very spacious closet for a nursery." I looked at the shelving.

"It's amazing, right? I never would have thought I'd have a home like this." She reached out and trailed her fingers over one of the racks. "I feel guilty. Is that crazy?"

"You shouldn't feel guilty but I get what you're saying." I reached out and touched her shoulder. "Don't feel guilty, just pay it forward when you can. If you get a chance, help promote the Returning Combat Veterans Affairs."

"I will." Her voice was quiet. "Somehow I'll pay it forward one day."

"But not right now. Right now, you're going to make some of those famous pork chops and tell me about your plans for the new baby." I followed her out of the closet and toward the kitchen. "Have you chosen a name?"

"Savannah." She smiled at me over her shoulder and caressed her considerable baby bump.

"You don't have much longer, do you?"

"Nope. We got this place in the nick of time." She grabbed some food from the fridge before digging through some boxes. "Do you see the pots in any of those boxes?"

I shifted boxes around until I found one labelled *pots* and pulled a few out. "Which one do you need?"

"These two and the small saucepan." She plucked them from my fingers and moved back to stove. "The pork chops have been marinating all day. Would you mind helping peel potatoes?"

"Sure." She set out a bag of small red potatoes and a knife. I used to help my mother make dinner when I was little, but that had been a long time ago. I dumped the potatoes in the sink to rinse them off and started peeling slowly. "I haven't done this in a long time."

"Oh, it's fine. Cyrus likes it when they have a little skin on them." She moved around the kitchen with an efficiency that I envied. I could cook most of the basics, though I'd never been fond of mashed potatoes. Not that I was going to tell her that. Or Jake for that matter.

I looked over my shoulder to where the guys were setting up a basketball hoop for Korbin. The little guy was with his grandparents for the night so they wouldn't have to worry about him running out a door while the movers were working.

"Speaking of Cyrus, how's he doing?" I kept my tone light but I noticed how her hands jerked. "I suppose the move has worn you all out."

"That's part of it." She glanced quickly to the windows. "He'd been having a lot of back pain. We'd chalked it up to using new muscles and adjusting to the prosthesis, but he had a CAT scan the other day and the results weren't good."

"Oh, Kyla, I'm so sorry to hear that." I turned to look at the other woman.

"We don't know anything definite yet, but it looks like he'll need more surgeries." Her face tightened in a way I hadn't seen before and I wondered just how bad things really were. She would find a way to explain a hurricane in happy tones.

"That's got to be frustrating." I stopped to look at her. "To heal from one surgery only to have to deal with another would be depressing."

"I always assumed he'd have to go through more surgeries. When he got back from Germany, he was a mess. They said his spine had suffered some serious damage and that it might cause him more trouble later on. It's one of the reasons I insist we bring the chair everywhere. He pushes himself too far."

"When are they going to do the surgery?" I turned back to my potatoes and concentrated on not cutting my fingers off.

"They wanted to do it next week." She sighed heavily. "But he wants to wait until after I have the baby."

"But can he wait? I mean, some of those things get a lot worse if you don't take care of it right away." I continued to peel the skin from the potatoes. I imagined it would be even more difficult to get the surgery done once the baby was present.

"They said he could wait a little while, but not long. I'm hoping it'll be a quick recovery." She looked around the room before lowering her voice. "I'm embarrassed to admit that I'm nervous about having to take care of a newborn, Korbin, and helping Cyrus."

I noticed that her knuckles were white where she gripped the giant spoon. She wasn't just worried, she was terrified.

"I'd be happy to help out. And I'm sure your parents will jump at the chance to help out with the kids. It's a grandparent thing, right? And if all else fails, we'll find a way to get you some help around the house." I offered my best reassuring smile. "I mean, I might not know much about cleaning houses, but I'm good at laundry. I clean a mean white load."

She laughed and went back to her food prep. "I'll take you up on that. Honestly, after having Korbin I've all but given up on separating laundry into whites, colors, and towels."

"Well, you call me and I'll sort it out for you." I looked at the potato that I'd massacred. "At this rate, we're only going to have half the amount of potatoes you were counting on."

"Ouch." She picked the potato from my fingers and shook her head. "That's pretty sad, Maddie."

"Well, I make an excellent boiled egg. I don't suppose we're having those for dinner."

"Actually, I have the makings for deviled eggs."

"Look at me. I'm contributing to dinner!" I went to the fridge and pulled the carton of eggs.

"Okay, Chef Ramsay. I'll believe it when I see it." Kyla flipped her hair over her shoulder and I laughed.

I was riding with Jake back to his house, content after a nice night with friends.

"What did you do with your pork chop?" Jake looked over at me.

"A vegetarian never gives up their secrets." I chuckled.

"I thought that was supposed to be magicians."

"In this case, it still applies." I couldn't stop my smug smile. "Actually, I told Kyla before you guys came in. I never even had one on my plate."

"Are you still hungry?"

"No, I ate more than my share of deviled eggs and mashed potatoes."

"Were they better than mine?" His smile reached from one ear to the other.

"Well, I never actually got to taste your potatoes. I just wore them."

"Hmm." His eyes darted over in my direction and there was no mistaking the heat. "And nothing else if I remember correctly."

"Unless you count that spectacular bruise."

"Maybe I should check that out and see how it's healing." His hand reached over to rest on my thigh.

"I didn't realize you were a doctor." I bit my cheek to keep from smiling.

"I'm not opposed to playing doctor." His hand on my thigh crept up a little, his thumb rubbing along the inseam of my jeans. "When was the last time you had a breast exam, Miss McGuire?"

"That was so lame it was painful." I laughed.

"Good thing I'm a pretend doctor." His hand slid up a little higher, his thumb rubbing circles at the junction of my legs.

Heat ran through my body and I knew I was blushing, but didn't care. Instead I spread my legs a little wider for him and he obligingly adjusted his hand so he could touch me a little more. When he used his thumb to flick open my jeans I sucked in a deep breath.

"Jake, someone will see us." I didn't stop him though as his fingers slid under my panties and along my skin. My breathing sped up and I bit my lip.

"You're already wet, Maddie." The growl in his voice sent shivers down my spine. His fingers slid against me and I couldn't help my gasp of pleasure. "Slide your jeans down so I can touch you better."

"You're going to get in an accident." I gasped and it sounded loud in the truck cab.

"No I'm not." He made a turn and pulled off the highway. "We aren't far from a little known hiking trail."

"What about the Secret Service?" I groaned and bit my lip as his finger circled my clit.

"They'll leave us alone." He pulled into a dark, empty parking lot. He pulled into a secluded spot and put the truck in park. "Now, those pants have to go."

I undid my seat belt before wiggling my pants down to my ankles. He turned me in my seat so I was facing him with my work boots in his lap. With deft fingers he undid the laces and threw them on the floor board and tugged my jeans all the way off.

"Jake!" I started to wiggle away, worried someone would see us.

"No one's going to see us, Maddie. The agents will make sure we're left alone." He didn't hold me in place, but I stopped fighting. "But I don't want to wait for two hours in traffic. I want you now."

His hands skimmed up my legs and then back down to my ankles. I let my knees fall open and ran a hand down my stomach. He groaned when I touched myself, his hungry eyes tracing every move.

"There's my siren." He shifted one of my legs behind him and leaned forward.

When his tongue joined my fingers I groaned. He knew exactly how to push me over the edge. Long strokes of his tongue that brushed against my fingers as I spread myself open were followed by long deep kisses that made my back arch.

I heard the zipper of his jeans before I felt the heat of his arousal against my leg. I opened my eyes to watch as he stroked himself from the base to the top of the head and then back down. I gripped his hair with my hands, unable to reach what I wanted to touch.

"Fuck, that's it." I ground my crotch against his face, whimpering as his scruff scratched my delicate skin. "God, you're so good at that."

He doubled his efforts, his thorough tongue driving me to moan loudly. If anyone was listening there would be no mistaking what was happening in the truck. I gripped one of my breasts and watched as his head moved between my legs.

"Fuck, Jake. Oh, fuck." I let go of my breast and held his head in place. "Don't you dare stop. Fuck, don't stop."

Stars exploded before my eyes and I flung an arm out to brace myself against the dashboard. He lifted his head and wiped a hand along his jaw.

"You're so fucking gorgeous when you come, Maddie." As I caught my breath he gripped my hips and pulled me onto his lap. "Ride me."

"Do you have a condom?" I wrapped my hand around his dick and he groaned loudly.

"Yes. In my pocket." He tried to reach behind him but we were a tangle of limbs.

"I'm on birth control." I looked in his eyes when he froze.

"Are you sure?" He cupped my face with his hands. "I'm clean. I got tested before we started dating but we can use the condom."

"I got tested after my last boyfriend." I gripped him tightly with my hands, stroking his shaft and he groaned. "That was a year ago."

"There wasn't anyone since then?" His dark eyes grew bright with emotion.

"Just you." I lifted myself above him before sliding down his shaft.

His loud groan was satisfying. He pulled my face down to his so he could claim my mouth. The kiss set every fiber in my being alight. There was something spectacular about how his touch made the rest of the world disappear.

He filled me completely and I was awed by how something so hard could feel so smooth and perfect inside of me.

"God, you feel so good." Jake pressed his mouth to my neck.

I couldn't find the right words to agree. Jake felt as if he'd been made for me. Our bodies fit together perfectly. I pushed up on my knees before sliding back down so that he stretched me in all the right ways.

His hands shoved my shirt and bra up before catching one of my breasts with his hot mouth. Work-roughened fingers gripped my hips as I moved over him.

I let my head fall back as he scraped his teeth across my breast and then captured the other one. His tongue swirled around the peak before sucking it into his mouth. He moved one of his hands from my hip to my free breast, rolling it in his hands before pinching the nipple. I hissed in pleasure and tangled my fingers in his hair.

"Fuck, you feel good." He pulled back to watch me as I moved. Arching my back thrust my exposed breasts forward and he filled his hands with them. "You're fucking perfect, Madeline."

"Took you long enough to realize it," I gasped.

"I'm stupid, so stupid." He gripped my hips urging me to move faster.

I leaned forward, bracing my arms on his shoulders. "You can't help it."

He laughed which made his dick jump inside of me and I gasped.

With deft fingers he reached between us and flicked that sensitive spot that would send me racing to the edge.

"Oh, God. I'm going to come." I lifted above him, need driving me faster.

He wrapped his free arm around my waist, slamming me against him. "That's it. Come for me baby. I want to watch you come."

Pleasure grew before shooting sparks through my system. I groaned as my body clenched around Jake, milking him. In a blink he was following suit, his body pumping into mine, wave after wave of his orgasm flooding into me.

He pressed his forehead to my chest, his breathing ragged. I leaned forward and pressed a kiss to the top of his head, my hair falling around us like a curtain.

"You've ruined me, Maddie." His voice was ragged with emotion as he looked up at me. "No one will ever compare to how you make me feel. No one could compare to you."

Tears formed in my eyes and I traced his face with my fingers. There was no turning back now. Jake had captured my heart completely.

I wanted to tell him, to tell him that I loved him, but I didn't want to scare him. I didn't want to send him running for the hills. The thought scared me. I wasn't sure how I would survive him leaving me. I'd never felt this way about another man and doubted that I ever would again.

Chapter 17

Jake

"That fucking aimbot!" I yelled into my headset. "There's no way that guy made that shot without help."

Puz grunted from where he sat next to me on the couch as I played video games.

"Dude, you were standing in the open. You might as well paint a bright orange X on your head," Cyrus replied.

"He shot me through a tree, Cy. A tree! That bastard is cheating!" I waited for my avatar to respawn so I could hunt down the cheater. "Where is he?"

"I didn't see who got you." Cyrus's distracted voice floated through my headset. "Ah, fucking cheating scumbag!"

"Ha, now you care!" I directed my little character to throw a bomb inside a tank before taking out the escaping avatars.

"No!" Cyrus's voice cut through my earphones, almost deafening me. "No!"

His voice dissolved into a mess of curses and half words.

"Holland, what's wrong?" My muscles tensed and I clenched the controller. "Holland! Report!"

There was no answer and my heart pounded in my chest as I waited for a response.

"I'm fine, Cap." His voice was shaky and in no way eased my nerves. "I'm fine."

"What happened?" I stared past the television, thinking of Cyrus's face at his house as we'd set up the basketball goal for his son.

"You ever wonder why we play this game?" His voice sounded off as if he was distracted, his mind somewhere else.

"Sometimes. I guess it's what we know."

"Yeah." He was quiet and I saw his avatar unmoving in the middle of a road. "We got fucked over there."

"A lot of us did." I swallowed and tried to calm my nerves as memories rushed back over me. I was barely aware of Puz whining next to me.

"I gotta have surgery again." His deep voice cracked and he cleared his throat.

"I heard." I set the controller down and squeezed my hands into fists.

I could hear Cyrus's labored breathing and I fought to stay calm, to sound calm.

"When does it stop?" Cyrus's voice got a little louder in my ear than required. "When will I be done losing bits of me? They're going to fuse my spine in three places. That's another year of physical therapy. Another year of Kyla having to take care of me like I'm one of the kids."

"Nah, man. It won't be that bad. Besides, you have a big family that is more than willing to help out and you'll be up and moving around again in no time."

"Don't try to feed me the bullshit, Simmon. Would you want your wife to have to change your diapers?" His voice took a slightly hysterical tone.

"Holland, get your shit together. Kyla doesn't care about that stuff. The surgery is meant to help you, not make it worse." Puz put a paw on my leg and I absentmindedly scratched his ear. "Look at how fast you bounced back already. This is a simple surgery, they fuse vertebrae on a regular basis now."

"You ever wonder why it was us? Why our 'copter got shot down? Why we lived while everyone else died?"

Bile rose in my throat. "Yeah, Cy. I've wondered those things, but that's a dead end. We'll never have those answers. We just have to push forward."

Silence was my only response and panic gripped my throat. "Cyrus, you still there?"

"Yeah. I'm here, man." I heard him take a deep breath. "Sorry. I need to find a different game."

"I bought the Lego Hobbit game the other day."

"Dude, your girlfriend is turning you into a dork." Cyrus laughed and I let loose the breath I'd been holding.

"Well, if you want something a little more tame, I think they sell a game where you can play with fluffy little animals. They dance and you can feed them and shit."

"Fuck you, Simmon. I'd rather fight dwarves and dragons. I'll get the Hobbit and I'll kick your ass at that."

"I didn't realize there were dwarves and dragons. Who's the dork now?"

"I heard your girl talking about them."

"Fuck you, Holland." I smiled, relieved to hear some of his normal spirit back in his voice.

"No thanks, man. You ain't my type." He chuckled. "I'm

signing off. Kyla is going to kick my ass when she realizes I've set up the game station and not the new crib."

"Derelict."

"You know it. Later." His avatar disappeared from the screen and I took a deep breath. Puz nuzzled my hand and looked up at me with his big dorky eyes.

"A poodle. You had to be part poodle." I lifted his ears and let them flop back on his head. "You're lucky you're cute. But if you tell anyone I said that, I'll deny it."

I inspected his stitches and then lifted his lips to check his teeth. Puz pushed at my hands with his paw. "It's not my fault you got your ass handed to you by a squirrel. Those stitches need to come out soon or your skin's going to grow over them."

He lifted his head as if shocked.

"It's not that bad. It'll take a few seconds." I ruffled his fur and he rolled over on his back so I could reach his belly. "You're a belly rub whore, you know that? And I could take the stitches out here, but since you like the vet better I'll take you there."

"Do you always hold full conversations with Puz?" Maddie skipped down the stairs and into the living room wearing one of my T-shirts.

I turned the game station off and threw the headset and controller on the table.

"Don't be jealous that he doesn't answer you." I stood up and went to the kitchen. She followed close behind me. "The Thai food arrived while you were in the shower."

"Thank goodness. I'm starving." She went straight to the cabinets and got out plates.

I watched as she stood on tiptoes to reach some glasses and my shirt skimmed the top of her thighs. It was a look I could get used to.

"So, what are we going to watch?" She looked at me over her shoulder as she spooned food onto her plate.

I moved up behind her and wrapped my hands around her waist. Leaning down I placed a kiss on her neck and smiled when she wiggled to get away. One of the things I'd learned over the last few weeks was that she was incredibly ticklish just below her ears.

"What do you want to watch?" I didn't care what was on the television as long as Maddie was beside me.

"Netflix released a new fantasy show that I've been dying to watch." She scooped a healthy serving of rice on her plate. "There's dragons and sword fighting, kick-ass damsels that are not in distress. I can't wait."

"Sure, but next time I get to pick." I looked down at her, trying to keep my horror from my face. Fantasy wasn't exactly my preferred genre.

"Come on. I think even you'll like this one." She handed me my plate.

I filled my dish with lots of goodies and carried it to the living room before going back to get us drinks.

"Who were you playing on your game?" Maddie crossed her legs on the couch and reached for her plate.

"Cyrus," I answered.

"It sounded like you were arguing." She used her chopsticks to scoop some food in her mouth.

"Not exactly." I took a drink from my beer bottle. This was territory dangerously close to things I didn't want to talk about with Maddie. "I think he had an episode of some kind."

"Hmm." She frowned and picked up her wineglass. "Was it bad?"

"They're never good." I shrugged and stuffed food in my

mouth. I rolled my shoulders to ease some of the tension that had gathered in the center.

"But some episodes are worse than others, right?" She went back to her food and I knew that she was choosing her words carefully, trying to not step on my toes, and that annoyed me.

"Maddie, you said you wouldn't tiptoe around me." I pointed my chopsticks at her.

"I'm not. I'm tiptoeing around what Cyrus went through." She rolled her eyes at me and I felt oddly better. "Kyla said he wasn't doing so well."

"The game triggered something and he got upset about his surgery." I shrugged. "We decided to play something else."

"He's trying to put it off until after the birth of his daughter." She pushed some of the food around on her plate. "Ew, there's a piece of chicken in my rice. Get it."

She held her plate out to me and I picked the piece off and popped it in my mouth. "Yummy."

She shuddered and went back to her vegetables. "Gross."

"When was the last time you had meat? You might like it."

"It's not whether or not I like it. It's about feeling bad for the animals." She shook her head. "Nope, I'll stick with what I eat now.

"So, back to Cyrus. Do you think he's seeing anyone about his episodes? I think Kyla is worried."

"We all have to see a military psych every so often. It's standard procedure."

"How often do you have to go?" She picked through her vegetables for a carrot and then a piece of pineapple.

"My mandatory evals are every six weeks." I shrugged. My hackles were rising and I rolled my shoulders to try and relax. I was already tense from the things Cyrus had said.

"You feel comfortable talking with him?" She took another sip of her wine.

"I told you I'd find someone, Maddie." I tried to keep the frustration off my face.

"I'm sorry." She reached over and touched my knee. "I just didn't know how it worked."

"I don't want to talk about that stuff with you, Maddie. I can't." How was I supposed to tell her what had happened, what I had done over there? She would never be able to look at me the same again and I couldn't bear that.

"It's fine, Jake. I don't want details, you know? I'm not asking for that. I just wanted to know that you were okay."

The concern on her face killed me.

"I haven't figured out who to talk to. I can't talk to the military psych. Anything I say in there would go straight to my mom." I sighed and set my plate down. My appetite was gone. "It can't be someone that would report to the Commander-in-Chief."

"That makes sense." She shoved some more food in her mouth. "Do you want help looking for someone? I could ask around."

"No." The word came out a little sharper than I had intended. "It's fine. I'll find someone."

She nodded her head but didn't meet my eyes.

"Tell me about your bill."

"I don't want to bore you." She waved her chopsticks in the air. "Honestly, it's just a bunch of grunt work right now."

"Have you gotten a lot of support so far?" Politicians should be jumping at the chance to help President McGuire's daughter.

"Some." A shadow crossed her face and she looked down at her plate.

"I would think they'd be lining up to be co-sponsors. You're the President's daughter."

"Not really." She grimaced and put her plate on the table next to mine.

"I'm missing something." I watched her face carefully.

She shrugged. "We're up against the big pharmaceutical companies. They have a lot of money to throw around and to fund campaigns. People don't want to piss them off."

"Is that all?" Something felt off, like she wasn't telling me everything.

"Pretty much. I mean, not everyone wants to help. My father has made some political enemies over the years. That's part of the job, I guess." She waved her hand in the air. "It'll all work out in the end. It's just going to take a lot of work."

I knew there was something she wasn't telling me, but I had no right to push. I had secrets, so she was entitled to her own.

"Come here." I leaned back on the couch and held my arms open. She scooted over and cuddled up against my chest. I reached the remote with my fingertips and turned on the show she had been talking about.

It opened with a couple of teenagers running from a bridge troll and I resigned myself to hating it. Of course, it wouldn't matter as long as I had my arms around Maddie. That made anything bearable.

Chapter 18

Jake

Six centimeters," Cyrus explained. "If she doesn't progress in the next hour or so, they're going to do a c-section."

The concern in his voice was palpable. Knowing that cesarean surgeries were performed on a regular basis around the world didn't make it any less scary. The thought of watching the mother of my child cut open on a table while they dug the baby free from her body made my heartbeat speed up and it wasn't even happening to me. My eyes darted at Maddie and I bit the inside of my cheek.

"It's going to be okay, Cy. I bet Kyla isn't worried at all."

"Kyla isn't scared of shit. She's coloring with Korbin right now like she isn't attached to a hundred different fucking machines." His voice dropped and I had a new understanding.

Every hospital smells the same, doesn't it? Antiseptic and cleaning products that barely cover the smell of blood. I can't go in one without going back to the tent in Afghanistan.

"Is there anyone else with you?" My fingers tightened on the phone. Flashes of the doctors and nurses in scrubs slid through my mind. I could imagine the beeping of machines and the odd combination of smells that included blood, vomit, and cleaning products.

I jerked when Maddie's small hand touched my leg. Her eyes were full of worry and she mouthed "let's go."

"My parents are flying in from Wisconsin and Kyla's parents are here, but exhausted. She's been in labor for over twenty-eight hours now." I could hear the desperation in his voice. "We're all tired. I'm not sure how she's still so damn chipper. She should be cursing and throwing things."

Maddie mimed spooning food into her mouth and I nodded my head.

"Why don't we bring you some food? Something better than hospital grub," I offered.

"Nah, that's too much trouble."

"We're coming no matter what, so we might as well get you some food on the way. Tell me what you'd prefer or I'm going to get a bunch of tacos."

"I fucking hate tacos and you know it." Cyrus's laugh was gruff but there. "Burgers would be good though. A real one. Korbin hates pickles though."

"Any other particulars?"

"Kyla can't eat anything and her parents ate earlier." He covered the phone for a second before coming back on. "Yeah, they don't want anything. Just me and Korbin. God, a juicy hamburger sounds perfect. Thanks."

Maddie leaned forward and whispered something to the driver.

"No problem, man." I hung up the phone.

"How's Kyla?" Maddie turned to me.

I tapped my phone on my leg. "Better than Cyrus. Apparently she's coloring with Korbin but they may have to do a c-section."

"I'm not sure anything would stop Kyla. She's like a force of nature. All sunshine and smiles."

"Smiles are a part of nature?" I raised an eyebrow.

"Oh you know what I meant." She smiled up at me as if to prove her point and it worked. I was awestruck. The green dress she was wearing highlighted her hazel eyes.

Lifting my hand I cupped her face. "Yeah, I get it now."

Her cheeks pinked and I brushed my thumb over her skin. Leaning closer I pressed my mouth to hers and instantly wished we didn't have to go to the hospital. She tasted like honey and all I wanted was to wrap my body around hers somewhere private.

I tangled my hand in the hair at the back of her neck. Her soft moan gave me the chance to capture her bottom lip with my teeth. She gripped my shirt with one hand and poured herself into the kiss. That was my Maddie, all or nothing.

When she finally pulled away there was fire in her eyes. I loosened my hold on her hair and stroked the skin of her neck.

"We need to spend more time together," she whispered.

I knew exactly what she meant.

"We're about to go on a whirlwind promotional tour." I placed a kiss on her nose.

"Not exactly romantic." She rolled her eyes.

"Everything is romantic with you," I answered.

She shook her head. "How do you manage to walk the line of corny and sexy so well? If that line came from someone else I'd have laughed."

"It's a gift."

"It's something all right." She chuckled. "I'm glad they're having the baby before we leave. Is Cyrus worried?"

"I think Cyrus would be worried if Kyla had a hangnail." I wove my fingers with hers. "But he did perk up at the thought of a burger."

"That's where we're headed right now," Maddie explained. "I figured we'd get him the good stuff and pick something up at the Shake Shack."

My stomach growled. "Maybe we should grab something for us too."

She patted my stomach and laughed.

"Sounds like a plan."

By the time we got to the hospital I'd eaten my burger and most of the fries. The driver dropped us off with our body-guards at the entrance and we managed to find our way to the waiting room.

There's a different feel in a maternity wing than in the rest of the hospital. Hope is heavy in the air and people are smiling, but the smells are the same. Everywhere I looked there were nurses and doctors rushing to and fro. My gut clenched and I started to sweat. No wonder Cyrus had sounded a bit panicked on the phone.

"Kyla Holland?" Maddie stepped up to the nurses' desk. She must have sensed my apprehension because despite my connection with Cyrus she took the lead.

"She's being prepped for surgery." A shorter woman with red hair looked up at Maddie and her eyes widened. "You're Maddie McGuire!"

"Yes, ma'am." Maddie gave her a small smile. "Is there somewhere we can wait?"

"Yes, the rest of the Holland family is over by the television. They put on Disney for the little boy." Her eyes moved to me before looking at our security detail. "I can try to find extra seats."

"No thank you." Tony smiled and I realized it was one of the few times I'd seen him do so. "We'll be fine."

"If you need anything let me know." The nurse's eyes darted down to where I was holding Maddie's hand and her smile grew. I'd completely forgotten that I'd threaded my fingers with hers after we got out of the car. A few other staff members had taken notice of us at this point.

"Thank you," I said.

"Maddie!" Korbin ran over to where we were standing, followed by an older woman with gray hair. He held up a red truck in one hand and wiped his nose with the other. "Look at my fruck!"

"That is an awesome truck!" Maddie knelt down and admired the fire truck.

"I'm so sorry. He's been cooped up all day." The woman scooped Korbin into her arms and deposited him on her hip. "I'm Karen, Kyla's mother."

Maddie stood up and shook her hand. "I'm Maddie and this is Jake. We're friends of Kyla and Cyrus."

"It's nice to meet you. Kyla thinks very highly of you." The woman smiled at us with weary eyes. "They're getting ready to do the c-section."

"How were she and Cyrus doing?" Maddie motioned to where an older man snored in a chair next to the television. "I think you were sitting over there."

"Oh, yes. That's Frank, my husband." She went back to her seat. "Excuse us, it's been a long two days."

"Fruck. Vroom!" Korbin waved the truck in the air and one of the wheels got tangled in his grandmother's hair.

"Oh, Korbin." The woman grabbed the truck and worked the wheel free from her hair. "No trucks in Nana's hair."

"Torry, Nana." Korbin brushed her hair with fingers. "Pretty hair."

Karen smiled at her grandson before leaning down to nuzzle him.

"Do you mind if we wait with you?"

"Of course." The woman gathered up some of the things they had strewn across other chairs. "And Kyla was chipper. You know how she is, contractions don't slow her down. Cyrus on the other hand . . ."

"What's wrong with Cyrus?" I cleared my throat, surprised I'd spoken up.

"He hates hospitals," Karen explained. "I think being here for so long was starting to get to him."

"Maybe they could give him something for his nerves?" Maddie suggested.

"Oh no, he'd never take those." Karen shook her head and waved her hand dismissively. "Just a case of the daddy jitters. He'll man up and deal with it. It's not him that's going through surgery, right?"

Maddie smiled but I could see the wheels turning behind those giant eyes. She was concerned and worried by how easily Cyrus's sweet mother-in-law brushed a serious ego under the rug. Either Cyrus had done a better job pretending around his extended family or they honestly dismissed this sign that something was wrong. It wouldn't be the first family that didn't see past the façade of PTSD.

My thoughts were a jumble of things as I half listened to

Maddie and Karen chat while stopping to answer Korbin's questions about the characters on the television.

"He doesn't normally watch this much television but I figured this was a special occasion." Karen frowned as Mickey Mouse did something called a Hotdog Dance.

My eyes glazed over as I watched Korbin bop along with the music and thought about how Cyrus was really feeling, the way his family seemed to have no clue he was dealing with something very serious.

Could I tell him to get help or to find someone to talk to? It felt incredibly hypocritical considering that I hadn't found a professional to share with yet. There were thousands of psychiatrists in the D.C. area alone. But who was trustworthy? And how could I know they would be the real deal and able to help and not just some quack that was waiting to collect insurance money?

I had no idea how long I'd been sitting there grasping Maddie's hand on one side while gripping the paper bag from the burger shop. It wasn't until a chime filled the waiting area that tore my gaze away from the laminated wood floors.

"What was that?" I looked around and noticed a bunch of excited smiles.

"It means a baby was born." Karen shook Frank's arm until he stirred in his chair.

"No creamer," he muttered.

"Wake up Frank. Wake up, you're still asleep." Karen shook his arm again. "The bell chimed. I bet it was Savannah making her debut."

"What?" The man blinked like an old owl wearing crooked glasses. "She had the baby?"

"I think so!"

"Think? You don't know yet?" The man had a mustache that reminded me of a walrus. It bobbed as he spoke and I was waiting for him to suck it in his mouth and then spit it back out at us. "You should've waited to wake me once you were sure."

"At least pretend to be a little excited!" Karen elbowed him in the gut. "Savannah will be our first granddaughter."

"But we don't know if that was even her!" Frank looked at us. "Are you waiting for a friend?"

"For your granddaughter," I explained.

"Oh?" He blinked at me and then Maddie. "Oh. You're Jake Simmon! And the President's daughter. Forgive me, dear. I can't think of your name right now."

"I'm Maddie." She offered a small smile. "Would you like to go ask the nurse who that bell was for?"

"I'm sure they'll tell us if it was."

A woman in scrubs came over to the group and nodded at us before turning to Kyla's parents. "Karen Philmont?"

"Yes, that's me." Karen smiled up at the nurse.

"Ma'am, Kyla would like for you to come back to the operating room." The nurse wasn't smiling and my stomach took a turn south.

"I thought she could only have one person with her." Karen shot a confused look at her husband.

"Yes, ma'am. Cyrus had an accident on the way to surgery. He's being admitted for his back. It looks like he's going to need to have surgery today as well."

"Oh my God." Karen covered her mouth. "Is he okay?"

"He's in a lot of pain and they're administering medication to help." She held her hand out to Karen. "We need to hurry. Kyla is ready for the c-section and I'm sure she wants you with her."

"Of course." She pushed her purse at Frank and stood up. "Watch Korbin. I'll let you know as soon as the baby is here."

"Go," Frank urged. "She needs you."

"Ma'am, is anyone with Cyrus?" I stood up and touched the nurse's shoulder.

"I'm not sure. If you go ask at the desk they will be able to direct you to where he is." Her eyes darted to where the Secret Service agents were standing.

"Thank you." I watched as the nurse escorted Karen through a set of doors that another nurse buzzed them through.

"Please go check on Cyrus. His family is in the air and I hate the thought of him being alone." Frank stood up and reached out to shake my hand. "Karen can be a bit oblivious at times, but I know that Cyrus is having a rough time. He needs a friend with him now."

"Yes, sir." I turned on my heel and headed for the desk while Maddie told Korbin she'd see him soon.

"Excuse me," I said. One of the nurses looked up at me with a bored expression. "Can you tell me where they've taken Cyrus Holland?"

"Are you a family member?"

"No, ma'am. He's a friend. We served in Afghanistan together and I was here for the birth of their daughter. I was told that there was an accident and he might need someone with him."

"You won't be allowed back to his room and I can't release any information to someone that isn't family."

I clenched my hands into fists and fought to keep from slamming them against the counter.

"Excuse me ma'am." Tony took a step forward and held out his badge. "The Vice President's son needs to see Mr. Holland as soon as possible."

A mulish look formed on the woman's face and she lifted her chin. "I don't care if he's the President. Only family members are allowed back with the patients."

"I'd be happy to call my father and see if he can reach the head surgeon." Maddie sidled up on my right side. "But I don't think we really need to bother him."

The nurse's mouth gaped open like a fish.

"You're just doing your job, but Mr. Holland's family won't be here for several hours. He needs someone with him right now. Cyrus's wife is about to have a c-section and he suffers from PTSD. Having a familiar face with him right now would go a long way."

I looked at Maddie, shocked that she had announced to the world Cyrus had PTSD. That wasn't something that you told strangers. They would look at Cyrus differently now, treat him differently. How could she treat it so carelessly?

"Considering what you just told me, I can see how he might benefit from a good friend." The nurse stood up and motioned for me to follow. "I think we can get one of you back to your friend with no trouble."

"I'll go." I stepped away from Maddie.

"Are you sure?" She looked up at me with worried eyes.

My anger bubbled just under the surface and I didn't trust myself to respond. Is that how she thought of me? As damaged goods?

"Jake?" She reached out and grabbed my hand.

"I need to get to Cyrus." I didn't look back at her.

"Stop, Jake," she whispered. "Jake! What did I do wrong?"

"You don't know he has PTSD." I lowered my voice. "They're going to put that in his record now. Anyone would be upset right now. His wife is having a baby while he's being prepped for surgery."

"I just assumed—"

"Did Kyla tell you he had PTSD?"

"No, but he has all the symptoms and she said he'd been having a hard time." Her eyes were wide and her skin was pale. "I just wanted him to have someone there for him. If I was him I'd be scared."

"Well, I'm going." I heaved a deep breath in frustration.

"I'll be right here if you need anything." She bit her bottom lip and there was no hiding the pain in her eyes. "I'll text you as soon as we hear about Kyla and Savannah."

"Thanks." I tried to reel in my frustration.

"I don't like it when you're mad at me, Jake." She squeezed my fingers.

"I'll let you know what's happening with Cyrus." I pecked her cheek before turning to follow the nurse.

My stomach churned as we walked the hallways and I had a brief moment of doubt as anxiety gripped my chest. Maybe I should have stayed in the maternity ward that sparkled with hope instead of diving into the depths of despair.

I looked back over my shoulder and saw Maddie watching me with a heartbroken expression.

Chapter 19

Maddie

No questions about my personal life." I looked at the television reporter sitting in the chair across from me.

"You're a politician, Maddie. You don't have a personal life." The woman looked in a small mirror as she touched up her lipstick. "Everything is free rein."

"Sally, I'm not a politician." I shook my head. "I'm here to talk about a charity. Anything else is off limits."

"We just want to hear that you're happy, dear. Give the public what they want and they'll repay you by donating to your little charity." She looked up at me from under false eyelashes. "Use your little relationship to promote your agenda."

I tried to swallow the bile in my throat. The thought of using something so personal to push an agenda was disgusting. Especially when things between me and Jake had felt so . . . askew. He acted like things were fine but they weren't.

"Fifteen seconds." One of the directors hollered across the

stage. Marilyn tossed her mirror and lipstick in a basket under her desk.

One of the stage hands counted down the last few seconds and the theme music started.

"We're here today with Maddie McGuire, America's First Daughter. In the last segment we addressed the charity that you are currently focusing on."

"Yes, the Returning Combat Veterans Affairs." I ignored the television sets pointed in our direction so we could see what we looked like. Nothing messed with your head as much as seeing your live interview happening in front of you.

"You've just finished your first house for the program." The other woman smiled politely at me.

"Yes, the family was just able to move in a little over a week ago." I smiled widely. "It was very rewarding to see them set-tled."

"A press release went out announcing the birth of their newest child. Were you present?" She smiled.

"Well, I was at the hospital, waiting on the happy news."

"Is it true that the father had an accident that resulted in him missing the birth of his new daughter?"

"Cyrus Holland is a multiple amputee survivor and he needed more surgery. Unfortunately it couldn't wait any longer." I worked to stay relaxed in my seat. I could only hope that I hadn't overstepped my bounds. "I've been told that he is doing very well, as is his wife and the new baby."

"That's good to hear. Now, is it true that Holland served with your boyfriend?" Her pleasant smile looked so innocent.

"If you're referring to Jake Simmon, then yes, Mr. Holland did serve with him in Afghanistan." My cheeks were starting to hurt from my fake smile and a tick developed in my left eye. Things had been rough between me and Jake since the hospital. He refused to talk about it, but I knew I'd upset him.

"Do you worry that this may look like favoritism?" Again, that bright cheery smile only served to increase my desire to deck the woman.

"Jake and I had absolutely no say in who received the home. There are a lot of different points that go into the decision process. Mr. Holland suffered extreme injuries that will keep him from having a full-time job. The fact that they had a child and another on the way with no home to call their own, also factored into the decision."

"But perhaps his name attracted the powers that be." She leaned forward a bit, hungry to make a story out of nothing.

"The family had been chosen before we even started helping build the house as far as I am aware." I narrowed my gaze. "And I wouldn't be any less happy if the home had gone to another deserving soldier and their family."

"Well, I have to ask you how your new relationship with Jake Simmon is progressing. Photos of you two are circulating around the world." A picture of us holding hands and walking down a sidewalk flashed on the screen behind us before being replaced of an image where we were embracing at the construction site. "People absolutely love seeing you together. Before you know it they'll have some cute couple nickname for you."

I fought to not gag and I knew my smile slipped because there was a gleam of victory in the reporter's eyes.

"Anything happening between the two of us will remain between us."

"Just a little girl talk? Between me and you, how are things going between you?"

"I tell you what, Sally. You tell me how your relationship is going. We can trade stories." It was mean, because as far as I knew, the woman was going through a divorce.

"Oh, my life is so boring. No one wants to hear about that."

"Your husband, is he still working for NBC? What's his name again?"

If Sally could spit venom from her eyes, I'd be dead. I might as well be sitting across from a dilophosaurus in a blond wig.

"Would you like to talk about the bill you're proposing? I have it on good authority that the Vice President is opposing your stance. She feels that it opens up other companies to serious trouble."

"The bill is still in the early stages. We want to present the best possible bill for the House to vote on. Nothing is finalized so I can't imagine what the Vice President would be opposed to. We don't have anything official for her to oppose." I braced my arms on the table and smiled.

"Perhaps it's not the bill she opposes?" Marilyn leaned forward. "We all know that the Vice President doesn't stand for things to be out of order. Perhaps she's not happy with her son's choice in girlfriends."

"I'm sure that our Vice President would never stoop to oppose a bill just because she disliked the person that wrote the bill." I shook my head dismissively.

"Then the Vice President approves of your relationship with her son?"

"You'd have to ask her that, Marilyn."

"I'll do that, Miss McGuire." There was an evil glint in the interviewer's eye that made my stomach clench.

"Right now most of my attention is focused on spotlighting the RCVA and their efforts to help our returning soldiers.

These men and women deserve our respect and need our help."

"Indeed, a very worthy cause. The link for the website is posted at the bottom of your television screens and we'll also have more information over on our website." The credit music started playing.

"Please check out the website. They're always looking for volunteers." I smiled brightly.

"We'll be back in a few with an up-and-coming Democratic star."

The theme music started and Sally looked at me with pure venom in her eyes. "You're a real bitch, McGuire. You know I'm going through a divorce."

"And I told you I didn't want to discuss my private life. I did nothing you didn't do." I reached around and turned off my mic before pulling it free from my jacket. I leaned toward the reporter and lowered my voice. "And you haven't seen me be a bitch yet."

"We'll see how you feel after my interview with VP Simmon."

I dropped the mic on the table and walked off. If I didn't get out of that studio quickly I would end up with an assault charge on my record.

I stretched in my seat and fought a yawn. We'd had interviews at all the papers in D.C. before going to Boston and New York. I couldn't even remember all of the different shows we'd been on over the last few weeks.

"How much longer?" I ground my palms against my eyes.

"It's another six hours before we get to D.C., ma'am," the driver explained from the front seat.

I looked over at Jake. "Why don't we stop? I need a bed and real food. Not fast food."

"That is a great idea." Jake grabbed my hand and brought it up to his mouth to kiss my fingers. The warmth of his kiss did wonders to loosen the chains around my heart. "I don't think I'm meant to sit in the backseat of a vehicle for this long."

He let go of my fingers and massaged his knee. He had his cane today and I knew that meant all of the traveling was catching up with him. He seemed to do better when he had steady movement in his schedule. His normal day included a good amount of exercise.

"There's a small inn not far from here, Miss McGuire. Your father stayed there during one of his campaigns, so we already know the layout." The agent in the front passenger seat turned to look at me. "It has a small restaurant downstairs that served some decent pub grub."

"That sounds perfect," Jake responded.

"You were on one of Daddy's tours?" I smiled at the older man.

"Yes ma'am. His first presidential campaign." His grin was fast. "Was a real treat to see him work a crowd."

"He has that *je ne sais quoi.*" I shook my head. "There's no explaining that special something that attracts people."

"I'd say the apple didn't fall far from the tree." He turned around in his seat so didn't see my ridiculous expression.

"You really don't want your face to freeze that way," Jake whispered.

I turned and glared at him. It wasn't like he wouldn't understand my shock. My father could talk to anyone or a room full of thousands of people and they all left feeling special. Even during the debates, his opponents seemed taken in by his cha-risma. That wasn't something I possessed. No. Instead of ele-gantly finding a way to deflect questions, I did something bitchy like turn the tables on the reporter.

Jake leaned close, his lips brushing my ear. "You don't real-ize it, but people flock to you. You make them comfortable, treat them no differently than you would the Queen of England or the Pope. The public loves that you are well spoken, but down to earth. I saw an article in the *New York Times* that called you the people's voice."

I chuckled a little and turned to meet his gaze. The world was in a sad state if they thought I was someone worth looking up to.

"But I don't even know what to do if there is a nuclear fall-out." I shrugged my shoulders.

"That was random, even for you." Jake tucked some of my hair out of my face.

"I can't be a role model or the voice of the people. I don't know how to get rid of cobwebs and I also don't know what to do if the country faces a catastrophe." I frowned.

"You better get us to that hotel quick. I think the President's daughter is suffering from a mental breakdown."

"Shut it." I elbowed him with a laugh. It was nice to have him joking with me again.

The little inn was adorable. A huge home was attached to a building with a restaurant sign and large oak trees offered plenty of shade. The staff was more than helpful, setting up a room block for us and the aides that had been traveling with us. There were only a few other patrons and most of them were in their rooms.

"Do you have a workout room?" Jake asked the front desk

clerk. She was younger than me and looked up at him with a dreamy smile.

"Yes we do, Jake. I mean, Mr. Simmon." Red colored her cheeks and I felt bad for her. Jake was worth blushing over. "It's at the end of the first floor hallway."

"I'm going to get some sleep." I stood on my tiptoes and kissed Jake. We'd paid for separate rooms at every place that we stayed even though we hadn't used both. It was just easier than dealing with the rumors ordering one room would start. "I don't think I can keep my eyes open for another minute."

"I need to stretch." He looked down at my face and I could see the tension lining his jaw.

"Sure." I smiled at him. "Wake me up when you're done and we can get some food."

"Get some rest, Maddie. We've been up for a day straight." He leaned over and pressed a soft kiss on the corner of my mouth. "I need to blow off some steam."

My mouth stretched open in a big yawn. "Okay. To be honest, the only thing I really want is to take this stupid dress suit off and sleep."

He grabbed the handles for our suitcases and we went upstairs to the rooms.

"You okay?" He stopped outside of the elevator and was rubbing his knee.

"I'm fine, Maddie." Annoyance laced his voice and I tried to not let it hurt my feelings. We were both tired and frustrated after the last few days. I couldn't wait to get back to swinging a hammer and ignoring the cameras.

I stopped at my door and pulled out the key card. I opened my door and propped it open with my hip before holding my hand out for my suitcase.

"Get some rest." He kissed the top of my head. "I'll see you in a little bit."

"See you later." I tugged the heavy suitcase into the room but Jake stopped the door from closing.

Jake held it open with his free hand. "I really am fine, Maddie. Sitting in the car for so long just got to me. I'm sorry I snapped at you."

"Jake, I asked because I care, not because I think less of you." My shoulders slumped. "I am allowed to care about you, right?"

"Yes," he said. He pulled me into a quick hug. "I'm an asshole and assholes need lots of care and patience."

"If you can ask if I'm tired or angry, I should be able to do the same, right? That's part of being in a relationship. Sharing each other's burdens and making sure we're okay." I rubbed my hands up my arms. "I don't like feeling as if I can't ask how you're doing."

"You're right, that's not working." He lifted my chin with one finger. "Since we are sharing, are you going to tell me what's going on with my mother?"

I jerked my chin from his grasp in shock. I'd been hoping that he hadn't seen or heard about that interview. I tugged the suit jacket off and threw it on the back of the desk chair. I kicked my shoes off and used my toes to fling them in the corner. "I'm tired and irritable. I'm sorry."

"Maddie." His voice took on a frustrated tone. "You only want to share my burdens, not the other way around. That isn't fair."

"It's not that." Was it? Was I being hypocritical? "It's not really a big deal. You know how reporters are always looking for sensationalized headlines."

"You and I both know that my mother is always a big deal. She has a way of jumping in and making sure she is in the thick of things." His eyes turned hard. "Did she threaten you?"

"Your mother doesn't scare me, Jake." I started to turn away from him and his fingers tightened.

"What did she do, Maddie?"

"She offered her help." I shrugged.

"What did she want in return?"

"It doesn't matter. I turned her down." My voice rose a little and I clenched my fingers into fists. "I'm not making any deals with the devil."

I froze and my eyes widened.

"Don't look like that." Laughter bubbled out of Jake. "She might be my mother but even I'm not immune to the stink of sulphur."

"I'm sorry, Jake." I shook my head and wiped at my face. "I'm tired."

"Me too." He moved his hands to my shoulders and massaged them gently. "I don't want you to deal with my mom by yourself."

"There's nothing to deal with, Jake. I told her no, that's the end." Just remembering how she wanted to change me hurt.

"She wanted you to leave me, didn't she?" Jake narrowed his eyes and lowered his voice. "She threatened the bill if you didn't."

I looked over his shoulder to the open door and quiet hallway.

"I don't want to talk about this right now," I explained. "Anyone can hear us."

"It's harder to open up than you thought, isn't it?" He frowned. "I'll try to be better but you do too. Being in the car that long felt like being trapped and I don't deal with that so well anymore. It means I have a shorter fuse right now."

"I didn't know . . . I'm sorry." I closed my eyes. "I shouldn't be so irritable."

"I think we've earned a chance to be irritable." He grabbed my fingers and brought them up to his mouth. "Look at us having our first argument."

"A milestone of sorts I guess." I rolled my eyes but couldn't help but smile. "Not much of a fight. No yelling or screaming. I didn't even get to throw a pillow."

"You flung some shoes across the room." He nodded toward the corner. "That should count for something."

"But I didn't fling them at your head." I pouted up at him. "If I'd realized that was my only chance I'd have aimed better."

"I'll have to remember to invest in a helmet if I piss you off again."

"You didn't piss me off, Jake." I frowned. "You hurt my feelings. There's a difference."

He didn't say anything for a minute and I wondered what he was thinking.

"I've never really done the long-term relationship thing before, Maddie. I've dated women, seen them for a while, but nothing serious. This is new for me and that means I'm going to make mistakes. I'm going to say stupid things and do something that pisses you off." He stepped closer and folded his arms around my waist. "But I promise that I'll never do it on purpose and I'll try to learn from my mistakes."

I rested my hands on his chest and pressed my head against his shoulder. "I'll be patient if you'll be patient. I'm going to make mistakes too."

"Anyone would be irritable after all of those interviews and constant travel. We'll be better in the morning. You get some rest and I'll work some steam off." He looked down at me and I met his gaze. "I heard they make waffles."

"I do like waffles." I pressed a kiss to his lips.

"I know."

Chapter 20

Jake

I'd been on the rowing machine for half an hour but still couldn't seem to work off the edge I'd been carrying the last week. I'd tried to text Cyrus earlier but hadn't gotten a response. I didn't want to text Kyla because she had more than enough on her plate.

Kyla was more than busy with a brand-new baby, a toddler, and a very sick husband. When I'd talked to her on the phone a few days ago, she'd done her best to sound chipper and on top of things, but her voice had cracked when explaining about Cyrus's back and the baby had been crying in the background.

Guilt ran rampant through my mind even though I knew that both sets of their parents were there to help. I didn't need a doctor to tell me that the guilt stemmed from our accident in Afghanistan. If I'd been a faster pilot or noticed the men on the ground, I could have avoided the accident that caused all of Cyrus's injuries and the rest of our squad would still be alive.

I gave up on the rowing machine and headed for the treadmill. Despite my preference for running outdoors it wasn't going to happen today. The inn was situated on a busy road and the weather was cold and wet. Maybe I could run long enough and far enough I wouldn't be worried about anything else.

The door opened and a few women walked into the gym with big smiles. I nodded briefly before turning back the window in front of the treadmill. I put my earbuds in but didn't turn on any music. My goal was to just be left alone.

Lost in my thoughts I didn't notice the flash of a camera phone. It wasn't until one of the Secret Service agents moved into my line of sight that I realized something was wrong. The agent's mouth turned down and he coughed into his hand. I slowed down the treadmill until I was at a steady jog. Pulling my earbuds out I looked around to see a curvy brunette in well-chosen exercise clothing staring up at me with a flirtatious smile.

"I'm sorry. I didn't mean to hog the machine." I turned it off and used my towel to wipe off the bar. "Here you go."

"Actually, I was wondering if you'd take a picture with me. Please?" She smiled up at me and despite the fact that I was sweaty and tired I nodded my head. I'd been trained to make the public happy and it took no time to take a picture.

"Sure." I stood there while she handed her phone to her friend. She wrapped her arm around my waist and pressed her head against my chest. I waited patiently while her friend took the picture, but couldn't make myself smile.

"Me too?" The friend smiled and stepped over to my other side before I could answer.

She lifted the camera in front of us and pressed her head to my side like her friend. There was a clicking sound and she checked the image before giggling.

"One more!" Her hand moved down my backside lower than was appropriate. "Just one more! Make a funny face!"

"Excuse me." I stepped away from the girls and nodded to the agent. "I've got to go."

"C'mon. Just one more?" She smiled up at me but I was out of patience.

"No." I turned away and one of them grabbed my arm. I jerked out of her hands with more strength than I should have and she fell back against the treadmill.

"Hey!"

"I'm sorry," I said. Leaning over I helped her up. "You shouldn't grab people. You startled me."

"I'm going to need you two to leave the room." One of the agents stepped between us.

"You don't own this building!"

"We just wanted a picture," the girl with the wandering hands explained. "He didn't have to freak out."

"You restrained Mr. Simmon. You can't treat people that way." The agent pointed toward the door. "Return to your rooms, please."

"We came here to work out." The first girl put her hands on her hip.

"Agent Destin will escort you back to your rooms." One of the men stepped forward and cupped her elbow.

"Hey!"

"Hush, Amanda." The second girl shook her head, her eyes wide with alarm.

"This is crazy!"

I listened as their voices faded down the hall. The lead agent looked out the door before nodding his head.

"They've gone up to the second floor. You're clear to leave."

"Thanks." I took the stairs closest to the gym and made it to my room on the fourth floor without any interruptions.

I took a quick shower and got dressed, still too antsy to sleep. My stomach grumbled and I decided that food might help. I stepped into the hallway and started for Maddie's room but stopped. She needed her sleep and I'd promised to wake her in the morning. I'd grab some grub by myself and maybe watch a game on the television at the bar.

"Going out, sir?" Tony stepped out of another door down the hall and I looked at him, confused. It took a second for me to realize that he was wearing civilian clothes and that was what was throwing me off.

"Thought I might get some food." I jerked my chin toward the stairs. "Are you off?"

"Mandatory shift change." He shrugged.

"Hungry?" I asked him.

"I wouldn't mind some company." He nodded his head and matched my stride.

There weren't many people in the tiny publike restaurant. There was a football game playing on a flat-screen television in the corner above the bar. The menus were on laminated card stock; nice and simple.

"I'm Matt," the waiter announced. He turned the chair backward and sat down. He was wearing a simple black shirt and had a pen stuck in the collar. "What can I get you guys to drink?"

"I'll take a soda." I tapped the menu against the table.

"Water," Tony said.

"Got it. Have you had a chance to look over the menu?" He plucked the card from my fingers and turned it over. "Here are the daily specials. Tonight is Shepherd's pie, one of my favorites."

"Sounds good to me."

Tony ordered a burger and shifted his chair so he could see the football game on the television.

"College game." He leaned back in his seat.

"Before Afghanistan I didn't really care about watching sports. I liked to play, but didn't see the point of watching it on television." I nodded my thanks to the waiter when he set my soda in front of me. "Now, it's just a nice way to spend an evening. Normal."

"If you can call grown men with their chests painted normal." Tony laughed.

We laughed as we watched the game and ate our dinner. I ordered a second soda and propped my leg up on the chair next to me. There were only a few other people left and no one was paying us any attention as we watched the game and talked bullshit.

"Did you see that? That was a bullshit call!" The waiter threw his towel at the television. Tony leaned back in his chair, the front two legs coming up off the floor while he laughed at the guy behind the bar.

I'd cleaned my plate and debated ordering another batch of onion rings when my phone rang. I pulled it out of my pocket and flicked the green icon to answer.

"Hey Kyla, how's it going?" I settled back into my chair.

"Jake?" Her voice was the exact opposite of every time I'd talked to her in the past. Gone was the bubbly, happy young woman; instead it sounded like someone had ripped her soul out.

"Kyla? What's wrong?" I leaned forward, every muscle in my body tense.

"Where are you? I can't get hold of Maddie." There was a wet sound and I could picture her wiping her nose on her arm. "Is Maddie with you?"

"No, she's asleep. What's wrong Kyla? Are you okay?"

Tony set the front of his chair back down on the floor and I saw his professional persona slide back into place. He sensed danger.

"No. No, I'm not okay." Her shaky voice sent my pulse into overdrive. "Is there anyone else with you?"

"Kyla, tell me what's wrong." She was scaring me. "Did something happen to the baby? Korbin?"

"No, no. Savannah and Korbin are fine." She sniffled into the phone. "We came home from the hospital today. Cyrus was supposed to meet with a home nurse."

I held my breath, trying to stay calm, but I knew whatever was coming would be bad.

"He's dead, Jake." A low keening sound followed her words that ended on a sob. "I didn't want you to find out on the news. He's gone."

"Cyrus? Cyrus is dead?" The wind left my lungs as if I'd been punched.

I sat there, listening to her cry as I tried to understand what could have happened, what could have gone wrong.

"Kyla?" I asked. Her crying had slowed and I tried to make out what she was saying.

"He killed himself. Why would he do that?" Kyla's broken voice was like a knife to my heart. "Why would he leave me?"

"He committed suicide?" I gripped the edge of the table so hard that my knuckles turned white. "What happened?"

"He said he wanted to nap and so I stayed out in the front of the house with the kids." She hiccupped. "My mom had run to the store to get some groceries."

I sucked in a deep breath and then another. I couldn't get enough. I shoved up from the chair I was sitting in and started to pace. Kyla was talking but I couldn't understand what she was saying. None of it made sense.

"I don't understand." I shook my head, trying to clear it.

"He shot himself, Jake. He left a note." She cleared her throat and took a breath. "It said he couldn't take care of us and didn't want to be a burden. He wasn't a burden. I don't know what I did that made him think he was a burden."

"You did nothing wrong, Kyla." I tangled my fingers in my hair and pulled. It was longer than it had been in years. "Listen to me. This isn't your fault."

The sound of her sobbing filled my ears until someone else took the phone from her.

"Jake?" Kyla's father's voice filled my ear. "Jake, is this you?"

"It's me." I stopped walking and stared at the wall.

"Kyla didn't want to upset you, but insisted on calling you herself." The old man coughed to clear his throat. "Reporters started showing up a little while ago and she panicked."

My throat tightened and I stared up at the ceiling. "She doesn't need to be worrying about me right now."

"She knew this would hit you hard." Kyla's father took a deep breath. "Is Maddie with you?"

"She's asleep." I was aware that someone was trying to get my attention, but I refused to look at them.

"Are you going to be okay?" The man lowered his voice.

"Yeah, yeah. I'm fine. Take care of Kyla." I swallowed the lump in my throat. "Tell her not to worry about us and let me know what I can do to help."

"Thanks, Jake. You'll tell Maddie?"

"Yeah, I'll tell Maddie." He hung up and I looked down at my phone.

"I really need to talk to you." Someone touched my shoulder but I didn't look up. "Jake, we need to make a statement."

I watched as the screen on my phone went dark.

"C'mon Jake." Martin, one of Mom's goons, shook my shoulder. "Snap out of it. We've got to be quick."

"Back off, Martin." I heard Tony in the distance.

"We have to get ahead of this now. Jesus, we can't wait for him to get his shit together." Martin's voice rose. "Jake, Jake! You need to get it together." His voice was drowned out by the ringing in my ears. "No wonder he fucking crashed in the desert."

I heard the sound of my phone smashing into the brick wall behind the bar, I heard Tony call for reinforcements, and I heard the sounds of my fists slamming into Martin, but nothing else. The only other sound was the ringing in my ears as I threw the pompous little shit to the ground.

Someone tried to restrain me and adrenaline surged through my veins. There was a crash somewhere and I heard the sound of someone holler and the shifting of feet. My vision narrowed and I dropped into defensive position. They weren't going to take me without a fight.

I shook my head hard enough to rattle my brain. I didn't even know who was after me, but it didn't matter in the end.

"Jake, it's okay." I heard a familiar voice but it was mixed in with the ringing and hollering.

Cyrus? No, Tony. A bodyguard.

The smell of blood filling my nostrils was quickly joined by the smell of smoke. My eyes stung as memories of being trapped under the helicopter wreckage flashed before my eyes. I could almost feel the heat from the fire as Cyrus called out for Kyla.

Something restrained my arms and I fought, the memory of not being able to move too real, too raw.

"Jake?" Someone called my name, breaking into my thoughts, and I jerked backward. My good leg caught on something and I couldn't keep my footing with the prosthetic. I went down on my side hard and something crashed under me. My head bounced off the floor and my vision doubled.

"Are you hurt?" The voice was above me, but I could barely make it out. "Jake, are you hurt?"

"Get him to his room."

"Call a doctor."

"Stop!" I roared. "Take them first!"

Tony moved into my view. "Jake, you're not in Afghanistan. Understand me?"

I stopped fighting and looked up at the man. No, I wasn't in Afghanistan any more, but it was still all my fault.

Chapter 21

Maddie

A loud banging shocked me awake. I could hear what sounded like arguing voices in the distance but dismissed it as a television. The room was dark when I finally opened my eyes. It took me a minute to remember where I was and why I was still wearing a button-down shirt. I rolled over in the bed and wiped at the drool that dried on my cheek.

My phone was flashing on the desk across the room but I ignored it and went to the bathroom instead. I was about to flush the toilet when someone knocked on my door again. There was no mistaking the angry voices in the hall now. I shot a frantic look around the dark room for my pants.

"Just a minute!" I found the lamp and switched it on. My pants were partially hidden under the desk and I quickly pulled them on.

The knocking came again only louder.

"Maddie, we need you." Tony's tight voice made me look up

in shock. In all the years I'd known him, he'd never once asked for my help.

I didn't bother to button my pants or find shoes, I threw open my door to find several agents surrounding a belligerent Jake. There was a nasty bruise along one of his cheekbones that would eventually turn ugly and he was limping as if something had happened to his prosthetic.

"I told you to leave her alone." Jake slammed his fist into the wall next to his room door.

"Jake?" I rushed forward but several of the agents blocked my way. "Jake! What's wrong?"

He didn't look at me, just stared at the hole in the wall. I wasn't sure he'd even heard me.

"Maddie, have you talked to Kyla?" Tony stepped into my line of vision and I was surprised to see blood dripping from his nose. "Have you checked your messages?"

"What?" My eyes went back to where Jake stared at the wall. "What happened to Jake?"

"Have you checked your phone, Maddie?" Tony reached a hand out toward me.

"Leave her alone." I barely recognized Jake's voice. He sounded like an animal, something wild and feral.

"Take him to his room." Tony gripped my shoulder and leaned down to whisper in my ear. "I need to talk to you. Alone."

That was when all hell broke loose in the hallway of a tiny hotel in the middle of nowhere.

"Don't you fucking touch her!" I wouldn't have known that rough growl was Jake's if I hadn't seen the words ripped from his mouth. "Don't you touch her. She doesn't belong in this!"

It took seconds before he'd escaped his retinue of agents, knocking two senseless before he had his arm around Tony's neck. One of the men pushed me out of the way and I fell against the half-open door to my room. It gave way and I slid to the ground in an undignified tangle of arms and legs.

I gasped loudly and touched my head gingerly.

Jake was an animal, his unintelligible roar filled the hallway and I cringed at the anguish in his voice. I'd seen him lose it, but never like this, not like he was somewhere else living something else. Someone slammed into his back and he fell with a loud grunt into the door frame before landing at my feet. He pushed up from the floor once before falling back down and not moving.

"Jake!" I scrambled to him, but he didn't move. Carefully I checked his face and head, looking for injuries. "Tony! He's not answering me."

Panic flooded my system as I cradled Jake's head in my lap, blood staining my fingertips from a cut near his temple.

"Get a doctor." Tony's cool voice snapped orders at the people around him. With deft fingers he checked Jake's scalp and neck. "He's knocked out but he'll be okay."

"Tony, what happened?" It took me a second to realize tears were running down my face and that's why I couldn't see clearly.

"Let's get him to his room and I'll explain." Tony and another agent hefted Jake's unconscious form from my lap before another one helped me to my feet.

They laid him on his bed and one of the agents brought wash rags and a bucket of ice. I stood off a little, not sure what to do. I didn't want them to move him any more than they already had, worried about trauma to his neck and head.

"Are you going to tell me what happened?" I stared at Tony as he checked Jake's head.

"Kyla called." Tony looked up at me from where he was holding ice against Jake's temple.

"Kyla?" I frowned as my stomach knotted. "What did she want?"

"From what I could hear, she tried to call you first, Maddie. She was scared of how Jake would take the news." Tony's eyes were shadowed. "Cyrus killed himself today. Said he didn't want to be a burden any longer."

"No, they just got back from the hospital. Things were going good." I shook my head. "They had a plan and people to help them."

"Sometimes that doesn't translate right for people. Cyrus wasn't just hurt on the outside. You noticed he was hiding things, seemed down at times." Tony's eyes shifted back to Jake before looking at me again. "Just like Jake has been hiding things."

"But he killed himself?" I reached behind me for something to balance my weight. The room shifted and despair crept up my throat. "Oh, God. Kyla and those sweet babies."

"I've called and people are there helping and keeping the media at bay."

"The media? Those fucking dick hounds are nosing around? That's the last thing that family needs!" Rage filled my chest.

"Calm down, Maddie. I know you want to help them, but you have a bigger job right now." He narrowed his eyes at me. "You've got to stay calm for Jake. He needs you right now and from what I know of him, he doesn't like to need anyone."

I looked at Jake where he lay on the white bedspread of the

hotel bed. I covered my mouth to try and keep the bile down and closed my eyes.

"He's going to think this is his fault." I sucked in as much air as I could and blew it back out. "Cyrus was the only member of his team to make it back from Afghanistan."

Tony nodded his head and looked back at Jake. "You can't make his guilt better, but you can be there while he works through it."

"He's supposed to be seeing someone. I promised him—I promised to treat him like I always would if he found someone to talk to about it all." I sat down on the other side of Jake and wrapped my fingers around his hand.

"The doctor is here." An agent I didn't recognize stuck his head in the door.

"Do we know this guy?" We couldn't let some random person come in and check out the Vice President's son.

One of the ladies from the PR firm walked in ahead of the doctor holding a stack of papers. "Doctor Bonnette has been informed of what will happen should any details of this visit be made public. He has also signed all of the correct security forms and has a clean record."

"Thank you, Nicole." I stood up and looked at the papers briefly before turning my gaze to the man holding a doctor's bag. It wasn't the leather ones you see in movies, more like a paramedic's bag; a black duffle bag covered in pockets and bursting at the seams. "Doctor Bonnette, thank you for coming."

"I'm happy to help." The older man moved to the bed and sat his bag on the floor. "Can you tell me what happened?"

Tony shot me a look before I could answer and replied instead. "It's been a long week, Doc. We were downstairs watching the game and had a few beers. Just blowing off some steam. Needless to say, the roughhousing got a little out of hand and Mr. Simmon's prosthetic gave out."

"I see." The man used a pen flashlight to check Jake's pupils. "And he hit his head at some point. The gash on his cheek shouldn't need stitches, but he's bruised up pretty good."

He stuck his penlight back in his pocket and traced Jake's skull with his fingers, gently checking for an indication that anything was amiss.

"I'm going to clean his cut and prescribe medicine for his pain. He's going to be miserable when he wakes up." He dug in his bag and found the supplies he needed. "Should I check his leg while I'm here?"

"Can that wait until he wakes up?" I leaned forward and watched as the doctor cleaned Jake's cut.

"Absolutely. My office is just down the road and I can be here in a matter of minutes." The doctor looked at me and narrowed his eyes. "Have you been hurt, Miss McGuire?"

"What? No, I'm fine." I leaned back away from him.

"Forgive me for saying this, but your eyes are red and you look as though you've had a nasty shock." His astute gaze ran over me and I felt as though I was naked. It was purely clinical, as though he sensed that there was more than we'd told him.

"It's been a long press junket. I'm tired." I ran a hand over my wrinkled shirt. "I was too tired to even change before calling it a night."

"Lots of water, rest, and good food should set you straight." He smiled and I was reminded of an old-timey doctor from a Rockwell painting.

"Thank you, Doctor Bonnette."

He closed up his bag and made his way out the door. I sat down next to Jake and touched his cheek.

"I don't think you should stay, Maddie." Tony stood next to the door. "It may not be wise to be here when he wakes up."

"I'm not leaving him to wake up alone in a strange hotel room." I glared at my longtime bodyguard. "I'm staying."

"You should go back across the hall. I can come get you if he wakes up."

"I love him," I explained. "I'm not going anywhere."

Tony nodded his head. "I'll be right outside."

After he walked out I padded across the hotel room and turned on the bathroom light before turning off the rest of the lights in the room. There was a soft tap on the door and my phone was slid underneath. I picked it up, noting my father's name and immediately answered.

"Daddy," I whispered.

"Are you okay, sweetheart?" He was alone. There was no noise of people in the background or papers being shuffled.

"Yes." I sniffled, hating that I was ready to fall apart just hearing my father's voice. "Jake isn't though."

"I heard." He sighed. "I don't think he's been okay for a while."

"No." I shook my head even though he couldn't see me.

"He does a hell of a job hiding it. I almost didn't catch what was happening." I could picture my father staring off into the distance blaming himself for Jake. "I'd hoped that giving him something hands-on would give him a chance to heal on the inside."

"He needs more than to be busy." I looked over to where Jake was lying motionless. "Today was bad."

"Did he hurt you?" My father's voice sharpened.

"No, no." I hurried to explain. "He had some sort of episode when he found out about his friend. He—he—"

"I already know." There was pain in my father's voice. I knew that the lives of each of the soldiers weighed heavily on him.

"Jake took the news hard." I wiped at my eyes. "Real hard."

"We'll get him help, Maddie." My father lowered his voice. "Do you love him?"

"Yes." I sniffled. "Very much."

"Then be patient. This isn't going to be an easy road."

"I know."

"For what it's worth, I think you made a good choice, Maddie. Jake is a fine young man that will take good care of you once he figures out how to take care of himself."

"I'll take care of both of us until then."

"That's my girl." I could hear him breathing softly on the other end of the phone call. "I'm proud of you, Madeline. You've grown into a brilliant young woman."

"Thank you, Daddy."

"I'll do my best to keep Virginia at bay, but there's only so much I can do when it comes to her son." This time his sigh was rueful. "She's going to make a powerful President. It's a shame she isn't so great at being a parent."

"Not everyone can be you," I teased.

"Get some rest. I'll be checking on you."

"Love you."

"Love you, too." The phone clicked off and I looked down at it for a minute before moving again.

I turned it off and slipped it back out under the door, knowing that Tony would put it away for me. I slipped my pants off and climbed into the bed next to Jake, snuggling as close as possible.

Hours could have passed while I lay there holding the man I loved. I tucked my body next to his, hoping that it would be a comfort when he finally woke to the reality of what had happened. My mind spun from Jake to Cyrus to Kyla and their families. The pain I felt in my heart couldn't come close to what everyone else was experiencing. I thought of the pictures Kyla had texted me of little Korbin holding his tiny sister, Savannah, and the picture of Savannah tucked next to her smiling father in a hospital bed.

"I fucked up so bad." I hadn't realized Jake was awake until his deep voice rumbled through the air. "If I'd just managed to control the helicopter none of this would have happened."

I didn't say anything, instead I squeezed his fingers tightly with my own.

"I thought that if I could make things right now, fix what I'd broken, it would be okay. But I can't fix this." His voice broke. "I'm supposed to be able to handle this, to take charge and figure out what to do next, but I don't know. I don't know and I can't fix it. I can't fix it."

"Shhh. No one needs you to fix anything right now, Jake." His arm wrapped around me and he buried his face in my hair.

"I don't know what to do." His hot breath fanned across my face.

"Hold on to me, Jake." I kissed his jaw and let him pull me tightly against his chest. "Hold on to me. That's all you need to do right now."

It wasn't until his breathing steadied letting me know that he was sound asleep that my tears ran free. It wasn't until I knew I wouldn't hurt him with my own inner pain that I let go. I ached for the man I loved, for the family I'd grown close to. I ached for Cyrus and the pain he must've felt.

My heart cried for every person that came home from war bearing this horrible truth. There were no winners in war. Everyone on both sides was damaged in some way.

Chapter 22

Maddie

He hadn't spoken to me since he woke up that morning. The silence was worse than his explosion the night before because it was as if he had disappeared inside himself.

Puz danced around our feet as we made our way back into Jake's house, but even his excitement at seeing us after a week was dimmed by our solemn moods. After going outside and doing his business, Puz was stuck to Jake like glue. There was no missing his concern over Jake's dark mood.

"Why don't I make us something to eat?" I headed for the fridge before looking through the contents.

"I think you should go, Maddie." His voice was even and sure.

"I don't have anything to do tomorrow. I can stay here." I didn't look at him, but continued to rummage through the food. If I looked at him, I might break into a million pieces. I didn't want to be sent away. Especially not when he was so desperately hurting.

"No, Maddie." He closed the refrigerator door.

I turned away from him and opened a cabinet instead. "Maybe soup? Or I think you had some of that nasty canned stew you like. I could make rice to go with it."

"Maddie, look at me." He sounded so confident, so sure in what he was about to do. "I want to be alone."

"I don't want to look at you, Jake. I don't want you to see whatever is on your face." I pulled the rice out of the cabinet and moved toward the stove. "I just want to be here with you."

"You have to go." He barricaded me in a corner with the cabinets and lifted my chin.

"No." I narrowed my eyes and fought to control my racing heart. "I'm staying."

"I don't want you here." His eyes were so dark, so full of pain that I'd have given anything to touch him, to hug him. "I want you to leave."

"You don't mean that, Jake. Being alone isn't the answer right now." The bag of rice I was holding shook. "You're hurting and I can help."

"No." He shook his head. "You can't help me. Having you here, moving around in my house just irritates me. I want you out."

"Jake," I whispered. That had hurt. "You don't mean that."

"Stop telling me what I mean," he snapped. "I know what words I'm using. I mean exactly what I'm saying. I don't need you here and I don't want you here. I want to be left alone."

"You're hurting me." I raised a hand to my chest in an attempt to soothe my heart. He wasn't touching me any longer, but I felt as if he was crushing my heart. "Don't say that, Jake."

"Go." He took a step back and pried my fingers from the rice bag.

"Don't," I whispered. "Please, don't push me out. I love you, Jake. I love you and I want to be with you."

His face froze for a half a second as if my words had shocked him back to reality, but then a black cloud filled his features.

"You don't love me, Maddie. You don't even know me." He slammed one of the cabinets shut and turned around. "Now, get out."

"Jake, you love me too. I know you do." I touched his shoulder.

He jerked away from my hand and whirled to face me with angry eyes. "You know nothing about me. Nothing. You don't know what I'm capable of or what I've done. You don't know how I feel right now or why I feel that way. You don't love me. And I don't love you. We had fun, but time is up. Move on and get over it."

I stepped back as if he had hit me, tears forming in my eyes. Puz whined in the background, his head going between me and his owner.

"That's not fucking fair, Jake. Not fair."

"Life isn't fair."

"No, it's not." I choked on a sob. "You're hurting. You don't know how to handle all of those emotions. I get that. But I don't accept that you don't love me. I've seen it in your eyes and I'm not giving up. I'll give you your space, but I'm not going away, Jake. What we have together isn't going away. I will be here for you."

I set the can of beef stew on the counter and walked out of the kitchen. Those few short steps were some of the hardest I'd ever taken. Walking out quietly was the last thing I wanted to do. I wanted to scream and throw things until Jake saw sense, but I knew that was the last thing that would work.

I went straight for the door, picking up my jacket and purse as I went. I opened the door and ran into the back of one of the agents.

"Mr. Simmon has asked to be left alone."

"I'm his mother," a woman explained. "And if that's not good enough then I'm the Vice President of this country. Now get out of my way."

I pushed the tears from my face before stepping around the agent. "He doesn't want to see anyone, Virginia."

"I see." Her eyes ran over my bag and jacket. "He's finally gotten you out of his system and you assume that means he doesn't want to see anyone."

"I'm not assuming anything. He made it very clear that he doesn't want to be bothered." I set my bag down and pulled my jacket on.

"Family isn't a bother. Family is there for you when your world falls apart. Family helps make the tough decisions." The older woman stepped closer and lowered her voice. "You aren't family. You're a distraction, a waste of time. You're nothing more than that slutty reporter I gave your story to. You just lasted a little longer than she did."

"You leaked my arrest to Veronica?" I hissed the words wishing that her comparison didn't hurt.

"Yes, I did. As soon as I saw Jake look at you, I knew I needed to get ahead of the damage you would wreck." Her smile made my stomach rebel and I thought I'd lose it on the sidewalk for everyone to see. "I'd hoped when he went home with her I wouldn't have to deal with you at all."

"You threw me under the bus. I can almost wrap my head around that," I said. "But to pimp out your own son? That's some sick shit, Virginia."

"Watch your mouth, little girl." She took a step toward me. "I do what is best for this family."

"No, leaving your son alone is what's best for your family right now, but that's not what you're here to do."

"Leave, Maddie. There isn't anything you can do." I looked past her to Jake's father. His expression was firm, but there was an uncomfortable pain lurking in his eyes. It was almost a shock to see him out of his military uniform and even more so to see him with his wife. What wasn't a shock were the reporters lining the street, complete with cameras.

"He needs to be with people that love him." I shook my head. "This is going to make things worse."

"Are you implying that I don't love my son?" Virginia's nostrils flared.

"I'm not implying anything. I'm saying it." I pointed my finger at the other woman, like a witch casting a curse. "You're only here for yourself. You wouldn't know love if it bit you on the fucking nose and refused to let it go. What are you going to do, Virginia? Drag him out here for pictures with you? Pretend like you knew anything about Cyrus and his family? I bet you're hoping he breaks down and does something that'll get you a bunch of pity votes. You're nothing but a self-centered, power-hungry bitch."

"Get out of my way, Maddie." Virginia narrowed her eyes.

"I'm standing on public property. A sidewalk. You can't tell me to leave for no reason."

"I swear to God that I will have you arrested for being a little bitch." Her voice hardened.

"You can't arrest me for calling it like I see it." I put my hands on my hips.

"You know what I can do? I can kill every bit of legislation you propose. You can kiss your little bill goodbye." Virginia licked her lips and brushed some of her hair away from her shoulder. "It'll never make it out of the House. And if you so much as dare show up near Jake again, I'll have him committed. Do you understand me?"

I launched myself at Virginia, ready to tear her face to shreds, but something heavy and solid caught me in a steel-like vise.

"Don't, Maddie," Jake whispered against my head. "Don't give her what she wants."

A sob broke free from my mouth. "Jake?"

"Go." He pushed me toward Tony but didn't look at me.

"Jake—" Tony managed to get a grip on my shoulders and turn me away from the scene on the sidewalk.

"Don't, Maddie." Tony's voice was next to my ear. "It's what she wants."

"Call off your dogs, Mom." Jake stood in front of his parents, back straight. "I'm not playing your games. You're not welcome here."

"I'm your mother. You can't kick me out."

"I can and I am." Jake's voice was hard.

Tony pulled me toward one of the black SUV's before shoving me into the backseat and I didn't get to hear the rest of Jake's words. I turned to try and watch what happened, but we were out of view within seconds.

Tears crowded my eyes the entire ride to the White House while Tony sat next to me, holding my hand. He didn't say anything, which was for the best considering that I probably wouldn't have heard anything.

Once I was safely locked away in my room I paced back and forth, feeling the need to do something and having no idea what to do.

I picked up my phone and dialed a number by heart.

"Virginia is going to kill our bill."

"Why would she do that?"

"Let's just say I'm not her favorite person right now."

"What if we take your name off?" Senator Fletcher's voice was soft. We both believed in the bill. It was a practical question.

"I don't know if that will work. She'd still think of it as mine." I thought about it. "It would probably be best if we waited."

Senator Fletcher sighed. "Something must've really cooked her beans."

"We had a very loud argument on the sidewalk in front of Jake's place." My voice broke on his name and I closed my eyes.

"How is he?" Her voice was gentle.

"I don't know. Not good." I chewed on my bottom lip.

"I'm sorry, Maddie."

"Thanks." Sorry was exactly how I felt. "I'll be in touch."

"Of course, darling."

The phone clicked off and I threw it against the wall.

Chapter 23

Jake

"You've got to stretch, reach for something better, Jake." The doctor's voice was soothing, patient. "Have you talked to any of your friends? What about Cyrus's wife? Or your sisters?"

I wanted to punch him in the face so I didn't respond. How did I know this man was my mother's little bitch? He hadn't mentioned Maddie.

"This anxiety and turmoil isn't good for you. How can we reach for something better? What would be better for you?"

I stared at him and crossed my arms. I wasn't talking to this dill-hole. I didn't care what kind of classical music played in his waiting room or how much he encouraged me to trust him. My mother had picked him out and that meant he was her puppet.

"Jake, trust is scary, but we can do this together."

"Trust?" I uncrossed my arms and leaned forward. "How can I trust you? My mother picked you. Do you know what that means? That means she knows she can control you, she can get to our confidential talks and then share the information with the rest of the world."

"That's not true. That's something you've worked up in your mind, but it doesn't make it reality." The doctor leaned back in his chair and held his pen between his hands.

"Reality." I snorted. "Reality is that you have no idea who you are dealing with, Doc. My mother is not a regular mother. She is the Vice President and you're a military psychologist. Anything I tell you will be on her desk within hours."

He scribbled on his giant yellow legal pad. I tried to not be annoyed by the scratching sounds.

"I'd like to prescribe some medication, but it's not going to work if you won't take it."

"And what are you prescribing medicine for? We've talked about nothing. You have no idea what to prescribe medicine for." I sneered at the man in his white lab coat.

"I believe you are suffering from a paranoid personality disorder that is heightened because of your depression. If we can help with your depression, then the rest will fall into line."

I stood up and stretched, making sure he realized how little I thought of his diagnosis.

"Time's up, Doc." I walked out the door and didn't look back. Even if I'd thought he genuinely cared or wanted to help, I wouldn't have talked to him. A military doctor was out of the question. A civilian doctor was also out of the question because I didn't trust my mother to not put pressure on some honest person to get the information she wanted. No reason to have my mom break anyone else in her attempt to reach the top.

I left the building and went straight for my truck. I'd started refusing the car service with the agents. I felt better in my own vehicle, I had more control when I was driving myself. I didn't like feeling as if I couldn't take care of myself or for people to look at me and think I was being driven around because I was broken.

And thanks to my mother, lots of people were looking at me as if I was a misshapen mound of human flesh. The only good thing about her shouting to the world that I was suffering from PTSD was that most of the reporters had backed off. It was interesting to see some of them developed a conscience. Not all of them, but more than I'd expected.

On my way home I passed a group of people running an animal adoption clinic outside of a pet store. I glimpsed the flash of light brown hair pulled into a ponytail and took my foot off the gas. As it hovered over the brake pedal I realized it wasn't Maddie, but someone much younger.

I hit the gas and scolded myself for hesitating. I'd been ignoring Maddie's phone calls and voice messages for over a week. I hid like a pathetic child when she showed up at my place every few days, turning up the television to drown out her knocking. Part of me wanted to see her so badly that I'd dialed her number a million times before pressing clear on my phone. The part of me that hit the cancel button was stronger, darker. I didn't want to poison Maddie.

She'd get over me and love someone else eventually.

I clenched the steering wheel and almost missed a stop sign. I slammed on the brakes and gritted my teeth.

I fucking hated that more than anything I hated in my life. Well, except for myself. She'd told me she loved me and I'd shoved her away, practically thrown her out the door.

Where she'd been accosted by my mother. I'd watched like a coward from behind a curtain while my mom tore the woman I loved down.

Until I couldn't take it anymore.

I didn't remember going down the steps, but I did remember the way Maddie had felt wrapped in my arms as I dragged her away. I remembered the tears in her eyes as I'd whispered into her ear. I don't know how I'd managed to tell my mother to stuff it in front of so many people, but it had to be because of Maddie and the way she believed in me.

It was in the way she looked at me, sought my opinion on things.

God, I missed her so bad it made me sick.

There was a parking spot in front of my row house and I just barely managed to fit the big truck in place.

I got out of the driver side and onto the sidewalk before I realized there was a girl on my steps. For half a heartbeat I thought Maddie was sitting there, waiting on me and I wasn't sure how I'd turn her away again. Not face to face. Then she moved from the shadows and I realized it was red hair, not light brown.

"Caro?"

My sister stood up and smiled at me. Her bright green eyes ran over my body and she cocked her head to the side. "Don't you own an iron?"

I looked down at my pants and frowned at the wrinkled jeans. I'd picked them up off the floor this morning when I'd crawled out of bed after another sleepless night.

"You came here to pick on my clothing?"

Honestly, I didn't care. I'd missed my younger sister. I wrapped my arms around her and pulled her against my chest.

She grunted with the impact of my hug. "I saw you on the news. I thought it was Bigfoot walking through downtown until I saw your name on the bottom of the screen. Seriously, what is with this?"

She pulled out of my arms and tugged on my beard.

"Ow, that's attached to my face." I brushed her hand away.

"Why is it attached to your face?" Her green eyes narrowed at me.

"I haven't shaved." I rolled my shoulders and walked up the steps to unlock the door. "C'mon."

She followed me inside and set her purse on the entry table. Puz jumped around our feet and she immediately fell to the floor and let him crawl in her lap. Caro had always loved animals, so I wasn't surprised.

"Jake, if you don't want to shave that's fine with me. If you want to look like Hagrid from *Harry Potter*, that's fine with me too. But what I don't know, is if it's fine with you." She cuddled Puz against her chest and looked up at me.

"What are you talking about?" I turned and looked at her. We'd barely gotten into my house before she'd decided to throw down the gauntlet. She pushed Puz off her lap and stood up again.

"You. I'm talking about you." She stepped closer to me and poked my shoulder. "You pull off the rugged, five o'clock shadow thing well, but you make a pretty pathetic Bigfoot."

"I'm not trying to be Bigfoot." I reached up to massage the back of my neck.

"Then what are you trying to be?"

"I don't know!" I threw my keys at the table in an explosion of paper rattling noise. "I don't know what the hell I'm doing."

Caro leaned over and picked up the papers and restacked them on the entry table. When she stood up she didn't say anything, just watched me. Caro was my middle sister and far more sympathetic than either me or Ari. The fact that she'd risked coming here near our mom meant she was genuinely worried about me. Guilt clutched at my throat once more.

"I don't know what I'm doing." I took a step forward and pulled her into a hug. "I'm sorry. I didn't mean to snap."

She squeezed me back. "Don't be sorry, Jake. Let's decide what you're doing and do that."

"When did you grow up?" I pulled back to really look at her. She had grown up. She was beautiful with a delicate little nose and bright, intelligent eyes. Her red hair glimmered in the sunlight filtering through the window in my door.

"While you were away at war." Her sad eyes were looking at my face the way I was analyzing hers. "You look tired."

"I can't sleep." I headed for the kitchen and she followed silently behind me.

One of the great things about Caro was that she never felt the need to fill any silence. If she decided to talk to someone about anything it was because she felt compelled to. I'd always thought that was why she'd gotten along so well with the horses at our family estate in Virginia. Caro spent every waking moment with the horses. When she was younger our mother had encouraged her to participate in different competitions. I'd suspected she'd hoped Caro would end up on an Olympic pedestal. But Caro had never really cared about the competition. She'd been in it for the horses and nothing else.

"Why didn't you go to the funeral?"

"Jesus, Caro. Let me make some coffee before you start in on me, okay?" I poured ground coffee into the filter and refilled the water.

"Do you have anything to eat with the coffee?" Caro opened a cabinet. "There are crackers in here, Jake. Nothing else." She pulled the rumpled package out and held it up for me to look at.

"I haven't gone shopping." The last time I'd gone grocery shopping was with Maddie before the press junket. My heart clenched at the reminder of how long it had been since we'd been normal.

As if the universe was intent on torturing me, my phone beeped. I picked it up, knowing without a doubt that it would be Maddie. She'd stopped calling and leaving voice mails. She knew me well enough to guess that I deleted them without listening to them.

She'd be right. It was painful to hear her voice.

But her text messages read like a book. She told me all about her day, the volunteer staff at RCVB, and about new animals at the shelter. The messages always ended asking about me and Puz and telling me she missed me.

I sat the phone back down without reading the text and turned to get a coffee cup.

"You didn't go to your friend's funeral. They made sure there was a chair next to Maddie." Caro's voice wasn't accusatory. She was merely stating a fact.

"No, I didn't." I looked at my sister and for once didn't hold back. "I couldn't, Caro"

"Have you seen his family? I saw their pictures in the news. They look like nice people." She didn't fidget, didn't look away from me. "They could probably use some friends. Maddie has been going over there every couple of days. She worries she's going to crowd them."

"She would." I looked at my sister. "Did Maddie ask you to come here?"

"No. I came because you didn't answer my phone calls. I

know what Maddie's been up to because she *has* answered my phone calls."

I grunted, not sure what to do with all of that information. Part of me was glad that Maddie hadn't punked out on her friends the way I had, but it also made me feel even guiltier.

"Hope you don't want creamer." I glanced in her direction. "Because as you saw, I'm out of everything."

"I gave up caffeine." Caro picked up my phone from the counter. "You really should put a pass code on your phone. She misses you, you know."

"Why did you give up caffeine?" I didn't look at her because I didn't want her to see how much I missed Maddie too.

"It made my anxiety worse." At that I did turn around to look at her.

"You—anxiety?" I frowned. Caro had been a sensitive, nervous girl growing up but I hadn't realized it had affected her so much.

"Yeah." She hopped on the counter and swung her legs. "I'd drink lots of caffeine when I was staying up to study. I started keeping a chart of my panic attacks and I realized they were worse when I was using lots of caffeine and not getting enough sleep."

"How long have you had panic attacks?" I turned to look at her fully, the familiar feeling of guilt gnawing at my stomach. Only she would think to keep a chart of her panic attacks.

"As long as I can remember."

"I'm sorry. I didn't know."

"It's okay." She smiled at me. "I mean, I see someone and I work through it."

"What about Mom?" Rage filled my body. She would use this to control Caro. "She'll use this, Caro!"

"She doesn't know." Her smile was so bright it lit up the room and her giggle loosened something in my chest. "It's liberating to have something she knows nothing about."

"But your security detail? The bills?"

"Skype appointments mean no one knows I see the doctor and what's the point of being a trust fund baby if I can't pay for my own doctor bills?" She shrugged.

"How did you find this doctor? I mean, if you only talk to him on the computer he might not even be a real doctor! What if he's using the bathroom or something when you call? Do you talk to him while he shits?"

She laughed so hard tears formed in her eyes. "It's a woman and no, I've never talked to her while she was going to the bathroom. She deals with a lot of high-profile clients."

"Who told you about her?" I poured my coffee and thought about it.

"Chance."

I looked over at her and raised an eyebrow. Chance was an actor that had attached himself to my sister when we'd been younger. He made our home life look like *Waltons* reruns. His mother was a mega-star and his father was from old money. Their lives had been splashed across media from the get-go. His father was a real dick and his mother wasn't exactly up for mother of the year award. Where his father was uptight and worried about appearances, Chance's mother, Merie, had been more about living life to the fullest. Needless to say, that marriage hadn't lasted and Chance had bounced between homes.

It was pretty bad when he thought our family was normal.

"How is Chance?" The last I'd heard, he was dating some glamorous model in Spain.

"Filming a new movie." Caro rolled her eyes. "Dating his co-star again."

"The same co-star he's dated before or dating another co-star?"

"This one is new. I like her and hate knowing that he's going to break her heart."

"Huh." I'd always thought there might be something between my sister and her well photographed friend, but as far as I knew it had remained platonic. "Maybe this one will stick."

"Mm-hmm. It's Chance, Jake. The only way it's going to stick is if she clubs him upside the head and drags him to her cave. The guy can't seem to stay satisfied." She fiddled with her shirt.

"And, uh, that upsets you?" I frowned, not sure if I was supposed to ask those kinds of questions.

"Oh, God. No. But I do feel bad for Claudia. She's nice, not spoiled by the glitz yet." She choked out a laugh. "Chance is good-looking, but it's never been like that for us. I don't know. I think I know too much about him."

"You're the one seeing the doctor." I looked down at my coffee. "I'm not exactly up for any sort of advice."

"I'm here to dole out the advice today." She jumped off the counter and walked around the kitchen looking at things. "You need to find someone to talk to. There isn't anything to be ashamed of."

"I'm not ashamed." My response was a little too fast, a little too loud. "Maybe I am. I don't know. I'm willing to talk to someone. I promised Mad—it's finding someone to talk to that's proving difficult. The faster Mom shoves doctors in my face, the faster I run in the opposite direction."

"It sucks being the Vice President's kid." Caro scrunched up her nose. "But you can find someone."

"Like your Skype doctor." I leveled my gaze on her.

"No. Dr. Darden is too gentle and patient for you." She sized me up with her eyes. "You need someone that's going to push you and not put up with your shit."

"Thank you, Doctor Caro. I didn't realize seeing a psychologist meant you became one."

"Har, har. It doesn't give me a license to practice, but being your sister means I have twenty-two years of experience dealing with you and your stubborn pride. You don't need someone mushy, feely. You need no-nonsense."

"I'll take that into consideration." I watched as she poked at all the little touches Maddie had added in the kitchen over the past weeks. "Do you want to go get dinner?"

"Am I going with my brother or with Bigfoot?"

"I'll change." I set my coffee down.

"And shower." She pointed at her face and made a circle motion. "And do something about all that."

"Some women like scruffy men."

"Scruffy, yes. Old Man Winter, no."

"It's not that long." I ran my hand over my chin noting that it was longer than I'd realized.

"Did you know your facial hair grows in uneven? That's why sexy men with beards take care of them. And there's something stuck in there, by the way. Otherwise you look like Bigfoot."

"So, did your Skype doctor give you a sense of humor too?"

"Find out at dinner." She walked out of the kitchen looking at everything in my place with interest. She lingered on things that Maddie had picked out, little ways she'd claimed the space. Puz's food and water bowl shaped like puzzle pieces. The spice rack she'd hung on one of the cabinets. "And I'm calling Ari. She's dying to see you. We can meet somewhere."

"Won't Mom know you're here then?" I stopped on the stairs before heading to my room.

"Mom already knows I'm here." She turned and looked at me. "Ari needed a break so I'm here to share the load."

I walked back down the stairs, wrapped an arm around her neck and kissed her head. "Thanks."

"You stink." She looked up at me. "And you're welcome."

Chapter 24

Maddie

The car ride to the Lilarian embassy was silent. Tony had been withdrawn and quieter than usual—even for him, but I had no idea why. Since he'd held my hand in the car from Jake's house he'd basically been mute.

I hadn't wanted to come to dinner by myself but no one was able to come with me. Phoebe was back in town but had been busy and couldn't come, to her utter disappointment. The last time we'd really talked she'd gushed about the pictures of me dancing with Alex in the papers and online.

I'd worn the same outfit I wore on my first date with Jake. Maybe it was because my heart was hurting and I'd felt sentimental when I saw it hanging up in my closet. Or maybe it was just because it was an outfit already put together. As lazy as I was, I knew I could have found something else to wear, but there'd been no denying the ache in my chest when I'd seen the clothes. I missed Jake so much, but I kept hoping he'd reach out to me. I was giving him his space, but I hadn't given up on us.

It had been weeks since I'd told him I loved him and he'd kicked me out. It had been weeks since I'd heard his voice or seen him face to face. And even though I knew he was hurting it had been so painful to lay it all out there and be told to leave. But I wasn't going to give up.

I knew that if he was trying to avoid me, he wasn't going to listen to voice mails, so short of stalking him and showing up places he might be, I sent him text messages. Only one every day so I didn't stress him out, but he knew someone out there loved him.

Cyrus's death scared me. It scared me that someone could seem so normal, so put together while talking about the future, and then dead the next day. Was Jake at that point? Would Jake commit suicide if he didn't find help?

That thought haunted me every single day.

I knew his mother had set up appointments for him, but from what I could gather, they'd all gone poorly. And they would continue to do so. Anyone his mother sent to him would fail for the sole reason that his mother had chosen them. Jake couldn't seem to open up. He was scared of what he'd find and he wasn't going to risk opening himself up to more hurt with a doctor he couldn't trust.

We pulled up in front of the Lilarian embassy and I looked out at the building. It stood out on Embassy Row and I found myself wondering if it had served as a church in a previous life. The building had Gothic turrets that stretched for the sky and stained glass covered the side facing the street. Ivy trailed along the steps and I found it charming that they'd let it grow instead of having it removed. Their flag flew high for everyone to see and armed guards stood at the door, but I'd lost my awe for armed strangers a long time ago.

Tony didn't say or ask anything, just waited for my signal to open the door. He never asked about Jake, but when we'd come back from one of the uneventful trips to see Jake, Tony would just nod and tell me to keep at it. There were times when I felt as if he had known things would work out this way, but I'd never understand how.

I stared out the window and nodded my head for Tony to open the door. One of the guards stepped forward and requested my name.

"Madeline McGuire." I held up my ID for one of the guards to inspect. "I'm having dinner with the Prince and Duchess."

"Yes, ma'am."

They led me inside, but Tony was asked to stay outside of the residential area. He settled into a chair near a group of Lilarian security playing some type of card game. His back was stiff and I knew that he wouldn't be joining in the fun. When Tony was on duty, there was no break in concentration.

"Maddie!" Samantha walked across a plush rug in bare feet, a gorgeous toddler with wavy brown hair tucked against her hip. She leaned forward and kissed my cheek.

"Samantha, thanks for having me over." I smiled down at the little girl looking at me. "Hi, I'm Maddie. What's your name?"

"Mah-tha." She smiled shyly up at me. "Wike Mad-dee."

"That's right. They both start with an 'M.'" Samantha bopped her hip up and down and elicited a giggle from her daughter. "You're so smart."

I watched the mother and daughter, my heart lifting a little at the normalcy of their exchange.

"Kick your shoes off, Maddie. We don't stand on ceremony

here." She smiled at me. "In fact, if you weren't coming tonight we'd probably be sitting on the floor watching television. Martha likes to picnic."

"Martha, I think we're going to get along perfectly." I smiled at the little girl and she buried her face in her mother's shoulder before peeking back up at me with big blue eyes while I took my shoes off and placed them near the door.

"Alex will be back soon. He had a call come in from home," Samantha explained.

"Everything okay?" I was a bit jealous of the way Samantha said *home*. I didn't really have one of those anymore. If I was being honest, I hadn't had one in almost eight years. The White House didn't feel like home. My dorm rooms hadn't felt like home. All of those were temporary and the word *home* implied something permanent.

"Oh, yeah. You know how it goes. Little things no one else seems capable of handling and he can fix with a simple yes or no." She looked at me over her shoulder and rolled her eyes. "Rules and etiquette. We have a fantastic staff, an amazing group of people, but some things just have to be approved by him."

"And by you?" I teased.

"God yes. Why do they need me to okay every single piece of silverware? It's a fork! You use it to put food in your mouth. Who the hell cares if it has a three leaf ivy pattern on the stem?"

"Who hell cares?" Martha held out her hands as if she just couldn't fathom it.

Samantha's face transformed into a mask of utter horror as she shook her head no. "That's a grown-up word, Martha. You can't say hell. Okay? Don't say hell in front of dada. Don't say hell at all."

"Mama say hell alls time." Martha cocked her head to the side and looked up at her mother with a confused expression.

I coughed into my hand, unable to contain my amusement any longer.

"Don't give me that look, you little monster! It doesn't work on me." She dug her fingers into her daughter's side until the little girl squealed in happiness.

"I hear my favorite girls." Alex's voice sounded around the corner.

"Don't say grown-up words." Samantha held up a finger to her lips before turning and smiling at her approaching husband. "There you are!"

Alex leaned down to kiss his wife and daughter before holding his hand out to me. "So good of you to join us tonight."

"Thank you for the invitation." I smiled up at the prince.

"I believe the chef said we were having chicken nuggets and cheese noodles." Alex made a serious face.

"Macaroni and cheese," Samantha explained.

"I'll skip the chicken nuggets but I'm down for some mac 'n' cheese."

"He's teasing you." Samantha handed her daughter over to her husband. "We're having spinach lasagna roll-ups. Is that okay? We can do something else if you'd prefer."

"That sounds delicious." I looked at the happy couple.

"Good." Alex transferred Martha to his back and ran-hopped his way out of the room. "Time to cook!"

"He's cooking?" I raised an eyebrow.

"Amazing, right?" Samantha's face took on a dreamy look. "He's really good in the kitchen."

"You, lucky, lucky woman." I shook my head.

She threaded her arm through mine as we followed her little family. "So very much. Now, tell me why your guy isn't with you."

"He's dealing with some things." I chewed on my lip. I'd texted Jake about the dinner, but as usual never got a response.

"I saw the news about your friend." Samantha squeezed my arm. "It's hard to lose the people we care about."

"Yes." I looked at Samantha. "Everyone responds to it differently."

"I suspect that Jake is letting his guilt eat at him." Her tone was soft. "I'm not trying to intrude, but I like you. And I like Jake. It makes me sad to see you hurting."

"I'm holding on to hope that he will find someone that can help him in ways I can't." My voice broke on that last word. "It's killing me, but he won't let me help. He won't talk to me at all. And I do mean at all. I haven't seen him in weeks."

I'd seen a picture of him with his sisters in the paper. He'd even been smiling, which was a vast improvement to the grimace he had been wearing, but it wasn't the same as seeing him in person. It had only highlighted how little I knew about what was happening with him.

She stopped me in the hallway. "What you need tonight is friends and a good home-cooked meal. We can give that to you and maybe the rest will fall in place."

Samantha's warm eyes filled with compassion.

"Thank you." I didn't think, just leaned forward and hugged the woman in front of me. It felt natural, like I'd known her my whole life. I was suddenly glad I'd come alone, because I wouldn't have been this open with anyone else to witness my perilous hold on my emotions.

When we entered the kitchen I tried to not laugh at the sight of a prince wearing a ruffled apron while his princess daughter pointed at her mother with a flour-covered hand.

"Where hell been?" The little girl put her hands on her hips and said something else I didn't understand.

"I see you've been teaching our daughter more English." Alex looked over his shoulder at Samantha who turned scarlet.

"You told her to say that!" Samantha put her hands on her hips, which made it clear where the little girl had learned that pose.

He chuckled but refused to own up to it. Instead he started ordering us about the kitchen and we fell into a comfortable conversation. It felt normal, routine.

It was fantastic. And exactly what I'd needed.

By the time dinner was ready, no one wanted to deal with a table and place settings. So we sat at the kitchen island and devoured the pan of vegetarian lasagna.

Martha ate far more than I would have thought possible before eventually throwing her fork on the counter and saying something in Lilarian.

"It's not nice to speak a different language around people who can't understand it." Alex pointed his fork at his daughter.

"No mo' zana." She leaned back and rubbed her belly. "No room!"

"And what about dessert? Is there no room for raspberry sherbet?" Samantha asked.

The little girl felt along her stomach as if she might find a little pocket of space. She lifted her hand, her finger and thumb spread apart. "This much room left."

"Then you can have that much sherbet." Samantha reached across the island and touched Martha's nose.

"No boop!"

Alex and Samantha both laughed but I wasn't sure if I'd heard correctly.

"What was that?"

"She doesn't want her mother to boop her nose."

"No nice." Martha shook her head.

"I see." I smiled at the little girl. "No boop."

The evening was so peaceful, I didn't realize how much time had passed until Martha fell asleep in Alex's lap. I looked down at my phone and frowned.

"Oh my gosh. It's after ten. I should let you get to sleep." I stood up and fought a yawn. I was more than ready to get some sleep myself.

"Come see us in Lilaria?" Samantha stood up from her spot on the fancy sofa.

"I'd love to." I hugged and tried to convey how much it meant by squeezing a little tighter. "Thank you so much for dinner."

"Any time." Samantha smiled up at me. "You've got my number. We'll be in touch."

"Would you mind putting Martha in bed? I'll be right up to tuck her in." Alex shifted the sleeping toddler to his wife's arms. "I'll see our guest out."

"Good night, little friend." I kissed my finger and touched it to her forehead.

Samantha smiled and disappeared down a corridor while I put my shoes back on.

"Maddie, I hope you don't mind, but I took the liberty of getting some information for you." Alex tucked his hands into his trouser pockets and shrugged sheepishly.

"What sort of information?" I got the last shoe on and looked over at the prince.

"When my father died, there was a doctor who I talked with for several years. I trust him with my life."

I felt my eyebrow raise, not sure where he was going with this information.

"The thing is, I know your friend has been having a difficult time." Alex rocked back on his heels a bit and glanced at me with gentle eyes. "And I know how hard it is to find someone you can trust to talk to. Especially, when you worry that someone might use that information to their advantage. Someone that might have means to getting your privileged conversations."

I closed my eyes. The last person you should have to worry about hurting you was your own mother.

"I didn't know you'd talked with someone. It must've been helpful."

"What I'm trying to highlight here is that no one knew. Dr. Beaudreau doesn't work for your government, he isn't a citizen that might experience pressure from influential people, and I happen to know he's in town right now."

"You think he would work with Jake?" I bit my lip. "From what I've heard Jake is refusing to talk to anyone, but maybe if it's someone from another country . . ."

"That was exactly my thought." He handed me a card and I looked it over. "This is his information."

"So I should just call him? Or try to give the information to Jake?"

"Maddie, I hope this doesn't offend you, but I've talked with the doctor and we had a slightly different idea."

When he was finished explaining, I felt hope flare in my chest. I looked up at Alex and fought the tears in my eyes.

"Thank you." I launched myself at him and he returned my hug.

"It was no problem."

"I guess we're even now." I sniffed and chuckled.

"Well, I do repay my debts." Alex led me to the front of the embassy. "We'll be in touch." He kissed my cheek before nodding at the guards to open the door.

Tony fell in step behind me and as I climbed in the car, I felt as if a weight had been lifted from my shoulders.

Chapter 25

Jake

There was a light tapping at my front door that immediately set Puz to barking.

Worried that it was Maddie, I peeked through the curtains to see a familiar blond head. Air left my lungs in a rush and I thought about pretending I wasn't home, but my conscience wouldn't let me.

"Kyla?" I opened the door and looked down at the petite woman. Her usual chipper face wasn't as peppy and there were circles under her eyes, but her smile was genuine when she saw me.

"Jake!" She reached out and immediately wrapped her arms around me. "I was worried you wouldn't answer the door."

"How'd you know I was home?" My truck was currently having the tires changed.

She looked up at me and her cheeks turned pink. "Well, I've been waiting. I saw you get dropped off, waited a little bit and then came over." She pointed at her car and that's when I realized she was alone. No family or children with her.

"Where are the kids? They're not in the car are they?" I frowned.

"God, no. They're with my mom." Kyla glared up at me. "I'm not going to leave my kids in the car, Jake."

"Sorry. Of course not." I scratched at the scruff on my chin.

"Are you going to invite me in?" She waited patiently, obviously expecting me to do just that.

I hadn't let anyone in the house except for my sisters. Not since I'd told Maddie to leave. But this was Kyla and I owed her.

"Uh, sure." I stepped out of the way while Puz jumped up and down like a possessed demon. "Calm down, Puz."

"Oh my God. He's missing a leg!" Kyla swept Puz up into her arms while he peppered her with kisses. "I mean, I knew that from Maddie, but still! He's so cute."

"Do you want something to drink? To sit down?" I was out of practice talking to people, even with someone friendly like Kyla.

"I can't stay long. I just came to tell you something." She set her keys down on my little table.

"What's that?" I looked down at her and frowned.

Instead of answering me she reared back and punched me in the gut. It was so unexpected I fell back against the wall and clutched my abs. I looked at the tiny woman with shock.

"Ow."

"Now, do you feel better?" She shook her hand.

"What?" I stared at her in disbelief.

"Do you feel better? You felt guilty about what happened and now I've punched you. We're even and you can stop hiding in your house." She inspected her hand before looking back at me. "I didn't really hurt you did I?"

"Uh, yeah." I pushed off the wall and forced my hand away

from my stomach. "Who the hell taught you to punch like that?"

"Cyrus." Instead of looking sad, she smiled up at me. "How'd I do? Did I really hurt you?"

"Yeah. Cyrus would be proud." I couldn't help the smile that tugged at my mouth. "Really proud."

"Good." She picked up her keys before looking back at me. "I didn't do it for me, you know. Cyrus wasn't your fault, Jake."

I didn't agree with her, but it seemed rude to explain that when she'd taken the time to drive over and punch me.

Her eyes finally took on some of the sorrow I'd expected. "Cyrus was Cyrus's fault. It's not my fault, it's not your fault. And God, I miss him so much there are times I don't think I'll ever survive but then I look at my kids and my mom and dad. I talk to his parents. And you know what?"

"What?"

"I realize that there are a lot of other people in my life to help fill the void he left." She looked away from me. "I'm not perfect and times I cry. I cry a lot. Sometimes I'm so angry at Cyrus I want to beat things. I want to scream at him for leaving me, leaving the kids. Then I cry again. But I keep going, Jake."

I didn't know what to say. I didn't know how to respond to something so honest.

Her eyes lifted to mine. "I keep going. And you have to keep going too. Do you understand me? You have to keep going and letting the other people that love you help fill that void you have inside. Cyrus hid that hole in him and it ate him up. You can't let that happen."

I looked down at this incredibly strong woman and couldn't find words to respond so I hugged her. Tears formed in my eyes and I took a deep breath.

Finally she pulled back and gripped my arms. "Do what you have to do to get better, okay? If you feel guilty and think you owe me somehow, then you can repay me by getting better. I want you to stop hiding in this house. I want you to call Maddie and tell her you love her, because I know you do. I've seen it all over your face when you're together."

"Okay." I wiped my nose with my arm. "I'm sorry, Kyla. I should have been able to help. If I hadn't missed those mercs while flying none of this would have happened."

"Don't make me punch you again." She laughed even as tears ran down her face. "This wasn't your fault, Jake. Blame the general that gave you the orders, blame the people that shot down your 'copter. Because none of this was your fault. So do what you have to to deal with all of this, to accept that it wasn't your fault."

I ducked my head, not wanting her to see me cry.

"And call your woman, Jake. She's hurting but doesn't want to make things tougher on you." Kyla mimed punching me again and I dodged out of the way. She really had landed a solid hit. "I've lost someone I loved, but she doesn't have to."

"I'll try." It was the best I could manage.

"And you need to come over next Friday. I'm having a barbeque and if you don't show up, I'm calling backup. Got it?" She pulled away from me and headed for the door. "I've got to go. This is the longest I've been away from the kids since . . . Well, it's never easy to leave a newborn."

"Thank you." I followed her to the door.

"For punching you? Anytime." She looked back at me with wide eyes. "Did I really do it right?"

"Yeah. You did it right."

She smiled and opened the door but stopped short.

"Hello, is Jake home?"

I peered past Kyla and frowned at the thin man wearing a tweed jacket and bow tie. I didn't recognize him and it was odd for the security detail to let a stranger past them without calling first.

"Yeah, I was just going." Kyla shrugged her shoulders. "Friday. My house. Or I send reinforcements that punch harder than I do."

"I hear you, Rocky."

"She seems like a lively young woman." The older man watched as Kyla crossed the street. "Is she your girlfriend?"

"What?" I looked at the man. "Who are you?"

"Beaudreau." The man handed me a card. "I'm a good friend of his royal highness, Prince Alex."

"Alex?" I looked down at his card. He had a PhD, but there was no other information to tell me why he was on my doorstep.

"May I come in?" The man nodded toward my house. Not really sure why I stepped back and let him walk inside.

"Why would the Prince of Lilaria send me a doctor?" I held the card up.

"He thought you might need someone to confide in. I'm a psychologist, Mr. Simmon." The little man looked around the entryway and I felt as though he was bookmarking everything for catalogue.

"I'm feeling a little slow here. I'm not really sure why you're here."

"Jake, do you mind if I call you that? I'm not much for formality." He cupped his hands behind his back. "Jake, let's be frank. You've experienced some serious trauma in the last year and a half. That could mean nothing or could mean everything. The fact is, you need someone to talk to. Someone you can trust."

"Why should I trust you?" I frowned and looked back at the card. "I don't know you. You could be a grocery clerk."

The man pulled out a phone and dialed a number. He listened for a minute before talking.

"Yes, I'm here. Yes. Of course." He handed me the phone. "Alex would like to speak with you."

I took the phone and held it up to my ear.

"Alex?" I couldn't keep the distrust from my tone.

"Jake, good. I'm glad he caught you." The Prince's voice answered me, but I was still suspicious. "I know this is weird, but I thought you might be having trouble finding someone to confide in. I also know, that like me, you're probably feeling stubborn and don't like being backed into a corner, but I have the best of intentions. Beaudreau was my psychologist when I was younger. I can personally vouch for him. But he has more going for him. He's not part of your military and he's not a U.S. citizen. No one can pressure him to share your confidential information. And even if they did pressure him, he'd likely tell them to stuff it."

I barked out a laugh, looking at the proper man in a bow tie standing in my foyer. The man looked like he wouldn't hurt a fly. Not on purpose.

"Give him a shot," Alex said.

"And how do I know this isn't some elaborate hoax? That you're really Prince Alex?"

"Maddie had dinner with me and Samantha last night. I count her a friend and would like to do the same with you. I hate seeing my friends hurt." He lowered his voice. "You don't let go of a woman like her."

I looked at the ceiling and then at the man standing in my parlor.

"I'm going to check this shit out." I threw the doctor's card in the bowl on the little table. "But if you are who you say you are, and this guy is who you say he is, then I'll give it a shot."

"Thank you." I could picture Alex smiling which made me frown. "You won't be disappointed."

"We'll see."

"Beaudreau is fucking fantastic." Alex laughed. "I'm not worried. I hope you're ready to be called on your bullshit. He might look like a stuffy professor, but that man doesn't pull any punches."

"I think I've been punched enough for today." I rubbed my chest, wondering if I'd have a bruise.

"You'll have to explain that to me over a beer sometime."

"I think we might be able to do that." I hung up the phone and frowned.

"Are you going to show me anywhere other than the entry-way?" Beaudreau asked.

"Fuck." I handed the man his phone back. "I guess so. Do you want to look at my baby photos too?"

"I doubt you have those here, but we can talk about that later." He smirked.

"So, Doc. Do you always make house calls?" I looked over my shoulder at the man as I led the way to the living room.

"Occasionally. I've been spending a lot of time in the States recently." He picked up a trinket Maddie had bought at a stand near the fresh market.

"Do you want a bottle of water? Soda or beer?" I headed

toward my kitchen, not really caring if he thought it was a bad idea. I rarely drank, but felt like I'd earned one today.

"Thanks, that would be great." He pulled his jacket off and hung it on the back of one of the kitchen table chairs.

I pulled two bottles out of the fridge and handed him one as he rolled up his sleeves.

"It's going to be a long night, isn't it?" I sat down in a chair and leaned back.

"You never know how these things will go." He opened his beer and lifted it up to me. "Have you decided to not double check my credentials?"

"It was Alex on the phone. If he trusts you, then I guess I can."

Beaudreau had been to my house every day for over a week. It hadn't been all bad, but he definitely punched harder than Kyla.

"Are you going to go?" The old man sat at my kitchen table.

"The barbeque?" I shrugged as if the whole thing didn't make me nervous. "I think so."

"Take Puz with you," he suggested. Yeah, he definitely saw through my bullshit.

I nodded my head.

"Will Maddie be there?"

I shrugged. "I don't know."

"Has she stopped texting you?" The old man leaned forward.

"No, but she hasn't mentioned the party." I took a swallow from my soda. "I don't know if that means she's not going, or that she doesn't want me to know she's going."

The bastard chuckled.

"I'm glad this is so funny for you."

"I'm looking forward to meeting Maddie. She sounds like an amazing young woman."

"She is."

"Eventually you have to decide if you're really going to let her go or if you're going to fight to keep her."

"Fight?" I looked up wondering if that meant there was something I didn't know. Had she finally given up on me?

"We are our worst enemies, Jake. From what you say, Maddie loves you, but eventually she will have to move on for her own mental health. If you want her, you're going to have to fight to keep her. Fight to make yourself better so you can be the person she knows you are."

"You're like a fucking Hallmark commercial."

"And you're not the first person to tell me that."

"Shit." I got up and threw my can in the recycling bin. "I hate this. I fucked up but I'm not sure what I've screwed up the worst. My head or Maddie."

"Never said this would be easy." The old man stood up and pulled on his jacket. "I've got an early flight, so I'm going to call it a night."

"Sure." I looked at the man. "I'll see you when you get back."

"Yes, you will." He slapped me on the shoulder and left my house whistling.

After he left I paced through my living room. My phone buzzed and I stopped to look at it.

KYLA: Get your ass over here.

"Puz!" I went to the door and grabbed his leash. "Let's go."

He sat patiently while I clipped his leash on and followed me with a wagging tail to the truck.

"Sir?" One of the agents walked over to my vehicle.

"I'm going to Kyla Holland's house."

"Yes, sir." The man raced back over to the black SUV.

"You sure you want to go?" I looked over at Puz.

He stood up in the passenger seat and barked.

"Fine."

Cars lined the street in front of the house I'd helped build with Maddie. I frowned and took a couple of breaths before heading out. It felt odd to see so many smiling faces at the home where my friend had died.

Music floated through the air from the backyard and I made my way toward the groups of people.

"Yo, man!" Tame came over and slapped me on the back. He was about my height, but leaner with blond shaggy hair. "You came! Kyla thought Shade and I were going to have to drag you out."

"Shade's here too?" I looked around. I saw the big man talking to a blonde woman with an ample figure.

"Yeah. This is what Cyrus wanted. A party with his friends." Tame gripped my shoulder. "So, we're here to have a good time and eat good food. The neighbors have all been real cool about it."

"That's great." I let my gaze run around the yard, but didn't see Maddie. Emotions bubbled under my surface but I couldn't sort them out. I was upset that she wasn't here, looking for me. I was relieved that I didn't have to face her yet.

"C'mon, let's get you a beer."

"I drove." I shook my head.

"You're the Vice President's son. I'm pretty sure you have a DD whenever you want one." Tame pulled me toward the house and nodded his head at our friend. "Shade has been trying to score with that little thing over there all night. Wanna make a bet?"

"Twenty says she gives him a fake number."

"No way, she's going to end up smacking him before the night's over. Do you remember Dallas?" He laughed.

"Okay, you're on."

Tame had a way of working a room that just pulled people toward him and he never seemed to leave anyone out. I'd been that way not that long ago but now I was happy to let him do all the work while I just enjoyed the company.

People shared stories about Cyrus that led to different stories. There were sad moments, but they always seemed cushioned by the good ones. It wasn't comfortable, but it also wasn't cold and distant. It felt like life. The good and the bad mixing together to form a tale about a young man taken too soon.

It was a while before I realized that Puz had disappeared with Korbin. The little boy had begged to play with the dog until I'd caved.

"Have you seen Puz?" I asked Tame. "Or Korbin?"

"I think Korbin took him into the backyard." My friend tilted his head toward the back of the house.

I slapped him on the back and headed for the back door. My chest had released over the last hour as I relaxed around people I'd known for years and for the first time in a long time, I felt like I could really breathe.

"Puz?" I opened the back door and took a deep breath, letting the crisp air curl through my lungs. "Korbin, where's Puz?"

The sleepy little boy was sitting on his grandfather's lap and pointed toward the bonfire.

A familiar form sat next to the fire, wrapped in a blanket, and cuddling my dog while talking to a few other women. A man was playing the guitar quietly and there was the smell of roasted marshmallows in the air. She moved and the fire glinted off her soft brown hair and the sound of her voice caressed my ears.

My heart stuttered and I almost missed a step on the stairs. I watched as Maddie scratched Puz's head and leaned down to whisper in his ear. I could imagine her telling him she missed him. I'd never wanted to be a dog so badly in my life. She laughed at something someone said and I swear my entire body came alive.

How had I stayed away from her for so long? How had I ever managed to tell her to leave? I loved her so much it hurt and that scared me. It scared the shit out of me.

But did I deserve her? Was I good for Maddie or would I just drag her down with me?

"Don't be such a pussy. Go talk to your woman," Kyla said from beside my elbow with a smile. "That's what Cyrus would say, right? Of course, I've never really cared for that comparison. Vaginas are a lot stronger than people give them credit for."

"You're something else." I laughed.

"I know." She leaned against my arm for a second, her head barely reaching my shoulder. "Thanks for coming."

"Yeah." I looked down at the infant in her arms and traced a finger over the pudgy little arm. "I'm sorry I haven't been here for you. For all of you."

"You can't help my family until you help yours first. Maddie is your family, you love her, Jake. Despite everything that went wrong, I wouldn't have traded a single second of my life with Cyrus." She looked around the backyard. "And I still have all this, all these people to be thankful for. Don't give up on being happy because of what might go wrong because a lot could go right."

I pulled her into a hug and kissed her head. She laughed but I heard her sniff. Before I could say anything else she pushed me toward the bonfire. "Go. Get woman. Argh."

I shook my head and started for the fire, but stopped when Puz ran straight to me and danced around my feet. I looked up expecting to see Maddie, but she was gone. The blanket she'd been wrapped in was laying on the chair as if she'd disappeared in a puff of smoke.

A sense of dread washed over me and I looked through the house.

"Hey, have you seen Maddie?" I asked Shade. He was nursing a beer in the kitchen.

"She left, man." He nodded toward the front of the house. "Looked upset. You do something stupid?"

"I've done nothing but be stupid." I shook my head.

Shade nodded his head. "Know how that goes."

"Don't tell me she slapped you." I narrowed my eyes at my giant friend.

"Nah, man. She left with someone else." He shrugged. "No big deal."

I looked back toward the front door. Shade's problem might not be a big deal, but Maddie was.

"I gotta go." I slapped his shoulder. "Better luck next time."

"You better do something big. A girl like Maddie deserves big things." He pointed at me. "She deserves better than stupid."

"You're right."

And I'd be damned if I wasn't going to pull out all the stops. I couldn't live without Maddie any longer. I needed her and I wasn't going to let her slip away. Doc had been right. I needed to fight for what I wanted.

And I wanted Maddie.

Chapter 26

Maddie

Istared up at my ceiling wishing I could sleep, but my dumbass brain had other plans. Instead of snoring I was going over the party in my head. I'd been so hopeful that evening, silently praying that Jake would show up—that I'd get to see him, maybe talk to him.

Instead I'd watched as he pulled Kyla into his arms and leaned down to kiss her. I'd sat there as my hope was ripped from my chest. It had felt like the world had crumbled under my feet as I stood and stumbled around the house toward the waiting car.

And my brain seemed stuck on instant replay. Everything about that night had gone wrong. Tony had gone on overload, thinking something had happened when I came barreling out to the street with snot streaming down my face and blinded by tears. His face had been a cold mask of fury. One of the other agents had to drag him back to the car.

It had taken a minute before he got in the car so we could

leave. Once in the vehicle he'd handed me a tissue and stared hard at the house as we drove away. He'd followed me to the residential suite, but I hadn't paid much attention to anything he'd said. In fact I didn't remember much of what had happened after I saw Jake and Kyla.

The rational part of my brain fought to not blow it out of proportion. It could have been incredibly platonic but that hurt too. I mean, Kyla just lost her husband and I couldn't imagine her jumping into someone else's arms. But it hurt that while pushing me away, Jake had found comfort somewhere else, even if it was in a friendly way. I hadn't been the one to help him and that hurt me.

My phone buzzed on the nightstand and I rolled over to pick it up. When I saw Phoebe's name I almost cried in relief.

"Phoebes?" I hit the green button and listened for the only voice that could talk me down from the ledge.

"Are you okay? I've had this horrible feeling and couldn't shake it." Her voice sounded distant.

"What, you're psychic now?" I brushed at the tears that gathered in my eyes at the sound of my best friend's voice.

"I'm just very in tune with your energy." Her voice sounded serious. "Now tell me what happened."

"I don't even know, Phoebe. I just don't know what's going on." I closed my eyes.

"This is about Jake, right? You guys are having trouble. I saw a picture of his mom arguing with you on some sidewalk." Her voice lowered. "Tell me what's happened."

"God, Phoebe. I fell in love with him." I choked on a sob and had to take a minute to calm down. "I can't go into it on the phone."

"Yeah, I get it." She sighed.

"He's got some issues to work through and doesn't want my help." I bit my lip.

"There's something else." Her voice took on a soothing tone.

"He didn't want *my* help." I emphasized *my* so she'd catch my drift.

There was silence from the other side of the phone for so long I thought she might have lost our connection.

"Phoebe?"

"I met this witch doctor while digging a well. I bet he'd give me something to shrink Jake's winky." Fury laced my normally peaceful friend's voice. "It's a powder that you drop in his food."

I suppressed a giggle. "His winky?"

"You know what I mean." Her voice got a little louder. "I'll do it. I can get it through customs."

"What, are you going to swallow a balloon full of winky-shrinking powder?" I grimaced.

"For you, I'd swallow two balloons." Her voice cracked. "I'm serious, Maddie. I'll do it."

"Have I told you lately that I love you?" I rolled over on to my back and wiped at my nose. "And I don't even know if it's anything other than friendship between them."

"Doesn't matter. He's letting someone else piece him back together. That was your job." I could imagine her sitting on a cot in a communal tent full of other volunteers. "That hurts."

"Yeah, it hurts." I closed my eyes, listening to the sound of voices in the background of Phoebe's current home. "I don't know what to think. There is nothing I can do."

"Yes there is. You can get some damn sleep, because I know it's late there, and in the morning you get up and you start working on the bill."

I closed my eyes. "His mom said she'd get it canned."

"That stank bitch!"

I sputtered a bit. "Stank bitch?"

"Yes! Stank, rotten, prissy-ass bitch!" She sucked in a breath. "Oh, I'd love five minutes in a room with her."

"Yeah, probably not a good idea." Virginia Simmon made generals sweat in their boots and dictators avoided her at the UN. "But I appreciate your willingness to face the beast."

Phoebe growled into the phone.

"Simmer down, Fluffy." I sat up in bed and rubbed my forehead.

"Why didn't you tell me that bottle-red horcrux was blackmailing your bill?" Phoebe practically hollered. "Who does she think she is, anyway? Lucille O'Ball? She'd be so lucky."

"There wasn't anything you could do." I shrugged even though she couldn't see me.

"Good grief, Maddie! Your dad is the frickin' President!" She lowered her voice. "He'd lose his shit if he knew his VP was blackmailing his daughter and I sure wouldn't want to be on the receiving end of him being pissed. Do you remember when North Korea decided to test missiles last year? No one is forgetting that speech he made. He was all righteous Bill Pullman from the movie *Independence Day.*"

"I don't need my dad to fight my battles." I tried to not sound petulant. "This is my deal, my project. I don't want anyone saying that the bill got passed because of my father."

"I get that." She sighed. "But you can't just let that bitch blackmail you."

"I—I don't know what I'm going to do yet." I picked at the blanket.

Phoebe groaned. "I'm sorry, Maddie. Now's not the time. You've got enough on your plate right now."

"It's okay." It wasn't, nothing was okay.

"It's not, but it will be, Maddie. I promise."

"Thanks, Phoebe." I threw myself back on my pillows. "I think I'm going to try and sleep now."

"Sure." Her voice was soft and I fought to ignore the pity. "Things are always better in the morning."

"Good night."

"Good night, Maddie." The phone clicked and I sat it back on my nightstand.

I don't know how long it took me to fall asleep, but morning came entirely too soon. As did the knock on my bedroom door.

I rolled over and covered my head with the blanket. I didn't want to talk to anyone, I didn't want to see anyone, and I definitely didn't want to get out of my bed.

"Maddie?" Tony's voice was quiet.

"Go away, Tony. I'm not getting up today."

"I'm sorry, Maddie." Something in his voice made me uncover my head. "This is important."

My stomach dropped but I threw the blanket off and stood up. Walking over to my bathroom I grabbed my robe and wrapped it around me. I stuffed my feet into my slippers and opened my bedroom door.

"The shift change is about to happen and I wanted to introduce you to my replacement." Tony looked past my shoulder.

"What?" I shoved my hair out of my face.

"I'm rotating out, but I wanted to introduce you to the new person. Mona is the best there is and I think you'll get along well."

"Rotate out? For vacation?"

"No, Maddie. It's time for me to move on."

My mouth opened but words wouldn't come out. Tony had

been my guard for the last two years and he was just going to leave now?

"Mona is on the young side, but has a lot of experience. I wouldn't trust anyone else." His eyes tightened and his jaw clenched. "I wouldn't leave you with just anyone."

"I don't understand." I shook my head. "You're leaving me?"

"It's time. Most agents don't stay this long with their charge." He stepped closer. "Can I come in?"

I stepped back so he could come in my room.

"I know my timing sucks, Maddie. I can't imagine how pissed you're going to be at me for this, but it needs to happen." He stuck his hands in his pockets. "I'm going to California."

"You're going to California? Why?" I wrapped my arms around my stomach. "Did I do something wrong?"

"No, that's the last thing I want you to think." He stood there looking so calm while my whole world fell apart. "I can't protect you anymore."

"Because . . . ?"

He pulled his hands out of his pockets and walked across my room to look out the window.

"Is it Dahlia?" I wracked my brain for reasons. "Does she miss her family?"

"Yes." He turned to look at me. "And no."

"I really need you to be straight right now, because I'm having the shittiest week ever and this is making it worse." Was there anyone that didn't want to run as far away from me as possible?

"I can't take care of you the way I should." His eyes were pained. "We're not supposed to become attached to our charges. It blinds us to what's going on, where danger could be coming from, and so far I've been lucky."

"So, you're leaving because you're my friend?" I rubbed my forehead with my fingers.

"You're like my little sister, Maddie." His eyebrows pulled together. "And that makes it hard for me to do my job. So I'm leaving before something bad happens."

"I don't get it." I sat down on the edge of my bed.

"I've been so worried about you, I can't do my job. My job isn't to make sure you're not unhappy, it's to make sure you're safe and well protected." He sat down next to me. "I'm sorry, Maddie."

"So, this is why most of the agents come and go so often." I rubbed my cheeks.

"Yeah," he agreed. "But you can always call me if you want to talk. And Dahlia has already started talking about a guest suite, so you could always escape to the West Coast if you need a break from D.C."

"This sucks, Tony."

"I know." He bumped my shoulder with his. "But you're going to like Mona."

"Mona, huh?" I sniffled and tried to get control of my emotions. Tony had been part of my life for years. I couldn't imagine not seeing him every week. It felt like part of my family was leaving. "With a name like that I bet she got made fun of a lot when she was little."

"I'm thinking it probably only happened once." He laughed. "She's a good apple."

"Only old people call other people good apples." I cut my eyes up at him.

"Well, I'm not getting any younger."

I snorted. "So, California. That's a big state. Care to narrow it down some?"

"Los Angeles." He shrugged. "Lots of big names in that area."

"Makes sense." I sighed. "So, are you going to make me godmother to your rugrats? Since I'm the little sister you never had?"

"Let's not count our eggs before they hatch." He pulled at his tie and I chuckled. "But if there are babies in my future, you'll get my vote."

"I'll remember that." I stood up and took a deep breath. I wasn't going to make this any harder on Tony. "Okay. Let's meet Mona."

He smiled at me sadly before nodding his head. I'd do my best to not make Tony feel bad. He'd put his life on hold to take care of me and I wouldn't be the reason he waited any longer.

Mona was nice and seemed to have a good sense of humor, but it would be a while before I really felt comfortable around her. Feeling like I couldn't hide in my room any longer I got dressed and decided to go to the animal shelter. Some manual labor might help take my mind off things for a little while.

Tony didn't stay after he introduced me to Mona, so she was with me while I cleaned dog kennels and talked to prospective adopters. Four hours, a few splinters, and a blister later, I was too tired to feel much of anything. The numbness lasted until I closed up the shop and left to find a tiny silver sports car next to our black SUV.

"Maddie." Veronica Whitmire climbed out of the vehicle. "Do you have a minute to talk?"

I froze in my steps. Ronnie was the last person I ever expected to see at the shelter.

Mona stepped in our path and blocked my view of the other woman while I tried to find my voice.

"I'm sorry, miss. You'll need to schedule an appointment if you want to talk to Madeline." The new agent's pose was relaxed but confident.

"Madeline? No one calls her that. Besides we're old friends." Ronnie laughed and my teeth snapped together.

Mona looked back at me, not knowing if Ronnie was lying or not, but obviously not trusting the tall blonde.

"What do you want, Ronnie?" If I let Mona railroad the reporter I'd be waking up to articles about hiding behind my Secret Service detail.

"I was wondering if you'd like to give a quote for the photo we're running tomorrow." She held up a picture, but I couldn't see what it was exactly.

I walked forward and took it from her proffered fingers. I fully expected to see me and the Vice President nose to nose snarling. Instead I sucked in a sharp breath and would have dropped the printout if my fingers hadn't clenched in shock.

Jake was standing next to Kyla at a store, his arm casually draped around her shoulders. Korbin was holding his other hand and pointing at a toy. All of their faces looked happy and relaxed.

I tried to find words but my heart squeezed in jealousy. He didn't want me around, but he was happy to spend all of his time with Kyla.

"I take it that you didn't know about their relationship?" Ronnie's face was so excited I felt like a bug caught in a spider's web.

I looked back at the picture and tried to find words, but they still eluded me. Anger and pain washed through my body. I took a step toward the other woman, ready to beat her until I felt better.

"If you want a quote, I suggest you contact the Press Secretary." Mona gently inserted herself between me and the reporter.

"That's fine. I'll just say that you declined to comment." Ronnie shrugged. "I think the readers can read between the lines."

"You—" I tried to shove past Mona but she was a lot stronger than I would have thought.

"I hope you like strip searches." Mona leaned toward Ronnie.

"Excuse me?" Ronnie took a step backward.

"Since you like harassment so much, I have a special list I'll add your name to. The next time you're at an event where any of the McGuire family is, you'll be escorted to a secure area where we can thoroughly check you for any type of nefarious devices and question your agenda."

"You can't do that." Ronnie frowned.

"When it comes to the protection of the McGuire family, I can pretty much do anything I deem necessary. And right now, I think it's necessary that you not be within one hundred yards of Miss McGuire."

"I—I—you can't do that." Ronnie backed up until she stumbled into her car.

"Why not? You think you are the only person that can do whatever you want?" Mona grasped my elbow with her fingers and gently started leading me toward the SUV.

"You'll ruin my career." Fury lit her face. "You can't do that!"

I felt like I was stuck in slow-motion as Ronnie pushed off her car and stepped toward Mona. I watched as Mona turned, a gleam in her eye, and laid Ronnie flat on her back.

I barked out a laugh before covering my mouth. The driver

of the SUV and another agent jumped out, guns drawn. Mona led me to the car, leaving the others to call for backup.

I sat in the front seat of the SUV and looked at Mona as she climbed into the driver side.

"I'm sorry I didn't know about Ronnie." Mona put the car in reverse and pulled away from the shelter. "I'm not sure what happened between you two, but she won't be getting near you again."

"You knocked Ronnie on her ass." I managed to keep my face straight.

"I've had worse first days." She shrugged as she pulled onto the highway.

"This week has been one of the shittiest I've had in a long time." I watched the other woman as she drove. "But watching you slam the skanky reporter into the dirt was definitely a highlight."

"Glad I could help." She looked over at me and smiled.

"Me too."

The last week had been a complete storm, but maybe I'd come out of it okay.

Maybe.

Chapter 27

Jake

Ialways thought the Eisenhower Building was an underrated building in Washington, D.C. The architecture was like the stuff I saw in Europe. I didn't know the terms for the roof or windows, but I knew enough to know it was beautiful. Of course, it wasn't just the door frames and bronze fixtures. It was the history and the power that walked the halls of the building now.

I could imagine Maddie telling me that Winston Churchill had walked the halls, that Theodore Roosevelt had once had an office in the Eisenhower Building. But it wasn't the ghosts of Christmas past that I was there to visit. It just happened that the powers-that-be walking those halls right now were related to me.

And she was going to be very pissed when I told her why I'd come to visit. Which was why I needed to pony up and take those final steps into the damn building.

The men at the gate inspected my ID and called my mother's office to let them know I was on my way. Her office was all aflutter, which didn't surprise me since she wasn't the kind of boss that would take kindly to someone playing solitaire. She wasn't going to win mother of the year any time soon, but she was one hell of a politician. My mother was going to shake the world as President one day.

If I wasn't so pissed at her all the time, I'd be proud of that fact. I sat down in a waiting chair and fought down my grimace. Doctor Beaudreau would think that I'd acknowledged there was something good in my mother was a step in the right direction. Of course, I'd never doubted my mother's ability to run the country. If anything, I'd always comforted myself with the fact that her family suffered for the greater good; that our sacrifices paved the road for a better future for the country.

And I was here to stop all of that.

"Your mother will see you now." The secretary stood up at her desk and motioned for me to go through the doors.

Once I was fully in her lair, my mother walked around from her desk and held her arms out.

"Jake." She gave me a light hug before stepping back to look me over. "You're looking good."

"Thanks." I looked away from her. "You've been busy."

"Campaign stuff." She motioned for me to sit down. "There's a never-ending list of things to do or worry about."

"You're up in the polls." I sat down on one of her couches.

"Yes, I am." She sat across from me and smiled. It was the smile I hated, the fake, patient political smile. She must've decided I needed to be handled with kid gloves. "So what brings you to my office?"

"I'm here to tell you it's over."

"You and Maddie?" She frowned. "I already knew that, Jake. You haven't seen her in weeks."

"Not Maddie." I ground my teeth together. "You."

"You're here to tell me I'm over." She shifted on the couch so she could cross her legs. "I'm not following you."

"No more rallying flag, no more shoving me in front of a camera, and you're going to stop blackmailing Maddie." I kept my voice calm and even.

"Excuse me?" Her eyebrows rose in a practiced move. "I'm not blackmailing anyone and the interviews you do are part of putting this family in the White House. You know this."

"No." My voice rose a notch and I cleared it before going on. "We're putting you in the White House and I'm done doing it."

"Jake—"

"No, I'm not done. My earliest memory is you telling me to smile for the camera. I did an interview from the hospital bed in Germany, two days after I woke from surgery. I've danced with who you told me to dance with, smiled at the cameras when you asked, and let you direct my personal life, but that ends now." I took a deep breath. "You're not going to bully Caro or Ari anymore, and you're not going to sink Maddie's bill just because you can."

"I realize you're going through a difficult time, but you don't get to walk into my office and dictate to me." She sat up straight. "I'm calling a doctor. You need to be medicated."

"You're not calling anyone." I leaned forward, resting my arms on my knees. "And you're not going to threaten to do it again."

It was my mother's turn to lean forward. "And why would I do that?"

"Because I will tell the world everything you don't want them to know."

"What could you possibly tell them?" Her eyes narrowed.

"I'll tell them that I was forced to give interviews while dealing with PTSD. I'll tell them that I was forced to do interviews or you would use my sisters for publicity." I didn't let my eyes leave hers. "I'll tell them that you used me to promote your campaign, that you blackmailed me into breaking up with Maddie, and that you threatened to have her bill canned. I'll tell them whatever it takes for you to lose voters."

"You're being ridiculous." She stood up and walked to her desk before walking to the window and then back to the couch.

If she was pacing, I was winning. I fought my smile and watched her calmly. Maybe this was going to be easier than I thought.

"Going to the press is a bad idea, son. Who do you think they will believe?" She crossed her arms. "I can make my case to the media just as easily."

"It's not about who they believe, it's about how many votes you're going to lose in the process." I sat back. "And you're too practical to ignore my point."

She didn't answer, instead she turned to look out the window. "You're doing this for Maddie."

I didn't respond at first. She wasn't looking at me, so I didn't have to worry about hiding my expression.

"It's not just about Maddie. It's about me, Ari, and Caro. It's about you not playing God with our lives."

"You didn't start acting out until you began to date Maddie." She turned to look at me. "I knew that girl wasn't any good. Her mother was—"

"Stop." I stood up. "I don't care why you think she's less

than us. Who fucking thinks that way, Mom? This is what I'm talking about. Maddie is the most thoughtful, patient, loving person I've ever met. She's brilliant and doesn't try to run over people. This is why I'm done being under your thumb. You don't get to choose who is worthy of being loved. Not by me."

Her entire body stilled. "You love her."

"What?"

"You love Maddie." Her eyes widened.

"Of course I love her."

"You would sell out your family for her?"

"I'm not selling out anyone." I slammed my hand against one of the many bookcases. "I'm standing up for the people I love, just like you should have been all these years. Why don't you get that?"

"You're threatening me for Maddie. I think I have a right to understand your relationship."

I swallowed the lump in my throat. I wasn't sure if I even had a relationship with Maddie anymore. She'd stopped texting me every day and the radio silence was killing me.

"It's not just Maddie. It's for Caro and Ari. They don't deserve to be pawns in your political game." I shook my head. "I'm doing this for me."

That last bit was thanks to all of the therapy I'd been doing every day. Somehow I'd come to terms with the fact that I deserved to be happy—to be more than my mother's chess piece.

"What exactly have I done that's so wrong?" She moved behind her desk. "What have I done that makes me such a horrible mother?"

"Besides pressuring me into joining the military? How about blackmailing my girlfriend? Or not allowing your children to be children? It's not a short list, Mom."

She leaned forward and braced her hands on her desk. "I've been grooming you for our life as the First Family. This is the dream, Jake. We're going to be able to fix the mess our country is and make it better."

"Save the spiel for someone who cares. Mom, that's your dream, not ours."

"It's our dream, our family legacy." She stood up straight as if I'd surprised her.

"Oh, yeah? When was the last time you asked any of us what our dreams were? What makes you so sure that being the First Family is what anyone else wants?"

She crossed her arms and I knew I'd won. My mother was too well trained to cross her arms in an argument. It was a sign of weakness, closing yourself off from assault. It didn't matter that I wasn't here to attack her. She felt threatened.

"Mom, you're going to make one hell of a President, but you were our mom first." I watched her as she began to pace behind her desk. "It's time you remember that we're your kids, not chess pieces on a board."

"I never meant for you to feel as though you weren't important."

"Then start letting us make our own choices. We're too much like you. The more you push us, the more we'll fight." It felt odd to have the upper hand with my mother. "I'm still going to vote for you. No one can do what you can for this country. I'm just asking for you to use a little of your magic for your kids for once."

"You're too old to believe in magic." She snorted.

"You have a way with people, a way of accomplishing what you feel is important. I'm just asking you to make Caro, Ari, and me important."

"You are important, Jake. You all are." She watched me with careful eyes. "You're right. I should have been more considerate of what you and your sisters needed."

"I've heard that accepting the blame when you make a mistake is a sign of good leadership."

She snorted loudly. "Who the hell said that?"

"A fortune cookie." I smiled.

She chuckled before walking around the desk and looking up at me.

"If you love Maddie, then I won't get in the way."

"And you won't block the animal testing bill?"

"No. Go forward with the legislation and my blessing." She sighed. "I don't have a problem with the bill actually. I'd sign it into effect if I was President."

"I'm going to hold you to that." I smiled. "And Ari and Caro?"

"I'll try to take their feelings into consideration." She narrowed her eyes.

"Mom."

"Caro is practically grown. I can't force her to do anything. And Ari is still too young to do whatever the hell she wants. If I didn't keep a rein on her she would change the color of the White House to Tardis Blue, or whatever the hell that flying box is painted."

"You just made a *Doctor Who* reference." I smiled. "Look at you paying attention to your daughter."

"Don't push it, Jake." She wrapped her arms around me and squeezed quickly before letting go. "Go before I change my mind."

"No changing your mind, Mom." I leveled my gaze at her. "I mean it. Or there is no deal."

"And you think I didn't raise you." She laughed. "You're negotiating like a pro."

"I learned from the best."

"Go away, Jake. I've got an appointment waiting."

"Yes, ma'am."

"And tell Maddie I won't kill her bill." She grunted. "But I won't put up with her yelling at me in public again."

"I'll ask her to not yell at you . . . in public." I ducked out the door before she could respond.

The secretary ushered an older gentleman into the room I just vacated and I blew out a deep breath. I felt like I had one hundred pounds lifted off my shoulders.

Now to see Senator Fletcher about a bill.

Chapter 28

Maddie

"Y ou're going to go blind," Phoebe tsked at me.

"I'm not staring at the sun, Phoebe." I rolled my eyes but turned off my phone and tucked it in my pocket. I might be annoyed with her right now, but I was really glad she was finally home.

"No, you're writhing in misery thinking Jake is in love with someone else." She pointed at me over the adoption desk at the shelter. "You keep staring at that picture of him and your friend trying to find a tiny detail to confirm your suspicion."

A photo of Jake helping Kyla carry something into her house had popped up on some site and spread across the media like wildfire. He was laughing with her while Korbin ran in the yard with Puz.

And every single time it showed up, it was like being shot in the heart. He looked happy, relaxed.

With another woman. And my stomach writhed with jealousy.

I'd seen them at the party a few days ago, talking and laughing. At first I'd thought that maybe he had come to see me, but then I'd watched as he kissed her head. I hadn't been able to get out of there fast enough.

All that time I'd been waiting, trying to give him a chance to work through what was bothering him. I'd told him I loved him and he'd told me to leave.

I'd been such a fool.

"I'm telling you, it's nothing. You know how the media works. This is a snapshot, a millisecond of time that was captured and spun in whatever way that would sell the most papers and get the most hits online." Phoebe frowned at me. "And if it isn't, I'm going to kick his stupid ass until he needs another prosthetic."

"Phoebe!" I wiped at my cheeks.

"That's what friends do, Maddie." She picked up the nail trimmers. "I'll cut a bitch."

I groaned.

"Get it? Because they're nail trimmers? I'll cut a bitch? Like a female dog?"

"Ugh. That was horrible, even for you." But it did make me laugh.

"Have you taken care of the new dog in kennel twelve?" She tapped the clipboard in front of her. "If my puns won't work, maybe manual labor will."

"You're a cruel and unusual friend, Phoebe."

"Thank you."

I spent the rest of my shift running around and delivering medicine and mucking cages. I wished it really had kept me from worrying over the picture.

"Yo, time to go!" Phoebe tapped her waterproof watch. "You've got that thing tonight, right?"

"Shit." I looked up and frowned. "Yeah, Dad's giving an award and I have to be there."

"Go get your Cinderella on." Phoebe pursed her lips. "Because you definitely look like a mistreated servant girl right now."

I picked up one of my feet and frowned at the mud and other brown matter stuck to my work boots. Maybe I'd find a fairy godmother on the way back to the White House.

Feeling guilty about being so disgusting I put my shoes in a plastic bag in the back of the car and sat on my jacket.

"Any new animals?" Mona asked.

"A few. There's a really cute little kitten. She's bound to get a home quick."

"It's the older ones that have a hard time." Mona said it like she worked with animals all the time. Maybe I could get her to volunteer on her off days.

"Yeah, and those are the ones that are already housebroken and kennel trained. It's a shame." I missed Tony, but I was really starting to like Mona.

"You'll find them homes." She smiled at me.

The staff was a flurry of excitement by the time I got to the residential suite. Bran was laying on one of the couches dressed in his tux while playing some kind of video game.

"Whoa. You stink." He looked up at me as I ran by.

"It's shit!" I laughed and slammed my door. I only had an hour before I'd be expected for pictures and that was definitely pressing it.

I rushed through the shower, barely taking the time to shave my legs so I'd have time to do something with my hair. It was too late for something intricate, so I'd have to settle with curling the ends.

I pulled a black dress from the closet and frowned. I didn't remember buying it, but it had my name pinned to it and was the right size. Deciding that it would be easier to just go with something plain, I pulled the dress on and turned to the mirror with a shock.

It was extremely form-fitting but still had a loose, flowing look to it. The neckline disappeared well below my breasts and the back was practically nonexistent.

"I thought that would look good on you." Abigail walked into the room. She was wearing a midnight-blue gown with her hair pulled up. "You're stunning, Maddie."

"You picked this out for me?" It was nothing like the safe, boring dresses she normally sent my way.

She walked over to stand next to me in the mirror. "I met your mother once. A long time before you were born. She was this lively woman that never seemed to be worried about boundaries and protocol. She was the definition of a carefree spirit. I didn't like her, I dismissed her for not seeing what I thought was the big picture."

"Uh, if you're going for a heart-to-heart—"

"Just listen. It took me years to realize I hadn't disliked your mother. I'd been jealous. I grew up with all these rules and requirements. They molded my whole life, defined who I was. When I was back in Colorado, I looked your mother up. I wanted to tell her that she had taught me something about myself." She fiddled with my dress and I realized she must really be nervous. "And that's how I met your father. Your mother had died a few months before I reached out to her."

"I didn't know that."

"I'm telling you this, because I know we haven't always seen eye to eye. But I love you, Maddie. When your father brought me into your family you became my daughter. I know I wasn't your mom, but I love you as if you were my own." She looked away from the mirror and I realized she had teared up. "And I'm proud of you."

"I love you, too." I reached up and squeezed her hand.

"Anyway, I bought this dress when I saw it, because I knew you would take Jake's breath away in it. I'm ashamed to admit I thought he'd be good for you, but now I see that you're good for him. You have this way of bringing out the best in people."

"Abigail, thank you so much, but Jake—"

"Isn't here yet. So you have plenty of time to finish getting ready. I think your hair looks lovely down." To add to my shock she leaned forward and kissed my cheek. "I'll see you downstairs."

"But Abigail . . ."

She walked right out of the room and pulled the door shut with her.

Jake was going to be here tonight?

I had two options. I could hide and pout or I could put on my battle armor and go downstairs.

Maybe I could do both.

I worked carefully on my makeup, taking the time to make sure my eyeliner was even and the foundation blended in perfectly. I flipped through my jewelry and picked out a pair of emerald earrings but decided against a necklace. This neckline wasn't meant to be accessorized.

I looked through my shoes, wishing I had something sexier to wear, but had to go with what was available. I had one pair of black stilettos and that would have to do.

By the time I was finished I had surprised myself. Standing in the mirror was an elegant woman with a slightly wild looking edge.

Jake had called me his fairy queen once. The woman looking back at me was dressed in sophisticated black and dripping with jewels, ready to do battle with magic.

If Jake didn't love me, then I'd make sure he regretted missing out.

I picked up a small jeweled bag and shoved the necessities in it.

"Maddie?" I turned around at the sound of my father's voice. "Wow. You're stunning."

"You're going to need a bib in that dress." Bran frowned, obviously horrified by my cleavage.

"I'll just borrow one of yours from the children's table." I smiled at him while he rolled his eyes.

"Abigail showed me the dress when it arrived. She definitely knows her stuff." My father picked up my hand and made me spin. "Jake isn't going to know what hit him."

"Listen, Jake and I haven't spoken in—in a while. So, just lay off the Jake stuff, okay?"

"He'd have to be stupid not to talk to you tonight," Bran said. "I mean, you're my sister so this—" he waved his hands in my direction "—is gross, but if you weren't my sister I'd say he was an idiot."

"I think there was a compliment in there somewhere." I frowned at my little brother. "Are you being nice to me?"

"I give up." Bran rolled his eyes and headed for Abigail.

My father held on to my hand when I started to follow Bran. "Are you okay?"

"I'm okay." I squeezed his fingers. "I will be okay."

He nodded his head. It was true. I would be okay. I just needed to make it through the night without making a fool of myself.

We posed for pictures and I managed to ignore Virginia and her frosty attitude, but it was nice to see Caro and Ari. Thankfully, Jake hadn't shown up for the photos.

In fact, I didn't see him until I sat down at the table. When I'd seen the name cards I'd thought of switching them in an effort to escape, but decided I needed to be an adult. If Jake had moved on with Kyla, I'd try to be happy for them.

And maybe think about letting Phoebe loose with the nail clippers.

"I wanted to tell you earlier, but you look amazing." Jake slipped into his seat, his eyes running over me hungrily.

"Thank you." I clenched my purse under the table and managed a polite smile.

"Maddie, I'd really like to talk to you." He touched my arm and electric sparks shot through my system. "There's been a lot going on."

"My father is about to make a speech." I nodded toward where my dad was standing.

"Later?"

I ignored him, focusing on my father. Tears stung at the corners of my eyes, but I'd be damned if I was going to ruin my war paint before he'd even told me he'd moved on.

"Please, Maddie? I owe you an explanation."

I jerked my chin once but didn't look at him again for the rest of the dinner. It was bad enough that he was next to me, his sleeve brushing my arm, his knee bumping into mine. Each touch was a knife to my heart.

By the time the food was whisked away, I'd started looking

for ways to avoid Jake. There were a few people in the room that I could count on for a dance. Possibly a few others. Then I could sneak out before anyone noticed.

I left the table in a hurry, desperate not to be stuck talking to Jake in front of all these people. That was when Senator Fletcher motioned for me to come over.

"Maddie, my dear, you are breathtaking." She leaned forward to kiss my cheek.

"Thank you. How are you?"

"I'm wonderful. Has Jake told you the news?"

"News?" I frowned.

"We have a sponsor and everything is set to move forward." The older woman's face beamed. "The Vice President even gave us her list of people. Jake talked her into backing your bill."

"He what?" My voice was a little louder than I'd intended.

"I thought you knew." She frowned. "I really shouldn't say anything else. It's his story to tell."

"I don't understand. You said you'd stop the bill."

"I did, dear. Just as you asked, but Jake came to my office this week and insisted we make it happen." She touched my arm. "Are you okay? You look pale."

"I—I'm confused, that's all." I sat down in a nearby chair. Was this his way of apologizing for leaving me? Or had Phoebe been right? He really did still love me.

"Maddie, will you dance with me?" Jake stood behind my chair and held his hand out to me. I looked around the room and willed a sibling connection with my brother. I could always dance with my brother. "Please?"

People were looking at us waiting to see how I would respond. I wanted to have something witty to say, some grand excuse, but I didn't trust myself to open my mouth.

Instead I looked up into his warm eyes and nodded yes.

He swept me into his arms and through the other dancers. Being in his arms was the most wonderful and most painful experience. I loved him enough to let him go if that's what he wanted, but I still had hope that he was here for me. It was that hope that tortured me.

"You're not looking at me." He leaned forward and his breath tickled my skin.

"Why did you reopen the bill?" I answered with my own question.

"Because I know how much it means to you." His hand on my waist pulled me a little closer. "Please look at me."

"I don't want to look at you, Jake." His thumb ran across my fingers in a soothing pattern.

"Why not?"

"I don't want to cry in front of all these people." My voice shook and I stared off to the side as we moved around the floor. "And if I look at you, I'm going to cry."

"We have to fix that, because I can't take my eyes off you."

Without another word he pulled me from the dance floor and up the grand staircase. After a quick look around, he pulled me into the Lincoln sitting room where he'd stolen a kiss months ago.

"Maddie, I need you to look at me when I say this." He tilted my chin up and I took a deep breath before opening my eyes. "There you are. God, I've missed you, Maddie. I've missed you more than I've missed anything in my life. Losing my leg was a cakewalk compared to not having you."

"I don't understand." I blinked as tears filled my eyes. "You told me to leave. I tried to be strong, to be patient, but then I saw you with Kyla."

"Saw me with Kyla? You mean that ridiculous picture of me helping her carry a sewing machine? Maddie, you know how the media spins things. Kyla is making baby clothes and selling them online."

"It's not just that." I started to look away. I didn't want him to see me cry, to see me so lost.

"Don't do that. I need to see your eyes, Maddie. Please, don't look away."

"I saw you at her house. I saw you kiss her and hold her." A sob broke free and I bit my lip.

"Shh. Don't cry. What are you talking about?" Realization dawned in his eyes. "Is that why you left that night? At the party?"

"I wasn't going to stay and watch the man I love with someone else." Anger burned quickly in my stomach. "I saw you. I wasn't going to hang around and have everyone pity me."

"Maddie, I'm not in love with Kyla." He chuckled and I clenched my teeth. "How could I be in love with Kyla when I'm in love with you?"

"I—I—you're confusing me. You admit that you did kiss her but love me?"

"Yes. I kissed her on the head just like I do all of my sisters."

"Like your sisters," I repeated.

"Madeline McGuire, I'm in love with you. What you saw was Kyla telling me to stop being a pussy and to go after the woman I loved." His eyes softened as he pulled me against him. "And that's what I'm doing. I'm fighting for the woman I love."

"She called you a pussy?" I frowned.

"Yes." He laughed.

"You love me." I hesitated with each word. "But you sent me away. I haven't seen you in weeks."

"Yes. I'm stupid and I'm bound to make more stupid mistakes but I'm never letting you go again. I'm not perfect. I'm broken on the outside and the inside, but I'm getting better. I want to be better for you and for me." He rested his forehead against mine. "No more keeping things bottled up. No more off-limit topics between us. If you want to know how I'm feeling or dealing, then I'll tell you. I've got a doctor but it's not something I can fix overnight."

"You're seeing Doctor Beaudreau?" I sniffed.

"Yes. More like he's seeing me. And he wants to meet you." His hands on my sides slid around to my back.

"You really love me."

"Maddie, I've loved you for as long as I can remember. I was just too stupid to realize it. You were right all those years ago. I'd been jealous of that little prick you were sneaking off with, I just didn't understand." He leaned down and caught my mouth with his and lightning shot through every cell in my body. "I love you when you wear men's work boots and crazy t-shirts."

He kissed me again and this time his hands moved slowly over my body, caressing and teasing.

"I love you when you dress like a fairy queen." His mouth was quick and soft. "I love you when you wear nothing but mashed potatoes in your hair."

I laughed as he kissed me.

"But most of all, I love you for being you. For being the hard worker, for loving with all your heart. I love the way you make me feel, the way you light up a room by just being you. I love it all, Maddie. Even your bad taste in movies."

This time his kiss lasted long enough to leave me breathless.

"I love you too, Jake."

This time when he kissed me, there were no barriers. His hands pressed me against him and I traced his shoulders with my hands before pulling at his shirt.

"I want you," I whispered. "I need you, Jake. I need to touch you and feel you."

His only response was to scoop me into his arms. I squeaked and he hushed me with another kiss, which was fine by me. I couldn't get enough of the way he tasted, the way he felt pressed against me.

I heard him open a door before taking us into a dark room.

"Jake, this is the Lincoln Bedroom."

"Is anyone staying here?" He looked around the room.

"No." I shook my head.

"Then no one will care." He sat me down on the floor before making sure the door was locked. "I don't want to wait any longer for you."

"Then don't." I hooked my fingers in his belt and pulled him to me, enjoying the soft groan that escaped his mouth.

"Mad—"

"Shh." I touched his lips. "Just kiss me, Jake."

I didn't give him time to change his mind. I pulled his head down to mine so I could claim his mouth. When he pulled at my dress, I didn't resist. I wanted my skin against his, to taste him, to touch him. I shoved his tuxedo jacket from his shoulders and made quick work of his belt.

Before I could slide his pants off his hips, his hands reached around my back and slowly unzipped my dress. With gentle fingers, he slid the straps off my shoulders, letting the dress fall open to expose my bare breasts.

"You're gorgeous." His words were husky as his eyes drank me in.

"Touch me, Jake."

He ran his fingers up my arms and over my shoulders, tracing my collarbone before lightly running over my breasts. I sucked in a breath when he cupped them in his hands. He used his thumbs to run over the peaks before gently pinching them. I arched my back and groaned.

Leaning down he caught one of my breasts with his mouth and I sagged against the wall. He sucked it into his mouth before scraping his teeth across the peak.

"Jake!" I cradled his head and moaned when he bit down gently.

"What do you want, Maddie?" He lifted his head to look at me.

"More. Everything." I gasped when he caught my other breast with his mouth. "I need you inside me, Jake."

He stood up and began stripping. His shirt landed with his jacket somewhere on the floor.

As soon as he let go, my dress fell to the floor in a whisper of fabric. I dropped to the floor and looked up at Jake. The heat in his eyes was all the encouragement I needed.

Wrapping my hand at his base I slid my hand around him before taking the rest of him in my mouth. His fingers ran through my hair and I moved my mouth down his shaft.

"Fuck, that feels good." He groaned when I sped up my attentions, sucking and licking as I went. "So good."

I took as much of him in as I could, hungry to produce more

of those delicious sounds he was making. Pulling back I ran my tongue along the bottom of his cock before sliding back down over his shaft and humming gently.

"Oh, Jesus. Sweet Maddie." His fingers tightened in my hair. "Maddie, that's too much, my love."

He grasped my shoulders and lifted me to my feet. He wasted no time, plundering my mouth with his own while his hands traced every curve, dipping under the lace panties I was wearing and it was my turn to groan.

"So wet, just for me."

"For you." I sucked in a breath as his fingers teased between my warm folds.

"I want to be buried right there. I want to watch you move underneath me."

He pulled me backward toward the large four-poster bed. He laid me on top of the bedspread and let his eyes run over me.

"Open for me, Maddie." He touched my knee and I let my legs spread apart. "So beautiful."

He traced the growing wet spot on my panties before gripping the material with two hands and ripping it apart.

"Oh," I gasped.

"Are you still on birth control?" He ran his hands along my inner thighs.

"Yes," I answered quickly.

"Thank God." He crawled up my body and positioned his cock at my entrance. "Are you ready, sweetheart?"

"Always." I reached up and traced his jaw with my fingers.

He turned his face to my hand and kissed my fingers as he slid inside.

I groaned and lifted my hips to meet him as he pressed his head against mine. "I love you, Maddie. You're my home, my family."

"I love you too, Jake." I pulled his face to mine as he moved above me. I ran my hands along his arms, back, and chest, before running down to cup his ass.

"It's been too long." He burrowed his head into the crook of my neck. "I've missed you so much, Maddie."

"Then don't wait any longer." I angled my hips upward to meet his thrust. "I'm so close."

He groaned loudly, his movements faster. "My sweet Maddie. My beautiful fairy queen."

"Close, so close." I wrapped one of my legs around his hips and my head fell back with the pleasure. "Perfect, my perfect man."

I gasped loudly when he stiffened over me, my muscles clenching as I fell over that beautiful edge with Jake.

When the world stopped spinning and the stars cleared from my eyes, I rubbed my face against his scratchy jaw.

He lifted up on his elbows and stared down at my face with awe.

"I swear, you must have fairy blood." He touched my nose gently before tracing my lips.

"I'm not sure about fairy blood, but my family is Irish."

"That must be it." He chuckled.

"So, is this it? What is our next step forward? More therapy?"

He rolled over, wrapping me in his arms and settling me on top of his chest.

"Next, we do everything together. Starting with a key to my place. Then we take it day after day, one step at a time."

"You want me to move in with you?" I looked up at him.

"Absolutely. If you're ready. The house doesn't feel the same without you."

"What else?"

"You finish school, we get a bill passed, and live happily ever after." He smiled down at me.

"I like the way that sounds." I snuggled closer to him.

"Me too." He sighed with contentment.

Epilogue

Almost two years later.

I can't believe this is happening." I gripped the arms of my chair and leaned forward to see better. I felt like my entire life was invested in this one moment and it was hard to breathe right. It had taken two times and a lot of changes to get the bill to where it was right now.

"Your proof is right there." Jake pointed at the television. "Two more votes and we have it."

Somehow, despite my distaste for politics, I'd found myself working on things I never would have dreamed of after college: bills to ensure clean drinking water, policy changes, and as the face of several charities.

"What if something goes wrong? What if someone changes their mind at the last minute." I lifted my hand to my mouth and chewed on my thumbnail. The newest President, Virginia Simmon, was sitting in the audience, smiling as if the bill had been her plan. She could still bomb the bill once it hit her desk, but I had hope she would do the right thing. After Jake had talked to her a couple of years ago, and the fiasco with Caro, she had truly seemed to take his words to heart. Either that or she had gotten soft once she was able to claim her prize title of President.

"Just wait." Jake sat calmly next to me. His face was serene but I could tell he was excited by the way his right leg bounced in place. He wasn't worried about his mother but he was focused on something. Our life had been full of happiness, but it had taken work and patience. He still saw Dr. Beaudreau, but not as often. He was so busy with RCVA that I'd been worried he might miss the actual vote.

"Another vote!" One of the aides shouted from another room while a cheer went up and I sucked in a breath, looking back at the TV.

"See? I told you that it was going to be fine." Jake lifted my hand to his mouth and pressed a kiss to my fingers.

"We might actually do this." I looked up at my boyfriend. "We really might accomplish this!"

A roar resounded from the other room just before a group of people flooded into our tiny office.

"We did it!"

"You did it!" I saw Tony and his wife's face swim into view briefly, the happy gurgling of their new baby melting into all the other noises.

"Way to go, Maddie!"

I refused to take my eyes from the television as people hugged me and slapped my back. I wasn't looking away until I saw that final vote roll over. I couldn't believe it until I saw it with my own eyes.

I stared unblinkingly at the ticker at the bottom of the screen. *C'mon. C'mon!*

Then it happened. There was no tick sound to mark the occasion, no burst of confetti, just a change in the count at the bottom of the screen, and a spattering of applause in the Senate Chamber. It took a second for the change in the count to register in my brain.

I looked up at Jake with big eyes.

"We did it," I whispered. "We really did it."

He scooped me into his arms and spun around the room, despite the amount of people crammed into the tiny space. I wrapped my arms around his shoulders and buried my face in his neck so no one could see my tears.

"I can't believe we did it."

"Yes, we did!" Jake smiled proudly down at me. "I never doubted it."

I stood on my tiptoes and kissed him. It wasn't an instant fix for all of the animals stuck in the lab, but it was a start. No new primates could be introduced into lab testing and the rest would be phased out over a few years. No one was opening cages to set puppies free tonight, but eventually they wouldn't be in testing cages at all.

I couldn't imagine a more perfect moment.

But I'd been wrong.

Jake pulled back from me and dropped to one knee before pulling a small box from his pocket.

"Ohmygawd!" One of the interns whispered loudly as everyone around us sucked in their breaths. These people had been working their fingers to the bones with us for years and based on the whispered *yes* in the background probably had a pool on when this would happen.

"Jake?" I looked down into his eyes and was moved by the deep emotion swirling there.

"Madeline McGuire, I'm not a perfect man, but I promise to strive for perfect every single day. I promise to love you every single day. I promise to do my best by you in every way. I will walk however many dogs you adopt, bottle feed however many kittens you bring home. I'll do it all, everything and anything, as long as I get to do it with you." He opened the box and I stared down at the pear-shaped diamond solitaire in awe. "Will you marry me?"

Tears gathered in my eyes as I stared down at the ring that had once been my mother's. He must have spoken to my father weeks before to be able to get the ring in our safety deposit box in Colorado.

"That's my mom's ring." I choked on the tears threatening to spill over. "You got my mom's ring."

"It was the only ring for you." He smiled up at me before raising an eyebrow. "So, what do you think? Spend eternity with me?"

"Yes." I slid to the floor in front of him. "Yes, to marrying you. Yes to eternity."

He held my shaking hand with his and slipped the ring onto my finger before lifting my fingers for another kiss.

"I love you, Maddie." He swooped me into his arms for a scorching kiss before pulling me up in his arms and spinning me around again.

There was no holding back the tears this time and I didn't care who saw them. The last year had been a lot of work, there had been ups and downs, but it had all been worth it with Jake by my side.

"I love you, Jake."

Acknowledgments

There are times that a book will fly out of an author so fast, she barely knows what she actually wrote. And then there are books that are painstakingly written in blood, sweat, and tears. *Bedmates* is one of those books. Not because I didn't love the story or the characters, but because I loved it all so much. This is a genuine work of love.

Jake and Maddie have lived with me for years now, bouncing around in my head and I'm so grateful to have the chance to share them with you and to the people that make that possible.

A huge shout-out to my agent, Rebecca Friedman and my editor, Tessa Woodward, for their saint-like patience. I'm surprised they didn't drive to Georgia and pry the manuscript from my fingers. I couldn't seem to let go.

As usual, I have to thank my husband. His patience and understanding is my life-line when I'm having a panicked author moment. A huge thanks to my daughter who always managed to remind me that there is more to life than the fictional characters living in my head.

Thank you to all of my friends and family that have supported me while I followed my dream. *Bedmates* is my tenth published novel and that is an amazing feeling.

Thank you to all of the readers that continue to support me and my books. Without you, other people wouldn't find the characters that drive me crazy at strange hours of the night. You guys make it all possible.

Roll out the red carpet for the next book in
Nichole Chase's American Royalty series,
Coming October 2017!

NICOLE CHASE lives in Georgia with her husband, toddler, superhero dog, Sulcata tortoise, and two cats. When not devouring novels by the dozens, you can find her writing, painting, crafting, or chasing her daughter around the house while making monster noises.

BOOKS BY NICHOLE CHASE

SUDDENLY ROYAL
Available in Paperback and Ebook

When a duchess from the small country of Lilaria invites her to dinner, Samantha Rousseau assumes it's to discuss a donation. The truth will change the course of her life in ways she never dreamed . . .

RECKLESSY ROYAL
Available in Paperback and Ebook

Catherine has spent her life being the perfect princess, and she's tired of waiting for someone good enough to come along. She has a plan, and it all hinges on seducing the one man who seems utterly unimpressed by all things royal. The one man she is tempted by more than any other . . .

RELUCTANTLY ROYAL
Available in Paperback and Ebook

Newly ordained Lady Meredith Thysmer has to seize her chance to make a better life for herself and her son. She's not afraid to use her best assets to get what she wants . . .

Maxwell Jameson Trevor, prince of Lilaria, hates his royal role, but Max's compassion, humor, and steadfast loyalty to Meredith and her son win her over. Somehow Meredith's got to find a way to seduce this reluctant royal.